RAVE REVIEWS FOR JULIE KENNER!

"Ms. Kenner is an up-and-coming author with a bright future ahead of her."

—ReaderToReader.com

"A fresh new voice in humorous romance."

—Sandra Hill, bestselling author of *My Fair Viking*

"Kenner has a way with dialogue; her one-liners are funny and fresh. Her comic timing is beautiful, almost Jennifer Crusie-esque."

—*All About Romance*

APHRODITE'S KISS

"A true original, filled with humor, adventure and fun!"

—*Romantic Times*

"Like a carnival fun house, full of surprises and just plain good old-fashioned entertainment."

—*Romance Reviews Today*

"Adorable characters and hilarious story lines set Julie Kenner apart. . . . *Aphrodite's Kiss* is pure delight!"

—Trish Jensen, author of *Stuck With You*

THE CAT'S FANCY

". . . funny, witty, and unbelievable erotic."

—*Affaire de Coeur*

"*The Cat's Fancy* deserves a place on any reader's keeper shelf!"

—*Romance Communications*

"Ms. Kenner's debut novel sets the stage for more glorious stories to come. I can't wait!"

—*The Belles & Beaux of Romance*

APHRODITE'S GIRDLE

•

"So the belt makes the wearer irresistible to whomever he or she desires," Zoë affirmed. She smiled, perhaps imagining the possibilities. "Is there more?"

Zephron nodded toward Hale. "Tell her."

Oh, great. A pop quiz. But he smiled and turned in his chair to face his sister more directly. "You know that Aphrodite—"

"Our great-great-great-great et cetera grandmother."

"—forged it centuries ago." When Zoë nodded, he continued. "Well, it has all sorts of powers. On a mortal, it causes what you said: love and adoration by whomever the mortal desires. It's sort of a sensual magnet. It also works even if there's no romantic desire, although the effect is much weaker. In that case, the wearer can persuade people to do what he or she wants." He paused. "On a Protector—"

"Let me guess," Zoë said. "On a Protector, the effect is even more intense. Love and adoration by everyone, no matter whether or not the wearer desires them. Mind-control, basically. So if Hieronymous got a hold of the thing . . ."

"Even Zephron would bend to his will," Hale finished. He and Zoë looked at each other, then turned to look at Zephron, who inclined his head in silent agreement.

"So where is it?" Zoë asked. "I mean, where in Los Angeles?"

"We don't know." Zephron's image turned, focusing entirely on Hale. "It is your job to find out."

Aphrodite's Passion

JULIE KENNER

LOVE SPELL BOOKS   NEW YORK CITY

A LOVE SPELL BOOK®

April 2002

Published by

Dorchester Publishing Co., Inc.
276 Fifth Avenue
New York, NY 10001

ISBN 0-505-52474-0

The name "Love Spell" and its logo are trademarks of Dorchester Publishing Co., Inc.

Printed in the United States of America.

Visit us on the web at www.dorchesterpub.com.

Special thanks to Cherif Fortin for helping with the cover model details. All embellishments are my own! Most of all, this book is dedicated to Catherine Elizabeth—a super baby.

Aphrodite's Passion

VENERATE COUNCIL OF PROTECTORS
1-800-555-HERO
www.superherocentral.com

Protecting Mortals Is Our Business!

URGENT COMMUNIQUE
FOR COUNCIL USE ONLY
Eyes Only

Hale
Protector First Class
California

Acknowledgment requested

Hale:

Council intelligence has detected an increase in Outcast activity, suggesting imminent adverse action by Hi-

1

eronymous. In light thereof, Zephron, High Elder of the Venerate Council, requests your presence within the next twenty-four hours at the American Operations Center, Washington, D.C., for immediate briefing and assignment.

Form 89-C(2)(a), on file with the Mortal-Protector Liaison Office (MLO), indicates that you have already been issued the following council-controlled items (to the extent such list is incorrect, please immediately submit Form 29-B(2)(a) in triplicate with all necessary corrections):

propulsion cloak, model E-10 (expert model);
and
standard issue cellular phone (speed dial included) with full web access, direct communication to Council headquarters, and projectile launch capability.

Upon your arrival at the Operations Center, you will be issued a Mission Essentials Kit, including all standard mission equipment. To the extent such equipment is utilized during the course of your mission, please file in triplicate (by no later than the fifteenth day of the first month after completion of your mission) Form 827A(4)(b) with the Mortal-Protector Liaison Office. Return all unused equipment to council headquarters.

We look forward to your prompt arrival at the Operations Center. Excuses for late arrivals will not be tolerated.

Enjoy the rest of your vacation!

Sincerely,

Phelonium Prigg

Phelonium Prigg
Assistant to Zephron, High Elder

PP:jbk

Chapter One

Hale propped himself up in the hotel bed and grimaced as the note from Prigg dissolved in a flurry of sparks and sputters.

Really.

Prigg's overdeveloped sense of drama could be so tiresome. A simple phone call would have worked just as well. Either way, though, the result was the same: Hale's long-awaited vacation was history. Which was especially frustrating as he had hotel reservations for two full weeks.

On the far side of the room, Elmer uncurled himself and stretched on the sofa cushion, his spiky fur standing on end as he yawned. *What's with the fireworks?* he chittered. *We got a new assignment?*

Hale shot a scowl in the ferret's direction. "*We* don't have an assignment. *I* have an assignment. Which means I have to go to work while you lounge about at home watching daytime television."

Elmer's fur puffed out even more and he emitted a high-pitched squeak, which for a ferret could be either a laugh or an indignant groan. Hale assumed that he was going for indignant.

I do not "lounge about," thank you very much. Elmer raised his furry little chin. *I study the market.*

Hale stifled a chortle. Ever since they'd arrived at the Los Angeles Airport, Elmer had been chattering on about becoming the funny but loveable family pet in some Hollywood sitcom. "If you say so." Hale turned away, ostensibly to check the clock, but mostly to hide his grin.

You just have no appreciation of artistic genius. All you appreciate are female br—

"Ah-ah-ah." Hale rolled over and held up a finger to silence his friend, who managed a tiny ferret shrug before snuggling back down to finish his nap. He and Elmer had been together for years, and he loved the mouthy little guy, but there were some things that just didn't need to be spoken aloud.

Not that Elmer was actually speaking. If the maid walked in, she would hear only Elmer's distinctive ferret squeak. But Hale was an animalinguist, which meant he could understand animal-speak—everything from the vague desires of most animals, to the more articulate thoughts of the more developed of their species. And, of course, he could understand with perfect clarity those animals, like Elmer, whose bloodline had been bred for generations to serve as companions to Protectors.

Some days he really regretted that particular talent.

With a groan, he slid out of bed then headed to the balcony that overlooked the secluded Southern California beach. He'd hoped to make it to Greece for some R & R. No such luck. Instead, he was stuck in a four-star hotel just north of Malibu. Not the vacation he'd dreamed of, but it did have a few advantages over his Manhattan apartment.

Like the dozen or so mortal women who frolicked and bounced on the sand below. Exactly the kind of amenities he looked for in a vacation location—plenty of extracurricular activities and a room with a view.

For more than a year, he'd been trying to get away from the daily grind. Being a superhero—especially a superhero with an undercover assignment as a romance cover model—took a lot out of a guy. He needed some serious down time, and now that he'd finally gotten some, Prigg was calling him back.

Life just wasn't fair. Especially considering he was staring out from a hotel balcony at a smorgasbord of delicious women he'd come to sample. Nothing long-term, mind you. He was a Protector, after all. He'd never get permanently involved with a mortal.

Then again, he didn't intend to get permanently involved with another Protector, either. Why would he? He was young, he was virile, and—if he believed his own press releases—he was one hot property. Why tie himself down? Why indeed? Especially when he could so easily find such delightful, fleeting diversions as the ones on the beach below.

He'd come on vacation with the hope of being well and truly diverted. Unfortunately, he'd been here for forty-eight hours already, and not one single blond, brunette, or red-headed diversion had graced his bed.

Pathetic.

Not that they'd turned him down, of course. That was one of the nice things about being him—women just didn't say no. Actually, the problem was much more basic. He simply hadn't yet gone outside and tried to lure any of the luscious ladies to his room.

Sighing, he drummed his fingers on the windowsill. Instead of playing beach volleyball with bronzed co-eds on Spring Break, he'd elected to stay in his hotel room for the last two days. Frowning, he felt his forehead with the back of his hand. No fever. Damn.

You're losing your touch, Elmer said.

Great. The ferret was awake again. "Not hardly. Just pacing myself."

Elmer didn't look convinced.

"I don't need a woman on my arm every minute. If I'd rather stay in the room and read"—he broke off, looking around the room to find the tattered paperback he'd found in the chest of drawers—"*Valley of the Dolls*, then that's my prerogative."

Not his usual reading fare, that's for sure. But it didn't much matter since he hadn't actually read a word. He'd been too frustrated to concentrate.

Uh-huh. Elmer shot him a look, then proceeded to scratch behind his ears.

"Just drop it," Hale commanded.

Drop it? Drop what? I'm not saying anything. Not one word. No, sirree.

"Elmer . . ."

What? I mean, I'm *sure as Cerberus not mentioning the fact that you haven't done the wild thing with a single female since Zoë and Taylor got hooked up. Nope. I'm not saying that at all.*

"For someone who's not talking, your mouth is sure moving a lot."

Harrumph! Elmer turned three circles on the cushion, then tucked his head under his paws to sulk. Subtle, he wasn't.

Hale scowled in the ferret's direction, then turned and scowled out the window. All in all, he was in a scowling kind of mood. Not that Elmer was right. He wasn't avoiding anything. Not women, and certainly not sex. The thought was preposterous. Ridiculous. Absolutely not true.

7

So what if he'd been a little off-kilter since his half-sister Zoë had tied the knot with that mortal guy? It wasn't as if Hale wanted the same thing. He shuddered. Certainly not.

More likely he was just distracted, that's all. Worried. About Zoë. Right. That had to be it. He was worried about his baby sister marrying a mortal.

Of course, Hale had to admit that Taylor was an all-right guy—for a non-Protector, anyway. And he loved Zoë, so Hale figured they'd probably be okay. After all, Zoë was a halfling. Maybe being part mortal made it easier to be in a mixed marriage.

But Hale was full-blooded, and he knew better than most that mortal-Protector relationships almost never lasted. Mortals couldn't handle the stress, and of the few Protectors who did get into such affairs, most went soft and abandoned their duties.

That wasn't for him. No, sir.

Fleeting entanglements, however, were a whole different story. That was the beauty of mortals, after all. Get in, get out, have a good time, then be on your way. No strings. No commitments. No guilt.

Not at all like with Protectors, who knew where to find you. There was no chance for truly casual sex there—not with the likelihood that last Friday's date might call up on your Council-sponsored cell phone at any time. No, Hale had learned the hard way that dating a Protector left open the possibility of a commitment, and that wasn't a possibility Hale wanted on the table.

He peered down toward the beach again and spotted a particularly lovely blond mortal sunbathing on a dark green towel. *Her.* That was the one. He'd just march down there, turn on the charm, and escort her right back up here. Then he'd lock Elmer in the bathroom and have a torrid afternoon with a very hot woman. He'd shake off this funk and be his old self again before he had to rush back to D.C. and do the superhero gig.

Yes, indeed, that's exactly what he'd do.

Flushed with purpose, he threw on some swimming trunks and headed out. In the breezy lobby, the cool tiles felt nice against his bare feet, and for a second he considered stopping in the bar, having an icy drink, and chatting with the owner about nothing in particular.

No. No stalling. Plan. Girl. *Go.*

His resolve restored, he marched out of the hotel and across the warm sand toward the blond beauty. She looked up when he approached. A beautiful face highlighted by vivid green eyes. Long, sleek legs. Breasts that begged to be touched. In other words, exactly the type of woman he was used to sharing a few sensual hours with. She was perfect, and her coy glance suggested she was more than willing.

So why did he suddenly have an urge to rush back to his hotel room and spend time with Jacqueline Susann instead of with this bikinied babe?

"Hi there." He pitched his voice low, using the tone that had never failed him.

The woman rolled over and propped herself up on one elbow. Her smile revealed flashing white teeth and infinite possibilities of the most decadent sort. "Well, hi yourself. I haven't seen you around here before."

"Maybe you haven't been looking."

"I guess not. Because believe me, I would have noticed you."

"Then it's a good thing I noticed you." Mentally, Hale patted himself on the back. Smooth. He hadn't lost his touch. No worries. No worries at all.

"Lucky me." She sat up, curling her legs under her, her posture designed for maximum male-appeal. Clearly, the girl was no stranger to flirtation. "Are you here for business . . . or pleasure?"

"Pleasure," Hale said. "Pure pleasure."

"How nice. I'm Bitsy, by the way."

"Hale."

Above her sunglasses, her brow furrowed as her lips pursed. "Hale?" The smile was back, this time accompanied by wide, interested eyes. She pointed a perfectly manicured nail at him. "I know you, right? You're on the cover of all those romance novels."

"Guilty." He tested his grin on her, pleased to see it seemed in working order.

"Are you here on a shoot?" She craned her neck looking around, probably for a camera crew. Considering how many celebrities frequented the hotel, Hale was surprised there wasn't one set up nearby.

"I'm on vacation. Relaxing. Meeting new people." *Trying to get myself out of a funk.*

"Well, the pleasure really is all mine, Hale." The woman tossed her hair back, then peeked under the strap of her bikini top—presumably checking her tan, but also revealing the enticing curve of a breast.

Hale swallowed, not nearly as enticed by the view as he would have expected. In fact, he suddenly had an overwhelming urge to go back to his room and watch a little Nick-at-Nite. For some inconceivable reason, this perfect specimen of a mortal woman just wasn't pushing his buttons.

Frustrating. Damned frustrating, and he didn't intend to tolerate it much longer.

"Come on," he said, more gruffly than he intended. "I'll buy you a drink."

If she thought his invitation was abrupt, she didn't say anything. Instead she gathered up her towel, wrapped a tiny sarong around her hips, then passed him her tote bag. "Carry for me?"

He resisted the urge to roll his eyes. "Sure. Let's go."

Twenty yards back to the hotel lobby. Twenty long, frustrating yards listening to the bikini babe ask him if he had a limo parked nearby and just how large was his expense account anyway? By the time they reached the lobby bar, the sad, inconceivable, inescapable truth had caught up with Hale and tackled him: There was no way on earth he was taking this woman up to his room.

Maybe Elmer was right. Maybe he was losing his touch. But it wasn't that he couldn't succeed with the ladies; it was that he didn't want to. Why? At the moment, he didn't care. All he wanted was to get out of there. But Bitsy's hand seemed glued to his forearm, and shaking her was going to prove difficult. Damn.

"Drink?" He steered her toward the bar.

"Sure." Bitsy was all smiles as she let go of his arm and perched on a stool.

He signaled to the owner, intending to order two of the bartender's special concoctions.

"Why don't you order us a bottle of Dom?" The blonde leaned close, her shoulder brushing against his forearm. "We can start our little celebration here, then move it to your room."

"Great," he said, sure his voice lacked even an ounce of enthusiasm. He nodded to the bartender, acknowledging the drink order even though he had no intention of having any himself. A drink like Dom could only be shared with a special lady, and Bitsy just didn't fit the bill. Hell, maybe no one did.

The problem now was how to extricate himself from this unwanted and impromptu date.

"You know," Bitsy began, taking a sip from the champagne flute put in front of her, "I've always wanted to be a model or an actress." She aimed a little pout in his direction. "Maybe you can help me? Do you know any directors?"

11

"I really don't—"

"My portfolio's in my car." She nodded toward the door. "Maybe you could buy me dinner and I could show you?"

"I'm not really—"

"I could show you more than that, too," she cajoled, stroking his arm.

He *had* to get out of there. "Look at that!" Hale pointed across the empty room.

"What?"

"Over there. Isn't that cool?"

The blonde squinted, swiveling on her stool to look in the general direction he was pointing. "I don't see anything," she said, turning back.

And Hale knew just how true that was. She really didn't see a thing, at least not him. He'd completely dematerialized. Invisibility was a rather handy superpower when you got right down to it.

"Hale? Where'd you go?" The woman twisted around, searching the room for him, until her gaze focused on the mirror that backed the bar's bottles of bourbon and rum. "Oh! There you are!"

Hale grimaced, realizing she must have seen his reflection.

In a second, she'd whipped back around so that she was looking in his direction—but again she couldn't see him. Confusion flashed across her perfectly made-up face.

"Where are you?" She turned in her chair to look toward the mirror again, so Hale dropped down below the bar.

That was the one annoying thing about his particular superpower. He could turn invisible, yes, but reflective surfaces still picked up his image. Usually that was little more than an annoyance. Right now, though, it might foil his entire plan for escape.

Very quietly he crouched down, making sure his head was below bar level as he crept away. Disgust with himself—a superhero—for taking the chicken's way out welled inside him, but not enough to suffer through an evening with this woman. No matter how ripe and lovely she was, he just wasn't interested.

Still invisible, he headed for the stairs, avoiding the polished elevator doors and all other reflective surfaces and cursing himself the whole way as the blonde's confused voice echoed after him. He had to be coming down with something. No other explanation made sense. He was Hale, Protector First Class, a direct descendant of Zeus, and he had a heck of a reputation with the ladies. The Hale he knew simply did *not* turn tail and run from bikini-clad women.

Hopping Hades, what was wrong with him? Flu? Leprosy? Consumption?

Whatever it was, the fact remained that he simply wasn't in the mood, despite how soft and willing the girl might be. As he climbed the stairs, her voice drifted up from the lobby, calling his name as she searched for him. She couldn't see him, but even so he raced ahead, zipping up the stairwell at lightning speed until he reached his room on the fifteenth floor. Only after he'd slammed the door behind him did he materialize.

Elmer looked up, his beady little eyes curious. He opened his mouth, but Hale held out a hand, in no mood to be razzed by his furry friend.

"Don't say a word. Not one word."

The ferret managed a shrug. *I wasn't going to say I told you so. Really I wasn't.*

"Just get ready," Hale growled. "We're leaving."

Chapter Two

"Sit. Sit. *Sit!*" Tracy sighed and dangled the doggy treat closer to Mistress Bettina's cold, wet nose. "Please, Missy, you're making me look bad—an animal trainer who can't handle her own dog?"

Apparently Mistress Bettina couldn't care less how Tracy looked, because the dog just sniffed, waggled her fuzzy little pedigreed butt, and yawned.

Resigned, Tracy tossed her the treat, which Missy promptly gobbled. "Thanks for nothing. Just remember who brushes you so that you turn all the boy dogs' heads."

"Does she talk back?"

Tracy yelped, her heart pounding as she turned around to face . . . *him*. Leon Palmer. America's latest heartthrob—and Tracy definitely counted herself among the Throbettes.

Behind her, Missy growled low in her throat. It was not particularly threatening considering the dog was tiny, but certainly not polite either. Tracy looked back over her shoulder. "Hush, girl. It's Leon Palmer."

Didn't Missy realize what a big deal this was—*the* Leon Palmer . . . talking to her, Tracy Tannin, assistant animal trainer and Hollywood nobody? She really couldn't believe it.

She wanted to savor the moment, but Missy's growls and yips weren't exactly enhancing the mood. She shot an apologetic smile Leon's way, then bent over and scooped up the dog, rubbing her between the ears until Missy finally settled down and Tracy could again concentrate on Leon.

He must be lost. After all, the trailer that Paws In Production used to house the animals' kennels was parked on a far corner of the backlot. It was well away from the day-to-day action of the filming of *Mrs. Dolittle, Private Eye*, so hardly any of the sitcom's crew ever wandered back here, and certainly none of the cast ever did. Especially not stars like Leon. Tracy considered swooning but decided it would be terribly uncool. Instead, she rubbed Missy's head, silently reassuring the dog that having Leon Palmer nearby was a good thing.

Leon grinned, apparently used to women staring at him in awe. After a moment, he flashed the full-blown for-the-photographers smile that was currently gracing a dozen entertainment magazines. "You okay? I didn't mean to startle you." His glance shot down toward Missy, his features tightening. "Or the dog," he added.

"Oh. No. I mean, yes. I'm fine." She squeezed her hands into fists and counted to ten. "I mean, don't worry about it. I just didn't realize anyone else was around. We're pretty secluded back here."

"I can see why."

The corner of her mouth drew down. "Huh?" Oh, he must mean keeping the cameras away from the smell and noise. "The animals are all trained. Well, all but Missy here, but she's not actually one of the company's. She's my dog, and she's untrainable." Tracy shrugged. "Anyway, all the other animals behave themselves."

His grin displayed that famous dimple. "No, no. I just mean that I can see why they'd keep *you* in seclusion." He leaned toward her. "Wouldn't want a pretty thing like you distracting the actors and making the actresses jealous."

"Oh. I . . ." She swallowed, wondering about his definition of pretty, but was flattered nonetheless. "Oh." She gulped again. "So, uh, how can I help you?"

"I was hoping to meet my new co-star before shooting started this morning." He paused, looking Tracy up and down. "Are you Melissa Carpenter?"

"I'm Tracy."

His polite expression faded.

"Mel's assistant," she added, pleased to see his smile return. Clutching a squirming Missy under one arm, Tracy wiped her free hand on her jeans, wishing she had worn some makeup, had brushed her hair, and hadn't been covered with fur. She held out her wiped-clean hand for him to shake, hoping it didn't reek of doggie sweat. "Good to meet you."

"The pleasure is all mine, Tracy. I'll have to come back here more often now that I know what treats the producers are hiding."

Tracy tried to smile, but wasn't sure she managed. Men never noticed her. *Never.* So she wasn't exactly sure what sort of response to make. Something more brilliant than drooling, that was for sure.

"Uh, fine. You can come by whenever. We've got lots of treats." She fished in her pocket, then held one out. "Mostly doggie treats."

He stared blankly then, almost as an afterthought, he cracked a tiny smile.

Good going, Trace. What a way with men.

"So, uh, can you introduce me to my co-star?" Leon asked after a moment.

Tracy cleared her throat. Best to focus on business and not attempt jokes. "Yes, well, she's still back at the compound. Mel does most of the training there." His "co-star" happened to be a particularly uncooperative female ferret named Penelope, and training the little beast was going terribly.

"That's too bad. I was hoping we could make friends today." He glanced at Missy, giving the dog a wary look. "I . . . uh . . . was hoping we could get used to each other."

"We were told those episodes didn't start shooting for another week or so. Did someone tell you she'd be here?"

"No." He waved off the question. "I just thought maybe I'd get lucky." He smiled and moved closer. A low growl rose from Missy's throat, and Leon jumped back. After a few seconds, he managed to regain his composure. He caught Tracy's gaze. "I just didn't realize *how* lucky."

Oh, my. He was flirting with her.

Unbelievable.

Tracy fought the urge to pinch herself and see if she was dreaming. Instead, she just rubbed Missy's head and forced herself to smile and act casual. Right. *Casual.* That was a much better plan than simply throwing herself at him.

His supremely confident expression suggested that he knew precisely how frazzled she was, and that he was more than happy to be the one frazzling her. Their gazes locked for a few seconds before his smile broadened. "Well, guess I better run. Don't be a stranger." One last show of pearly white teeth, then he turned away.

Tracy waved after him, her hand still limp in the air when Mel wandered up to the trailer a few moments later.

"Are you saluting? Or is this some weird new Southern California religious thing I just haven't heard about?"

17

Melissa had moved to Los Angeles from Ohio years ago, and her favorite pastime was picking on Tracy's hometown. Usually it got a rise out of her, but not today. Today, Tracy just lowered her hand, smiled at her boss, and passed her the dog. "He was here," she said.

"He?" Melissa asked, shifting Missy under her arm. "Who he?"

"Leon Palmer." Tracy whispered the name as if it were the key phrase of an incantation. "He asked for you."

"Burke told me Leon was scared of ferrets," Mel explained. "He probably came here trying to convince me to tell the show to use another dog or cat or something."

Tracy frowned. "Really? He sounded excited about meeting Penelope. He even looked disappointed that she wasn't here."

Mel rolled her eyes. "Well, then he's a good actor, because Burke told me yesterday that the whole cast knows the ferret's being trained at the compound until we start rehearsals."

Tracy wasn't sure what to say to that. "Well, whatever his reasoning for coming back here, the point is that he ended up staying and flirting with me."

"And this is a good thing?" Mel asked—as if Tracy had just revealed she was next in line for a brain transplant.

"*Any* man flirting with me is a good thing." Tracy sighed. She was practically the invisible girl. Plain-Jane Tracy Tannin, the poor little Hollywood flop who hadn't inherited her movie-star grandmother's exotic looks or her father's classic features. Not that it usually bothered her, but on occasion it would be nice to be noticed. And now, to be noticed by a guy she'd had a crush on for months . . .

"The man practically oozes ulterior motives," Mel said. "He probably figured you could get him out of the Penelope mess as easy as I could."

18

Tracy crossed her arms, determined to savor the moment. "No way. I told him you were training her, not me." She refused to believe Leon just wanted something. He'd seemed so sweet, so sincere. And, besides, he knew darn well that Mel was in charge of the animals. How much power did he think an assistant had? She stood up straighter, hoping to convince herself as much as her boss. "He was *flirting*, Mel. I know flirting when I see it."

"Forgive me if I don't drool."

"Oh, come on. You have to admit he's cute."

Mel looked at her over the top of her aviator sunglasses. "I'll go you one better, kid. I think the man's positively gorgeous."

"See?"

"See what? See you making a fool out of yourself?"

Tracy scowled. "Okay. You win. I admit I might be getting a little bit carried away, but I haven't even had a date in six months—"

"Maybe the men just can't catch you. You work so much."

"I work for you, remember?" Tracy countered.

"And I appreciate it," Mel said, the sincerity in her voice ringing through. Although Mel had been in the business for years, she'd only recently opened her own company, and—except for the two college interns who fed the animals and cleaned cages—Tracy was Mel's one and only employee. At first, Tracy knew, Mel had struggled just to bring in enough money to buy food for the animals and pay Tracy's salary. But now, Paws In Production was taking off, its animals regularly appearing on *Mrs. Dolittle* and a few movies that were filming around town. The company's success meant that Mel was leaving a lot of the daily details to Tracy while Mel ran around town, having meetings, interviewing potential employees, and generally building up the company.

19

All in all, the situation was great for Mel and for Tracy, who'd gained a lot more experience than she'd anticipated when she'd first hired on after her grandmother died. The only downside was that she often needed to work long hours, and that put a crimp in her social life. Not that she'd ever had much of a social life to begin with.

"Well, how much I work isn't the point. The fact is, men don't notice me. Therefore, I happen to think that a guy like Leon Palmer—who could have any woman he wanted—flirting with me is a pretty cool thing."

"Fine. Whatever. But don't start thinking something's going to come of it. He flirts with everybody and dates someone new every week. The guy's a jerk."

"He seemed perfectly nice just now." A little arrogant, maybe, but Tracy had met enough Hollywood types to know that was often just a cover for insecurity. Of course Missy hadn't exactly been her usual friendly self, but it wasn't as if the dog was *always* a good judge of character.

"If he was nice, it was only because he wanted something. Or else he has a brain tumor."

Tracy crossed her arms and tapped her foot. "You're not being helpful. Come on. Tell me what I should do now."

"Be afraid. Be very afraid."

Tracy kept on tapping, her mouth firmly closed.

Mel sighed, her long fingers stroking Missy's head before she put the dog back on the ground. "That's my best advice. I don't even like the guy. I mean, jeez, if you're going to go all ga-ga over some unattainable guy, couldn't it be someone you can fantasize about? I mean Leon Palmer is so *not* fantasy material."

Tracy laughed. "I can fantasize about him just fine."

"I was thinking someone a little more removed from reality. Someone safe. Like one of the models on those romance novels you're always reading."

20

Tracy's cheeks warmed at her employer's perceptiveness. So what if she had a little crush on a romance cover model? Her fantasies were perfectly innocent. And considering how boring her reality was, she didn't intend to give them up.

"I bet those guys are arrogant and conceited, too," Mel continued. "But at least you won't have to see it every day at work."

"Now *they're* arrogant, too? You've never even met one." Tracy cocked her head. "You've got issues, Mel. Deep, dark issues."

"What are those guys' names?" Mel asked, like a dog with a bone. "The ones on the covers you're always drooling over?"

"Cherif Fortin's one," Tracy mumbled. She tried to control her embarrassment. Mel might have issues, but apparently they were going to explore Tracy's. "And there's also John DeSalvo."

"Yeah, but there's that one you really like. The dark-haired guy with those amazing blue eyes."

"Hale. His name is Hale."

"Just Hale?"

Tracy shrugged. "Maybe it's like Cher. Or Madonna. I don't know." She let her head fall back as she sighed. Hale was always so nice in her fantasies. He'd come to her house dressed in a tux, planning to take her dancing. They'd never get further than the foyer, though; they'd whirl and twirl to the music until that last final note when they'd kiss . . .

Mentally, she sighed. Such a nice fantasy.

"Earth to Tracy, Earth to Tracy. Come in, Tracy."

"Sorry. Distracted." She shook her head, feeling a bit like Missy shaking off a bath. "Anyway, it doesn't matter. Hale's total fantasy, and if my crush goes any further than the two of us, I'll have to hurt you."

21

"Uh-huh." Mel's mouth twitched. "What I'm saying is, you should try to hook up with a real man, not some fantasy guy—"

"Leon's real."

"—But if you're going to fantasize, at least do it about someone better than Leon."

Tracy sighed. All her life, she'd been the invisible one, fading into the background against the bright light that was her grandmother. To be noticed—especially by a guy like Leon—well, that was a dream come true.

Mel didn't look particularly sympathetic.

"Just help me out here, okay?" Tracy pleaded.

"I already gave you my best advice—run far, run fast."

"Mel . . ."

"Okay. Okay. All I can say is talk to the guy. You know. Be yourself."

"Myself?"

"Well, yeah. I mean, who else are you going to be?"

Who else, indeed? Tracy looked down at her tattered jeans and skinny legs. She didn't have a mirror, but she didn't need one to know that her shoulder-length, straight brown hair wasn't exactly high-fashion. She'd pulled it back with a rubber band and as usual, a million tiny wisps had escaped to frame her face. For a model the look might be sexy. On Tracy, it just looked messy.

"Maybe I'll be myself tomorrow. That gives me time to figure out what I'm supposed to look like."

Instead of a sarcastic comment, Mel just gave her a stare, the tiny lines at the corners of her eyes softening the expression. "Is this really a guy you want to reinvent yourself for? I mean, fantasies are one thing. Do you really even *want* this guy?"

Tracy sighed, cracking the door for the truth that was pounding away to be let in. "I don't know. Probably not for good." He was arrogant, true, and the movie mags did peg him with a different woman every week. But if a guy like Leon wanted her, even for a day, maybe she wasn't as plain as she'd always thought. "He doesn't have to be *the* guy, does he? Maybe he can just be *a* guy."

"So, what are you saying? You're going to have a fling with Leon Palmer?" Incredulity filled Mel's voice.

"Maybe." Tracy stood up a little straighter. The idea did have a certain appeal. "Yeah. Maybe I am. He certainly seemed interested enough." And that little fact flattered the heck out of her. Maybe Leon Palmer wasn't Mr. Right, but at the moment she didn't even have a Mr. Right Now. And who better to fill that role than a handsome television star? She stifled a grin. *In today's episode, Mr. Right Now will be played by Leon Palmer.*

Her boss's stern expression drew her out of her goofy reverie.

"It's not like I'm going to marry him, Mel. I just want to see where this leads. I think he really liked me." Tracy heard the desperation in her voice and added, "And I haven't had a guy like Leon flirt with me in, well, never."

Mel's expression softened, then turned motherly. "All right. Go for it. Have a good time. Get all dolled up and knock him dead. Sound like a plan?"

"Absolutely." Except for the butterflies jumping around in her stomach, not to mention the niggling feeling that pursuing Leon was utterly insane.

She pushed the thought away and smiled at her boss. "Thanks, Mel. I'll knock him dead if it kills me."

Hale yawned and stretched as he wondered what the heck was going on. He would have stood up and paced, killing time by looking out the windows, but the American Ops Center of the Venerate Council of Protectors was hidden deep below the Washington Monument. Windows wouldn't have provided much of a view.

We go to California, we end up back here. My nerves can't take this, I tell you. Up, down. Land, take off. Fly here. Drive there. I have sensitive sensibilities, you know. Stability. That's what I need. Stability and a little R & R. Elmer perched on the armrest of Hale's chair, a morose expression plastered on his little face. He sighed deeply. *You really do have the worst luck with vacations.*

That Hale did, but he wasn't in the mood to discuss it. Nor did he want to probe how thrilled he'd been to have an excuse to escape Bitsy and those other bathing beauties on the West Coast. *That* was a new neurosis he'd examine on his own.

He turned to Zoë, who was staring openly at the ferret.

"What's he chattering on about?" she asked.

"It's the onset of ferret psychosis. Ignore him."

Elmer managed the ferret version of a glower, which Hale ignored as he continued to focus on his sister. "They really didn't tell you anything about why we're here?"

She shook her head, her coppery hair flying. "Nope."

Hale frowned. He hated not knowing what was going on.

"I got a communiqué, same as you," Zoë added. She took a deep breath and snuggled back into one of the overstuffed recliners that surrounded the hologram dais. "I just think this is so cool, don't you? We must be getting assigned to work together on a mission." She bounced a little in her seat. "I can't wait."

"Hold your horses, kid. We don't know why we're here. For all we know it's a surprise party for Dad."

His half-sister rolled her eyes and looked smug. Heck, she was probably right, and Hale needed to get over feeling so protective of her. Just a few months ago, she might have been a halfling, unskilled at handling her superpowers. But she'd proved herself by saving the world. Not too many people—Protector or not—had that particular claim to fame.

Still, though, he was her older brother, and it was his prerogative to worry. "Where's Taylor?" he asked.

"Back in Los Angeles, of course."

"He didn't mind you coming out here?"

She laughed. "He knows what I do, Hale. Heck, he's involved in half my missions."

Hale nodded, that particular fact making him more than a little nervous. Taylor's private-investigation business might be the perfect front for a crime-fighting Protector, but Hale hated the thought of his little sister relying so much on a mortal. Of course, considering his sister had gone and actually *married* said mortal, it wasn't as if he could reason with her.

"Admit it," she said, her voice teasing. "You like him."

He mumbled something noncommittal.

"Come on. I saw you two last month watching *Star Wars* together."

"It's a good movie."

"And you were awfully complimentary when he helped you catch those counterfeiters."

"The guy's smart. I never said he wasn't."

"And you let him drive your Ferrari."

"I keep it parked in your garage. It's not like I need it in Manhattan. It would be rude not to let him drive it."

"And . . ." The corner of her mouth twitched.

"And he's a good guy." Hale shrugged, giving in. "You know I like him. I'm just a little wary of . . ."

"Yeah?" she prompted.

His shoulders sagged. "I'm sorry, kid. It's just that I—"

"—have a problem with mortals. I know."

Hale drummed his fingers on his thigh, irritated. His "problem" wasn't exactly unreasonable. Mortal-Protector relationships didn't work. Oh, sure, maybe the odd couple,

like Zoë and Taylor, or Hale's friend Starbuck and his fiancée Jenny, but more often than not, mortals were not to
be trusted. They'd tear your heart out and leave it bleeding
on the floor.

Heck. Zoë should know that. It's what her mom had
done to their father. Hale had been a little kid at the time,
and when Tessa had found out Donis's secret, she'd told
him to get out of her life and stay out. By default, she'd
told Hale the same, and he'd lost a woman who'd come
damn close to being the only mother he could remember.
It had hurt like hell, and even though Donis and Tessa were
back together, that didn't erase the past hurt. His father
might be able to forgive and forget, but Hale was smarter
than that.

As if the past didn't hold enough red flags for Hale, now
Donis was cutting back on his Protector assignments. He
said it was because he wanted to retire and spend more
time with Tessa, but Hale had to wonder how much was
because Tessa was demanding Donis change his lifestyle.
She was making Hale's father re-examine his priorities, and
that, to Hale, was bad.

Zoë shot him a peevish look. "One of these days, I hope
you meet a mortal woman who'll bring you to your knees."

*And then we'll have to enroll you in a twelve-step program
for mortal-phobes,* Elmer chittered, shaking so hard with
silent ferret laughter that he almost fell off the armrest.

"Don't hold your breath, kiddo," Hale said to Zoë. Protect mortals? Sure. Sleep with them? No problem. Fall for
them? Never. For good measure, he turned to glare at Elmer. "And you behave."

"Shhh." Zoë suddenly held a finger to her lips, her eyes
widening. "I hear something."

Zoë superpowers included super senses, so Hale didn't
doubt her, though he did wonder what his sister could possibly be hearing considering the viewing room was sup-

posedly soundproofed and cut off from the buzzing computers and clackety-clack of keyboards out in the central processing area. He didn't have long to wonder. Soon enough Zephron's image appeared on the dais in front of them, and Hale realized his sister had heard the faint whirring of the hologram projector.

They both sat back and waited for the High Elder to inform them of their mission. Since most tasks were assigned by simple communiqué—or even the much simpler telephone—Hale knew it must be important. A summons to the Ops Center suggested the direst of straits. Plus, the message he'd received in California had mentioned Hieronymous.

Something was definitely amiss.

"We have located Aphrodite's girdle," Zephron said without preamble.

Hale and Zoë exchanged a look. Elmer's fur spiked out, and the ferret crept up the chair to perch at Hale's shoulder. Just the mention of Aphrodite's girdle was sobering, especially since only a few months before, Zoë had been forced to save the planet by recovering the mystical stone centerpiece of the belt from Hieronymous's minions. The stone loose in the world had been dangerous enough. The girdle loose in the world . . . well, the consequences could be devastating.

"Where?" Zoë asked.

"Los Angeles."

She leaned back. "Since I'm the only Protector who actually lives in L.A., I guess that means it'll be my job."

Zephron's image flickered. "Not entirely. Hale has the primary responsibility for this mission. You'll be providing backup. This task is critical, however, and I wanted you here for a full briefing."

"I understand." She clasped her hands in her lap, showing no sign of distress, and Hale felt a swell of pride.

"So, why me and not Zoë?" he asked, even while Elmer started singing.

Hooray for Hollywood. Tra la la la la la la Hollywood . . .

Zephron raised an eyebrow, but essentially ignored the frantically hopping ferret. "I'll explain in a moment. First, to bring you up to speed, the girdle has been missing for years."

"Centuries, I thought."

"That is what you were meant to think. In truth, the belt surfaced once in recent history. Early in the twentieth century the Elders of the Council became aware of a mortal who possessed the belt but we were unable to reacquire it. Now, we have again detected its presence." The Elder sighed. "Hieronymous's spies have undoubtedly informed him of this development as well."

Hale nodded in understanding. His uncle, Hieronymous, had once been a powerful Protector. But his ambition was to control mortals, not keep them safe and he'd been Outcast for years. Forbidden to use his powers under threat of the direst punishment, Hieronymous had been somewhat kept under control. Slowly but surely, however, the man was organizing an underground band of other Outcasts. He also had recruited a few Protectors—traitors who had yet to be discovered—within the Council. As soon as he had the chance, Hale and the other Protectors knew, Hieronymous would try to overthrow them.

He'd already used his halfling son, Mordi, as part of his first serious attempt, the one Zoë had managed to foil. But if Hieronymous got his hands on Aphrodite's girdle, he'd have another clear shot at the prize. That would be a bad deal all around for Protectors . . . and pretty much the end of the line for mortal freedom.

Well, that sucks, Elmer said. Hale just nodded. The ferret's assessment summed up the situation quite nicely.

"I only know a little bit about the belt," Zoë admitted, shooting Hale a scathing look.

He slunk further down into his chair. The belt had been the focus of a little white lie he'd told his sister not too long ago, when she'd been pitted against Mordi. The verdict was still out on their cousin's loyalty—whether he was for the Council or his father—but there was no question that the verdict had been reached on Hale's lie: Zoë was still miffed about that.

"I know it makes the wearer irresistible to whomever he or she desires," his sister continued. "It's like a focused aphrodisiac on the object of your affections." She smiled, perhaps imagining the possibilities. "Aphrodite certainly had an obsession for that kind of thing. But that's all I know. Is there more?"

Zephron nodded toward Hale. "Tell her."

Oh, great. A pop quiz. But he smiled and turned in his chair to face his sister more directly. "You know that Aphrodite—"

"Our great-great-great-great-et-cetera grandmother."

"—forged it centuries ago." When Zoë nodded, he continued. "Well, it has all sorts of powers. On a mortal, it causes what you said—love and adoration by whomever the mortal desires. It's sort of a sensual magnet. It also works even if there's no romantic desire, although the effect is much weaker."

Zoë frowned. "I'm not following."

Hale's brow furrowed as he tried to think of an example. "Okay, let's say you're a mortal and you have the belt. Whoever you desire—romantically, sensually, sexually, *whatever*—is going to love and adore you."

"Like a love potion."

"Right," Hale said, looking to Zephron for confirmation.

"Very true," the Elder said.

"I understand that," Zoë said. "But you said it works even if I don't desire the guy."

"Right." Hale shrugged. "Maybe you're in a department store and want better service. Or a movie's sold out and you're wishing the manager would let you in anyway."

Zoë grinned. "Well, heck, that sounds better."

"What do you mean?" Hale asked.

"I've already got Taylor. But premium seats at a movie sound great."

Hale rolled his eyes, continuing with his explanation. "That's if it's a *mortal* who's wearing it. But on a Protector—"

"Let me guess," Zoë said. "On a Protector, the effect is even more intense. Love and adoration by everyone—no matter whether or not the wearer desires them. Mind-control, basically. So if Hieronymous got a hold of the thing . . ."

"Even Zephron would bend to his will," Hale finished.

They looked at each other, then turned to look at Zephron, who inclined his head in silent agreement.

Wow, squeaked Elmer. *This just keeps getting better and better*. Most ferrets hadn't mastered sarcasm. Elmer had it down pat.

"No kidding," Hale said.

"So where is it?" Zoë asked. "I mean, where in Los Angeles?"

"We don't know." Zephron's image turned, focusing entirely on Hale. "It is your job to find out."

"No prob—"

"Uh, question." Hale's sister pressed her lips together, clearly sorry for interrupting, but not sorry enough to wait.

"Yes, young Zoë?" Zephron looked at her, his eyes warm and grandfatherly. Hale bit back a smile. His little sister had certainly wormed her way into the heart of the usually stern High Elder.

"I realize I'm still new, but . . . well . . . how'd it get away the first time?"

Zephron's face tightened, his expression more serious than Hale could ever remember seeing. "It was missing for a long time during the silent-film era. Then, a young actress named Tahlula Tannin acquired the belt. We still don't know how. When we became aware that she had it, the Council's inner circle rallied to recover it. Our mission failed."

"Why?" Zoë asked the question on Hale's tongue.

"At the time, the inner circle consisted of my father and your grandfather."

"Oh." That pretty much said it all. Their Grandfather Hector had sired both Donis and Hieronymous. Zoë and Hale's dad took after his mother, whereas Hieronymous was more like his father. Not exactly the most upstanding Protector ever.

"So Grandfather Hector stole the belt from this Tahlula person?" Hale asked.

Zephron shook his head. "I almost wish he had. The belt is protected by Aphrodite's magic. We don't know all the rules, but we do know that no Protector can take it from a mortal. It must be given to him freely by whatever mortal has possession of it. If not, the Protector who steals it loses his powers forever."

"Wow," Zoë said.

"Precisely," Zephron agreed. "Our problem lay within a power struggle between my father and your grandfather. Each tried to acquire the belt. They wined and dined Ms. Tannin, seeking to persuade her to make a gift of the belt, but to no avail. Your grandfather did manage to acquire the stone centerpiece before it was lost again—that is another story—but the woman would not give up the girdle itself. My father visited her in a final effort to persuade her, but by the time he arrived the belt was gone. She wouldn't

31

say where she had taken it, but there was never any indication again that the woman had it in her possession. Despite our surveillance."

"And it's never been located since?" Hale asked.

"Never."

"We failed?" Zoë sounded vaguely disappointed.

"I'm afraid it does happen, child. If every mission were successful, we would not be so concerned about Hieronymous's efforts to rally all Outcasts."

Zoë nodded, but didn't look too happy. "How can you know it's in Los Angeles but not know where exactly? For that matter, what do you mean when you say you 'became aware' this Tahlula woman had it?"

Zephron beamed as if at a prize pupil. "An excellent question, my dear." He turned to Hale. "Care to venture a guess?"

"A tracking device, probably." A number of Council artifacts could be traced through Protector technology.

"Essentially, yes," Zephron agreed. "Your ancestor, Aphrodite, bequeathed the girdle to the mortal world." His face reflected a hint of disapproval. "She was always a prankster, that woman. At any rate, her magic protects the belt. The Council can hone in on its location, but only if a mortal is actually wearing it. The longer the mortal wears the belt, the more specifically we can pinpoint the location."

"Like a phone tap," Zoë said.

"Exactly." Zephron nodded. "But if the belt is unworn, it is completely invisible to us."

"It's gold mesh, right?" Zoë asked. "With a stone in the center?"

Zephron nodded, then turned, fumbling out of the range of the hologram projector. When he came back into view, he was holding a belt. "This is what it looks like," he said, holding it out for Hale and Zoë to inspect. "My father had this duplicate crafted. He thought to interest Tahlula in an exchange, but she showed no interest in the bargain."

"When did it last show up?" Hale asked. "The real deal, I mean. Not the duplicate."

"A week ago. A mere blip. So now you will resort to more conventional methods to locate it."

"Taylor can help," Zoë suggested.

"Not necessary," Hale said.

Zoë crossed her arms over her chest. "Watch it, big brother. Taylor's perfectly capable, and he works with me all the time."

Hale grumbled an assent. If he didn't agree, he'd never hear the end of it. Besides, the guy *was* a private investigator. Even if he was a mortal, too.

"I suggest you begin your investigation with Tahlula Tannin," Zephron said. "The last time we saw it, the belt was in her possession. Perhaps it has not gone as far as we thought."

"We'll start with her family," Hale said. "Maybe someone inherited it." He turned to Zoë with a bit of a peace offering. "Taylor can start there, trying to track down who she left her property to."

Zephron smiled. "She has a granddaughter—Tracy. In fact, you might say that this woman is the reason *you* are being assigned to this matter." He gave Hale a pointed look. "And since it is most likely this granddaughter inherited the belt, we've already retrieved the information on her current job in Los Angeles."

Woo-hoo, a girl! That's right up your alley, Hale! Elmer chittered.

Hale couldn't argue with that. Or, at least, it had *once* been up his alley. He hoped it still was. "I can be there within an hour." He glanced down at his watch. Considering the time change, that would put him there in the afternoon. Propulsion cloaks were a fabulous thing. He could fly to L.A. and check out the granddaughter while

33

Taylor tried to find out about Tahlula's will. It wasn't guaranteed to work, but it was a solid start.

He frowned, remembering Zephron's words. "What do you mean that Tracy's the reason I'm being assigned this mission?"

For a moment, he thought the Elder wouldn't answer. Then Zephron pulled himself up to his full height. "Clearly this is an important task—the fate of the world depends on its success. Normally, we would assign a team of Protectors—"

"Thanks for the vote of confidence," Hale said, not sure where Zephron was going.

"—but in this case," Zephron continued, "I've decided to assign only you." He nodded toward Zoë. "And your sister, of course. She can provide assistance."

"I'm flattered," Hale said, sure that the reason for his assignment wasn't simply that Zephron thought he was supremely exceptional. Hale had an ego, sure. But he was also realistic. "But why me?"

"As I already explained, the mortal in possession of the belt must give it to a Protector voluntarily. We can't simply steal it, since our powers would disappear." He took a breath. "As I mentioned, we do not know all the details of how the belt protects itself and its mortal owner. However, anecdotal evidence suggests that that once a mortal wears the belt, he or she will be so enamored of the power and magic that they will not want to part with it. A request to simply give it away would likely be futile."

Hale frowned. "Okay. But I still don't understand why me."

For a moment, Zephron actually looked embarrassed. "If the owner feels a bond—a connection—with the Protector, that fact can be used to our benefit to persuade the owner to hand over the belt voluntarily." Zephron's face became stern. "Neither Hector nor my father were able to persuade Tahlula, I'm afraid. Tahlula had not truly connected with them." He looked Hale in the eye. "You must make that connection. Befriend this mortal. Persuade this mortal. Our survival—and the survival of every mortal on earth—depends on it."

"And you really think *Hale's* the best for this assignment?" Zoë asked, her voice pitched high with disbelief.

As Elmer chittered in agreement, Hale also had to concur. "You want me—*me?*—to befriend a mortal?" He looked at Zephron. "You've known me my whole life. Why in Hades would you shoulder *me* with this assignment?" It was almost as if Zephron wanted him to fail—or had some other unspoken agenda. It just didn't make sense.

"You have befriended mortals in the past," Zephron said. "Taylor, for example."

Zoë nodded. "That's true. And Hoop, Deena and Lane," she added, referring to all the mortals Hale had met when Zoë had battled Mordi.

"Yes, but they're not . . . I'm not . . ." He trailed off. As much as he hated to admit it, he had befriended them. *Damn.*

"You are also an excellent Protector," Zephron continued. "And you can be very persuasive when it suits you." He looked Hale in the eye, and Hale was sure he saw a hint of amusement flickering in the Elder's gaze. "In other words, I'm positive you will prevail."

Hale nodded in silent acknowledgment of the compliment, then tried another tack. "As much as I might enjoy making another mortal friend," he lied, "I'm wondering if it's really necessary."

"Of course it is," Zoë said. "Didn't you hear Zephron? Hieronymous? End of the world? A generally bad situation all the way around?"

"I mean, why don't we just let Taylor or some other mortal steal the thing? As I've pointed out many times, they

35

don't have any powers to lose." He turned to Zoë and lifted an eyebrow. "And it would prove that mortals are good for something."

"I assure you," Zephron said, "mortals are good for many things. But not this."

"Why?" he and Zoë asked in unison.

"Aphrodite's enchantment again. No mortal can steal the belt. It simply isn't possible. A mortal can receive it as a gift or an inheritance or buy it in a thrift shop if the owner has thrown it away, but a mortal cannot simply take it." He shrugged. "It's impossible. The belt will not leave its rightful owner unless the owner gives it away or it is stolen by a Protector—who would then lose his powers."

A darned finicky fashion accessory, if you ask me, Elmer piped up. Hale tried his best to ignore him.

"Just remember," Zephron added. "When we find the belt's owner, your mission will include providing protection. Any mortal in possession of the girdle will be in danger from Heironymous."

"Protection from what? He can't steal the thing," Zoë spoke up. "We just went over that." Her eyes went wide. "Can he kill her and just take it?"

Zephron shook his head. "If the mortal owner of the belt dies at the hand of another, the belt's powers die as well."

Hale rubbed his temples. "So, let's see if I'm following— we can't enlist a mortal to steal the belt for us because Grandma decided that wasn't part of the playbook. And we can't steal it because we'd lose our powers. Assuming she won't hand it over if I just ask nicely, that means I'll have to"—he shuddered—"*befriend* this Tracy person or whoever has the belt in order to convince her to give it up to me voluntarily."

Zephron nodded. "Precisely."

"Not that I'm complaining about the whole mortal bonding thing," Hale lied—he *was* complaining, and loudly—

"but isn't it unnecessary? I mean, there's no way Hierony-mous could befriend anybody, much less a mortal."

"True," Zephron acknowledged. "But there are many other methods of persuasion. Torture, for example."

"Oh," Zoë whispered, swallowing.

"Hieronymous could also send one of his minions to per-suade the owner with soft words and romantic evenings," Zephron added. "Or, he could simply resort to other means."

"Other means?" Zoë repeated.

"Hieronymous has minions, many of whom would sac-rifice their powers for his approval. The curse extends only to stealing the belt. Not receiving it."

Rules, rules, rules, Elmer said. *You protectors and your rules. I swear, you need a manual to keep up.*

"Anything else we need to know?" Hale asked, silently agreeing with the ferret.

"No," Zephron said. "As I said, we do not fully under-stand the belt. At this point, you know everything we've confirmed."

Hale nodded. So, that was it. Their mission was about to begin. He squeezed the armrest and looked at Zoë. She nodded, almost imperceptibly, and Hale knew they were thinking on the same lines. If Hieronymous's followers were so loyal, then Uncle H's threat to the Council was growing exponentially every day. Once again, they needed to foil their uncle in order to save the world.

But what the heck? He was up to the challenge. And what was the point of being a superhero if there wasn't a little drama in your life?

Mordichai watched as Hieronymous drummed his fingers on the heavy oak desk. *Tap, tap. Tap, tap.* His father's in-cessant habit drove him crazy, and if it didn't stop soon,

Mordi was sure to let out a howl loud enough to shake the heavens.

Or maybe not. No one lost his patience with Hieronymous. Least of all his son.

"It's there. Aphrodite's girdle." Hieronymous stood up, his fingers twitching as if he were stifling the urge to rub his hands together with glee. "We've seen the flicker from the monitoring device."

He pointed toward the bank of monitors on the far side of the room. As usual, ten of the twelve were displaying various financial programs. The eleventh showed an empty stone cell, manacles on the wall, with only a single red chair in the center.

Mordi frowned, trying to figure out what his father was doing monitoring an old castle. "The belt's in a dungeon?"

Hieronymous shot him a look of contempt. "That 'dungeon' as you call it, is part of an old movie set that one of my investment companies is considering acquiring."

Mordi fought a smile. Hieronymous himself owned nothing. Instead, his property was owned by offshore corporations shielding other offshore corporations. Nothing traceable back to Hieronymous—which was just the way he liked it.

"Why?" Mordi asked.

"I took a fancy to it," his father said. Mordi imagined that was true. Hieronymous would probably live in a castle once—if—he overthrew the Council. "And it may come in useful someday." Hieronymous pointed a finger toward the last monitor, the one in the middle displaying the Los Angeles skyline. "But you are not here to learn about my investments. Aphrodite's girdle is somewhere in that city, and we don't have a clue where."

"I know, Father."

"You *know?*" Hieronymous sneered. "Or you understand?"

38

Mordi sat up straighter, sucking in a strengthening breath. "I understand."

"Do you?" His father's voice was low, menacing. "Tell me, son, what it is you understand?"

Mordi sighed. He'd failed his father recently, and winning back the old man's trust was proving tricky. Not that Hieronymous had *ever* really had faith in Mordi. No, Mordi was a halfling—a by-product of a tryst with a mortal—and apparently that fact didn't sit well with dear old Dad. Which meant that time and again Mordi found himself beating his brains out to win respect.

"I understand that Aphrodite's girdle is somewhere in Los Angeles. I understand that you need it, that with it you can rally the Outcasts and overcome the Council."

"How?"

Mordichai sighed, hating having to prove himself at every turn. "The girdle will make you invincible. No one will be able to stop you or refuse you. That treaty the Council is trying to work out with the mortal government will be just so much paper. You'll be the top dog. You'll be the head honcho. You'll be the king of the world," he added, imagining his father living in his newly acquired castle.

A thin smile touched his father's lips, and his eyes got a faraway expression. "Exactly. A Protector who wears the girdle, even an Outcast, is like a god. I shall rule as our race was meant to rule—not taking a backseat to those mortals and their pesky problems. They should be serving us, not the other way around."

Hieronymous waved a hand in the air as he paced the length of the room, his heels clicking on the hardwood floor. "Treaties and politics and secret negotiations, all for what end? So that perhaps Protectors can come out in the light and be seen for what we really are? Bah. Zephron and his stable of flunkies are fools. We should not negotiate with those ridiculous mortals. We should simply take over—

and crush the mortals like the insects they are."

He turned to Mordi, his eyes aglow with the lust for power. "With the girdle, I can escape this prison." His arm swept the luxurious highrise in midtown Manhattan that most mortals would kill for. "I can fulfill my destiny."

"You just need me to find and get it for you," Mordi said dryly. As an Outcast, Hieronymous was forbidden to use his powers. If he did—and if he was caught—the punishment was severe. Though Mordichai was not a full-fledged member of the Council, his status as a probationer didn't put any such restrictions on him.

Hieronymous aimed one curt nod in his direction. Not an overwhelming display of affection, but the man wasn't the type to dole out bucketfuls of praise. "Exactly. No matter how you failed me in the past, it seems that I do have some use left for you. As I cannot use my power to locate the belt's owner—or convince the owner to give the belt to me—I will have to rely on you. I have no choice." Again he waved a hand, as if sweeping away a gnat. "And, of course, you shall have to prove yourself to be the heir to my kingdom." The last was spoken casually, an afterthought intended to placate.

"Yes, Father," Mordi said. A slow fury rose in him, urging him to lash out, to unleash every bit of hurt and anger toward the man, but he held back. Instead, he simply sat holding his tongue and remembering why he was there.

Because the truth was, he *did* have to find the girdle. And he had to get it away from its owner. Only one question remained. Once he held it in his hands, what would he do? Would he turn it over to his father? Would he deliver it to the Council? Or would Mordichai have the last laugh after all?

Chapter Three

Tracy frowned at the broom-and-dustpan-type devices leaning against the Paws In Production trailer. Not the most pleasant of tasks, pooper-scoopering unfortunately came with the territory.

The crew was wrapping up as she headed toward the three set pieces that had been used for the day's shoot. The premise of this show was pretty simple, and sometimes Tracy found herself wondering at its overnight success. The elderly Mrs. Dolittle, a vet in a small coastal town, treated a bunch of animals—domestic and exotic—and each week she and her nephew got entangled in some wild and wacky crime that one of her animal patients somehow helped her solve.

Unlike her literary counterpart, Mrs. Dolittle didn't talk to the animals. That was Tracy and Mel's job—talking to them and making sure they knew their cues and what to do when the camera turned their way.

Julie Kenner

Mel had left early to tackle a day full of meetings, and none of the interns were scheduled to work. Which left Tracy to handle the parade scene—complete with a Bengal tiger and Mrs. Dolittle's dog Pepper. The scene had gone fine, but now Tracy was stuck with the unpleasant task of cleaning up.

Tightening her stomach, Tracy took her bucket, and headed out toward the parade route. This was definitely not the part of the job she liked best, but at least Mel or one of the interns usually shared it. Considering the company belonged to Mel, and Tracy was only an employee, the woman could easily have put her on permanent poop patrol.

She'd just filled one bucket and was heading back to the trailer to dump it when Tracy saw him again. Leon leaned against the Volkswagon Beetle he drove in the show, his wavy brown hair gilded by the afternoon light. A group of extras stood around chatting with him. Her first instinct was to turn and run—she wasn't exactly at her best—but then he waved in her direction and smiled.

She swallowed. Mel had said to talk to him, to be herself. He'd liked her before, surely he'd like her still. Taking a deep breath, she marched toward him. When she was near enough, she waved back. He blinked but didn't respond. Had he seen her?

Summoning all her courage, she continued on. When she reached the far side of the car, she stopped and smiled. He looked up, his eyes vacant, then he looked off somewhere over her and smiled. A blond extra in a too-tight tank top appeared in Tracy's peripheral vision.

Tracy suddenly felt cold. She considered just turning away and running as fast as she could back toward the trailer, but no, she was a grown woman. She might as well act like one.

"Hi, Leon," she began.

He turned back to her, obviously put out. "Can I help you?"

She was beginning to have a very bad feeling about this. "No. I mean yes. I mean, I just wanted to say hello." She lowered the bucket so it was hidden behind the car, feeling lower than low because she was on poop patrol. "We, uh, met this morning. Over at the trailer. You were looking for Melissa. Remember?"

The blond extra gave Tracy the once-over, then turned away, apparently convinced she wasn't a threat.

"Oh, yeah." Leon smiled, and a wave of relief crashed over her. "Elizabeth, right?"

"Tracy," she said, her mouth dry.

"Oh. Oh, *right*." He flashed his I'm-so-cool grin. "Sorry. I just didn't recognize you." His voice suggested that he was still clueless.

The creep. He hadn't been flirting with *her*, he'd just been flirting to get something he wanted. Exactly what Mel had claimed—and what Tracy had foolishly denied. Lord, she was stupid!

The tears that welled in her eyes only added to her humiliation, and she took a step backward, desperate to get away. Unfortunately she misjudged her footing and somehow managed to slip off the curb. Her arms flailed as she tried to balance, but it just wasn't working. She tumbled forward.

Horrified, Tracy watched as the bucket flew out of her hands and landed on the roof of the Beetle. Like smelly missiles, the stinky contents shot out toward the far side of the car as Leon and the extras—as if in slow motion—gasped and backed away.

They didn't move fast enough.

The splattering mess missed most of the extras.

It didn't miss Leon.

And as he stood there, his eyes wide while tiger poop clung to his hair and clothes, all Tracy could think was that this time, at least, he wouldn't forget her.

She walloped him! Elmer howled. *Way to go, girl!*

"Shhh," Hale whispered. He almost wished he'd brought popcorn, the show going on below his rooftop perch was so much fun. "They'll hear you."

We're two stories above. And you're invisible.

"Then they'll see *you*. Would you be quiet?"

They'll just think I'm a squirrel.

"Elmer . . ." He was in no mood to argue with the ferret. "Just be quiet, okay? I'm trying to watch the subject."

Subject, smubject. You're watching the female scenery.

True enough. The women hovering around the now-fuming Leon Palmer were nice enough eye-candy. But it was Tracy Tannin who caught his attention. Any woman who could stand firm after throwing animal excrement on a famous actor like Palmer—smarmy cretin though he was—deserved Hale's utmost respect.

Not that Tracy looked to be proud of herself. More like she wanted to crawl under a rock. In fact, she seemed so miserable that it was all Hale could do to keep from materializing, hopping down from his perch on the roof, and giving her a hearty congratulatory handshake and slap on the back.

Not that he really would, of course. Materializing in front of mortals always caused such a stir—they just didn't understand.

Besides, at the moment he was only here to observe. Soon enough his sister might discover that this woman had indeed inherited Aphrodite's girdle. Then he would have to get close enough to sweet-talk the belt away.

Still, while he might want to get *close*—in the way he typically did with mortal females—buddying up didn't sit nearly as well. What had Zephron been thinking? Hale was the last Protector on Earth who should be trying to befriend a mortal. And the fact that Tracy Tannin intrigued him didn't change that assessment one bit.

At the moment, the object of his surveillance had a horrified look on her face. Even so, he thought he saw something hidden beneath the surface. A glimmer of amusement, maybe? A swell of satisfaction? He couldn't tell, but he hoped he was right. She'd taken Palmer down a notch or two, and she deserved to be pleased.

"Just *look* what you've done!" the actor yelled, his words becoming more coherent as he quit sputtering.

Tracy cringed. "I'm sorry. Really. I'm so, so sorry." But the corner of her mouth suggested that she was having a hard time holding in laughter. She took a step toward him, a rag she'd pulled from her back pocket held out like a peace offering. "Can I help?"

"Yes, you can help," he growled. "You can stay the hell away from me."

This guy was a definite jerk, in Hale's estimation. All around Palmer, his little throng of hangers-on was dissipating, probably to escape the smell or to find washcloths of their own. Suddenly alone, the actor looked even more pitiful, and Hale silently urged Tracy to lay into him for being rude. To tell him he'd only got what he deserved.

She didn't, of course. Clearly, the girl had more class than Hale.

Taking a cautious step backward, she held on tight to her bucket. "Well, I really am sorry, Leon. And if I can't help, I guess I'll just . . ." She trailed off, ending by gesturing over her shoulder with her thumb. "Right. I'm . . . uh . . . going now."

With that, she turned and ran, her now-empty pooper-scooper bucket swinging as she sprinted through the back lot.

Left behind, Leon muttered curses and used a handkerchief to wipe off his jeans and shirt. Hale didn't intend to let it be that easy for him, though.

One of the best superpowers he had was telekinesis—he could levitate even the nastiest things without touching them. So, every time superjerk tried to wipe himself clean, Hale just lifted some of the mess back up and splattered it on him.

"What the . . . ?" Leon shrieked.

You're very bad.

"He deserves it."

Power exploitation . . . Elmer chided in a singsong little voice, reminding Hale about the cardinal rule for Protectors.

"He deserves it," Hale repeated. "He'll think it's the wind. And rules are made to be broken." Even so, he stopped. He'd made his point.

He had better things to do than watch this creep try to clean himself. After all, he'd come all the way to Los Angeles on a really good tail-wind so that he could spend the evening keeping Tracy Tannin under surveillance. Considering how intrigued he was by the girl, Hale was more than happy to trade punishing Leon for watching her.

Utter and complete mortification. No other words described how Tracy felt. If she could have dissolved into the asphalt, she would have, but unfortunately, her dissolving skills were sadly lacking. The best she could do was lie prostrate on the pavement, and somehow that just wasn't the same.

She checked the inside of the Paws In Production trailer, then remembered that Mel was still at her meeting. Missy was all alone, eating kibble in her kennel.

"Hey, little girl," Tracy said, unlocking the cage then patting her leg. Missy trotted to the edge of the second-tier cage, sniffed the air, then presented Tracy with a hopeful glance.

"No way, kiddo. It's barely two feet. You can jump down."

The little con artist whined, then flopped onto her belly, her paws in front of her and her eyes soulful.

"Oh, you're a ham." Tracy tapped her foot and waited for Missy to come to her senses. Naturally, the dog didn't. "Fine." She scooped the fluffball up, closed and locked the cage, then headed out of the trailer to her car.

"You're a lot of trouble, you know that?"

Missy whined, and Tracy felt absolutely certain it was a sound of apology.

"It's been a horrific day," Tracy said as she opened the passenger door and set Missy inside. "I think we deserve a treat. What do you think?"

At the word *treat*, Missy opened her mouth and let loose a high-pitched *arf* of agreement.

"Good. Because I'm thinking ice cream's on the agenda." Lots of ice cream. Bucketsful. No, *gallons*-full. Which, of course, raised the age-old question. How many spoonfuls of ice cream does it take to cure a really bad day?

Tracy had absolutely no idea, but she intended to find out.

She slid into the driver's seat of her ancient Nova and waited for Missy to quit gnawing at the fur of her thigh. As soon as the dog was settled, Tracy cranked the engine, ready to head for Ventura Boulevard and some chocolate chocolate-chip.

Nothing.

She cranked again.

Still nothing.

Either her battery was dead, or cosmic forces were conspiring to keep her away from frozen confections. Considering she had no intention of giving in to the cosmos, she assumed the problem was merely a dead battery.

What an annoyance. Still, when you got right down to it, wasn't that pretty much what she expected today?

She popped the hood and got out of the car, leaving the door open in case Missy wanted to hop out and sniff around. Tracy had never been able to make heads or tails out of the mechanical mess under the hood of a car, and today wasn't any exception. Considering her troubles in the past, the battery was probably dead, which meant she'd have to find someone to jump-start it. But since the lot was empty, "someone" probably translated to the Auto Club.

Rummaging in her purse, she located her cell phone under a bag of doggie treats. Unfortunately, she didn't have nearly as much luck finding her Auto Club card.

Fine. No problem. She'd just call information, get the number, then wait on hold for a million years while they looked her up in the system. What else could go wrong?

Just as she started to dial, Missy started barking like crazy. Tracy turned around, intending to glare at the dog, and found herself glaring instead into the most gorgeous pair of Paul Newman eyes she'd ever seen.

"Oh!" Through sheer luck, she managed not to drop her cell phone. Her jaw wasn't nearly as cooperative, and she fought to reassemble her face into some sort of expression that didn't scream *lust! Woman who never gets any right here!*

"Problem?" The man's deep, smooth voice was just as easy on her ears as the rest of him was on her eyes.

"No. No problem at all." Except that she couldn't stop staring. He seemed so familiar somehow, but she couldn't quite place him.

Her brain kicked into gear. Or her mouth did, at last. "Yes!" She coughed. "I mean, yes, actually, I do have a problem." With a quick nod, she indicated the offending vehicle. "It's being uncooperative."

48

"I find that hard to believe." His smile revealed a dimple, and once again Tracy was struck by how familiar he looked. As if she'd looked at him every day of her life. "I can't imagine anything not going out of its way to please you."

She squinted at him, not sure why another gorgeous man was flirting with her, but considering the day's events, she wasn't inclined to fall into that trap again. "As remarkable as it might seem, there aren't many things in this world that fall over themselves to do my bidding. If there were, maybe I wouldn't be getting ready to scour the backlot for jumper cables."

The man's mouth twitched.

"Glad to provide you with some entertainment," she snapped.

The man laughed outright. "I get the feeling you're not having the best day."

"I'm having a *lousy* day, thank you very much." Then, running her hands through her hair, she sighed. "I'm sorry. It's not your fault, and I'm taking it out on you. I promise, I'm not usually such a bitch."

Again, that incredible smile. "I believe you."

Missy wandered over, sniffed the man's shoes, then plunked herself down on the asphalt and waited for him to scratch her head. He complied almost immediately, earning him at least two brownie points in Tracy's book, and probably lifelong infatuation from Missy.

"Right. Well." Something about this guy made her incredibly nervous. Not that the *something* was any great mystery. He was some sort of Greek god, and she'd never exactly been at ease with men of the supergorgeous variety.

Still, one of the nice things about growing up as Tahlula Tannin's granddaughter was that Tracy had met more than her share of incredibly good-looking people. And through

49

each encounter, though she'd felt uncomfortable, she'd had to be on her best behavior. So, with her grandmother's etiquette lessons spurring her on, she held out her hand in greeting. "I'm Tracy, by the way. And you are . . ."

"Incredibly pleased to meet you."

His hand closed over hers, sending a flood of rather disconcerting tingly sensations racing through her body. Within seconds, the fact that he'd failed to answer her question ceased to bother her.

He nodded toward the car. "Can I help?"

"I think the battery's dead."

"No problem." He headed over to the area behind the Paws trailer, and for the first time she noticed the sleek, black Ferrari parked there. As Mel would say, another two points in the mystery guy's favor.

"I didn't think a car like that would need jumper cables," she said.

He aimed a devilish grin her direction. "Well, I don't keep them for me. But it's a heck of an efficient way to meet women."

Okay, this guy was a hoot. He was doing *way* too good a job at lifting her foul mood. "Does it work?"

"Ask me in a few minutes."

Well, that did it. A bubble of laughter escaped her.

He waved the jumper cables in her direction. "Met you, didn't I?"

"Oh, I get it," she said with good-natured sarcasm. "You hang around in parking lots waiting for women with dead batteries." Even as she said the words, she couldn't believe how flirtsy she was being with this stranger. It was so un-Tracy-like. Tahlula would be proud. Mel would be ecstatic.

"Do you have a problem with that?"

The husky tone of his voice zinged straight to her knees, and Tracy grabbed the roof of her car for support. "No. It's just that . . ." She trailed off, suddenly fresh out of flirty comments. After a second, she just shrugged. "I'm *so* not good at this."

"I don't buy that." He lifted the hood of her car and propped it up, then turned back to face her, his eyes smoldering. "I bet you're very, very good at everything."

Okay. He won. No way could she compete with this guy in a flirting contest. As she concentrated on standing up straight, her cheeks burned from what had to be a blush worthy of the record books. She'd better get this conversation back on business. "Um . . . so, it is the battery, right?"

As she nodded toward the engine, she thought she detected a glimmer of disappointment in his eyes, but it faded as quickly as it had appeared. "I'll know in just a sec."

In about twelve efficient movements, he'd made it back to his Ferrari, climbed in, and pulled up in front of her car. A few more mechanical-guy-type actions and he had the jumper cables hooked up between the batteries. To Tracy's delight, the macho-guy routine required him to bend over the hood, and she got quite a nice view.

"All done," he said, standing back up.

"You're speedy."

"Believe me, sweetheart, I can also go slow." His dimple made a quick appearance, then he got serious again. "Now hop in and see if you can start her up."

She did, and the Nova hummed to life. Sticking her head out the open door, she flashed him her winningest smile. "You're wonderful."

"Glad you think so. Drive it around for a bit so it can build a charge back up."

"I will." A moment of awkward silence. "Thanks."

Their eyes met for a brief, heart-stopping, delightful second. Tracy said a silent prayer that he would ask her out for coffee, and then immediately took it back. Sometimes it was nicer to live with a fantasy. In a fantasy, they'd spend the evening together, then head down in his Ferrari to the beach, where they'd walk together in the surf as the sun set against the horizon. Perfect. In reality, she'd probably spill coffee all over herself and not have a single interesting thing to say.

"I'll be seeing you around, Tracy," the man said, unhooking the cables and taking a step back toward his car.

"Mmmm-hmmm . . ." As her fantasy dissolved, she caught herself nodding like an idiot, then jumped out of her car and rushed toward him. "Wait!"

Curiosity and amusement reflected in his eyes as he turned back to her.

"You don't work for the show. What are you doing around here?"

"Just my job."

"Your job?" As far as she could tell, he hadn't done anything more than jump-start her car. "What job?"

"Helping damsels in distress, of course."

"Oh." For a second there, she even believed him. Then she saw his grin and rolled her eyes. "Sorry. Guess I shouldn't look a gift horse in the mouth. Never mind my question. Thank you. I really appreciate your help."

"Anytime."

And with that, he turned around and headed for his Ferrari. The view of him leaving proved to be just as enticing as the eyeful she'd gotten while he'd been under the hood. With some effort, Tracy managed to stifle a sigh.

Maybe the cosmos was on her side after all. Certainly this anonymous hunk of a Good Samaritan had added a bit of joy to an otherwise rotten day. And who knew? If the rest of the evening went as well, she might actually recover from her little incident with Leon without being scarred for life.

Chapter Four

Taylor looked at his wife—he still loved the sound of that, *wife*—and smiled. Zoë was always a bundle of energy, but right now he thought that if she let herself go, she'd literally bounce from one wall of their little kitchen to the other.

"Thanks for helping," she said, blowing him a kiss.

"No problem." He checked his watch as he leaned back in his chair. "I can always fit saving the world into my busy schedule."

From the living room his friend and partner, Hoop, guffawed. "Don't tease her, Taylor. She can beat you up."

Hoop's fiancée, Deena, scowled at the game board, then invaded Madagascar. "She can beat us *all* up," Deena announced. She aimed a grin Zoë's way, and Taylor had to smile. The blonde and Zoë had become fast friends when Zoë was an elementary school librarian. And Taylor had Deena to thank in part for his first date with Zoë. "Of course, she can't beat us at Risk," Deena added. She nodded toward the board. "Hoop and I are creaming all of you."

"Who can beat who up?" Lane asked, appearing in the living room after putting her son Davy down for the night. Since her landlord had decided to convert her apartment complex to condos, Taylor's foster sister and her child were temporarily camping out in the guest room. Lane and Davy had played their own parts when Zoë had saved the world recently. Taylor shuddered, remembering how close both his foster sister and her son had come to danger. Fortunately, Zoë had been there on each occasion and had saved them. It had taken some getting used to, but loving a superhero had certain benefits.

Lane held up a hand. "Wait, I know." She flashed a grin Taylor's way. "*Zoë* can beat *you* up."

"It's not being beat up I'm worried about." Taylor laughed. "She might decide I have to sleep on the couch."

"Speaking of . . ." Lane aimed for the huge living room couch and dropped, clearly exhausted, onto one of its cushions. She motioned toward the game board. "Is it my turn yet?"

From his perch on the couch's armrest, Hale mumbled something.

"What?" Taylor asked, even though he could guess what his brother-in-law was saying. The man was always making wisecracks at the expense of mortals—even his sister's friends. It drove all of them nuts, especially because they all knew that, deep down, he was a good guy.

"Nothing," Hale said, all innocence. He let loose a rip-roaring sneeze and immediately disappeared.

Deena looked up for a second before looking back at the game board, unimpressed with Hale's vanishing act.

"Stupid allergies." Hale's disembodied voice floated out of thin air.

Zoë rolled her eyes and, before Taylor even had time to

blink, his wife had leaped across the room and nestled into his lap. It had taken him a while to get used to how quickly she could move, especially now that her skills were developed, but he wouldn't have it any other way.

"You're not sleeping anywhere but my bed, mister. Those are the rules." She planted a light kiss on his cheek.

He tightened his grip around her waist. "Wouldn't want to break the rules." Their eyes caught, and he remembered all over again why he loved her.

"Uh, people?" Hale's voice broke through Taylor's Zoë-induced haze. "I came here to find out what you learned while I was watching Tracy. Can we get to work and desist with the public displays of affection?"

"It's our house," Zoë murmured. "It's not public at all."

"Then desist with the private displays, too," Hale said, shimmering as he materialized again. "Call me crazy, but I thought that since you folks called yourselves private investigators, you might have done a little investigating."

"We call ourselves investigators?" Hoop asked, to no one in particular. "Damn. And here I thought we called ourselves psychic crime fighters."

Deena groaned and threw a gamepiece at him. He just laughed as it bounced harmlessly off his head.

"My brother's getting surly," Zoë said, her voice dreamy against Taylor's ear. "And Hoop's getting goofy."

"Tell me something I don't know," Taylor murmured back.

Hale's exasperated sigh echoed through the room, and Taylor and Zoë laughed.

"Guess it's time to give him the full report," Taylor said.

Finally! Whenever Zoë and Taylor got lost in that mushzone, Hale wondered if he would ever manage to yank them out of it. Part of him even envied them, but that wasn't something he particularly wanted to think about.

Especially since Tracy Tannin's face kept popping into his head.

He'd gone to that lot solely to familiarize himself with the girl in case they were right and she'd inherited the belt. She hadn't been wearing it. And while that certainly didn't mean anything, now he found himself thinking about her at the oddest moments. Worse, he found himself thinking that if she *didn't* have the belt—and if the mission ended up calling for no interaction between him and Tracy Tannin—he was going to be sorely disappointed. Especially since the adorable mortal might just prove to be the cure for his recent lack of interest in the female of the species.

Right now, though, he just needed to know what Taylor had discovered. "Anytime this year would be good," he called into the kitchen, scowling at his brother-in-law who was still cuddling Zoë.

Taylor kissed Zoë's ear, then slid her off his lap. "Let's go calm down your brother," he said. Taking her hand, he tugged her into the living room toward the couch, the pair looking perfectly comfortable together. Two halves of a whole. The unexpected thought cast a wave of melancholy over Hale, and he cringed. Just because he'd never experienced that kind of closeness didn't mean he needed to start feeling all mushy. He was here on a job, and once it was over he could get back to his vacation and do a little female grazing. Somehow, some way, he'd get himself back into the groove.

"Okay, brother mine," Taylor said, as he moved to the computer hutch. Hale got a glimpse of the monitor as Taylor sat down in the desk chair. The Venerate Council's "News In Brief" page was up. The council had its own website, with a stellar search engine that accessed all sorts of supposedly inaccessible files. Being a superhero only went so far. They were living in an information age, after all, and crime-fighting superheroes needed all the information they could get. Taylor wasn't a Protector, of course, but considering he was partnered with Zoë, Zephron had given him permission to access the site. Apparently Taylor had been using the search engine, and Hale could see the large point headlines from across the room:

Mortal-Protector Treaty talks continue. Controversy rages! Click here for point/counterpoint!

Rumors abound—Has Aphrodite's Girdle been found? Follow this link for the latest news and commentary.

All Protectors with undercover assignments in the mortal world are required to complete Form 789-A(5)—Statement of Undercover Operations—and to file same with the Mortal-Protector Liaison Office. Click here to download applicable forms and instructions.

Hale made a mental note to get his Form 789 in on time as he waited for Taylor to quit rummaging through the papers on his desk.

"Okay," Taylor said. "Listen to this." He held up a computer print-out and started reading. "Beloved silent film star . . . blah, blah . . . survived by her granddaughter, Tracy Tannin . . . yadda, yadda . . . Okay, here we go—Tracy inherited the house and everything else."

With one easy jump, Hale hopped to the top of the computer hutch and sat there, his feet swinging in front of the monitor. That Tracy had been the only real beneficiary was excellent. Spending some quality time with the woman was something he could handle just fine—and now she was even more entrenched as their primary lead.

"Do you mind?" Taylor asked.

"Sorry." Hale dematerialized, clearing Taylor's view. "This means that if Tahlula still had the belt when she died, now it's Tracy's."

"Right-o," Taylor agreed.

"I take it Tracy wasn't wearing the belt this afternoon," Zoë said.

"Nope," Hale agreed. "Besides, if she were, it would have shown up on the tracking device. According to Zephron, it hasn't blipped again."

"So, we don't know for sure that Tracy has it," Zoë said.

Unfortunately, Zoë was right. He looked down at Taylor and materialized.

"So what's our next step, Mr. Investigator?"

"Way ahead of you." Taylor tapped a few more keys as Zoë wandered over. Hoop and Deena stayed put in front of their game. Lane got up, but as soon as she did, Zoë turned to her.

"You might as well go check on him," she said.

Lane's shoulders sagged. "I just got him put down. What's up now?"

"*He* is. Or he will be."

Lane's mouth twisted. "You're sure?"

"You know that little noise he makes before he wakes up with a nightmare?"

"He's making it?"

"Sorry. You want me to go check on him?"

Lane just shook her head. "No thanks. It's all part of mommy duty. You'll get there soon enough."

Hale's stomach tightened, and he examined his sister's face, wondering if . . .

"Quit fretting," she said to Hale as she noticed his expression. "Not now. But hopefully someday."

Surprisingly, Hale realized he was slightly disappointed. Maybe he wasn't ready for fatherhood—or even husband-hood—but uncle-hood might be fun.

"Hale?" Zoë squinted at him. "Are you okay?"

"Fine," he said, his voice gruff. Hopping Hades, what was wrong with him? Frustrated, he kicked at the side of the computer hutch. "So what have you got in mind?" he demanded, glaring at Taylor.

"You move in," the mortal said.

Hale balked. "Excuse me?"

"I said—"

"Move in?" Hoop interrupted. "Why not just let Superjock play the invisible man?" he asked, twirling a Risk gamepiece between his fingers. "He can snoop all around her place and no one will be the wiser."

Hale wasn't too keen on the Superjock nickname, and he shifted his glare from Taylor to Hoop.

"What? You can't do that? You guys got Protector police or something?" Hoop asked.

"There's that whole treaty thing," Deena answered. "They're not allowed to break into someone's house and start rummaging through their things." She cocked her head, then looked from Zoë to where Hale was perched. "Are you?"

"No." Hale agreed, half-wishing they were allowed. He turned back to Taylor. "What did you mean I 'move in?' "

Taylor pointed to the monitor, which Hale couldn't see from his perch on the hutch. "Today's classified ads. Tracy's looking for a roommate. Move in, and suddenly you're all set to form that strong, devoted bond of Mortal-Protector friendship that Zephron told you and Zoë about." Taylor paused. "And that I know you're so looking forward to."

Hale scowled at Taylor, sure his brother-in-law was being sarcastic, but the mortal just smiled innocently. "Not happening," Hale said.

"The bond, or the moving in?"

"The moving in," Hale said. "For the good of the mission, I'll get the girl to bond with me. I'll make that connection. I'll do whatever it takes to persuade her. But believe me, I don't need to move in to do that."

59

"Uh-huh." Taylor's voice was dubious.

"She only has to bond with me," Hale said. "Not me with her." Which was fortunate, since he didn't intend to share any sort of emotional bond with a mortal. The fact that he'd become friends with these mortals was simply a testament to how much he loved Zoë. And his sister's little in-crowd of mortals was unique, anyway. Hale put up with them, but that didn't mean he was suddenly opening his arms to the friendship of the whole mortal population.

Frustrated, he hopped off the hutch and moved to the sofa, flopping back against the cushions. He couldn't keep the kind of distance he wanted if he was living on top of her. Not that being *on top of her* would be all that unpleasant, but that wasn't his mission. No, for some inexplicable reason, Zephron had picked Hale to befriend the mortal. To make nice with the girl, get her to trust him, and then persuade her to give up the belt.

Still, Zoë and Taylor were probably right. Moving in would help. But Hale just couldn't stomach it. Eating breakfast together and sharing the living room television . . . well, those were intimate moments. Getting-to-know you moments. Exactly the kind of moments Hale had no in interest in having with a mortal. "Ah, hell," he muttered, letting his head fall back against the sofa. He'd never thought he was wrong for a mission before, but this time . . .

What had Zephron been thinking?

"Not that I'm agreeing with my brother's logic," Zoë said, looking from him to Taylor, "but we don't even know that Tracy has the belt. It would probably be premature for him to try and be her roomie."

"Exactly," Hale said, latching on to the excuse. "The belt only blipped on the monitor. We don't know who has it. It's probably Tracy, sure, but it could just as easily be in a box at the Salvation Army."

"Any reason why we don't just *ask* her if she has the belt?" Deena wondered aloud. "And if she does, then just ask her to hand it over." She looked from Hale to Zoë to Taylor in turn. "I mean, unless there's a rule, shouldn't you try that first?"

Hale turned to look at his sister's friend more directly. One thing he'd learned about Deena: she always said what was on her mind. "Let's say I ask her for the belt. If she does have it, she's not going to want to give it up. For one, it belonged to her grandmother. For another, Zephron explained about how she'll want to keep it. What do I do if she says no?"

Deena shrugged. "Seduce her, I guess. Isn't that right up your alley?"

It was, though after Bitsy, Hale had been a little worried. Not that he intended to explore his concerns with Deena. Instead, he just said, "If I've already asked her for it, and *then* I seduce her, she'll assume I'm only after the belt."

"And she'll be right," Hoop piped up.

"Oh." Deena gnawed on her lower lip. "Well, you could tell her the truth."

"Oh, yeah. That'd go over big." He looked over to where Elmer was asleep on a chair. "Hey, Elmer. You listening to this?"

A pair of sleepy ferret eyes blinked up at him. *What? Listening to what?*

Hale didn't explain. "Let's see how this would go over, shall we?" He nodded from Deena to Elmer. "Pretend Elmer's Tracy." He stood up straighter and said in his most polite voice, "Hi, Tracy. You don't know me, but my name's Hale. I'm a superhero. Do you happen to own an ugly belt that's been imbued with magical powers by Aphrodite? You do? Well, I'm here to take it off your hands."

Elmer yawned. *You're insane. All of you. I can't believe you woke me up for this.*

"So, what's he saying?" Deena asked.

"He's calling 911 to have me committed."

Deena opened her mouth—probably to argue—but then just nodded. "Okay. So maybe telling the truth isn't the best idea."

"Maybe not," Hale agreed, as he tried unsuccessfully to grab hold of an idea that was brewing in the back of his mind. "Although the seduction part might be fun." That, of course, was an understatement. Especially since he had an inkling that the intriguing Miss Tannin just might be the woman to pull him out of his funk.

Taylor snorted, but didn't say anything.

"What?" Hale asked.

Taylor shrugged. "I just think it's a little odd that a man who considers mortals so far beneath him spends his spare time seducing them."

His eyes met Hale's, and Hale decided that maybe the man had taken offense to his past mortal-bashing. At least a little.

The P.I.'s perceptive, you know, Elmer chittered, crawling up onto the back of the sofa and letting his legs hang down over the cushions.

"I like women," Hale explained. "Mortal. Protector. I just like women."

"Uh-huh. Are you sure there isn't something else going on?"

"Taylor . . ." Zoë put her hand on her husband's arm.

"Like what?" Hale asked, ignoring her. He was surprised to hear this from Taylor, but he wanted it out in the open.

"Like maybe you're scared to hang around longer than a night. Afraid that if you stay with any one woman too long, you'll start to feel that mortals aren't so bad after all. Or is it that you're afraid if you fall for one, you'll have a weak spot? Your very own Achilles' heel. After all, Achilles was probably your seventy-fifth cousin twice removed, right? If you fell for a mortal, suddenly you'd be vulnerable. Because if she gets put in danger because of you . . ." Taylor shrugged. "Sometimes it's just easier to keep your distance."

"Sweetheart . . ." Zoë shook her head.

"Just calling it like I see it," he said.

Hale's fingers itched to wipe the smug look off his brother-in-law's face, but he had to admit that the thought of Tracy in danger made his stomach twist. Still, just because he cared about one girl's well-being didn't mean he was suddenly desperate to feel something romantic. It didn't work that way. He was a Protector. He protected. Mortals needed protecting. That was all.

After a few deep breaths, the blood quit pounding in his ears. With supreme effort, he managed to sound calm and rational when he answered. "You're barking up the wrong tree, buddy."

For a second, he thought Taylor was going to argue; instead, the man shrugged. "Fine. Whatever you say."

"Thank you."

"Since you're not worried, then you should have no problem moving in with Ms. Tannin, getting the belt and saving the world."

Great. They'd come back full circle to the roommate idea. "She might not even have the thing," Hale protested weakly. "And there's no point in me moving in if the belt's at Big Bob's Flea Market."

"So find out for sure," Taylor said. "But if you aren't certain by the end of the day tomorrow, then see about moving in before someone else does and we lose that angle altogether. If it turns out she doesn't have it, you can just move out." He focused on Hale's eyes. "Unless you think you can't handle living that close to a mortal. I mean, I know all you superheroes have a few weaknesses. . . ."

Hale scowled as Taylor trailed off. He'd walked right into this one, and now he was stuck. Stuck with Tracy under one roof.

"It's perfect," Deena said.

Hale opened his mouth to argue, but couldn't find the words. Unfortunately for him, moving in made some sense. Tracy Tannin was a woman and their best lead. Tracy needed a roommate. And Hale was nothing if not experienced in getting what he wanted from women.

Conjuring a smile, he glanced around the room, then at Zoë. They all thought this was funny, did they? Him being saddled with a mortal roommate. Well, let them laugh.

"Fine. Unless we find out for sure by tomorrow night that the belt's somewhere else altogether, I'll see about moving in."

He was strong; he could do this. Heck, he was a Protector First Class. A superhero. A direct descendent of Zeus. An experienced lover and a master of women. He could live with a mortal. For the mission, he could suck it up and do it.

And the only thing that made him the tiniest bit nervous was just how much he was anticipating sharing close quarters with the likes of Tracy Tannin.

Chapter Five

Barring the brief interlude with the anonymous stranger, Tracy's evening had continued in the tiger-poop vein. Apparently her life was destined to be little more than large blocks of mortification occasionally broken up by brief stints of lust and longing.

A bummer, but so far she'd learned to live with it.

After the stranger had left, Tracy's day had managed a nosedive from its new high all the way back down into the Guinness Book of Terrible Days, culminating in a run-in with her ex-boyfriend, Walter the Worm, who hadn't even recognized her. Granted, it had been four years. Also granted, she'd had the frizzy perm from hell when they'd broken up. But that didn't change the fact that her face was exactly the same—a face that, apparently, was entirely unmemorable.

Except for one bright spot with the stranger, it had been a truly sucky day all around.

Now, Tracy was camped out in her attic, trying to forget. Her whole life she'd had two favorite places to hide when things weren't going well—her grandmother's attic and the ocean. Today, she'd opted for home, and as she sat cross-legged on the floor, a steaming cup of coffee within arm's reach and boxes of her grandmother's memorabilia surrounding her, the day's bad mood started to melt away.

Missy wandered through the attic, her toenails clicking on the flooring as she sniffed and resniffed each and every box.

"Those are just for your *nose,* little girl. Don't go marking any territory up here."

Missy whined, but hopefully intended to obey. Not for the first time, Tracy wondered if her grandmother's death wasn't as hard on Missy as it was on her. After all, Missy had been Tahlula's pride and joy. Surely the dog missed her as much as Tracy did.

Keeping an eye on the little fluffball, Tracy pulled the first box between her legs. She'd promised the curator of the Los Angeles Film Museum that she'd donate some of her grandmother's souvenirs for an upcoming exhibit called Goddesses of the Silver Screen. Since Tahlula Tannin was one of the first huge Hollywood stars, the curator was hot to get some of her belongings.

As she opened the lid and dug in, Tracy's eyes brimmed with tears. A faded color photograph topped the stack. From it, her grandmother's image smiled at her, along with Tracy's parents and Tracy herself, a skinny little kid with bony knees and shiny patent leather shoes, decked out in a crinoline dress.

Her chin quivered, and she swiped the tears away, feeling foolishly melancholy. "Get a grip, Trace." She put the picture back, firmly closing the box. "It's not like you haven't had a great life." She had. Thoroughly pampered by a grandmother who adored her, doted on by her grandmother's friends, Tracy'd had a near-idyllic childhood, despite the car wreck that had taken her parents so many years ago.

And now, at twenty-seven, she owned a fabulous house in one of the most coveted neighborhoods in Beverly Hills. Assuming she could somehow manage to pay the taxes—and that was a big assumption—no one could ever take from her that part of her heritage.

A sudden rush of tears spilled out and she let herself go, bawling like a baby until her insides were all dried out. As soon as the bout was over, she scrubbed her palms over her face, frowning against the unexpected onslaught of emotion. Considering how much she usually loved to rummage around in her grandmother's souvenirs, the crying jag had caught her off guard, and she floundered for a reason—air pollution? The sad state of politics in America? PMS?

Not hardly. She hugged her knees to her chest and rocked back and forth on the hardwood floor, knowing full well what was wrong. She was all alone in a very big world. Despite her job, despite Mistress Bettina, and despite her friendship with Mel, for the first time in her life, Tracy was really and truly alone. She missed her grandmother, who'd adored her unconditionally.

Grandma Tahlula had taken care of Tracy since she'd been a little girl, and in Tahlula's later days, Tracy had taken care of her grandmother. Tracy sniffed, remembering the vibrant, kind woman who'd been a Hollywood staple throughout her life. From silent films, to opulent musicals and, finally, to smaller, grandmotherly parts in sitcoms or made-for-TV movies.

Tahlula had worked well into her nineties, and she would have kept on working if the cancer hadn't gotten her. It had drained the woman's energy, not to mention her bank account, and it had broken Tracy's heart to watch her grandmother fade away.

Grandma Tahlula had been gone for a year, and now loneliness pressed closer with each passing day. Even though she'd meant it when she'd told Mel she wanted a fling, Tracy had to wonder if, deep down, she really didn't want much more than that. To love and be loved.

She shook her head, frustrated with herself. One last body-shaking hiccup, and she finally got her breathing under control.

Missy trotted over, sniffed Tracy's shoes, then whined and covered her eyes with her paws.

"I'm okay, girl. Just sentimental from looking through Gram's old stuff. That's all."

She wiped her nose with the back of her hand. Sure. Just sentimental. Nothing more.

Nothing except for Leon and Walter and everything else all piled on top.

Stop it! Tracy slammed a fist against the side of the box, scaring Missy. She was beginning to get on her own nerves. Walter and Leon were both jerks. Big, fat, hairy jerks. Who wanted 'em? Not her. That's for darn sure.

Standing up, she squared her shoulders and moved on to the box marked for the museum. Since she'd already been through that stuff once, surely there wouldn't be much in there to inspire another bout of waterworks.

Her grandmother's publicity photos from her early film days were on top, and Tracy pulled out the first—a black and white glossy in soft focus showing Tahlula in a flowing white gown belted at her waist. Tracy framed the image of her grandmother's face with her fingers and peered at the makeshift cameo. For a time, Tahlula Tannin had been considered the most beautiful star on the Hollywood scene, and fans had clamored for a glimpse of her. That generation's Marilyn Monroe, Tahlula had never wanted for attention. She had an aura, an almost magical quality, and she seemed to radiate beauty. Tracy pulled out the rest of the photos, and in each, Tahlula was similarly dressed— and looked just as stunning.

From another box Tracy located another studio photo, this one taken a few years later. In it, her grandmother was wearing a simple unadorned black dress. Unlike the photos in the first box, Tahlula didn't seem to pop off the emulsion. Tracy frowned. How odd. The focus was harsher, revealing the firm angles of Tahlula's cheekbones and jaw. Striking, yes. Pretty, absolutely. But the stuff legends were made of?

Tracy scowled at the photo, feeling a little disloyal, but it was an empirical fact: Her grandmother was pretty, yes. But drop-dead gorgeous? Not really. At least, not in this picture. Tracy pressed her lips together, struggling with the truth. It wasn't her grandmother's looks that had shot her to the pinnacle of success, but something else: a confidence, a bearing, a way of holding herself that was best captured in the photos from the first box.

Tracy sighed. She hadn't inherited her grandmother's looks or the older woman's panache.

Pity.

Shaking her head, she pulled herself out of her funk. She'd come up to the attic to forget her pathetic luck with men; dragging herself into the doldrums had not been part of the agenda. Okay. Fine. She needed happy thoughts. Raindrops on roses. Bright copper kettles. It's a small world after all.

Running her hands through her hair, she stifled a near-hysterical giggle. Maybe she should run downstairs and eat something, since she seemed to be bordering on delirium. Mentally she ran through the contents of her refrigerator: a jar of kosher dill pickles, a bag of slightly limp carrots, some freshly ground coffee. She frowned. Too bad she hadn't

Julie Kenner

managed to get any ice cream earlier. And then she remembered—there was an entire tube of slice-and-bake
cookies in the freezer.

Cookies. She turned the word over in her head, anticipating the fresh-baked smell and then the melting chocolate on her tongue. Oh, yeah. Hanging out in the attic might
be a temporary cure for the Leon's-an-ass-and-Walter's-a-
jerk doldrums, but cookies were a downright panacea.

Nibbling on her lower lip, she glanced at the box in front
of her. She'd finish this box, then she'd go make cookies.
That seemed like a reasonable, rational plan.

Her mouth watering, she pulled out the next photo. It
was of a birthday party. With cake. Creamy, moist, gooey
cake. She licked her lips, catching herself before she
drooled on the pictures. The museum probably wouldn't
appreciate soggy prints.

So much for reasonable and rational. Apparently those
virtues were no match for cookie lust.

Despite a beautiful wrought-iron gate, the security at Tracy
Tannin's house wasn't exactly stellar. A thief could get
through easily enough. For a superhero, it was a piece of
cake.

Hale reminded himself that he was here only to scope
out the territory. Until he found out if Tracy had the belt,
there was no reason to apply to be her roommate. And
even though he still wasn't too crazy about the roommate
plan, more and more he was hoping that Tracy really did
have the belt. Because he had concocted a plan of his own.

For the last hour or so, he'd been thinking about what
Deena had said: *Seduce the girl.* And although he'd dismissed the comment at the time, now he was thinking his
sister's friend had a point.

Seduction *was* his specialty, after all. And while Hale
might be the wrong superhero to form a warm, fuzzy,

70

touchy-feely bond with the girl, he was definitely the right choice to romance the belt away from her.

So that was his plan. If she had the belt, he'd connect with her, all right. Sexually, sensually. Hell, those were the kind of connections he was used to making. The kind of connections he was good at. And on more than one occasion he'd exercised his powers of persuasion on mortal females he'd seduced. So why not do the same with Tracy?

It wasn't the plan Zephron had outlined, but the Elder had picked Hale specifically for the mission. And it wasn't as if Hale's particular talent with the ladies was unknown. So maybe this is what the Elder had planned all along. Considering that Hale wasn't a likely choice to play buddy-up-to-the-mortal, the possibility made a lot of sense.

And even if Zephron hadn't planned on Hale seducing the girl, it didn't matter, because at the end of the day, Hale would convince Tracy to turn over the belt. He'd just do it *his* way.

As soon as he made the decision, Hale felt one-hundred percent better about the mission. Befriending a mortal made him shudder. But seducing a mortal . . . a little hot sex and some close cuddling without all those pesky emotions interfering . . . Well, that was his specialty.

Or it had been. He frowned. For the sake of the mission—not to mention his own sanity—he certainly hoped it still was.

Turning his attention back to the matter at hand, he crept through the yard toward the front of the house.

Are we snooping? Elmer asked from his perch on Hale's shoulder.

"We're not snooping," Hale whispered back, pulling himself from his thoughts. "We're investigating. There's a difference."

Uh-huh.

Hale ignored him and dematerialized as they approached the house. The grounds were private, and Hale hadn't noticed anyone except himself skulking about, but he wanted to make himself as unobtrusive as possible. As he peered through the cut-glass windows bracketing the front door, he considered simply breaking in and wandering through the house. But that was against the rules, he reminded himself. Not that Hale *always* followed the rules, but he knew the boundaries. Zephron would never approve of indiscriminate behavior—on this of all missions.

There was nothing of particular interest to Hale in the front hallway, so he jumped off the porch—Elmer's claws digging into him for purchase—and crept through the shrubbery toward the next window. Beyond it was some sort of den, with overstuffed chairs and lots of bookshelves, but nothing that attracted Hale's attention.

At least, not until he saw her. She was looking just as she had on the backlot. He studied her face. She had straight brown hair that reached just past her shoulders, a slim aristocratic nose, and eyes that seemed a little sad. Her face was striking, but not beautiful. Certainly it was not the kind of face he'd normally find attractive—but there was something unique about it. Something that had pulled him in that afternoon, and it was still pulling. He smiled and almost rubbed his hands together, pleased that he'd decided to go the seduction route. Yes, indeed—that was one decision he wasn't going to regret. And now, more than ever, he hoped she had the damn belt.

There she is. There's Tracy Tannin.

Elmer's voice pulled Hale out of his reverie, and he instinctively ducked. Though he was completely invisible, she could still see the ferret. Luck was on his side, though. The woman didn't even look in his direction. Instead, she just passed through the room, two boxes in her arms.

Hale followed, stumbling as he tried to catch a glimpse of her through the next set of windows. He hadn't wanted to lose sight of her, but already she had passed out of his range of vision.

Nothing in the next room. "Where'd she go?" Even to his own ears, his voice sounded frantic.

How in Hades should I know? It's your sister with the x-ray vision. Not me.

"Hold on." With super speed, Hale raced to another window, determined to find her. On his shoulder Elmer stumbled then latched on, his claws digging in deep enough this time to draw blood.

"Would you be careful!" Hale hissed. Peering through the window, he saw nothing.

Me? Hopping Hades! You're the one rushing around in the hydrangea bushes. Ha! I knew you were smitten. I just knew it!

"Smitten? What? Have you been watching old movies again? She's not my type at all, and you know it." That was true enough, and he hardly intended to admit to Elmer how intriguing she was. But just because he'd happily bed her didn't mean he was smitten. Smitten implied more than just sex and attraction. Hale had never been smitten by a woman in his life—and he didn't intend to start now.

I didn't say she was your usual fare. I said you had the hots for her.

"Well, maybe I do," he admitted. And frankly, having the hots for someone felt damn nice. Considering the recent decline in his libido, this sudden burst of sexual interest in a woman was downright welcome. Tracy Tannin might be nothing more than an average mortal, but his attraction to her meant that his engine didn't need tuning. No sir, all his parts were in perfect working order.

Thank Zeus.

At the moment, he wasn't inclined to examine why a woman so far from his usual speed had managed to rev his motor. Only the bottom line mattered, and that was simple: Tracy had pulled him out of his funk, and now he wanted her. Wanted to touch her. Wanted to stroke her. Just plain *wanted* her. In his bed. For a few hours. That, at least, was familiar territory. Maybe his taste had changed. He'd never gone for the less than voluptuous type before, but the end result would still be the same: a delightful diversion between the sheets.

There she is! Elmer screeched, bobbing up and down.

Hale looked over in time to catch the direction Elmer pointed—through a pantry and out into a large, well-lit kitchen. Unfortunately, Hale could only make out Tracy's shadow as she passed in front of the louvered doors.

"That way," he whispered, nodding to the side. "There's got to be a window over there." Trying not to seem too anxious, he half-ran, half-levitated his way around the corner of the house.

I haven't seen you in this much of a rush since that Hieronymous flunkie was spitting fireballs at you.

Hale ignored the ferret, not only because he didn't have a snappy comeback, but also because he'd found Tracy again. She was right there in front of him, standing before the kitchen counter, her hair hanging loose in front of her face as she sliced cookie dough and placed it on a sheet.

Are we going to snoop around some more, or are we just gonna watch Martha Stewart here?

Hale scowled but didn't answer. For the next few minutes, he simply watched as Tracy put the cookie sheet into the oven, then poured herself a cup of coffee and crossed to the massive kitchen table. The window was open, and the savory smells coming through it wafted toward him. Hale's stomach growled, and he stepped back, afraid she'd hear.

Her head did cock slightly, but she didn't move, and after a few seconds, she turned her attention to a box perched on one of the chairs. She pulled it open and began drawing items out at random.

Even though her back was to him and Hale could hardly see what she was doing, he would have been happy to stand there forever. He tried to shake off the unusual—and not entirely welcome—feeling. He simply wasn't the type to get all mushy for a woman.

And yet there was something about this one. Something that drew him in. Something that—

The girdle!

She'd shifted slightly, and Hale caught a glimpse of it in her hand. The evening light coming in through the kitchen window caught the gold weave of the belt, casting it in a mystical glow.

She had the girdle! Elation rose in his chest even as the rest of his body started to tingle.

Tracy had Aphrodite's girdle, and that meant Hale's mission—his official, formally sanctioned Protector assignment—was to get in there, seduce the girl, and get that belt.

He smiled. Damn, but there were days when he really liked his job.

Chapter Six

Mistress Bettina snored on the rag rug in front of the sink as Tracy dangled the belt before herself, letting it catch the orangish light from the setting sun. Funky in a retro sort of way, the belt practically screamed Goodwill.

When she'd found it last week, Tracy's first thought had been to give the thing to charity or donate it to the L.A. Film Museum. Holding it now, though, she hesitated. Part of her wanted to keep it for sentimental reasons.

Frowning, she put the belt back on the table as she reached into the box to see what other goodies she'd almost let go. Rummaging down to the bottom, her fingers closed on a silky length of material, which when removed turned out to be the scarf that Tahlula had worn when she'd played the part of Amelia Earhart. Maybe if Tracy dressed like her grandmother, some of the woman's trademark poise would rub off.

"Zank you, dahlink," she said to Missy as she slid the scarf around her own neck and struck a pose. "Eet is not every day zat a lowly chef like myself receives zee Nobel Prize for cookies. Zee honor, eet is—how you say?—tremendous."

Missy looked up, yawned, then drooled. Tracy dropped her shoulders. So much for that idea.

Still, she fingered the scarf, enjoying the way wearing it made her feel. Even if she couldn't entirely imitate her grandmother's poise, looking classy had to count for something.

Her gaze drifted to the belt, and she reached for it. It was made out of a pliable golden metal, but the main portion appeared to be one solid piece. The two ends were more of a mesh, also gold, and very, very retro. Right smack in the middle was a funky brown stone that clearly wasn't the original centerpiece of the belt, and Tracy assumed her grandmother had either not liked the original color or had simply lost the first stone.

All in all, the thing was odd-looking, but in a fashionable sort of way; its uniqueness saved it from a diagnosis of ugliness. Tracy could almost imagine some Paris designer slapping it on a runway model. And it kind of looked familiar. Intrigued, Tracy stared at the belt, trying to remember where she'd seen it before.

Her grandmother's pictures! Realizing the answer, Tracy started pawing like a madwoman through the photos she had of Tahlula's silent-film days. Sure enough, in almost every single one, her grandmother was wearing the funky belt.

Bizarre.

Tracy had never thought of Tahlula as the superstitious type, but maybe that wasn't the kind of thing a grandmother discussed with her granddaughter.

It was also odd that Tracy had never noticed her grandmother wearing the belt in later years. Had she just been supremely unobservant? Frowning, she dug into the second box for the photos from Tahlula's later years. No belt. Also bizarre. For some reason, her grandmother had stopped wearing the thing. But why? Tracy shrugged. It could be for any reason. Heck, maybe Tahlula's taste had changed.

Turning her attention back to the belt, Tracy twisted the pliable metal between her fingers and tried to conjure an image of her grandmother as a young woman. That's when she noticed it: something etched on the inside of the buckle. But not professionally. More like scratched there with the sharp edge of a pair of scissors.

Holding the buckle up to the dim light, Tracy squinted, trying to make out the inscription. It was barely readable, but she finally got it: TRACY, DARLING. BE CAREFUL WHAT YOU WISH FOR. LOVE, GRANDMA.

Tracy sucked in a breath. The belt was meant for her, complete with a mysterious message. How very odd. And how very unlike her grandmother.

Tahlula Tannin had loved letting Tracy play with the clothes and jewelry that she would one day inherit. They had played dress-up together and had tea parties and generally had a wonderful time.

So why hadn't Tahlula ever shown Tracy the belt?

The phone rang, the shrill noise echoing through the house, but Tracy barely even heard, too wrapped up was she in memories. Once again, she tried to remember if she'd seen Tahlula actually wearing the belt. She didn't think so. Around the house, her grandmother had often tried to escape her star persona and just puttered around in a housedress.

The situation just didn't make any sense. Clearly the belt was important. So why had Tahlula worn it all the time during her early film days, then stopped?

Maybe she'd only worn it when she wanted to be "on" and up for the camera or her fans. Maybe, like Tracy, Tahlula knew the belt was odd, and it had been a symbol of her film career. Maybe it was her personal talisman, and she only quit wearing it when she felt like her career had really taken off. Tracy would probably never know—all she knew was that her grandmother had thought the belt was important.

And it looked like she'd wanted it to be Tracy's.

Tracy slipped it around her waist, enjoying the way it seemed to meld to her almost non-existent curves. The belt felt right, natural. As if out of everything her grandmother had willed to her, this was the one thing into which she'd put her heart and soul. So why had she shoved it into a box instead of leaving it where Tracy would find it?

The phone rang again, and Missy started running in circles, her toenails skittering on the slick tile floor.

What the heck, Tracy thought, totally uninterested in the skittering dog or the ringing phone. Instead, her attention was totally focused on the belt. It had done well by her grandmother; maybe now it could be Tracy's very own self-proclaimed good-luck charm.

Releasing the clasp, she let the belt slip off her hips, catching it before it fell to the ground. Though metal, it was remarkably light, and she let it hang over her open palm, her brow furrowing as she considered what to do. The belt was so gaudy that the fashion police would never approve of it for daily wear. But Tracy was so intrigued that that didn't matter. If Madonna got away with wearing a bra instead of a blouse, surely no one in Los Angeles would freak out if Tracy Tannin wore her grandmother's belt. Right? Right.

As she dropped the belt back into the box, she made up her mind; she'd wear it to work tomorrow. After all, her wardrobe could use some spice. And—especially after the episodes with Leon and Walter—her luck definitely could use a boost.

"I come bearing coffee cake."

Tracy stifled a giggle as she listened to the disembodied voice from the phone. After about two dozen more rings she had clued in to the fact that her machine wasn't working, and she'd answered. Now she was talking to Mel, who had called from a few blocks away on her cell phone.

"Is that a threat?" Tracy teased.

"It's a promise. And a bribe. We need to talk. And I want to hear more about what happened after you showered Leon with tiger excrement."

Tracy ran her hands through her hair. "If that's what you want to talk about, I'm tempted not to let you in."

"Ah, but then you wouldn't get the coffee cake."

"You drive a hard bargain," Tracy admitted, trying to keep the smile out of her voice.

"Nah. I just play dirty."

After hanging up, Tracy packed all her grandma's stuff back into the boxes, then headed from the kitchen to the front door. She stepped onto the front porch just as Melissa maneuvered her hulking Jeep Grand Cherokee up the drive.

The yard was a mess, but Tracy couldn't afford a gardener and she didn't have time to take care of it by herself. She was grateful her grandmother had willed her the sprawling old estate, but it would have been nice if the woman had left her a little money to take care of it, too. As it was, Tracy was scrambling to come up with enough money to pay the property taxes. While she was scrambling, things like landscaping and fixing the pool would have to wait. A roommate would help, but so far no one had called.

By Hollywood standards, the place wasn't huge. A three-acre lot and a five-thousand-square-foot house. But it was located in Beverly Hills just off Sunset Boulevard. Which meant it had the three desirable things in the world of real estate: location, location, location.

Even though she had to scrimp to afford taxes, Tracy loved the place—just as her grandmother had. The year after *Gone With the Wind* premiered, Tahlula Tannin had decided she needed land as much as Scarlet did. She'd used the fortune she'd earned starring on the silver screen in the days before income taxes to buy this Beverly Hills manor and a little beach house in Malibu. She'd coveted the role of Scarlet and, for whatever reason, had named the beach house Atlanta, and the Beverly Hills house Tara-too.

In a twist of fate worthy of Hollywood, the beach house had succumbed to one of Malibu's famous fires, but Tara-too still stood. It was a bit rough around the edges these days, but Tracy couldn't dream of living anywhere else.

True to her word, Melissa bounded up the front steps with a box from the La Brea Bakery. "Ta-da!"

Tracy bent low and sniffed the box, her mood already improving as she savored the decadent pastry smells that escaped. "If you weren't already my best friend, I'd give you the job."

"That's serious stuff," Melissa said, following her through the marble foyer to the recently modernized kitchen. "What could I finagle if I'd brought an entire Italian cream cake?"

"You wouldn't believe me if I told you." Tracy cut them both very large pieces, then passed a plate to Melissa. "I'm baking cookies. But I think I need this, too."

Mel's eyebrows went up. "Either your day improved, or it got a hell of a lot worse."

Tracy shoveled a huge bite into her mouth. "Bof," she mumbled.

"Excuse me?"

She chewed, swallowed, and tried again. "Both. First it got better. Then it got worse."

"Worse than the pooper-scooper incident?"

"Oh, yeah. I can't even begin to tell you how much worse. So much worse, that the word doesn't do it justice."

"Rotten?"

"More."

"Horrid?"

"Not even close."

Melissa shrugged. "I give up."

"What's the absolute best?"

Mel squinted. "Best of what?"

"Just a word to describe the best. The top. The pinnacle."

"Orgasmic," Mel said without a pause.

"Fine." Tracy nodded, then took another bite. "I had the most anti-orgasmic, frigid evening from hell." She met Mel's eyes. "And the last hour I spent in the attic going through my grandmother's things. A hard-core dose of added sentimentality, you know?"

Mel nodded, and Tracy knew she really did understand.

"Well, tell," Mel said. "Don't leave me sitting here all curious."

Tracy leaned forward, glad to finally have an audience for bitching about the lousy, horrible, no-good, very bad evening. "Well, you know about how it started. I mean, this morning was okay, but then that whole thing with Leon."

The corner of Mel's mouth twisted as she held back laughter. "Tiger poop. I love it."

"Trust me. Leon did not love it. Leon did not love me. Leon was furious."

"But he won't forget you."

At that, Tracy smiled. "Believe me, I've been consoling myself with that all day." She waved a hand in the air. "Afterward, though, it got better."

Mel leaned forward. "You're blushing. What happened?"

"I am not!" But Tracy's hands automatically went to her cheeks. "Anyway, you'd blush, too. This guy was gorgeous. And he was flirting with me. Really."

"Who?"

"I have no idea." She proceeded to tell Mel the whole story, starting with her dead battery and ending with the oh-so-nice view she'd had of the stranger's backside.

Mel sighed. "That's great." She crumpled her napkin and tossed it at Tracy. "But I can't believe you didn't get a name. A phone number. Heck, did you even get his license plate number?"

"Nope. Not a thing. Which is a shame, too, because the day dropped to an all-time low after he left."

"Lower than tiger poop?" Mel asked with a smile.

Tracy half-shrugged. "Okay, maybe not lower, but it definitely dropped to that general vicinity. That's for sure."

"Poor baby." Melissa swallowed her last bite of cake, then cut herself another piece. "Tell Auntie Mel all about it."

Tracy rolled her eyes but complied. The fact was, she wanted all the sympathy she could get. "After the stranger left, it was ice cream."

"Doesn't sound so bad."

"An entire cone, dumped all over me when some jerk in a pinstripe suit scared Missy."

Mel made a wooshing motion over her head. "You lost me. Suit? Missy? Where's the ice cream?"

"I took Missy to the Promenade for a walk, and I wanted some ice cream, so I bought a cone. But then some jerk came along and scared Missy. She yanked the leash, I tripped, and all three scoops of double mocha chocolate chip landed on my shirt."

"That is a tragedy," Mel agreed soberly. "The ice cream, I mean."

83

"I know." Tracy nodded, still mourning the lost chocolate. "That's my absolute favorite flavor. But it gets even better."

Mel cocked her head. "By 'better' you mean worse?"

"Of course."

"Something in this world is worse than wasted ice cream?" Mel asked in mock horror.

Tracy stifled a grin, not quite ready to have her mood lifted. "Very little, true. But this definitely qualifies."

"So tell."

Tracy finished off her slice of coffee cake, then slid her fork directly into its pan, snagging a huge slab. "Walter," she said, then shoved the piece in her mouth.

"Walter? Your ex, Walter?"

Still chewing, Tracy nodded. "One and the same." Four years ago, she'd shared eight lousy months with Walter. Lousy because she'd thought they were getting along just fine until one day—about a week after they'd moved in together—he'd said he needed more space. She'd suggested they rent a bigger apartment.

Apparently that wasn't the kind of space he meant, because he'd moved out the next day—taking her television with him—and she hadn't seen him since. For a while, Tracy had entertained the vague hope that he'd been kidnapped by aliens and had been living the last four years in the Mother Ship, having all sorts of gruesome experiments performed on him. It turned out he'd just moved to San Diego.

Mel's blue eyes were huge. "What about him?"

"He was in the coffee shop."

"Coffee shop? I thought you were eating ice cream."

Tracy nodded. "I was. But after the whole shirt fiasco, I headed for the car. Only the battery was dead again. I guess I didn't let it run long enough."

"Figures."

"That's what I thought. Pretty much par for the course considering the day I was having." She contemplated the cake, decided one benefit of having skinny thighs was that she could pig out, and cut another piece. "Anyway, I was parked in front of the coffee shop, and so I tied Missy's leash to the bike rack and went in, figuring maybe somebody had jumper cables."

"And Walter saw you."

"Oh, yeah. He saw me, all right." She leaned forward, wishing she could adequately convey the utter humiliating ickiness of the situation. "He looked right at me . . . and didn't have a clue who I was."

"Oh."

Tracy stifled a grin. Seeing her friend this speechless was almost worth her humiliation.

Mel frowned, clearly searching for a reply. "Maybe he was preoccupied?"

"That's what I thought. So I said, 'Hey Walter. Have you got jumper cables with you?' He just sort of gaped at me, then asked if we'd met." With a sigh, she flopped back against her chair. "If it weren't so utterly pathetic, it would be hysterical."

"Oh yeah. A laugh a minute."

Tracy got up and poured Mel a fragrant cup of coffee, then got one for herself. She leaned back against the counter, letting the healing smell surround her. "It's like I said earlier. Men just don't notice me."

"It's not men. It's Walter. He's a first-class creep. The man has so many women in his eye, it's a wonder he can pick out any face."

"I'm willing to agree with you on that." It turned out Walter had had something of a roving eye. Not that Tracy was surprised. She had yet to go out with a man who didn't suffer from the grass-is-greener syndrome. And Tracy was grass that perpetually needed watering.

She sighed, wondering if she'd ever find a man who'd stick around. "The thing is, even *creeps* remember the women they've slept with. Don't they? I know my hair's changed, but he couldn't even place me. Totally clueless." She took a sip of coffee, then shook her head. "This doesn't speak well of my skill in *that* particular department."

"I'm sure you're fine in that department." A devious grin spread across Mel's face. "But it never hurts to practice. Maybe I could set you up with—"

"Your leftovers? No, thank you." Tracy sighed. She wanted her own men, men who chose her for her. It wasn't as if she needed to be a knockout like her grandmother, though that would certainly be nice. She just wanted to be noticed. "I'm too shy and I'm too plain."

"Shy? Oh, please."

"Maybe not around you, but I don't do well around new people."

"Oh, Trace. Who does?"

"You do. My grandmother did."

"I fake it. I'm *always* worrying about what people think. And I bet your grandmother was painfully shy. That's probably how she ended up in movies—so she could live another life."

"Maybe." Tracy's brow furrowed as she considered the point. The truth was, her grandmother never had liked public appearances, and she'd always called them a necessary evil. "But that still doesn't help when I'm trying to meet a guy."

"You know what they say. Picture them naked. It'll put you at ease."

Tracy laughed. "If I'd pictured Leon naked earlier today, I would've keeled over from heart failure. Yowza."

"And you're not plain," Mel added, apparently unwilling to acknowledge Leon-the-jerk's oh-so-substantial attributes.

"Of course I'm plain. It's a universal truth. Like gravity. The world is round. We need oxygen to breathe. Tracy Tannin is plain."

Mel aimed her gaze at the ceiling and held out her hands in a silent plea.

"Seriously. I'm too skinny. I've got no boobs, no hips, not one single curve—"

"Worked for Kate Moss."

"—and there's nothing at all interesting about my face," she finished, shooting Mel a do-you-mind look. "It's just *there*. Surrounded by perfectly straight, stringy hair that frizzes if I perm it."

She swallowed yet another sigh of self-pity. "My family's overflowing with beauty. So how the heck did I get stuck with the recessive dull, dull, dull gene?"

"You may not be drop-dead gorgeous, but I think you're plenty pretty."

"Then why didn't my own ex-boyfriend recognize me?"

"Well . . ." Mel floundered, and Tracy shrugged. Pathetic or not, she'd gotten her point across.

"I'm forgettable. And I hate it." Tracy frowned. "No, it's worse than that. I'm not forgettable—I'm invisible. I mean, even when I was with Walter, everything was so . . . passionless. He treated me like I was a piece of furniture. Not a woman." She frowned. "I'm not making sense, I know, but it's—"

"No, you are. You want to feel the earth move."

Tracy pounded her fork on the table. "Exactly. I may not be looking for the love of my life—hell, right now I probably wouldn't know him if I tripped over him. But I still want—"

"A fling. Like we were talking about before." Mel grinned. "A wild, hot, passionate, *throbbing* kind of fling."

"Yes. Exactly," Tracy said. "That's precisely what I need." She gnawed on her lower lip, feeling wanton and decadent. "I want to experience that sizzle, that passion. But . . ."

"But you're not interested in commitment," Mel put in.

"Not yet," Tracy agreed. *Sometime, yes.* "Right now, I just want—"

"Fire."

She nodded, liking the sound of that. "Enough fire to burn me down to my toes." Smiling, she caught Mel's eye. "A flaming fling. That's what I'm looking for."

"With Leon?" Mel's voice rose, incredulous.

Tracy shrugged. "I guess he's out of the running." As nice as that fantasy might be, the realization of it didn't look too likely. Tracy blinked, steering her thoughts back to her friend. "This is all just silly. For one thing, I'm too chicken to have a fling. For another, no male worth anything is going to want to have a fling with me." She held up her hands. "I'm right back where I started. Boring, plain, and pretty damn close to invisible."

"I don't believe that," Mel said. "But if you do, we'll just figure out a way to show you off." She tapped her lip, thinking. "We can find some way to add a little pizazz to your looks. You know. Give you a new image. A touch more sex appeal."

"More? I don't have any."

Mel shot her a stern glance but basically ignored the comment. "A look to boost your confidence."

"Well, I don't know what could do that," Tracy complained. Although it wasn't exactly true. The one thing she did have was her grandmother's belt. It had certainly made her feel better just holding it. Maybe it would help her land just the right guy to show her the passion she craved. Of course, maybe it wouldn't.

But one thing Tracy knew for sure: wearing the belt certainly couldn't make her any worse off than she already was.

Are you one lucky Protector, or what? Elmer squeaked. *She wants a fling. Flings are your specialty. Zephron sure picked the right guy for this job!*

Still crouched outside the window, Hale nodded. "Exactly what I'm thinking," he acknowledged.

On his shoulder Elmer swiveled, managing to get his face right in front of Hale's. *Excuse me? What are you cooking up in that libidinized brain of yours?*

Hale stifled a laugh. "Just a little seduction. Nothing out of the ordinary."

A seduction? The ferret snorted. *Why am I not surprised?* His tail swished in front of Hale's face as he shifted his perch. *I know Zephron wanted you to . . . uh . . . connect with this girl, but I don't think* that's *what he had in mind.*

Hale rolled his eyes. This was his lucky day, and he didn't intend to let the ferret's prudishness mar that. Only rarely did one of his assignments involve seducing a woman who so clearly wanted to be seduced.

A little wine. A few roses. Some well-placed sweet words.

A fire crackling in the hearth—well, it was summer, so maybe nix the fire. Perhaps a midnight swim instead. Their bodies slick and wet, pressed up together. Close. Tight.

He imagined her breath soft against his ear. Her skin smooth beneath his fingertips. Her breasts, ripe and ready as he bent low, peeling off her bathing suit to reveal—

He fought a shiver, his body reacting more than he'd anticipated to his little fantasy.

Oh, yeah. He was back in form and more than up for the job of seducing Tracy Tannin. In fact, he couldn't wait to get down to business.

Chapter Seven

"Any nibbles yet on your roommate ad?" Mel asked.

"Not a thing. But it's only run the one day." Tracy pulled a rubber band out of her pocket and yanked her hair into a ponytail. Some days she considered whacking it all off—it really was a pain—but she'd never quite worked up the nerve.

The kitchen timer chirped, and she headed to the oven, slipping a baker's mitt on as she walked.

"Something yummy, I hope."

"You just had coffee cake."

"So did you," Mel countered. "And it's not like the dessert police are going to come get us. So what is it?" She sniffed. "Chocolate chip?"

"Slice-and-bake special," Tracy confirmed, opening the oven door.

"You've got milk, right?"

"Of course." Tracy shot Mel a glance as she started sliding the cookies onto a serving tray. "What kind of establishment do you think I'm running here?"

"Speaking of that"—Mel motioned around the kitchen—"I meant to ask earlier. What are you doing in here?" She ran her finger along the edge of one of the photos of Tracy's grandmother. "Is this the stuff for the museum?"

Tracy plopped a plate of warm, gooey cookies in front of her.

"I think I love you," Mel said.

"Of course. I feed you."

"Seriously, what's all this stuff for?"

"Well, I thought I'd donate it all to the museum . . . but now I'm thinking I might keep some of the clothes."

Mel leaned over the back of the chair and grabbed the white scarf Tracy had tried on earlier. "So you've decided your new image is vintage?"

"Maybe."

"I was expecting you to go more for *Vogue* or *Cosmo*. You know—something hip for the Los Angeles dating scene."

"That's still a possibility," Tracy said, taking the scarf back.

"Speaking of dating, you didn't do something stupid and advertise for only a *female* roomie, did you?"

"Are you nuts?" Tracy took a bite of cookie, slid down her chair in a moment of pure ecstasy, then sighed. "I'm a natural man-repellant. Why on earth would I bother going to the trouble of limiting my roommates to girls?"

"Dunno. False sense of modesty maybe."

"Oh, please. This house is huge. And I'm trying to rent out an entire suite with a private entrance. A family of twelve could move in and I'd never even notice."

Okay. So maybe that was an exaggeration. But the house did have more space than she needed. The second floor was home to three bedroom suites, one with an outside entrance off the balcony. The lower level had the kitchen, ballroom, study, formal living room, dining room, and maid's quarters. It also had Tracy's favorite—a private screening room with comfy chairs and a lounge area where Tahlula used to entertain. Tracy had never had a party there, but she did love to watch television in style.

Tracy shook her head and gave her boss a questioning look. "Hey. Now that I think about it, what are you doing here? I mean other than eating and gossiping. I thought you had to work with Penelope tonight."

"That was my plan, but then I had to get ready for some meetings tomorrow. Not that it matters. Penelope's having problems."

"Penelope always has problems. That's why we're having problems with Penelope."

"Yeah," Mel agreed. "Well, this time Penelope's having about eight little problems."

Tracy shook her head slowly. "You're not saying—"

"Yup. Preggers."

"Well, heck. Guess that means she's off the show."

"And we have to find a replacement. Pronto." Mel turned to face the big window at the far end of the kitchen. After a second, she frowned. "Or maybe I just found a replacement." She took off her glasses and rubbed her eyes.

"Excuse me?"

Mel pointed. "There's a ferret in your window." She squinted. "Or there was."

Tracy whipped around, but didn't see a thing. "A ferret? What? Just hanging out on my windowsill?"

"More like hovering in midair, actually." Mel's brow furrowed as she shrugged. "You don't see that every day."

"I don't think you see that at all."

Mel held up her hands. "Hey, I didn't put him there. It's your house."

"Well, it's not my ferret. I think you're imagining things. You've just got ferrets on the brain."

"Probably. Either that or not enough caffeine. Or maybe too much sugar." She didn't look convinced, but Mel shook her head and turned back to Tracy. "Anyway, as I was saying, we've got big problems. I've already called all our competitors. Los Angeles is severely lacking in trained ferrets at the moment." A pensive expression crossed her face. "Maybe they could rewrite the script for a great big rat. Or a potbellied pig. We've got a great trained pig."

"Maybe we could find a ferret in San Diego."

"Or Ventura," Mel said. "But I doubt it."

"I don't know," Tracy said. "I guess we just play it by ear and hope we find one. If not, Leon can co-star with a pig. And that," she added, "would be very appropriate."

A television show! Elmer squeaked, his little squeals cutting into Hale's eardrums. *My heroine, my darling.* He gazed up from their hiding place under Tracy's window, an expression of longing on his little face. *I want to marry that woman.*

"Would you be quiet?" Hale asked. "I'm trying to think." They'd cut it too close a minute ago, and Tracy's friend had almost discovered them. Now they were well below the window level, so anyone peering out wouldn't see the ferret floating on Hale's invisible shoulder.

What's there to think about? Elmer asked. *It's perfect. It's wonderful. You talk to her. She trains me. You'll be around her all the time. What could be better?*

"Just about anything, I imagine."

Elmer snorted. *Oh, sure. Guess you're the only one allowed to be famous. Not little old Elmer. No, sir. No fame for the ferret.*

Hale rolled his eyes. When he had first accepted his alter-ego role, no one had expected how popular his face—or thighs, pecs, and biceps—would turn out to be. But Zephron had insisted that Hale could hide in plain view. The very conspicuousness of being a cover model would lend him an inconspicuousness as a superhero. While he'd complained at first, in truth Hale didn't mind. Not that he'd ever admit it to Elmer—who gave him plenty of grief about dressing up like a pirate or a medieval lord—but Hale thoroughly enjoyed the job.

But the thought of Elmer in front of a camera . . .

Well, frankly, that was more than a little scary. Elmer being Elmer was often too much to handle. Elmer being a television star . . . he'd have sunglasses, an entourage, his very own limo driver. Hale shook her head. That might be a little much to take.

Still, he had to admit this did seem perfect. And he knew from experience he'd never hear the end of it if he didn't at least let the little guy have a shot.

"Fine," he said, giving in. "I'll call my agent in the morning and see if he can line up an audition for you." He rubbed his temples. Marty was an excellent agent, but also an opportunist. Hale couldn't even begin to imagine how the man would twist this rather bizarre scenario to his advantage.

Serious television, Elmer said, his squeaky voice practically a sigh. *I wonder if I'll get a credit at the beginning. Maybe I'll even get my own trailer!*

Hale stifled a sigh, wondering what exactly he'd gotten himself into.

"Here." In his Manhattan apartment, Hieronymous pointed to the bank of monitors, all displaying various areas of Los Angeles. "Right in the middle of Beverly Hills." He drummed his fingers on his desktop and looked up at Clyde, his Chief of Guards.

"Surely Tahlula didn't die with the girdle still in her possession?"

Hieronymous frowned, hating the idea that all these years it had been right there for the picking. "I wouldn't have thought so. Tahlula Tannin knew full well the power of the belt, and yet she ceased wearing it. What mortal could resist the lure of Aphrodite's girdle?"

"You can't resist, Master. And if you can't, surely no mortal can."

With a growl, Hieronymous rounded on Clyde, his black robe flying out from behind him. "It is not a question of *resistance*, fool," he hissed. Gathering himself, he stood up straighter, then spoke slowly, as if to an idiot. Which, in his opinion, was often an accurate description of Clyde. "The girdle is a tool—a tool I intend to use for the greater good of our race."

"Of course, Sire." Clyde bowed his head.

Fools. He was surrounded by fools. His staff, his son. How was a supreme being like himself supposed to reach his destiny if he didn't have quality help? Really, would his problems never end?

With a sigh, he looked back at the monitors and dismissed the question. "Perhaps Tahlula misplaced it. Perhaps she gave it to charity or to a relative, who has only just put it on. The cause of its disappearance is immaterial at this point." He lifted his head, his jaw firm as he looked into Clyde's eyes. "We do not even know that the signal came from Tahlula's house. It wasn't strong enough to pinpoint anything more than Beverly Hills."

"Has Mordichai checked in?"

"Ah, yes, my son. My secret weapon. The one who will bring the belt to me."

"So he's got a bead on it, huh?"

Hieronymous stifled a sigh. Apparently Clyde was immune to sarcasm. "My son is alone in Los Angeles searching for a missing artifact. Unless he stumbled onto something in the"—he glanced at his Rolex—"two hours since he arrived, I don't think that he has a bead on anything." A pity, too. He needed that girdle. And he needed Mordichai to get it for him.

"Did you get your message to him?" Clyde asked.

Hieronymous fought the urge to sneer. "Of course. Do you think I would sit on such a crucial bit of information?" Just that afternoon, his key spy within the Council had delivered a message—Hieronymous's niece and nephew, Zoë and Hale, had been assigned to locate the girdle and return it to the Council. Pesky little interfering brats.

"Mordichai knows what is at stake. And he knows that in order to win the prize—and to win my approval—he will have to thwart his cousins' efforts."

"Sire . . ." Clyde's voice trailed off, his eyes lowered.

"What is it now?"

"Are you sure using your son is a good idea? I mean, Zoë barely has her skills under control. But Hale . . . well, he's one of the best the Council has."

Heironymous laughed. "One of the best? I'm surprised you give him so much credit."

Clyde stood up straighter. "I could easily best him, of course. And given the opportunity, I'll be happy to do it—"

"Yes, yes. I'm aware of the fact that Hale is the very Protector who discovered your duplicity." Hieronymous drummed his fingers on his desk. "Pity, too. You were so much more useful to me when you were still in the Council. But now, an Outcast." He met Clyde's eyes. "Tsk, tsk."

"For the opportunity to best Hale, I'd gladly use my Protector skills—even if it means risking punishment."

"Really?" Hieronymous filed away that little tidbit. Outcasts retained their power, but were forbidden to use their skills. If the Council discovered and prosecuted a violation, the punishment was severe—and permanent.

Clyde's face tightened. "My point is that I don't think your son is a match for Hale. After all, Mordi's only a—"

Hieronymous's head jerked up, and Clyde took a step backward, his mouth snapping shut.

"Only a *what?*"

"I just wonder if there isn't a better agent to send," Clyde continued, talking to the floor. "I mean, Mordichai is a halfling, after all."

"He may be a halfling, but he is also my son. And unlike Zoë, he has been trained—by me—since birth. He has the power to conjure fire, and the power to shapeshift. He is perfect for this job." More important, perhaps, Hieronymous had no other choice. Certainly he had other agents, but what would stop them from claiming the belt for their own?

In a flash, he answered his own question. Henchmen. The slimy, stupid creatures would be perfect. A mortal couldn't steal the belt, so he couldn't use his smarter human minions, but Henchmen . . . Unlike Protectors, they had no powers to lose. And they had the added benefit of being entirely loyal to whoever freed them from the catacombs.

Yes, perhaps Henchmen were the answer.

With a smile, he turned back to Clyde. "What you say has merit. Rather than place all this responsibility on my son, we'll send in my little pets."

Clyde practically preened; clearly the oaf thought that he was responsible for giving Hieronymous the idea. "And Mordichai?" he asked.

"My son will remain on the assignment. Henchmen may be persistent, but they do not always succeed." Sadly, the creatures were rather dim-witted. He drummed his fingers on his desktop. "Consider the Henchmen a backup plan."

"Yes, Sire." Clyde didn't look pleased, and Hieronymous knew he was concerned about Mordichai's trustworthiness. Not to mention his ability to get the job done. As much as his Chief of Guards annoyed him at times, Hieronymous had to admit the man was as loyal as they came.

In this case, however, Clyde was wrong. Mordichai could be trusted. He might have disappointed Hieronymous in the past—as a halfling, the boy's skills were sadly lacking—but Mordichai would never turn on his father. For one thing, the boy simply didn't have that kind of courage. For another, Mordi had been raised on Hieronymous's promises that he would be second only to his father in his new world order.

Whether or not Mordi would actually see such a position of power was neither here nor there. For the time being, such a plan served Hieronymous well—and kept his son on a sufficiently short leash.

Chapter Eight

The next morning Tracy wore her grandmother's belt, and by the time she rolled through the gate onto the backlot, the day already seemed brighter, the world cheerier, the people friendlier. Okay, maybe not the brighter and cheerier part—except that it was a truly gorgeous, smog-free day—but the people . . . Well, something was definitely up with the people.

Tracy's first stop had been the coffee shop near her house. Usually she waited until she got closer to the backlot, but she'd been running late and hadn't had time to make any coffee on her own. Her choices had been simple: stop for coffee even though the local dive had the rudest counter clerks imaginable, or pass out from caffeine withdrawal as she coasted down Laurel Canyon.

Tracy had chosen to face the coffee shop creeps, hoping beyond hope that—for once—it wouldn't be an entirely miserable experience.

And this morning they weren't so creepy. At least not to her anyway. Instead, everyone in the shop had practically bent over backwards for her. First, the folks waiting in line had offered to let her cut ahead, which was what she'd desperately wished for the second she saw the line snaking out the door.

As if that wasn't weird enough, the guy working the counter actually remembered that she always ordered a double non-fat latte. Then he gave it to her gratis—and apologized for the place being so crowded.

Okaaaaay.

That was weird-morning-incident number-one.

After that, she'd cruised over the canyon to Studio City. Apparently she'd cruised a little too fast, since she'd ended up getting pulled over by one of Los Angeles's finest. Another speeding ticket wasn't going to make her insurance company very happy, and so she'd sat in the car clutching her registration and insurance, silently willing the officer to let her off with a warning.

Amazingly enough, he had.

Shaking her head, Tracy had crept away, carefully watching her speed, using her blinker, and generally driving like her grandmother had. Now, as she crawled through the studio gate at a snail's pace, Tracy was beginning to wonder if she wasn't leading a charmed life.

But why?

Then she remembered the belt. It had to be psychological. Mind over matter. The belt had made her grandmother confident, and now it was bolstering Tracy's confidence in the same way.

Didn't all those pop psychology gurus say you had to believe in yourself before anyone would do anything for you? Well, apparently that little theory was true.

Amazing.

She maneuvered the backlot on autopilot, finally parking in front of the Paws In Production trailer. Chris, the intern, had arrived first, and the portable kennels were already lined up in front, each with an animal itching to get out.

Since Mel wasn't anywhere in sight—she'd likely already left for her meetings—Tracy opened Peanut's kennel and urged the dachshund forward. "Come on girl. We're running late." Tracy jiggled her fanny pack filled with doggie treats, and Peanut waddled out of the cage. Chris passed Tracy the day's call sheet as he moved to clean the cage.

By the time they reached the soundstage, shooting was already in progress. Fortunately, today's script didn't call for Peanut to do anything more involved than stealing Leon's chair when he got up to talk to Mrs. Dolittle, so the fact that they were late shouldn't really matter.

Even so, all eyes turned to her as soon as they walked in. Tracy gulped, stopped, and started to feel a bit like Charlton Heston in *Planet of the Apes*—a single human on display for the apes to examine. Everyone was staring, and Leon was positively gaping.

"Uh . . . hi." Deciding that being strictly professional was the better part of valor, she bent down, unclipped Peanut's leash, and gave the dog the signal to go to her first mark at the base of Leon's chair.

As Peanut rushed toward the chair, Leon rushed toward Tracy. "Are you all right? You're late."

"I'm fine." Newfound confidence or not, being the center of attention wasn't sitting well, and Tracy felt her cheeks burn. Her gaze darted around the room, and she gratefully noted that everyone else had gone back to their business. "I got pulled over this morning, so I was running a little behind."

"No!" He couldn't have sounded more angst-ridden if he'd been performing *Hamlet*. "I've got friends in the de-

101

partment. We'll challenge the ticket. I mean, this is outrageous. This is absurd. This is—"

"No big deal." She grabbed his flailing wrist. "Seriously. It's okay. I just got a warning." She frowned, though, wondering why Leon was suddenly being nice to her again.

"That's a relief," he said, and took her hand. "Seriously, though, if you need anything, anything at all, you just let me know."

"First positions!" The voice of the assistant director, Gary, echoed through the soundstage.

Leon ignored him, still holding Tracy's hand, a puppy-dog expression on his face.

She waited for him to say something. And waited. And waited.

Nothing. He just kept staring. Tracy'd never really understood the expression "goo-goo-eyed," but in this case, it seemed to fit perfectly.

"Uh, listen, Leon. About yesterday." Somehow an apology seemed appropriate, despite the fact that he'd been such a jerk. Besides, she didn't have anything else to say. "I'm really sorry I tripped and . . . uh . . . spilled the . . . uh . . . the uh . . . the—"

"Crap all over me?" Leon chuckled. "Wasn't that a riot? Took me an hour in the shower to get rid of the smell. Talk about an unexpected adventure." Again, that award-winning smile. "But I guess I deserved it. I was so preoccupied when you came over, I think I came off rather rude."

She gaped. Was he actually apologizing?

He took her hand. "Can you ever forgive me?"

Yup. That was definitely an apology. She blinked, too flabbergasted to form a coherent sentence.

"Leon!" Gary howled. "You want to grace us with your presence?"

"Be right there," he hollered back, but didn't make any attempt to move away from Tracy.

She squinted at him, trying to find the catch. "So, you really aren't mad?"

"At you?" His eyes, warm and soft, seemed to surround her, and she squirmed under his gaze, not entirely sure she was comfortable. "Sugarplum, how could I be mad at you?"

"Well, I just thought . . ." She trailed off, trying to figure out what he was up to.

"*Now*, Leon." This time, the voice came from the director himself.

Leon squeezed Tracy's hand. "*Au revoir, ma cheri.*"

She blinked as he headed onto the set. *What a bizarre morning.* There wasn't any time to take stock, though. She needed to focus on Peanut and making sure the dog made it to each of her marks, didn't miss a cue, and looked sufficiently cute and cuddly, with just a touch of doggie astuteness.

As the scene opened, Mrs. Dolittle and her nephew Brent, played by Leon, were bantering about the latest murder in their sleepy little hometown. Plopped near Leon's feet, Peanut looked half-dead. Tracy signaled to her, and the dog perked up. Another signal, and she scratched at the base of Leon's chair.

As scripted, Leon reached down and rubbed her ears, his conversation with his pretend aunt never faltering. Peanut sat back on her haunches and stared at him, her eyes big and pitiful. Then, the big finale. Tracy knew what would happen from rehearsals. Leon would get up to make a point, Peanut—at Tracy's signal—would sneak onto the chair, and then Leon would come back and just barely miss sitting on the dog. In editing, the laugh track would be bumped up a few decibels.

It wasn't Shakespeare, but it paid the bills.

Except something wasn't right. Glancing up from where she crouched, Tracy saw Leon staring at her, his eyes wide and adoring.

"Cut!"

She'd tuned everything out except for her cues for Peanut, and now she looked around to figure out what was going on. "What happened?" she whispered to a nearby grip she'd always thought had the cutest smile.

"Leon flubbed his lines."

"Oh." She frowned. "Then why's Burke glaring at me?" The director, well known for his temper, was directing equal doses of his world famous glare at Tracy and at Leon.

The grip sidled closer. "Because instead of saying he and Lori were going to see what they could find out at the morgue, Leon said that he and *Tracy* were going."

She swallowed. Lori was Leon's girlfriend in the show. So it made sense Burke would be ticked if he thought Tracy was distracting his star. She hoped like heck he wasn't mad at her. She needed this gig, and even if Mel wouldn't fire her, Burke could kick her off the backlot.

She glared at Leon, angry that he'd put her in this position. Was this revenge for yesterday?

"You two an item?" the cute grip asked, interrupting her thoughts.

"What?" she asked, trying to pick up the thread of conversation. "Who?"

He nodded in the direction she was looking—toward Leon, who was wiggling his fingers in a tiny little wave even as the A.D. tried to get everyone back to places.

An item? Her and Leon? She almost laughed out loud, then remembered the way he'd just apologized, not to mention the strange passion she'd seen in those eyes. They weren't an item, but something was definitely up.

"Um, no. Not at all."

"Good." The grip's smile broadened. "I was hoping maybe we could go out to dinner sometime after the shoot. I think we've probably got a lot in common."

She glanced at his Dance 'Til You Puke T-shirt. "You think?"

"Well, uh, sure. I mean, you like animals. I've got a cat. Or my roommate does."

Tracy's brow furrowed. "Right."

She had no idea what else to say, but fortunately, the assistant director called for quiet and she was saved from responding. The grip headed back to his station, and Tracy shook her head. Weird.

The actors started the scene again, and once again Leon managed to flub his lines. And again. And again. Finally Burke decided to wrap for the day, even though it wasn't even lunchtime. He stormed off the set, sending Leon a look that could melt glass. The look he shot Tracy was cooler—but decidedly confused.

Not quite ready to deal with any of it, Tracy called to Peanut, leashed the dog, then headed for the door, hoping to avoid another encounter with the cute grip with the bad taste in T-shirts. Leon caught up with her before she'd gone ten feet.

"You're leaving? So soon?" He stepped closer, into that little realm of air she considered her personal space.

Without thinking, she took a step backward. He moved too, closing the distance. She cleared her throat. "Well, yes. I need to get Peanut back."

"Can't you stay and chat?"

Her brow furrowed as she gestured toward the door. "I really should go," she said, not at all sure what Leon was up to.

"How about tonight? Coffee? Dessert? I promise I'll make it worth your while."

He took her hand, and Tracy gasped with surprise. Part of her wanted to say no. After the way he'd treated her, Leon Palmer wasn't exactly high on her list. But at the same time, he was being so conciliatory . . .

"Please." He squeezed her fingers.

"I don't know."

"I really feel I need to make it up to you. Please."

Her shoulders sagged and she capitulated. "I guess that would be okay."

In an elegant gesture, he raised her hand to his lips and kissed the tips of her fingers. Tracy tried not to melt. "I'll pick you up at eight," he said, and Tracy could only nod, wondering if she'd done the right thing.

When he walked away, she twisted around, wondering if anyone had witnessed their encounter. It was then that she saw the tall, dark Adonis standing on the far side of the soundstage, his face hidden by the shadows. But he wasn't hidden enough that she couldn't feel the way his eyes were watching her, or see the firm set of his jaw as he frowned.

His shape was somehow familiar, but she couldn't place it. Still, something about this man called to her. Something mysterious and provocative. Her stomach fluttered. Part of her wanted to cross the darkened soundstage and speak to him. To ask why he was watching her. Why he was frowning.

She took a step closer before the realization of her own boldness stopped her cold. And that's when he shifted, the light catching the angular planes of his chiseled features, and she realized where she'd seen him before.

Yesterday's mysterious stranger.

What on earth was he doing watching her from the shadows? She bit her lip, trying to decide if she should approach him, ask him that very thing. But the reality was, she didn't know this man at all.

It had been an odd, confusing day, and her mind was all a muddle. Best to leave now and sort it all out later. Or not sort it out.

Frankly, she wasn't entirely sure the day was sort-out-able.

Chapter Nine

She's wearing the belt! Elmer squeaked. *And that guy was being a complete dunderhead. It works! It really works!*

Hale clenched his fists at his sides. Elmer was right—that Leon Palmer fellow had practically fallen all over Tracy. Not that Hale minded seeing the little worm manipulated; under normal circumstances, Hale would be perfectly content to see Leon put under a spell for the rest of his life. But these weren't normal circumstances at all. If Leon was fawning all over Tracy, that meant that she must actually be attracted to the guy. Which was crazy. Couldn't Tracy see that the man wasn't sincere, belt or not? This Leon fellow didn't really care about her. Even more, from what Hale could tell, he was a bumbling idiot. How could Tracy just have agreed to go out with him?

Because she wanted him. She *desired* him. And the belt had given her what she wanted. Hale wondered what else she'd want before the day was through. As Zephron had

108

explained, the belt worked on both a sensual and a non-sensual level. She might *want* Leon, but she might also simply want better service at the dry cleaners. Or a better job. Or who knows what.

Still, at the moment, Hale couldn't be concerned with that. No, Leon was the problem. Tracy had actually smiled at Leon, and Hale's stomach had done flip-flops. Anger, frustration, *jealousy?* He didn't know, and he didn't care. All he knew was that the realization that Tracy actually liked this mortal cretin irritated him. He shoved the emotion away. He didn't care about Tracy's love interests. Of course he didn't.

Who Tracy liked, who Tracy dated, who Tracy made love with had absolutely no bearing on his life. None. Zip. Nada. She could do whatever she wanted. With whomever she wanted. Even annoying cretins like Leon Palmer.

Except it *was* his business. The truth was a blow he didn't expect. If his ancestor's magic girdle had anything to do with who Tracy dated and who Tracy slept with, then it very much was his concern.

Oddly, that fact cheered him; he now had a reason to care if Tracy liked Leon Palmer. And if he had anything to say about it, he intended to make sure that Tracy never fell for the bastard.

Yo! Hale my man! You wanna say something to your little buddy? Like why we're still standing here when the girl's gone?

At that, Hale blinked. Sure enough, while he'd been thinking about her love life, Tracy had slipped out the soundstage door. He rushed forward, desperate not to lose sight of her, then forced himself to stop. He'd never stumbled over himself to get to a woman . . . and he didn't intend to start now. No matter how much the woman in question was beginning to get under his skin. And no matter the importance of the belt she was wearing.

Slowly and calmly, he headed toward the door.

So where are we going?

"Her trailer." As it was, they should have been there long before. Hale had called his agent the previous night and explained that Elmer had a lead on a gig, and so Hale would be ferret-sitting instead of modeling for a while. Not one to miss an opportunity, Marty had immediately signed Elmer, then called Paws In Production and made all the necessary arrangements. All Hale had to do was show up with Elmer and sit on the sidelines and watch.

He grimaced. Frankly, he wasn't really a sidelines kind of guy. But in this case, it was a great cover. While Elmer was taking Hollywood—or at least Studio City—by storm, Hale could be working his mission. Working Tracy, that is.

Besides, the closer he got to the girl, the sooner he could seduce her out of the belt. . . .

Every time you seduce a woman, I get the short end of the stick, Elmer said, as if he could read Hale's mind. The ferret sighed. *You disappear with some female and I end up stuck in some hotel room, or holed up with Zoë and Taylor. And they don't even get HBO.* Another sigh. *I hope you realize how much I sacrifice for you. A television show is the least I deserve. The least, I tell you!*

Out of the corner of his eye, he could see Elmer's glare. He rolled his shoulder, causing the ferret to wobble.

Watch it, there!

"Me? You're the one complaining about my mission. Zephron would be ashamed."

Superheroing by seduction? the ferret teased. *I don't know. Doesn't sound very chivalrous. Let's see. Your sister has super senses. So does that mean you have a super shl—*

"Watch it." Hale tried to keep a stern face, but had trouble not laughing. "I'm just doing my job."

Tracy wanted a seduction. He'd give her a seduction. For the good of the mission, he'd give her the decadent fling of a lifetime. They'd connect, all right. But on a sensual level. Just sex. Nothing more. As Hale knew, sex could be damn persuasive. But there'd be no long talks where they really got to know each other. No lazy picnics on the beach. No way. Not with Tracy. Not with anyone.

At the end of the day, she'd have her fling and Hale would have the belt. Then he'd go far, far away, and forget he ever saw this mortal woman who somehow managed to tie his stomach in knots with just her smile.

"At any rate," Hale said, trying to shift his thoughts from the way Tracy's face glowed when she smiled. "Last night, you were perfectly keen on the seduction plan."

Elmer sighed, apparently sensing defeat. *In theory, sure. But like I said, every time you decide to seduce some mortal cupcake, I end up stuck in a hotel room for hours watching bad television.*

"You like bad television." So much that it was scary. "And if I move in with her, too, you'll have a whole suite of rooms."

You'll forget to feed me. In case you don't remember, I have trouble operating can openers. And it's not like this girl's house will have room service. . . .

Well, Elmer had a point. Hale had to admit he did tend to get tunnel vision whenever he went after a female. He just liked to focus all his attention on the particular woman of the hour. Nothing wrong with that, was there?

Besides, this is my chance to be a star! Let's concentrate on me for a moment, shall we? And could you put a little spring in your step? I'd like to get there before they hire another ferret.

Hale fought a grin, but walked a bit faster. "You're not here to be a star," he pointed out. "You're here on a mission. Not to get your name on the Hollywood Walk of Fame."

Harrumph.

Other than the tiny snort, Elmer kept quiet. Hale wasn't sure if the ferret had come to his senses or if he was just mentally mapping out his coming career. At the moment, it didn't matter; whatever his motivation, the little guy was keeping quiet.

They turned a corner and the Paws In Production trailer came into view. Tracy was right there, right in front of him. And even though she wasn't smiling that killer smile, his stomach was reacting.

Damn. No way could he be more than just sexually attracted to this mortal. No way at all.

Firm, athletic legs filled out jeans that were slightly damp and covered with dog hair. In one hand she held a hose, and in the other a squirming, lathered dog. The dog wasn't as articulate as Elmer, but to Hale's ear, its displeasure at being soaped up was loud and clear.

Tracy could tell, too. Even without speaking Dog. She was straddling the poor thing, mumbling to it about keeping still, one hand holding down the canine's rump as the other tried to work up a good lather.

She tries to do that to me, and we're outta here, Elmer chittered. *Not that I'm against a vigorous massage, mind you. I just prefer one without the bubbles.*

Hale bit back a chuckle. To his way of thinking, Elmer was crazy. Being bathed by Tracy Tannin sounded like a little slice of heaven.

The dog jerked free, then shook vigorously, drenching Tracy in a shower of suds. She jumped back, still holding onto the dog's leash, and Hale could see the stream of bubbles that festooned her forehead, as if she'd used a soapy hand to wipe her hair from her eyes.

All in all, she was a mess. Hale thought she looked completely adorable.

As he approached, Tracy looked up, her perfect green eyes bright and curious.

He could tell the instant she recognized him, because her mouth formed a little O and her eyes registered pure delight.

"You," she said. Her gaze shifted to his shoulder and Elmer, and her head cocked slightly.

After a moment, a slow smile spread across her face. With each infinitesimal increase in the expression, a band around Hale's heart burst. Just being the recipient of this glowing welcome was like winning a prize, and Hale found himself wondering how he could bottle the warm, happy moment and keep it forever.

With a quick shake of his head, he banished such foolish thoughts. Ridiculous. He was here on a mission. The fact that he was attracted to this mortal would help make her seduction easier, that's all. He certainly didn't need to lose himself to sentimentality.

"I don't believe it. You're the guy from the other day."

"Guilty," he said.

"And you're the ferret guy, too?"

She wiped a hand on her jeans and took a small step toward him, keeping her other hand on her dog's leash. "Mel left a message that someone was coming to audition, but I never expected it was *you*." She shook her head. "Talk about a small world."

"I'm just considering myself lucky to see you again." He closed his fingers around hers. Despite all the work she surely did with her hands, her skin was warm and soft. He wondered if the rest of her was just as caressable. He intended to find out.

A tiny V appeared above her nose as her brow furrowed. She was still looking at him, still holding his hand.

He scowled, uncomfortable under her assessment, and strangely fearful that upon this second, closer inspection she would somehow find him lacking. "Problem?"

113

Immediately she dropped his hand and backed away, her eyes wide. "No. Not at all. Sorry." The crease in her forehead reappeared. "It's just that . . . I thought you looked so familiar the other day. And you still do. Only I can't place it. You almost look like . . . I mean, I think I've seen . . ." She took a deep breath. "This may sound silly, but are you—"

"Hale!"

At the new voice, Tracy's mouth fell open and she took a step backward, almost stumbling over her soapy dog as she looked from Hale to some spot over his shoulder, then back again.

Hale turned to look behind him. A tall, thin man with graying hair and a slight limp was making his way toward the trailer. As soon as he got there, he slapped Hale heartily on the back, almost dislodging Elmer, who squeaked in protest:

Watch it, buddy. Ferret hitching a ride here.

"Good to see you. So glad you're here. I'm Burke Cunningham. I produce *Mrs. Dolittle* and direct most of the episodes." He turned to Tracy, his face lighting up. "And this little gal here helps us a lot in that department. Couldn't do it without her, could we, Trace?"

She looked mildly bewildered. "Uh, no, sir."

"Excellent! Excellent, my dear." He wrapped his arm around Tracy's shoulders and gave her a fatherly squeeze. "Wonderful girl," he said, looking at Hale. "Pleasure to work with. The utmost professional."

Tracy's brow furrowed, but she didn't say anything—even though Burke still had her shoulders in a lock and she looked decidedly uncomfortable.

The producer flashed a Hollywood smile Hale's way. "I'm so glad the ferret belongs to you." He rubbed his hands together. "I have a little proposition for you," he added. Hale swallowed, wondering what was coming.

"You really are Hale?" Tracy asked, worming her way out from under Burke's arm. "As in the cover-model Hale? *You're* the ferret guy?"

"One and the same," he admitted, the fact that she knew who he was thrilling him more than it should.

"I'm hoping Hale will join us for a few weeks," Burke said. "Celebrity guest appearances." He rubbed his hands together. "Could be quite a ratings boost."

Oh, no you don't! Elmer squeaked.

"Guest appearance?" Hale asked at exactly the same time. Elmer would never speak to him again if he stole the ferret's limelight.

"Well, yes. I got the idea when Marty called about the ferret. It's a brilliant plan, if I do say so, myself." Burke squinted at Hale. "So, how about it?"

For a second, Hale was tempted. Then he caught a glance of his furry friend's little face, and he knew that he could never intentionally steal Elmer's thunder. "Sorry. I'm on vacation. This is Elmer's gig."

Burke shot him a cross look and, for a moment, Hale thought the producer was going to argue. Then he cleared his throat and said, "I see. Well, we're certainly glad to have the ferret."

Hale flashed a cover-model smile. "And he's glad he's here." He looked pointedly at Elmer.

I know, I know. Don't say you never did me any favors.

Hale stifled his urge to smile, focusing on Burke, whose attention had turned back to Tracy. The man certainly seemed obsessed. No great mystery there, though. Not only was the girl damned appealing, she was wearing the belt. Clearly, the accessory lived up to its hype.

Not that Burke was fawning over her in a sexual way. It was more like he was reaffirming that she had a job. Tracy must have been wanting reassurance that her job was safe, and the belt was providing her that. He started to wonder what else she might want, then realized that Burke was staring at him, clearly waiting for some comment.

Hale cleared his throat. "Elmer and I appreciate the welcome. I'm sure he'll enjoy the next couple of weeks." Silently, he urged Burke to leave. He wanted time *alone* with Tracy.

"Elmer's episodes start shooting late next week," Burke said. "I sent a script to Marty, but I think Tracy here may have one she can show you if you're interested."

Tracy nodded, her eyes never leaving Hale. "Um, yeah. I have one in the trailer."

"Well, there you go!" Burke walloped Hale on the back again. "I'll leave you in Ms. Tannin's good hands, then. Pleasure meeting you." He aimed a huge smile Tracy's way. "Until next week, my dear. And you're doing a fabulous job." Then he scurried off. Considering how much he'd been eyeing Tracy, Hale wasn't sorry to see him go.

"Well," Tracy said, wiping her palms on her damp jeans. "I guess it's just you and me."

With a smile, Hale turned to face her full on. He liked the sound of that.

Hale. *The* Hale. Completely hunky object of her non-Leon fantasies. And he was standing right in front of her. Towering over her, actually, which was no small feat considering she was five feet nine in her stockings. She couldn't believe she hadn't recognized him the other day, but she supposed the fact that he was wearing clothes instead of an open, flowing silk shirt or chain mail made all the difference.

It was a miracle. It was fabulous.

She glanced down, quickly assessing how grungy she looked.

It was a nightmare.

Meeting Hale wearing damp jeans and soap suds and wrestling a soggy dachshund wasn't exactly the scenario she'd played out in her head on those long weekends curled up with a steamy romance novel.

Especially when he looked so positively delicious. Tall and dark, he was just like some Greek god who'd just stepped off a *Baywatch* set. Right now he was wearing jeans, a black T-shirt, and black sport coat, but Tracy knew well enough what his chest and arms looked like under all that pesky material. She imagined him flexing his muscles and bursting out of the tailored linen jacket. She'd seen enough of his skin on the covers of her novels to know just how he'd look, and one word pretty much summed that up. *Yum.*

He looked like a dream, and Tracy looked like something the dog dragged in. Life really wasn't fair.

Not that there was anything she could do about it now. She'd just have to be polite and not melt at his feet.

"So." She floundered, her hand twirling as she searched for something brilliant, witty, and utterly unforgettable to say. "Guess you didn't have any trouble finding the place. I mean, since you'd already been here and everything." So much for brilliant and unforgettable.

"No problem at all." Amusement danced in his eyes. They were the oddest shade of blue: deep like the sea, but accented with flecks of green and gold. Magical eyes.

She shivered, unsettled by her reaction to him. Sure she'd lusted over his body, but now that he was here in front of her, it wasn't his body at all that attracted her. Well, maybe a little. He *was* put together in the most amazing way. But more than that was the way he'd acted around her the other day. Like he genuinely liked her. Like he was interested in her. Really and truly interested.

She even saw it in his face. Not just his eyes, either—though his stormy eyes were fabulous—but in an openness

117

in the way he looked at her. Like he'd move mountains to protect her. Like she was his entire world.

No one had ever looked at her like that before. Not Leon when he was begging for a date, not Walter back when they were living together. Not anyone. And the longer he looked at her like that, the more under his spell she'd fall.

Blinking, she shook her head. *Get a grip, girl!* Jeesh, she'd been reading too many books with this man on the cover, and now she was falling for an image manufactured by those publishers. The truth was he barely knew her, and he certainly didn't have any reason to be interested in her *that way*. For that matter, she didn't really know him either. And she'd do well to tamp down on her raging hormones.

Taking a deep breath, she bent down and concentrated on Peanut, using a nearby towel to dry the dog. Sure, the dachshund would be just fine for a few more minutes, but Tracy needed an excuse not to look at Hale. Because if she looked, she'd simply stare. And if she stared, she'd drool. And drooling wasn't on the Miss Manners top-ten list.

But turning away was impolite. Since staring was dangerous and turning away wasn't a good option either, she stood back up, concentrating on the ferret on his shoulder. "So this is our new star." She glanced to Hale's face. "Is he trained?"

She met Hale's eyes. Damn! Now she was in trouble.

For some reason, the question seemed to amuse him. "Trained? Oh, yeah. Elmer's the Shamu of ferrets." The corner of his mouth twitched, and the little guy on his shoulder started chattering away. "Will you be quiet?" Hale snapped.

Her eyes widened. "I'm sorry?"

"Not you. Elmer."

Sure enough, the ferret's little mouth was now clamped firmly closed.

"Not too shabby," she said.

For a second, Hale looked confused. Then he laughed, the sound delighting her. "Right. Yes, well. I told you he was trained."

"And smart, too."

"Well, he knows the word 'quiet.' I use it around him a lot." His gentle smile warmed her, and Tracy again had the distinct feeling that there was more than just politeness in his expression.

Mentally, she shook her head, more forcefully this time. Nonsense. She was rolling in nonsense. Guys like Hale weren't interested in her. Then again, neither were guys like Leon, but he'd been quite the puppy dog just an hour ago.

Standing up a little straighter, she returned his smile. Maybe she didn't have her grandmother's charisma, but she hardly needed a paper bag over her head. And as for conjuring confidence when faced with gorgeous male specimens, that was why she'd worn her talisman. It seemed to be working.

Her fingers skimmed her waist and the cool metal of her good-luck-charm belt. So long as she was wearing it, she'd do just fine talking with these fabulous specimens of male-dom. All she had to do was keep telling herself that. Maybe eventually, she'd actually believe it.

"Well," she said briskly. "Maybe we should get started." She held out her hands. "Can I hold him?"

Curiously, the ferret squeaked and shimmied on Hale's shoulder, then jumped straight into Tracy's arms.

Surprised, she just held the little furball, then looked up at Hale. "I'll take that as a yes?"

A wry grin crossed his face. "He also knows the word 'hold.' "

"I guess you were right. He is well trained."

"He's got attitude, though." Hale aimed a pointed look the ferret's direction. "Lots and lots of attitude."

Elmer stretched out in Tracy's arms, his belly up, a contented look on his furry little face. "I see what you mean," she said, stroking his tummy.

He made a soft sound, half-squeak and half-sigh.

"No kidding," Hale said.

"I'm sorry?" she said and frowned. She wasn't following.

He shook his head. "Just agreeing with the ferret."

"Agreeing with him?" She laughed. "What? Do you speak Ferret?"

"Of course." He spoke perfectly straight-faced, but the laughter in his eyes gave him away. "He was talking about what ecstasy it was to have you stroking him like that."

The twinkle in Hale's eyes faded, his irises darkening as he took a step toward her, close enough that she could smell the subtle scent of his cologne. "I was just agreeing." His low whisper tickled her ear.

"I . . . oh." Heat curled through her body, starting at her toes and radiating up until she was sure her cheeks burned bright red. He was flirting with her again. Rather blatantly, for that matter. And despite the jolt of confidence she'd hoped for from the belt, she couldn't think of a single thing to say.

So much for relying on fashion to see you through a crisis.

"No response?" His delicious grin teased her, but she wasn't any closer to having anything intelligent or flirty to say.

She tried to catch his eye, tried to think of a snappy comeback, but couldn't quite manage. "I'm working on it," she mumbled.

The man was toying with her, that much was clear. Maybe he was truly attracted to her and maybe he wasn't, but she supposed it didn't matter. He'd grabbed the upper hand and she needed to get it back. No way was she going to dissolve into a puddle of feminine mush. That would hardly wow the man. Besides, considering Mel's workload, Tracy would probably be the one in charge of training his ferret, and that meant she'd be working closely with Hale. Which meant she needed to at least keep up the pretense of being professional.

It might sound awfully appealing, but she'd read enough articles in *Cosmo* to know that lust and the working girl could be a very bad combination. At least until she could figure out how to be around Hale and not feel like she was teetering on a sensual precipice.

Lust was one thing. Out-of-control was something entirely different.

Determined, she pulled herself up, practicing the kind of posture that would make her grandmother proud. She was in control. Professional. That was her, all right. True, the effect might be slightly diminished by the fact that she was holding a writhing ferret, but there wasn't anything she could do about that.

"Maybe we should head inside and take a look at that script." There. That sounded in control.

"You lead. I'm happy to follow."

There wasn't anything suggestive about his words or his tone. But somehow Tracy just knew. It was in the way he looked at her. In that little light in his eyes, and in the way his gaze never left her face.

She swallowed. If Hale wasn't truly interested in her, he was doing a damn fine imitation. Turning away, she hid a secret smile. This had started out as one of the most bizarre days of her life. It looked like it was going to stay that way.

As she walked along, she cast a sideways glance at Hale. Yup. Definitely bizarre. But also very, very nice.

Chapter Ten

The inside of the trailer smelled vaguely like wet fur, and Hale had to smile. Considering how much time he spent with Elmer, the smell reminded him of home.

Of course, his apartment was significantly bigger. The quarters inside the trailer were decidedly cramped, and the company intern left as they arrived—simply to give them more room. Not that Hale minded the tight quarters. At the moment, it put him in deliciously close contact with Tracy. He was content to simply stand there forever.

Unfortunately, Tracy wasn't.

Without meeting his eyes, she cleared her throat, then shifted her weight from one foot to another, rocking Elmer, who was still in her arms. Hale got the impression that she wasn't sure where to go or where to turn. He wanted to just open his arms and invite her in.

For just a moment, their eyes met, and he saw a glimmer of desire in her emerald-green irises. Excellent. That meant he was already halfway to seduction. In no time at all, the mission would be accomplished and he'd be on a beach finishing his vacation.

After a few seconds, the expression disappeared and her eyes were again aimed at the floor.

"So," he said, trying for levity. "What's a nice girl like you doing in a place like this?" He wanted—no, *needed*—to seduce her. But coming on too strong might scare her away.

It worked; she laughed. A genuine laugh that burst out so fast she slapped a hand over her mouth, almost dropping Elmer in the process.

Watch it! Some of us can't levitate, you know!

A flurry of movement near him caught Hale's eye, and he turned to look into the sleepy eyes of a female ferret. "Well, hi, there. What's your name?" he said.

Penelope. The high-pitched female ferret voice wasn't as refined as Elmer's, but it had a hint of Elmer's intelligence, and Hale wondered about the female's bloodline.

"That's Penelope," Tracy said, and Hale got the impression she was relieved to be talking about her animals instead of herself.

Penelope's gaze drifted to Elmer. *Hiya, handsome.*

If Elmer could have blushed, Hale expected that he would have done so. Instead, he just burrowed his head under Tracy's arm. Hale rubbed his hand over his mouth to hide his grin. Who would have thought Elmer would be the shy, silent type?

"She's who Elmer's replacing," Tracy added, shifting him. "Pregnant ferrets have a tendency not to train well."

Excuse me? Elmer's head popped up. *I'm replacing a girl! I don't think so.*

Calm down studmuffin, Penelope said. *If you're any kind of an actor, I'm sure you'll do just fine.*

Uh-oh. Anyone challenging Elmer's acting skills was sure to get a rise, and Hale aimed a stern glare in Elmer's direction, silently warning him to watch it.

Surprisingly, the ferret didn't seem to need prompting. Instead, the little guy was practically preening from Penelope's attention. *Sweetheart, my acting skills are up there with the best. If there was a Best Ferret category at the Academy Awards, I'd win it.*

Good for you, champ, she squeaked.

Elmer did a little ferret dance, and Hale stifled the urge to roll his eyes.

Tracy scratched Elmer's head, then rubbed under his chin when he turned over, his paws spread. "Excitable, isn't he?"

"You have no idea," Hale said. How long, he wondered, would it be before she stroked *his* body, her soft hands exploring *his* skin? Soon. But not soon enough, that was for damn sure.

He stifled a groan. Pretty pathetic, being jealous of one's ferret.

Tracy's perfect, pink tongue slipped out, moistening her lips as she glanced at him. "Um . . . yes, well, I guess we should take a look at the script. I figure you'll want to be around for Elmer's scenes, right?"

Hale nodded. "Absolutely."

She turned away from him to squeeze sideways between the kennels and a table piled with bags of pet food and doggie toys. "Sorry about the mess."

It wasn't the mess Hale minded. It was the dust. Tiny particles of animal fur mixed with bits of dirt and all of it suspended in the smoggy Los Angeles air. Not a good mix for a guy with allergies. His nose twitched and he tried to hold back a sneeze.

No such luck.

A-a-a-choo!

Hale popped out of the visible realm, silently cursing, and reminding himself again that a trip to the drugstore really was crucial. With focused effort, he tried to ward off another sneeze and materialize before the girl turned back around.

No such luck.

"Bless you," she said, peering over her shoulder toward where he had been. "Hale?" She blinked, then turned in a circle. "Where'd you go?"

Damn! He ducked under the table and concentrated on materializing. "Down here," he said, as soon as he'd become visible.

"Of course you are." In front of him, her feet shuffled. Then her knees appeared, followed by all of her. "Any reason we're down here on the floor?"

Because my man Hale can't be bothered with allergy shots, Elmer chittered.

Hale ignored the ferret as he tried to think of a reasonable response. "Uh, just checking for mice." Oh, yeah, *that* was brilliant. "Elmer doesn't work well if there are mice around."

Oh, sure. You act like an idiot and I get blamed.

Hale stood up, then aimed a glare toward Elmer.

Tracy followed, her expression curious but, thankfully, she didn't challenge him. "No mice," she said. Her hand swept the trailer, pointing out the stacks of kennels. "Not the trained kind or the roaming-free kind. Hardly any animals today, actually." At the moment, the kennels were all empty except for Penelope's and, now, a still-damp dog.

"Where are the rest of the inmates?" he joked, happy to be back in a somewhat normal conversation.

A smile twisted her lips. "Mel's compound. Today we were only shooting with Peanut. Penelope's only here so we can keep an eye on her during her pregnancy." Her arm swept the bank of cages. "Next week, these kennels will all be full. We're going to shoot a scene in Mrs. Dolittle's clinic. You know, one of those supposedly funny scenes where the animals get loose and wreak havoc?"

Hale shot a wry glance in Elmer's direction, but the ferret didn't even notice as he was making eyes at Penelope. "I can imagine."

She put Elmer down on the table and pulled out a chair, gesturing for Hale to take the other. "Sorry about the tight fit."

"Doesn't bother me at all." His arm brushed against hers as he sat. "I like tight fits."

Oh, puh-leaze. Ferrets couldn't exactly roll their eyes, but Elmer came awfully close. Apparently, he was paying attention again.

"Oh." The pink returned to her cheeks. Mighty Zeus, the woman was adorable. "Right. Well . . . the script."

"The script," he repeated.

She nodded. Then she asked, "So, how has Elmer worked in the past? Do his old trainers have any tricks I should know about?"

"Oh. Well . . ." he stammered. "Elmer's a quick study."

"He is?" She turned to face Hale, her eyes dancing. "That's good to know. How about you? Are you a quick study, too?" For just a second, the small smile hung on her lips; then she turned away—as if she'd hit her maximum flirting potential. Too bad. He liked that light in her eyes. And he wanted to be the one who put it there.

She might want a fling—if what she'd told her friend Mel was true—but clearly she didn't have any experience in initiating one. Fortunately, Hale had plenty of experience, and he was only too happy to take the lead. For the good of the mission, of course.

He let his gaze roam over her, drawing a deep satisfaction from the tiny goose bumps he saw on her arms in the wake of his lazy examination. "I'm a quick study when I want to be."

"Oh." She flipped a page of the script, her eyes glued to the paper. "So, um, will you be coming out to the compound every day?"

He sat back. "Compound?"

What compound? Elmer squeaked, managing to look both curious and terrified.

"Mel's ranch. It's where all the animals stay. I just assumed Elmer . . ."

Oh no. I'm not staying with a bunch of inarticulate dogs and cats. Unless . . . He drifted off, looking Penelope's way.

The female ferret chittered. *In my condition? Don't even think about it, big guy. I stay in the house. You'd be out in the shed with the others.*

"I don't think Elmer would thrive in that kind of environment," Hale said. He shot a look toward the little guy that he hoped conveyed the need for silence.

"Oh, dear. I'm sure that's what Mel had in mind. Especially since we need to start some pretty intensive training if we don't want to throw the show's schedule off."

"Isn't there some other way we could work this?" No matter how short this mission turned out to be, he had to live with Elmer for the rest of his life. And if he left the furry little critter in a wire kennel with a bowl of food, instead of a plush hotel room with HBO and room service, well, he'd never hear the end of it.

"I don't know. I suppose we could . . ." She drifted off with a frown.

"What?"

"I'm not even sure Mel would agree." She caught his eye. "This is her business, you know. But considering Mel's schedule this week, I'll probably be the one training Elmer. So we could work at my house every evening." She looked at him, as if gauging his reaction. "You'd have to bring

Elmer over every night. And you might find the whole process pretty tiresome."

"Not at all. Besides, he'll do better if I'm there."

"Well . . ." Hesitation still lurked in her voice as she toyed with the script. "We'll ask Mel. If she agrees and you're okay with it, then I guess we can try."

"Actually, I have a better idea." He leaned forward, putting the plan he'd made with Taylor and Zoë into action. "Someone told me you're looking for a roommate."

Her eyes went wide. Then she quickly dipped her head and focused on her fingernails. "Well. Um. Yeah. Yeah, I am."

"At the moment, I'm living in a hotel. A nice hotel, but it's still a hotel."

"And you'd want to move in with me? But don't you have an apartment somewhere?" Her voice squeaked, and he knew he'd thrown her off balance. Well, what the heck. He was pretty off balance right now, himself.

"Manhattan," he said. "And I wouldn't be moving in for good. Just while Elmer's on the show. That would give you some income while you're looking for a full-time roommate." Even to his own ears, it sounded like a perfectly reasonable plan. There was no hint of the seduction he had planned shining through. None at all.

Elmer snorted.

"Well . . ." She trailed off, and Hale put on his responsible, upstanding citizen face. "I guess it could work out. But are you sure you want to do this? I mean, it's not like there's room service."

Told you. Now I really am going to starve!

"And the pool hasn't been cleaned in a year." Tracy nibbled on her lower lip. "I doubt it's what you're used to."

"I'm sure it's perfect."

She cocked her head, watching him. "Okay," she said, the word almost a sigh. As if she knew she was doing a foolish thing, but couldn't help herself. Well, that made two of them.

"I guess we've got a deal." She shrugged again. "I've . . . um . . . got plans tonight. Why don't you move in tomorrow evening?"

Hale leaned back in his chair, thoroughly satisfied with himself. "I have an even better idea," he said, taking the next step toward a wild, wanton fling. "After I drop my stuff off tomorrow, why don't I take you out for a night on the town?"

From his perch on the roof of the Paws In Production trailer, Mordichai tapped his fingers on his thigh, pondering the situation. He pulled his cloak tighter around him, knowing he was safe from prying eyes. His prototype model 47A Propulsion Cloak included an invisibility feature as well as a supercharged propulsion pack for fast getaways.

Hale wasn't the only one who could slip in and out undetected. And unlike his cousin, Mordi didn't fade away during an allergy attack. All he had to worry about was undercharged batteries.

Now here he was at the start of his mission, and he hadn't a clue what step to take next. Right after he'd received the message from his father about Zoë and Hale being on the case, the tracking monitor had started blipping its little heart out. This Tracy Tannin girl had put on the belt, and anyone who might be looking could zero in on her.

Unfortunately, Hale had gotten to her before him. Still, Mordi was here now. He was on the case. He was *da man*. He had the girl in his sights. For once, he had the chance to best his cousin—and he intended to make the most of it.

The question was, now that he'd found the girl, what did he do with her? Especially since it wasn't Tracy he cared about, but the damn belt.

Lucky for him, the belt's location hadn't proved to be a huge mystery. Too bad for him, the girl seemed attached to the thing. He wondered if she was wearing it because of its dubious fashionable qualities or because she'd discovered its magical properties.

For the moment, he assumed the former—even though it meant the girl had pretty lousy taste in clothes. Considering the short amount of time she'd worn the thing, he doubted she could have yet clued in to its more mysterious capabilities.

Unfortunately, time wasn't on Mordi's side. And once she figured out the belt's qualities, she was never going to want to give it up. Not to him, not to Hale, not to anyone.

He drummed his fingers on the roof—softly, so that no one inside the trailer would hear—and considered his predicament. If he didn't acquire the belt, his father would disown him. Or worse. But as a Probationary Status Council Member, if he went after the belt for himself and got caught, he could pretty much kiss his Council membership good-bye.

He needed to decide what he wanted—his father, his career, or something entirely different. His own path, wherever that might lead.

All his life, he'd only wanted his father's approval, his father's love. But now he'd passed his twenty-fifth birthday. He was a grown man, old enough to be a member of the Council. And certainly old enough to know that Hieronymous loved no one except Hieronymous. If Mordi tried hard enough, worked hard enough, and never stumbled again, he might—*might*—earn his father's respect. Maybe even his admiration.

But his love?

Not hardly. And it was about damn time that Mordi came to grips with that fact.

No, the only one who cared about Mordi was Mordi. And he cared a great deal.

Under the camouflage of his invisibility cloak, he stroked his chin. Hieronymous wanted the belt, but maybe Mordichai did, too. And if Mordi managed to acquire it—and if he kept it—well, that would certainly make dear old Dad sit up and take notice.

The only problem was how. How could he get his hands on that belt?

Well, that was why he was camped out on a trailer roof in the middle of the San Fernando Valley, the blazing sun above hot enough to melt the tar on the shingles.

Too bad Hale had beat him to the punch. The mission would have been so much easier if Mordi had located the girl first. Zeus knew, his cousin had all the right equipment to charm the belt right off Tracy. And, unfortunately, Mordi wasn't any match for Hale where women were concerned.

Unless . . .

Shifting a little—the sun-warmed roof shingles were beginning to irritate his rear end—he tried to catch onto the tail end of that fleeting thought. This Tracy Tannin seemed pretty average as mortals went. What was it that mortal women wanted? What was it all those Oprah-like daytime talk shows were always touting? A man who understood them. Who could talk to them. Who really, really listened.

That sure wouldn't be Hale. His cousin wasn't exactly known for his sensitive side where women were concerned. Especially mortal women.

But Mordi was half-mortal. Not that he had a particular fondness for them—his mother had been mortal, after all—but he at least knew how to walk the walk and talk the talk.

So, in this particular instance, Mordi just might be able to best Hale after all.

Chapter Eleven

"So . . . I guess I'll see you tomorrow night, right?" Tracy leaned against the door of her car, still not believing Hale had asked her out. First Leon, now him! Her luck was certainly changing. The cover model stood mere inches away, and she loved the easy familiarity they'd already developed. Her eyes drifted to his shoulder where Elmer usually perched; then she remembered that Hale had left the ferret sitting in the front seat of his Ferrari with strict instructions to "hang tight."

He actually seemed to think the animal not only understood, but would obey. No question about it—the man had some eccentricities. She supposed that should scare her off—isn't that what all those women's mags said?—but with Hale, they just seemed to draw her closer. She'd known him for what? No time at all, really. And already she was smitten.

Mentally she grinned. The word was a little corny, but it described her situation completely. *Smitten*. Not that she'd had far to fall. She'd already been entranced by the fantasy Hale she'd made up to go along with his cover persona. Now she only hoped he'd live up to her imagination.

Of course, at the moment he still hadn't answered her question. He was just looking at her with a curious expression. Perhaps he didn't think his fame and eccentricities meshed all that well with her normal, boring little life. Maybe he'd rethought his offer.

A thoroughly depressing thought. Best to just take the plunge and find out. "Um? Hale? Tomorrow? Are we still on?" So much for being articulate. They'd just spent two hours in close quarters, laughing and being perfectly comfortable, but with the return of her insecurity, so came the return of mush-brain.

But Hale's eyes brightened, as if he'd been far, far away and she'd only just pulled him back. Then a lazy grin spread across his face. "You can count on it."

She almost exhaled in relief, but managed to catch herself. Instead, she just said, "Good."

One simple word, but it conveyed so much. At least she hoped it did. Her first reaction to having Hale move in might have been nerves, but that had soon been replaced by an all-over tingling. Excitement. Anticipation. It was so much more than she felt for her date with Leon. She almost wished she could cancel tonight, but she'd never had quite so much attention from the male of the species, and she didn't intend to count her eggs before her chickens hatched. Or something like that.

Still, she shivered, thinking about tomorrow with Hale rather than tonight with Leon. Instead of just dropping her off after their date, he'd be coming in, too. In such close quarters together, who knows what might happen?

Something interesting, she hoped.

Hale's masculine scent teased her as he leaned past, reaching for the door handle, and she just about melted on the spot. Instinctively, she stepped closer, wanting more of him, then realized what she was doing. She pressed back against the hot metal of her car—it might have been baking in the sun all day, but the heat it generated wasn't any match for the temperature of her blood right now.

The dimple in Hale's cheek appeared, as if he knew the effect he was having on her. But he didn't say a word, just pulled the car door open for her. Feeling slightly foolish, she slid inside. He closed the door after her, then stepped back from the car.

In an instant, she had the window rolled down, not wanting to let him get away quite so quickly. Then she just stared at him, realizing she didn't know what to say, and hoping she didn't look like a total idiot.

Fat chance.

"So," she finally managed. "I guess I'm out of here."

He didn't answer right away, and she wished she could slink down into the driver's seat and disappear. Then she took another look at him, and realized his nose was twitching as he fought a sneeze.

"Hale?"

Sniff, sniff, twitch, twitch. He waved his hand in some vague gesture. "Right. Great. Drive safe," he managed. His voice was nasal and his nose was still twitching.

He looked so darn uncomfortable, she fought a chuckle. "Well," she said. "Tomorrow, then."

He nodded, then half-waved, his face contorted with the effort.

Amused, she pulled away, figuring if he was going to so much trouble not to let loose with a rip-roaring sneeze in front of her, she might as well be accommodating. She'd barely traveled any distance at all when she heard the loud *A-a-choo!* She hit the brake, then leaned out the window and glanced back, expecting to see Hale standing there looking pleased with himself for holding it until she'd left.

He wasn't there. Odd. He had to be there. She'd just heard him. She remembered the way he'd dropped out of sight in the trailer. The man certainly had a knack for disappearing.

Frowning, she ducked back in the car, her eyes automatically going to the rearview mirror. *There he was.*

Okay, now that was weird. She glanced at the mirror again, only to see Hale darting toward the trailer. She popped her head out the window to call to him, but he was gone. The man certainly could move fast.

She tapped the accelerator, and almost sideswiped Leon. The actor was standing in the road, a lovesick-puppy look on his face. Still bewildered about Hale, Tracy waved, swerved around him, then pulled out the studio gate. He hollered after her, "See you tonight!"

Just yesterday, she'd been manless. Today, America's latest heartthrob had the hots for her, and a disappearing cover model had not only asked her out, but asked to move in. Not bad for one day.

The morning might have started out weird, but it was wrapping up nicely. Thoroughly satisfied with herself, she turned onto Ventura Boulevard, wondering what the next twenty-four hours would bring.

Two Henchmen crouched behind a dumpster just outside the studio gate, the fat one scratching under where his arms would be if he'd been remotely human.

"Tha's her. Tha's the girl. Weesa supposed to get the girl."

The skinny one turned and bopped him alongside the head. Or, the head-type part. "Not the girl. Master says we gotsa get the belt."

"The belt. Righta." He turned, his huge folds of slimy flesh jiggling as he looked toward Tracy's car. It turned onto Ventura Boulevard, brakelights flashing briefly as she careened around the corner. "She'sa going-gone. We go now?"

He started to run after the car, but the skinny one caught his tail and pulled him back. He settled with a wet *ker-plap* on the concrete.

Another bop on his face. "Not go now. *Change* now."

"Right-o." The fat one's facial features squinched up with concentration, and then he started to shimmer and shake, the folds of his flesh and slime dissolving and changing until he was no longer a fat creature but a plump man, decked out in denim bib overalls.

The skinny one followed suit, transforming into a tall, skinny man with a shock of red hair. His wore faded green fatigues that appeared two sizes too big.

The transformation complete, they faced each other. "We go," said the skinny one.

"Weesa go now," concurred the fat one. And with that, they took off down the road in the direction where Tracy's taillights had disappeared.

Hale slipped behind a building before rematerializing, two things at the forefront of his mind. One, Tracy Tannin had managed to get under his skin in the most deliciously distracting of ways. Two, he really needed to find some allergy medicine.

But as pressing as that second need was, Zeus help him, he had to see Tracy again. They'd pored over that sitcom script for hours, sitting side by side as they discussed the various tricks Elmer would be expected to perform.

Through it all, Hale had to fight to concentrate on the work rather than on the minty scent of her shampoo. By the time they'd finished the first read-through, he'd been desperate to leave, desperate to get outside and clear his head.

But time pressure wouldn't allow him time to clear his head. If he was going to get close to Tracy and get the belt away from her, then Tracy needed to fall for him—and fall hard. And fast. With her wearing the belt now, it was only a matter of time before Hieronymous tracked her down. After she'd agreed to let him move in, he'd thought he was in the clear. Then Tracy had reminded him about her plans tonight—her plans with Leon.

The fact that she was going out with Leon mucked everything up. If Tracy was also dating Leon, Hale's talents in the bedroom might not be enough to persuade her to part with the belt. Hale couldn't imagine the risk was high, but what if she actually fell for this guy?

Not that he actually would admit the possibility that Leon could rank over him in any woman's mind, but why take the chance? He needed to make damn certain that he spent time with Tracy *before* she went out with Leon, and that their time together beat the pants off any piddly little date activities Leon might dream up.

Of course, there was always Plan B. He could follow Tracy and Leon on their date, stay invisible, and secretly intercede if any sort of warm fuzzy moments seemed to be lurking on the horizon. Screw chivalry. As far as Hale knew, chivalry didn't count when another man had his sights set on your girl.

Blinking, he squeezed his hands into fists. What was he thinking? She wasn't his "girl." At most, she was his temporary fling. Or *his mission*. His "girl" implied a level of commitment and permanency, and Hale had no intention of falling into that trap. No intention whatsoever.

His resolve renewed, he dematerialized again and took off running at top speed toward the studio gate.

Mordi smiled, not believing his luck. Hale and Tracy had parted ways, and now Mordi had the entire evening to ingratiate himself to her. How perfectly thoughtful of Hale to leave his cousin such a wonderful opening.

He considered shifting into a dog or a bird and following her by foot or by air, then decided that the old-fashioned approach would work best. Hopping down from the trailer roof, he headed to the Porshe he'd rented that morning. It had cost a fortune to wrangle the thing for the weekend; he might as well use it.

The sleek machine took curves like a dream, and in no time at all he saw Tracy two blocks ahead, zipping down the street in her ancient Chevy. She turned off of Ventura onto Laurel Canyon, heading into the valley, and that's when he saw them. The two men running after her car. Only they weren't men. Nope. Not by a long shot.

On the surface they might look human. And certainly no passing mortal would give them a second glance—except for the fact that they were racing down the street after a car, a nail gun aimed at its back tires. But simply on the sake of appearance, these guys could fit in among any mortals quite nicely.

But like any of Protector blood, Mordi saw past the surface. Henchmen had to work hard to maintain the illusion of humanity. Mortals couldn't see the effort; Protectors could. And right at the moment he saw a beanpole of a Henchman and his huffing, puffing, rotund slimeball buddy closing in on Tracy.

Closing in on the belt.

Damn his father!

Not that Mordi should have been surprised, but just once why couldn't Hieronymous believe in him? Was it really necessary to send Henchmen to do the very thing he was assigned to do?

He scowled, pondering the possibilities.

What if Hieronymous had decided he couldn't trust his son to acquire the belt and turn it over to Daddy Dearest? Wouldn't that be a pickle?

It raised an interesting conundrum. Did Mordi let the Henchmen get the belt, and ruin his chance to obtain the prize himself, or did he swoop down and protect Tracy from his father's stinky little beasts? He'd preferred the latter, but then word would get back to Hieronymous and Mordi would be in the doghouse. Again.

He was still pondering the dilemma when the solution materialized about three blocks behind the Henchmen. Mordi half-snorted. Leave it to Hale to rush to a woman's rescue. With his chiseled looks and buff body, all he needed was a white stallion.

Show-off.

Not that Mordi begrudged Hale his looks—hell, Mordi wasn't any slouch in the appearance department—but somehow Hale was just, well, *Hale*. Probably a product of all that cover modeling. Surely eight hours under a photographer's lights with a half-naked woman in your arms did wonders for a guy's ego.

Mordi liked his cousin well enough, but the guy definitely believed his own press. And right now, he was racing to play the hero to Tracy. Damn.

Mordi considered showing himself and running to her rescue first—then he'd be the hero instead of Hale. But since Hale had clearly seen the Henchmen, that would never do. Already, because of his father, his cousin would suspect him of duplicity. Even though Mordi had nothing to do with the Henchmen, best not to foster any suspicions in Hale's mind.

No, he'd just kick back and wait.

After more than twenty-five years of living in his father's shadow, if there was one thing Mordi was good at, it was waiting.

Chapter Twelve

Ker-thwonk! Thud, thud, thud.

Tracy groaned, trying to keep her car under control even as she tried to figure out what had suddenly gone so wrong. Then it hit her. A flat tire.

Damn! Well, what did she expect? She was driving a thirteen-year-old Chevy Nova. Not exactly the car folks in Beverly Hills expected to see, but at least it was paid for. And, except for the occasional dead battery, it usually ran just fine.

Right now, though, she was cursing it. Already she barely had time to run to the mall and interrogate the cosmetic-counter ladies for tips on how she could look presentable. How the heck was she supposed to change a tire *and* do her shopping *and* still manage to get changed in time for a date?

Not that she was in *that* much of a hurry. After all, since Burke had shut production down early, she had a few hours to play with. And even though she would have preferred to spend more time with Hale and Elmer, she figured she'd need as much time as she could get to look beautiful.

As close to beautiful as she could manage, that is. Which probably wouldn't be very close, but maybe she could land in the general vicinity of passable.

The car pulled to the right, and Tracy fought to keep it on a straight path until she could pull off the street into a parking lot. Dragging the wheel to the left with a string of colorful curses, she finally managed to squeeze over a lane and pull into the lot of a greasy spoon that advertised chicken and waffles.

Hopefully, she wouldn't be overcome with hunger until *after* she'd managed to change the tire.

With a groan, she slipped out of her car and popped the trunk, then proceeded to dig through the bags of pet food and animal toys looking for her jack. No luck.

Well, fine. If she had to empty her trunk in the middle of a parking lot and do this methodically, then that's exactly what she'd do. Right away, she started hauling out bags—puppy chow, dog chow, ferret chow. If she looked long enough she'd probably find a bag of tiger chow, too.

Finally, she reached the bottom of her trunk. She was just about to lift the little panel that hid the spare tire when she saw them—a thin man in fatigues and his rather round companion. In farmer-style overalls, the second guy looked like he belonged with milk cows, not on a street in Los Angeles. But Tracy had long since learned not to bat an eye where fashion in the City of Angels was concerned.

The men were walking toward her, and she didn't have any real reason to feel nervous. For all she knew, they were suffering from chicken and waffle cravings. Except, she *did* feel nervous. She made a point of rummaging a little faster, the adrenaline rush building until she felt her fingers close over the cool metal of a tire iron.

"Hey, lady. Shesa pretty lady, yes?"

She turned, facing them straight on, the tire iron gripped tight in her hand.

"Oh, yes. Pretty. Weesa like pretty ladies."

What she wanted to do was take a step backward, but since her car was blocking any escape, that wasn't an option. Instead she hefted the iron, and tried to summon her most authoritative voice. The one she used with misbehaving dogs.

"Sorry, guys. I'm busy. I'd appreciate it if you'd leave me alone."

The fat one nudged the skinny one, nearly knocking him over. "D'you hear that? Sheesa wants us to leave. Not nice, lady."

"We leave," the skinny one said. "You gives it to us, and we leave now."

It? What *it?*

The skinny one wasn't staring at anything except the tire iron she was holding at her waist. Did he want that? 'Cause if he did, at the moment, she'd be happy to give it to him. . . .

"Give *now*." He moved toward her, and she held the iron up, brandishing it a bit until he moved back. Where the hell was everybody? This parking lot was hidden from the street by some brush, but this was a restaurant. Where were all the patrons? Where was the cavalry? Didn't anyone eat anything but tofu in this town?

Without warning, the skinny one lunged. Tracy reacted automatically, her throat releasing a high-pitched scream even as she hauled off and hit her assailant in the gut with the tire iron. She might not have played softball since junior high, but she had to mentally congratulate herself on the force of her blow.

Of course, while she was busy congratulating herself, the guy was busy recovering. And it didn't seem to take him

143

anytime at all. The fat one was getting into the act too, now, so she had two thugs advancing on her.

Wildly she swung the tire iron, connecting with the solid bone of the skinny one's jaw before moving on to whonk the shorter, fat one across the top of his skull. Oddly enough, she didn't hear bone cracking. Instead, she had the weirdest sensation of dragging an oar through pudding.

She blinked, but didn't have time to ponder the oddity. Everything was happening too quickly and as she took a deep breath, they advanced. Closer and closer, until—

"Gentlemen, I suggest you leave the lady alone."

Hale!

Like some foolish twit in a scary movie, Tracy dropped the tire iron and ran to his side, grateful when he swung his arm around her and pulled her close.

"You okay?"

She nodded.

"Sorry I didn't get here sooner."

"Sorry?" How on earth could he be sorry? "I'm just glad you're here at all." She frowned. "Why *are* you here?" But she didn't really want an answer. At the moment, she didn't care. She just wanted to be held. Just wanted to be taken care of.

And Hale was just the man she would have chosen to be her hero.

"I'm here to fight the bad guys, of course," Hale said, keeping an eye on Dopey and Grumpy.

The bad guys in question shifted in front of him, moving from side to side, foot to foot. Hale let them squirm. At the moment, there wasn't anything he could do with them, so he might as well let them stew.

Gently, he kissed the top of Tracy's head, the sweet smell of her shampoo intoxicating him. "Can't let *Henchmen* wander the streets of L.A. picking on beautiful women." He threw in the word to let the Henchmen know that he knew what they were—and that he was a Protector. It was a bluff, of course. If they ran, he couldn't catch them. Not without revealing himself to Tracy.

Which was too bad, since he'd thoroughly enjoy beating them to a pulp. But since he couldn't beat them with his brawn, he could only hope to outwit them with his brain.

Considering how dumb Henchmen tended to be, that shouldn't be too much of a problem.

"Should we call the police?" Tracy asked.

A slow grin crossed Hale's face. "Actually, I think that's a perfect plan." He produced his cell phone.

While Hale could easily see past their disguise, mortals wouldn't be able to. And though a county jail cell wasn't going to be able to hold the slimy critters for long, it would certainly put a crimp in Uncle H's style when he learned that his thugs got picked up for assault and attempted robbery. Even so, Hale had to mentally congratulate his uncle. A mortal couldn't steal the belt, and what Protector would want to? But slimy, vile Henchmen suited Hieronymous's needs to a T. It had been a clever tactic, using them.

Dopey took a step backward, getting ready to bolt.

"I wouldn't, if I were you," Hale said. The creature stopped, its eyes narrowed. It weighed its options as Tracy dialed Hale's phone.

Fortunately Hieronymous—or that maniac Clyde—must have drilled into the Henchmen's heads that they weren't to raise any mortal suspicions. In no time at all, cops had arrived and had them in cuffs. The two flabbergasted blobs were shoved into the backseat of a cruiser.

Hale glanced at his watch, wondering if even an hour would pass before these friendly neighborhood thugs performed their little jail-break routine. Well, it didn't matter to him. He already knew what he needed to. It was time to institute a twenty-four-hour watch on Tracy.

Beside him, she relaxed, clearly pleased to see her assailants hauled off in cuffs.

"Better?" he asked.

"I've lived in L.A. my whole life, but I've never been mugged before." She looked up at him, the smile on her face only slightly distracted. "I've even taken self-defense classes for years. Not that you could tell. All I did was swing a tire iron."

"It worked, though."

"Well, sort of. Since you showed up before they clobbered me." She cocked her head. "Why *did* you show up?"

"Oh. I was just heading to my sister's place, and I saw you back here. Guess we go home the same way."

She nodded, but still looked confused. "From the road, you saw me?"

"Absolutely."

"Even though this lot curves around behind the restaurant?"

"Must've been the angle."

"So you were really just driving by?"

"That's my story, and I'm sticking to it."

"Uh-huh." The corner of her lip twitched as she fought a smile. "Well, where's Elmer?"

Good question. Unfortunately, he didn't have a good answer. "Still in my car, of course."

"In your car? In this heat?"

"It's a convertible."

"Oh." She frowned. "Aren't you afraid he's going to run away?"

"He's trained, remember?"

"Uh-huh." She didn't look convinced. "So where is it?"

"Where's what?"

"Are we playing twenty questions? Your car. Where's your car?"

"Right. Of course. My car." One heck of a long way away. He probably should have driven it. "Uh, it's around here somewhere."

"Okay. Well, how did you get here?"

"Here? American Airlines has plenty of regular flights from New York. I just caught one and voila!" A lie, of course. He'd come to L.A. under his own power. But since she wasn't talking about that—and he damn well knew it— he didn't regret the lie too much.

Her eyebrows lifted above the rims of her sunglasses, her foot tapping a rhythm in time with the *whoosh, whoosh* of the passing traffic. "That's not exactly what I meant."

"Oh." He added the proper note of enthusiasm to his voice. "Oh! You mean *here*. In this parking lot. With you."

"Yup."

So much for stalling. Clearly he hadn't thought this out well enough beforehand. Glancing around, he noticed the grocery store across the street. "I wanted . . . uh . . . lettuce. So I left after you. And then I pulled into the store and saw you. So I came over here to help."

"A salad man, huh?"

He hated salad. "Absolutely."

"Mmm-hmm." She shielded her eyes and looked toward the Gelson's supermarket. "Should we go get Elmer?"

"Oh, no. He likes the peace and quiet. Thrives on it, really."

"Uh-huh."

Enough of this. He took the tire iron from her hand. "Why don't you let me change that flat for you?"

"Sure." This time when she smiled, it seemed slightly shy, not confused. "That would be nice."

Much better. Something physical he could do and do well. And it was a good thing, too; he obviously didn't make the best liar on the planet. The only tricky part would be remembering that he had to change this tire like a mortal guy: no slipping off the lug nuts with his thumb and forefinger, no using super speed to have the new tire on in the blink of an eye. But even doing it the annoying, slow way, he still had her spare tire on and ready to go in well under five minutes.

Finished, he looked up. "All done."

"Bravo!" She clapped, looking completely enamored, and Hale decided there was something to all that clichéd talk about knights on white horses and damsels in distress.

"Listen—" he said.

"Could I—" she began at the same time.

They both laughed, and then he said, "Go ahead."

Again, a shy grin flitted across her face. "I just thought that since you rescued me, the least I could do was buy you a cup of coffee. There's a coffee shop right across the street next to the grocery store." She glanced at her watch. "I can't stay for too long, but maybe a quick one?" Immediately, her cheeks turned pink, and he realized she must be remembering her date with Leon.

All the more reason to spend some quality time with her.

"That would be great. But I'm buying."

"Why? Because you're a guy?"

Holy Hera, she was priceless. "No. Because I want to."

Ten minutes later they were tucked into a corner booth at Jumbo Java, a slice of truly decadent chocolate cake on the table between them.

She nabbed a tiny bit of the cake with her fork. "So, tell me about being a cover model. Is it a fabulous life?"

"Sometimes." He couldn't tell her the full story of what he did, of course, but it was nice to be able to share a little piece of his life. "I enjoy it. The shoots, seeing myself on book covers. The fans."

After she swallowed, she grabbed another forkful of cake. "Must be very glamorous."

"Sometimes. Mostly it's rush, rush to get to a shoot, a few hours under the hot lights in costume, and a lot of waiting. But the personal appearances are great. I love meeting the fans."

"Sounds wonderful," she said, and he stifled a grin as she forked up a huge bite of cake dripping with icing.

Behind her, a guy who looked like a reject from a rock band slid into a booth, his eyes scouring Tracy before he turned the other direction. Hale scowled, something about the green-eyed man flickering in his memory.

"Hale?"

He looked up, shaking off his random thoughts. "Sorry, I got distracted. It *is* wonderful, but it can be exhausting."

"I understand exhausting," she agreed. "Mel's just getting Paws off the ground, so we're both working a lot of hours." Tracy took another bite, then smiled. "But I love it. I've always loved working with animals. In fact, about the only job I'd like better would be training animals at Sea World."

The image of Tracy in a skintight wetsuit was enough to bring a smile to his face. "Really?"

"The ocean," she said. "I love the ocean. The beach, the surf. I always have. It's where I go to wind down." She shrugged. "Actually, it's just as well I don't work with marine life. If I lived and breathed the ocean, it would probably lose a lot of its mystique."

Hale nodded, understanding what she meant. He loved the ocean, too, but he'd never bought a beach house. Somehow, escaping to the shore was more enticing than simply being able to walk out his back door into the sand.

"I know exactly what you mean," he said.

"You do?" she asked, sounding pleased. When he nodded, her smile broadened. "Guess that's one more thing we have in common," she said.

"One more?"

149

"Yeah," she said, the corner of her mouth twitching. "I really love salads, too."

Hale laughed, enjoying this outing with Tracy more than he should be for a simple seduction.

"Tracy?" A male voice said, and Hale fought a wave of irritation at being interrupted. "Tracy, I'm so glad to see you again."

A blond guy, about six feet tall with football-player shoulders, joined them at the table, a steaming to-go cup in his hand.

"Hi, Walter."

While Walter looked ecstatic, Tracy appeared less than thrilled. "What's up?" Her voice was polite enough, but underneath, Hale thought he detected a note of irritation. Under the circumstances, he was pretty annoyed himself. At the moment, he had absolutely no interest in sharing Tracy with anybody.

"Listen," Walter said. "I'm sorry about yesterday. Of *course* I recognized you. I'd just . . . uh . . . drunk too much coffee. Moving back to town and all, I've been living on Diet Coke and coffee. Caffeine high, you know. And I was distracted. That girl I was with . . . uh, she wasn't a girlfriend. No. She was, uh, a rep. For an air-conditioning company. My new apartment is so hot—"

"Uh, Walter? I'm kind of in the middle of something here." She nodded toward Hale.

"Oh. Right." The guy took a few steps backward. "Well, I'll just get going, then." He fished in his coat pocket. "But call me, okay? Here's my card." He plunked a business card down on the table, then slinked out of the coffee shop. Hale couldn't remember the last time he was so glad to see someone go.

"Friend of yours?"

"Sorry." Her cheeks flushed pink. "Ex-boyfriend. I bumped into him yesterday and he didn't even recognize me." She shrugged, then grabbed some more cake with her fork. "Weird. Especially since yesterday I was wishing that he *had* recognized me—and wishing that he'd fawn all over me because his life had become such a shambles since he left me."

"He left you?"

Tracy nodded.

"I find that hard to believe." What Hale didn't find hard to believe was Walter's little love-Tracy-fest just now. She was wearing the belt, after all. And that was some pretty potent magic.

"Anyway, I don't want to talk about him." She smiled, an expression meant just for him. "What were we talking about?"

"Jobs. Tell me about your job."

"I love it, but it's definitely not glamorous. Not like yours."

"Don't knock it. Every job has its downside." In Hale's case, those personal appearances that he loved had made his face recognizable. Hale couldn't do the anonymous superhero routine, and his Council assignments had been chosen accordingly. At first, he'd resented his mortal job. Now, however, he'd meshed the two lives. And, frankly, he wouldn't have it any other way.

"Yeah." Tracy's mouth twitched, and he knew she was fighting laughter. "The downside of my job's tiger poop. Or maybe that's an upside." She lost her battle and erupted into a fit of laughter. "Sorry," she said, after a few heaving breaths. "I just had the most bizarre day yesterday. Walter wasn't even half of it."

"Want to fill me in?"

She shook her head. "Nope." The laughter in her eyes changed to something else. Something softer. "But maybe another time. I think you'd be fun to swap stories with."

151

He took her hand, his gaze meeting hers. "Sweetheart, I promise you. You won't find many men with better stories than me." That, of course, was the understatement of the year.

"Really?" One of her eyebrows went up, matching the note of interest in her voice. "So don't keep me in suspense. Share."

After a second, he nodded. What the heck? She wouldn't believe him anyway. "You already know about my day job—"

"You mean there's another?"

"Absolutely. I may seem like just a mild-mannered cover model, but by night I'm Super Hale, protector of the weak. Defender of the innocent. Leaper of tall buildings."

Her mouth twitched. "I thought you were eccentric when you talked to your ferret. I guess I should learn to trust those first impressions, huh?"

"Always trust first impressions," he told her. Not bad advice. Except that his first impression of Tracy had been more than he wanted to think about.

"So, you're just passing through? Or are you here to rescue some diplomat or something?"

"Nothing as small as that, this time. I'm here to save the world."

"I guess I should feel honored you spent some time rescuing little old me."

"Not at all. You're the key to everything."

"Oh?" Her eyebrow rose again. "I'm the key to saving the world? Careful. You'll give me a big head."

"A pretty one, though."

"Mmm-hmmm." She cocked her head. "Okay. I'll bite. How am I the key to saving the world?"

"Protecting you protects the world." As would getting that belt off her waist. But that part he couldn't mention without pushing his luck. Reaching across the table, he took her hand, working to make his voice teasing. "Protect you from harm, and the world just transforms into a better place."

"I didn't know I ranked so high in the universal hierarchy."

"Sweetheart, don't ever underestimate yourself."

The shy grin was back. "So I've got a date with a superhero, huh?"

"Lucky you."

She leaned over the table toward him, her eyes dancing. "Anything I should know about the care and feeding of superheroes?"

"Be sweet to us." He traced his fingertips over the palm of her hand. "And never say no. It's not good karma."

A blush crept up her neck, turning her ears a delightful shade of pink. "Thanks for the tip. I'll keep that in mind."

Their eyes met and held, locked together by a force he'd never quite experienced before. For a few minutes, they just held hands, and then she blinked, her gaze drifting to the tabletop as she pulled her fingers from his. The moment vanished, but he knew in his gut they'd taken a big first step.

"Wow," she said, nodding toward the empty plate. "We managed to finish it all off."

Hale just nodded and agreed. The woman was perfectly adorable. So why point out that he hadn't even taken one single bite?

Chapter Thirteen

If she weren't driving, Tracy would have hugged herself, she was so happy. As it was, she considered pulling off to the side of the road so she could do that very thing.

Not that hugging herself was what she truly wanted. No, she wanted *Hale* to hug her. To hold her close like he had after those thugs had harassed her. As it was, he'd kissed her cheek after walking her back to her car. She might never wash that particular spot again.

That impromptu date she'd just left had been absolutely fabulous. He might be a famous cover model, but he was also down to earth, sexy as all get-out, and one hell of a knight in shining armor. Plus, he made her laugh.

In other words, he was perfect.

And those little quirks like talking to his ferret, they only seemed more endearing now.

Smiling, she remembered his concocted story about being a superhero. The man was a goofball—and, she had to say, she liked that in a guy.

Besides, in her book, he *was* a superhero. He'd sure as heck rescued her.

Shivering, she recalled the nasty gleam in those creeps' eyes as they'd stared at her. Odd, because her purse had been in the car. What was it they'd wanted? The only thing she'd been holding was the tire iron, and unless they'd been fired from the Auto Club and were holding a grudge, she doubted that was what they were after.

Which left only one thing. Her.

Ick. Major, big-time ick.

Thank goodness Hale had showed up when he did. Maybe she'd acted like a frail little flower of a woman, but that didn't change the fact that when he'd held her tight in the circle of his arms, she'd felt safer and more wonderful than she'd ever felt before.

And what a nice feeling.

All the nicer since he'd seemed content to hold her forever. And when they'd gone to the coffee bar, he hadn't wanted to leave. Finally, she'd had to pull the plug so she'd have time to get ready for her date with Leon.

Sighing, she squirmed in her seat, delighted by the truth that had been so very apparent. *He liked her.* Hale really and truly liked her! She was certain of it, and the feeling warmed her to her toes.

Cover model Hale and TV heartthrob Leon Palmer. Both wanting her. Amazing. All it had taken was a little shot of confidence, and suddenly she had famous dates for the whole weekend. Mentally, she thanked her grandmother.

Digging her cell phone out of her purse, she turned into the mall. Confident, she might be. An educated consumer, she wasn't. And since she'd spent her date-prep time with Hale, she had about three seconds to blow in, get enough makeup to try to turn herself into a glamour queen, and get out again.

"I need help," she said the second Mel answered the phone.

"Undoubtedly. But I'm not a licensed psychotherapist."

"Ha-ha. That's not what I need help with."

"Trust me," Mel quipped. "It is."

Tracy took the phone away from her ear just long enough to scowl at it. "*Not* helpful. I'm at the mall now, and I've got about fifteen minutes to get inside, get to the cosmetics counter, and figure out what I'm supposed to be buying."

"*You're* braving a department store cosmetics counter? By yourself? You do need help."

Tracy rolled her eyes as she turned into a parking place and killed her car's engine. "I told you. So, are you going to help, or are you just going to tease me?"

"Just tease, I'm afraid. I'm still in the meeting. We're on a break. I've got about five minutes."

Tracy slumped. "Damn. I really need advice."

"That's what they've got salesgirls for. What store are you near?"

Tracy told her.

"Lower level, near the shoes," Mel—a walking encyclopedia of malls—said.

"Gotcha." Tracy entered near the men's clothing, made a right turn at evening wear, and ran smack-dab into shoes. Like Mel had promised, just a few yards ahead glistened rows and rows of gleaming glass cubicles filled with beauty products that were sure to transform even the ugliest duckling into a swan. At least that's what Tracy hoped.

"Okay. I'm in," Tracy said, feeling a little like an undercover operative.

"What are your choices?"

"Clinique. Prescriptives. Estee Lauder. And about a billion more." She proceeded to rattle off the brands that were camped out at the various stations. "We could pretty much make over the world from this one store."

"Start with Clinique and work your way down."

Once again, Tracy glanced at the phone, her eyebrows raised with disbelief.

"Trace?" Mel's voice filtered through. "Where'd you go?"

"Are you insane?" Tracy asked, pulling the phone back to her ear. "I've got less than a half hour."

"Well, then," Mel said, the hint of a laugh in her voice. "I guess you'd better get cracking."

"Henchmen!" Zoë knew her voice was squeaking, but she couldn't help it. "Hieronymous sent henchmen? To the San Fernando Valley?"

" 'Fraid so." Hale's voice came through crystal clear on the Council-issued cell phone. "And they've already located Tracy."

"Well, heck," she said, fighting a shiver.

A low laugh from the other end of the phone. "My sentiments were a little more strongly worded, but essentially the same," Hale said.

"So what are you going to do?"

"Not me. You."

"Me? It's your mission. How's it going, anyway? Are you best friends yet?" she asked, trying to keep the smile out of her voice.

He didn't answer right away, and that alone was enough to make Zoë suspicious. "Hale?"

"I'm, uh, not exactly doing the friendship routine."

Zoë stiffened. "What?" Surely Hale wasn't abandoning the mission—was he? "What in Hades are you talking about?"

"I've got another plan. Another way to connect with the girl."

"Another—"

"Trust me. My new plan is right up my alley."

And that's when she realized. "You're going to get the girl into your bed." She drew in a deep breath. "Apollo's Apples, big brother. Do you ever think about anything else?" Her brother really did have a one-track mind. Not that she could wholly argue with his logic. This new approach did make sense. It sure seemed more likely to succeed than hoping Hale could make Tracy his new best friend. She stifled a sigh. Deep down, she knew Hale really didn't mind mortals, liked them even. She just wished he'd realize it, too.

"Right now." he growled, "I'm thinking about her safety. Can you go after her? I just left her. She'll get suspicious if I show up again."

He had a point. "Okay. So what do you need me to do?"

"Just watch her. I'll take over tonight."

Zoë scowled, thinking about Hale's plan of attack. "Yeah. I bet you will."

"She's got a date," he growled. "Tonight, I'm just an observer."

He sounded more irritated about Tracy's date than Zoë would have expected. She wondered if the cause was the inconvenience for his mission, or something else entirely. Interesting. Very, very interesting.

"Zo?"

"Sorry. I'm still here."

"Well, get going. She said she was going shopping. I'm assuming she went to that mall on Riverside."

"Don't worry," Zoë assured him before she hung up. "I'll find her."

There were times when having x-ray vision came in very handy. In no time at all, Zoë was cruising outside the mall, peering in through the brick and mortar. No Tracy in the first store, or the second. She was just starting to get discouraged when she looked through the walls at the last department store. Yup. There Tracy was—hanging out with one of these perfectly complexioned women in white lab coats.

Mission accomplished.

Zoë was just about to head through the door and casually bump into Tracy, when she saw something else that stopped her dead in her tracks—a third person chatting with Tracy and the salesgirl. *Mordichai.*

Well, if that wasn't just great.

Now she really needed to get to Tracy, and fast. She seriously doubted Mordi could sweet-talk the girl out of the belt in a few minutes, but Zoë knew better than to underestimate him.

As she half-ran into the building, she focused her super hearing toward the cosmetics counter. Eavesdropping simply wasn't eavesdropping where saving the world was involved.

"This is definitely your color," the salesgirl was saying.

"You think? I don't usually wear base."

"Trust me. It's a perfect match. See?"

Zoë slid her glasses down her nose, looking through a couple of walls and several racks of clothes to see the woman hand Tracy a mirror. She then turned to Mordi and asked, "Don't you think the color is perfect on her?"

"Well, I'm not certain why a woman as lovely as this needs makeup at all, but if she's dead set on getting it, then I'd have to agree." Mordi's voice came through loud and clear. And with a definite hint of suck-uppiness. Zoë's cousin wanted something from Tracy, and he wasn't wasting any time.

As the salesgirl started rummaging through drawers, pulling out samples, Tracy sat down on one of the stools. She smiled at Mordi. "I can't believe we ran into each other here," she said.

Zoë almost stopped in her tracks. Tracy and Mordichai *knew* each other? Impossible.

"Heck, I can't believe you recognize me from one television news segment six months ago," Tracy added.

"It was a fascinating segment. Training kangaroos, I believe. At any rate, I tried to catch you at your trailer to introduce myself. It's such a coincidence we shop at the same mall."

So they didn't know each other. Not yet, anyway. But what was Mordi's game?

"You're really doing a feature film? Well, Mel's the one to talk to. The company belongs to her, you know."

"I like to talk with the staff members first, particularly where animal training is involved." He leaned closer, and Zoë widened her eyes. "I like to stay especially close to the trainers who'll be doing the actual work."

Beginning to understand her cousin's game, Zoe picked up her pace. Apparently, Mordi was trying to do more than just befriend the girl—he was out-and-out flirting with her! Zoë scowled. The last thing she wanted was Mordi weaseling into Tracy's bed. Especially now that Hale was trying to do that very thing.

"Lovely belt you're wearing," Mordi said. Zoë stiffened. Okay, she was definitely going to have to wedge herself in the middle of this little tête-à-tête. Rounding the corner, she adjusted her speed to a fast walk, then pretended to look down at her watch as she barreled forward. Just as she'd planned, she slammed straight into Mordi just as he was bending over for a closer look at the belt.

"Oh!" Zoë cried. "I'm so sorry." She looked up, feigning surprise. "Mordi! How wild to run into you here. Literally."

To his credit, Mordi masked his irritation and showed only surprise. "Zoë." Then, almost an afterthought. "What a pleasure."

Zoe turned to Tracy. "Hi. I'm Mordi's cousin."

"I'm Tracy."

"How do you know Mordi?" Zoë asked.

"How do I . . ." A pink tinge colored Tracy's cheeks, and Zoë saw that Mordi had turned on the charm—and it had been starting to work. "We, uh, don't actually know each other. We just met. I was shopping—"

The salesgirl interrupted. "I picked out several shades of blush and some coordinating eye shadows," she said, stepping back to join them. "Of course, we'll also need to pick out eyeliners and eyebrow pencils. Probably a concealer and moisturizer, too. But don't worry. We'll take good care of you." She reached out to pat Tracy's hand, then stopped midway, apparently noticing Zoë and Mordi. "Or don't you want the makeup anymore?"

"No!" Tracy answered the salesgirl after a moment. Her head was spinning, and it wasn't due to the seemingly endless array of cosmetics to choose from. No, this head spin was a direct result of yet another man putting the moves on her.

Astounding. She'd come in for a drive-by makeover and ended up on the verge of making another date. No wonder she was reeling. And here was the guy's cousin appearing out of nowhere. Talk about odd. Never once had she met a guy's family *before* the first date.

"I'll put it back, then," the salesgirl answered, her unhappiness at her lost commission reflecting in her face.

"No, no. I still want it. I, uh, just bumped into some friends." She turned to the guy who'd been hitting on her, amazed at how refined and polished he seemed. Almost British. He was the antithesis of Leon's laid-back Hollywood good looks, and certainly nothing like Hale's sultry sex appeal. For reasons she couldn't fathom, suddenly she was attracting men in droves.

Who would have guessed it—Tracy Tannin, male magnet?

This mind-over-matter thing worked like gangbusters.

Mel would be proud.

"Now, just sit still," the salesgirl said, looming over her with various brushes and bottles.

It wasn't easy sitting still with a perfect stranger poking at her face, but somehow Tracy managed.

Through the whole process, Zoë and Mordi kept talking. Tracy tried not to listen in, but that wasn't really possible with them standing so close. And, in truth, she was curious.

"So, you're filming a movie with animals?" Zoë asked, her voice light and airy.

Tracy frowned, wondering how the girl knew they'd been discussing that. She and this Mordichai guy had been talking about his project long before his cousin had arrived at the counter.

"No, no," the salesgirl interrupted, before she could ask. "You need to smile. Like this." She demonstrated, showing off teeth too white to be human. "If you frown, I'm just going to have to redo your lips."

Well, so much for that. Apparently, putting on makeup required being mute.

In front of her, Mordi was shifting his weight from one foot to the other, looking distinctly uncomfortable. "Animals. Yes. I certainly am."

His manner was odd. But maybe it was a mystery better solved later.

His cousin continued: "How nice for you. I always knew you had a variety of talents. And a particular penchant for dogs, if I remember right."

The woman smiled sweetly, and that's when Tracy noticed that she had one blue eye and one gray—just one more thing that made Zoë absolutely striking, even in the boring jumpsuit she wore. Tracy sincerely doubted this girl had trouble getting dates. Then she noticed the wedding ring. Figures.

"I have a lot of interests," Mordi said.

"I wonder if it's wise to divide your loyalties like that," Zoë said.

Although both seemed perfectly civil, Tracy couldn't help but feel there was a lot going unsaid between these two. Eavesdropping could be *so* confusing.

"Trust me, cousin. I'm not divided at all."

"I'm *so* glad to hear it." Zoë sounded thrilled. She glanced between Tracy and Mordi. "So, you're planning to get Tracy here involved in your movie?"

Mordi half-rolled his eyes. "She's an animal trainer."

At that, Zoë turned to Tracy, a huge smile on her face. "Tracy *Tannin?*"

Tracy nodded, wondering if she was branded.

"How wonderful to meet you. I'm Zoë—Hale's sister." Her smile widened. "We just got off the phone. He told me so much about you."

Chapter Fourteen

Hale's *sister?*

Tracy's jaw practically dropped onto the counter; then she jerked her head around to look at Zoë more directly—managing to totally mess up her eyeliner in the process.

"Oh!" the salesgirl cried, dragging the soft pencil across Tracy's cheek.

"Sister?" Tracy said aloud, wondering what Hale could have said.

"Yeah. He and Elmer are really excited about working with you." She turned to Mordi with another sweet smile. "I don't suppose you have a role for Elmer? He's quite the little entertainer."

A thin smile touched Mordichai's lips. "No. No role." He turned to Tracy and gave an apologetic shrug. "I think I'll leave you two to catch up."

"Oh." She frowned. Or started to until the salesgirl *tsk-*

tsk'd. "Well, I'd love to talk more about your project. Maybe you could call next week?"

The man nodded; then Tracy extricated herself from the makeover maven long enough to extract a business card. "My cell phone number's on the back."

He took her hand, then kissed her fingertips. "You'll definitely be hearing from me."

"Oh, wow," the salesgirl confided as Mordi disappeared down an aisle. "Is he ever a dream."

"Mordi?" Zoë's face scrunched up, like she'd just tasted something unusual but not entirely unpleasant. "I never really thought about it."

"He's your cousin. Why would you?"

"True," Zoë admitted. She met Tracy's eyes. "What do you think? Dreamy, or not?"

Tracy found herself allowing, "There's definite dream potential there. The way he talks for one thing. Is he British?"

"Boarding school."

"Ah," Tracy and the salesgirl said at exactly the same time. "Well, *that's* pretty dreamy. As for the rest of him . . ."

"What?" Hale's sister bounced a little, looking just as eager as a kid at Christmas.

"Nothing."

"Tracy! What?"

She stifled a laugh. They'd known each other all of three minutes, and already this Zoë was pestering her just like Mel. "I was just going to say that Mordi's voice is dreamy—and he's cute and all—but compared to Hale . . . well, there is no comparison."

"Well, I don't know who this Hale person is," the salesgirl said. "But, girl, you must have it bad for him."

A smile lit up Zoë's face. "He's my brother, but empirically, I'd have to agree." She leaned closer. "And if you ever want to know where to find a website showing pictures of him in a loincloth, just let me know."

"Really?" Tracy asked.

"Where?" the salesgirl echoed.

Zoë laughed. "Do you have a computer?"

"Um, yeah." Tracy squinted, trying to figure out when this conversation had gotten so out of control.

"Remind me sometime, and I'll show you the web page. I could even show you tonight if you want."

Tonight. "I can't. I have a date." She glanced at her watch, suddenly realizing how late it had gotten. No time to dilly-dally.

"I'll take it all," she told the salesgirl.

"All this makeup?"

Tracy nodded. She couldn't really afford it, but she considered the makeup ammunition. Besides, she was putting it on a credit card. "Finish me quick and then ring it all up. I've got to run."

"But I need to show you how to apply it."

"Am I good for tonight?"

"Hold still," the salesgirl said, "while I add some powder and mascara."

Tracy did. "This isn't what I expected when I got up this morning," she said.

"What isn't?" Zoë asked.

"All of this. Your brother. My date tonight with Leon Palmer. Making friends in the mall. It's all kind of strange and unusual."

Zoë's smile was warm and inviting. "I guess the question is, do you have a problem with strange and unusual?"

Tracy knew that Zoë meant the question lightly, but something in her voice gave Tracy pause, and she considered the question honestly. "No," she finally said with a small smile. "No, I don't. In fact, I think I prefer strange and unusual. I mean, who wants their life to be entirely normal?"

"I'm glad to hear it."

Tracy started to ask why, but the salesgirl got into the conversation first, announcing the price for Tracy's war chest of makeup.

"Ouch." She looked at Zoë. "It's been a strange and unusual day already. And expensive. Very, very expensive."

Hale kicked back in Zoë's living room, still on a caffeine buzz from the three lattes he'd had with Tracy before she'd insisted that she really had to run. He'd spent practically the entire day with her, and still her image filled his mind.

As obsessions went, this particular one was rather nice.

Absently, he drummed his fingers on the armrest of the sofa, his foot tapping out a rhythm against the coffee table as he waited for his sister to get home.

She'd called him just a few minutes before to report in. Apparently, it was a good thing he'd sent her. Mordichai had been there, sniffing around, and that definitely meant this mission was going to get tougher. Since Zoë couldn't wrangle an invite to Tracy's house, they'd sent Hoop and Taylor to sneak onto the property and keep an eye on the situation while Hale took a break to gather some things for his overnight stakeout and to be debriefed by Zoë.

From a logistics end, then, all was well. From a mission standpoint, Hale wasn't so sure. The combined presence of Henchmen and Mordichai was definitely disturbing. He didn't know if the Henchmen were loyal to Mordi or Uncle H, though Hale would assume Hieronymous. Mordi didn't seem the type to use the foul beasts. Of course, Hale wasn't very trusting of Mordi's loyalties.

The only thing he did trust was that Tracy Tannin was the object of way too much attention. And strangely, all his priorities had shifted. At the moment, retrieving the belt didn't seem quite as important as making sure nothing bad happened to her.

"Antsy?" Zoë asked, walking into the room.

With an effort, Hale stopped drumming his fingers and tapping his foot. "Just thinking. About the mission."

"Yeah?" She looked disbelieving.

Hale scowled but didn't comment.

His sister dropped down onto the couch next to Elmer, who looked up and yawned. She reached over and started scratching behind his ears, and the little guy writhed with pleasure.

Heaven, Elmer said. *I love this woman.*

Hale rolled his eyes.

So, are you going to tell her?

"What?"

You know. . . .

Hale had no clue what the ferret was going on about.

"What's he saying?" Zoë asked.

"He's just being Elmer. All over the map and generally incomprehensible."

"I'm not buying that. I think he's talking about whatever put that pensive mood on your face."

"You know, you can be a real pest."

She shrugged. "I'm your sister. Isn't that what you expect?"

Don't dis this woman, Elmer squeaked. *She feeds me when you forget. And you should tell her. Tell her you've got the hots for Tracy. A mortal. She'll love that. And that you're acting screwy about it. I mean I've seen you seduce mortals before, and usually you're in and out before I can say, "boo." No pandering, no deep thoughts. But with this gal . . . you haven't been yourself. And it's not just the mission. Nope. Something's up. Something's definitely up. . . .*

Hale rubbed his forehead with his forefinger and thumb, wishing that the insightful little beast hadn't zeroed in on the exact problem. But there wasn't any escaping the truth. The fact remained that Hale was craving more than just a romp between the sheets. But that wasn't something he wanted to confess to his sister.

Go on! Tell her. Maybe she can give you some advice.

Great. Now Elmer thought he needed advice with women. Any minute now, the sky was going to start falling.

"*Now* what's he saying?"

"He's saying you should leave me alone. I'm older. You're supposed to trust me."

I did not say that.

"Oh, puh-lease." Zoë propped a leg under her, clearly settling in.

Hale sighed. He hadn't really expected that she'd drop it, but a guy could hope, couldn't he? "I wasn't thinking about anything in particular. Just pondering what Mordi was planning at the mall. And I was vegging a bit while I waited for you."

Not exactly a lie. His body *was* vegging; it was his mind that was going a million miles an hour thinking about Tracy. About the way she smelled. The warmth of her hand when he'd held it. The way her simple, straight hair highlighted those fabulous cheekbones. The fire he saw in her eyes, and whether or not it would ignite to a full-fledged blaze in bed.

Damn. He was beginning to sound like the inside of one of the romance novels he posed for. What was happening to him? He'd never felt this way when he was pursuing the many other women he'd lusted after. No, this was something else all together. Hopping Hades, whatever this was, it wasn't an emotion he particularly wanted to deal with. So how did he explain all this to his sister?

Certainly he couldn't relate that the thought of being near Tracy made him as fidgety as Superman in a kryptonite museum. If he showed even the slightest weakness in that direction, his sister would go off on him about what a hypocrite he was, falling for a mortal. Heck, she might even

169

try to get him and Tracy Tannin together for keeps. And that was even scarier than failing the mission and Hieronymous taking over the world.

"You said we needed to debrief," Hale reminded her.

"Right." His sister sucked in a breath. "Well, she likes you, Hale."

"Isn't that the idea?"

"No. I mean, yes." She ran her hands through her hair, then sighed. "I mean, she *really* likes you."

Zoë's assessment pleased him more than it probably should, and he had no clue why it should bother her. "So?"

"So . . . I like Tracy."

There were times when his sister drove him nuts. "Just spit it out, kid. What are you trying to say?"

"She's nice. I like her. And I know we have to get the belt from her, and I know that we have to do whatever it takes. . . ."

"But?"

"But now you're planning this big seduction scene and, well, I just don't want her to get hurt."

"She won't get hurt."

"But—"

Hale hardened himself to his protective feelings and said, "Trust me, Zo. This girl only wants a fling. I heard her say so."

At that, his sister looked him straight in the eye. Her dual-colored irises somehow made her pensive stare even more intense. "Just like *you* only want a fling."

"Exactly," he said. And he meant it. But even so, he felt the corners of his mouth turn down into a frown. Of course he only wanted a fling. A quick seduction. Just like he'd been saying all along.

And Tracy didn't want any more than that. Which made the plan perfect. Absolutely perfect.

Except, somehow he couldn't stop frowning.

Zoë was still staring at him, that curious expression on her face. He waved a hand. "Tell me about Mordi."

For a second, he thought she was going to argue, but then her shoulders relaxed and she nodded. "Not a whole lot more to tell. I was surprised he was at the mall. I bet he's been following—"

"He has." An image of his cousin's vivid green eyes in the coffee shop popped into Hale's head. "I saw him. I just didn't realize it was him."

"Shapeshifting," Zoë said, half under her breath.

"Yup. Pesky power when you're trying to keep track of a guy." Protectors could often recognize their own in shifted form, but unless they had Zoë's super senses, they had to be paying close attention. Otherwise, a shapeshifter could easily escape notice.

"Should we report him to the Council? He might be violating probation."

For a second, Hale considered it, then shook his head slowly. "No. So far he hasn't done anything wrong." He looked at Zoë. "Has he?"

"Not in front of me. I mean, he clearly wants to get close to Tracy—I think he may be planning his own seduction—and he was making me awfully nervous."

The thought of Mordi getting close to Tracy pissed Hale off more than it should. He told himself it was because Mordi could compromise the mission. In truth, though, his annoyance stemmed from something else. Something he didn't want to examine too closely. He aimed a frown in Zoe's direction. "Send an e-mail to Zephron and let him know what's going on. We have to be careful. If Mordi's working for his dad . . ."

Zoë sighed. "I'd really hoped he'd gotten his act together."

"So had I. But Uncle H is his father. You'd have to be pretty strong to break free of a parent's influence—even if he is an Outcast.

171

"Yeah. Well, I hope he does."

They sat in silence for a while, and Hale had a feeling he knew what was coming next. He was wrong.

"You should do something nice for her," his sister finally said.

"I should what?"

"Do something nice for Tracy. Women like that. And you're supposed to get her to like you, right?"

She had him there. "So you think I should . . . do what exactly?"

"I don't know. You said the grounds at the house are a wreck. Maybe you could fix them up for her. Shouldn't take you too long."

"You didn't see them."

Zoë shot him a look, clearly not appreciating his attempt at levity. "Well, it would be a nice thing to do."

"So, between protecting her, seducing her, and trying to sweet-talk her out of the belt, I'm also supposed to be her groundskeeper?" It wasn't a bad idea, actually. He'd like to do something nice for Tracy. In fact, Hale was somewhat irritated he hadn't thought of this idea himself.

A devious smile touched his sister's lips. "Yeah, well, you know what women think of sexy gardeners. I mean, there's that whole Lady Chatterley thing."

At the thought of a D. H. Lawrence moment happening between him and Tracy, every ounce of blood in Hale's body rushed to his groin. He bit the inside of his cheek to bring himself back to earth.

"Trust me," he said, as soon as he could talk normally. "I'll get the belt, no matter what tricks I have to use."

"Yes, Hale. But I think you should do it just because it's a nice thing. Not just to get the belt."

"Zoë . . ."

"What?" Her eyes were wide, and innocent, then she smiled. "I like her. I like you. What's wrong with a little matchmaking?"

"She's mortal, Zo. She's mortal, and neither one of us is interested in more than a fling."

Zoë smiled. "We'll see."

Hale just shook his head, determined not to encourage her. There was no reasoning with Zoë when she got something stuck in her mind. In the meantime, he intended to stick with the program. Which meant not falling for Tracy Tannin.

Zoë sighed. "Fine, you're on your own." She got up and headed for the kitchen. When she came back, she tossed him a crumpled-up paper sack. "What's a stakeout without a few snacks?"

Hale peered inside. A peanut butter and jelly sandwich, two Snickers bars, an apple, and a cardboard box filled with grape juice. Hale wasn't certain if he was on a stakeout or heading off to school. He had to smile; sometimes Zoë's previous job as an elementary school librarian seemed perfect for her personality.

"Thanks, kid."

She grinned. "You better get going. Time for you to relieve Hoop and Taylor."

Lane joined them from the back rooms. "Oh, sure. Leave when the mortal walks into the room."

Zoë laughed, but Hale thought it sounded like a pretty reasonable plan.

"Is Davy asleep?" Zoë asked.

"Yup. We just finished another Harry Potter chapter. I don't have any idea if he's really following the story, but I'm having a great time." She walked over to the hall table and picked up Zoë's key ring. "Can I borrow your car? I need to grab a few things at the grocery store."

"Sure," Zoë agreed.

"What's wrong with your . . . that thing you call a car?" Hale asked.

"Hey. Don't dis the Gremlin. Usually she runs great, but Taylor's fiddling with something, and he pulled off some belts."

Hale shrugged. "I could put it back together for you."

The look Lane flashed him was one of pure disdain. "You'd fix my car? For me? A mere mortal?" She fluttered her hand over her heart. "I'm in awe. That's something a *friend* would do."

Hale stifled the urge to roll his eyes. "I'm here to help. That's my job, after all."

"Helping us poor defenseless little mortals?"

Annoyed that his uncharacteristic generosity was being thrown back in his face, Hale snapped, "Pretty much. Yeah."

Lane crossed her arms over her chest. "You know, it's not such a big deal to befriend a mortal. A lot of us are capable of watching out for ourselves."

Hale thought of Tracy and the way she'd swung that tire iron. "I know," he said.

Lane's eyes widened as she turned to look at Zoë, whose eyes were equally wide. Clearly, neither woman had been expecting that response. "Oh," Lane said.

In truth, he wasn't ready to believe it. Not completely. The thought of a mortal—especially Tracy—having to defend herself against Hieronymous, for example. Hale shivered, not liking the image at all, and especially not liking the way his priorities had changed. His first instinct now was to rescue the girl—no matter the cost to whatever mission he was on. What was happening to him?

Vulnerable. Just like Taylor said. Mortals made a Protector weak. Emotionally, professionally. All around.

Not a good thing.

Yet Lane wasn't talking about befriending mortals like Tracy. She was just talking about appreciating your average mortal on your average day. And under those circumstances, Hale had no problems keeping a focus on his professional career.

"Maybe it's like helping a lady across the street," he said. He wanted to explain the reason he liked to help mortals, but also felt more comfortable keeping them at a distance. "She could do just fine on her own, but it feels nice to be useful."

"Useful? Not superior?"

"That, too." Hell, that was the truth. He smiled to take the edge off his words, though.

Lane shook her head, a small grin dancing on her lips. "You should just admit it, you know," she said.

He lifted an eyebrow. "Admit what?"

"You like us. Mortals. Me. Deena and Hoop. Taylor. We're not so bad."

He grunted, not willing to articulate more of a response.

Lane shook her head. "If you ever find a woman out there who understands you, you better grab her up. Because there can't be very many of them."

"Hear, hear," Zoë piped up. She gave Hale a meaningful look.

"I'm leaving," he said, pointedly avoiding their last comments. "Taylor and Hoop are expecting me."

"You gonna be okay hanging outside all night?" Lane asked.

He held up his backpack complete with his Mission Essential Kit, Propulsion Cloak, and the lunch Zoë had packed him. "And I can run really fast, too. I'll be fine."

"Sorry. Sometimes when I'm around you, I tend to forget that you're supposedly a superhero."

She bounced out of the way just in time to miss the pillow he threw at her.

"So you're really just going to lurk around outside this girl's house all night?"

"That's my plan."

"Isn't that going to get really boring?"

"Just like a cop on a stakeout. It comes with the job, I'm afraid." Of course, with his allergies, he was going to keep disappearing and reappearing like some schizophrenic ghost.

"Is Elmer going?" Zoë asked.

Elmer's happy where he is. The ferret's bored, sleepy voice drifted to Hale from the other side of the room, where he was curled up in a beanbag chair watching *Kindergarten Cop.*

Hale laughed. "Are you kidding? He's got videos, the remote control, and a plate of treats. The guy's not going anywhere. Heck, you guys are better to him than room service."

Lane laughed. "I guess." She looked at Zoë. "I suppose it's better that your brother will be out there watching over Tracy, but it still seems weird to me. *Staking out the good guys.*"

It didn't seem weird to Hale at all. He needed to protect Tracy, and he intended to go to whatever lengths were needed. The odds were slim Hieronymous would try anything in Tracy's own house—what with the eminent traceability of such an action back to him if he failed—but Hale didn't intend to take any chances. And there was always Leon to protect her from.

Truth be told, he was looking forward to this part of the assignment. Maybe he couldn't talk to her. Maybe she wouldn't even know that he was there. But the simple fact remained that, more than anything, he was thrilled that his job called for him to drive to Beverly Hills and satisfy his urge for one more glimpse of Tracy Tannin.

Chapter Fifteen

After dismissing Taylor and Hoop, Hale had circled the house, giving it a thorough once-over. Now he levitated under Tracy's bedroom window, invisible and feeling rather guilty for peeping—but not guilty enough to leave. The mission required that he protect the girl; it was simply his good luck that this particular aspect of his task overlapped with his desire to see her again.

And he did *need* to see her. He needed to confirm she was still all right, and he was more than willing to sacrifice good manners to satisfy that hunger.

At first he thought her bedroom was empty. He was about to let loose with a particularly vivid stream of curses when the door to the adjoining bathroom opened and Tracy stepped out. She was holding a glass of white wine and wearing an open terry-cloth robe over bikini panties and a plain white bra. Nothing remotely Frederick's of Hollywood about this girl's underwear, that was for sure. No lace. No satin. Cotton all the way.

And yet it didn't matter. Sears or Victoria's Secret, Hale's reaction would have been the same: an exquisite tightening in his groin, a dry mouth, a strong desire to throw himself through the window and beg her to make love with him.

Drawing on every ounce of strength he had, he resisted the urge. The only upside of such a foolhardy plan would be touching her. The downside would be the sting of her palm against his cheek. And her telling him to get lost. Or worse, her having him arrested. The Mortal-Protector Liaison Office would just love getting him out of that kind of bind.

He knew he should quit watching, knew he'd crossed some line of decency, but somehow he couldn't convince his feet to get him away from there. She'd mesmerized him, and he concentrated on watching her, on memorizing the way she moved.

Lean and lithe, Tracy Tannin had the grace of a cat, but she didn't seem to realize it. Somehow she seemed uncomfortable in her own skin, and Hale longed to demonstrate to her—inch by delightful inch—just how spectacular her body was.

He was daydreaming about that very thing when she passed in front of the window. Out of the corner of his eye, he noticed the paperback tucked under her arm.

He squinted. Was that . . . ?

Levitating closer, he tried for a better look, then sneezed and ended up crashing into the window, totally materialized, with his palms flat against the pane. Immediately he threw himself back and dematerialized again—but not before Tracy heard the thud and whipped around to face where he'd been. She rushed over to the window, probably fearing burglars, and pressed her face to the glass.

Only the thin pane separated them. Hale held his breath, fearing that even though he was invisible, somehow she'd see him.

Foolish, he knew. What he should be worried about was that she'd notice the fading handprint on her window, just a few inches below her nose.

Yet it didn't matter. At the moment, he wasn't thinking about the handprint at all—or his mission. He'd gotten a good look at the book she was clutching. It was his picture. Right there. On the cover. She was holding a book with his half-naked image on the cover. Soon, very soon, they'd be hot and heavy into their wild fling, and she'd be holding the real thing. Him. Her. Together. *Naked.*

He couldn't wait.

Someone had been outside her window. Impossible, she knew, since she was on the second floor. But, reasonable or not, she couldn't shake the spooky feeling.

Unnerved, she looked around for Mistress Bettina. Some watchdog. The little fluffball was probably curled up in front of the stove downstairs, blissfully asleep.

Feeling foolish, Tracy pressed her nose to the window-pane and looked around. *Nothing.*

For half a second, she considered calling Melissa's cell phone, then decided she was acting like a girly-girl. She'd already scoped the area, and nothing was out there. It was probably just that her nerves were on edge, which made some sense considering she was about to go out on a date with Leon Palmer. Pouring herself a glass of wine had probably been a bad idea, but she'd hoped it would relax her. Instead it seemed to have her jumping at shadows.

Still, it couldn't hurt to check out the noise. Taking a deep breath, she pulled up the window sash and leaned outside. Nothing.

Yep. Her imagination was playing tricks on her. Since her grandmother's death, she'd been hearing more acutely this old house's creaks and groans. That was one of the reasons she'd wanted a roomie. Well, that and the need for tax money.

So it had just been the wine. Or maybe she was hearing the house settling. Whatever the reason, right then, a male roommate sounded like a pretty good idea. Fortunately Hale would be here tomorrow. And he fit all her requirements for a live-in knight: strong, hunky, dripping with testosterone.

Sighing, she imagined the scene. She'd be in her room, minding her own business, and hear a noise. She'd scream, and he'd come running. No. Wait. Take two. He'd leap from the shower, wrap a towel loosely around his hips, *then* he'd come running.

"Much better." She whispered the words, her eyes closed as she conjured the face of her sexy, strong, soon-to-be roommate.

Her book had fallen to the floor when she'd opened the window, and now she picked it up again, her fingers tracing Hale's image on the cover. She still couldn't believe he had been flirting with her, and the memory of their afternoon together was intoxicating.

She brought herself back to reality with a shake. At the moment, Hale wasn't the man of the hour; Leon was. In fact, Leon was the man of the less-than-half-an-hour, and Tracy really needed to get her butt in gear if she was going to get dressed in time.

She might have suddenly become the Belle of the Ball, but that didn't change the fact that she was as nervous as she could ever remember being. To soothe her nerves, she punched the play button on her CD player, and the room immediately filled with the sounds of the surf beating against a beach. For as long as she could remember, she'd loved the ocean—the expanse of it, its depth, its mysteries. Listening to recorded surf wasn't the same, but it was better than nothing. And at the moment, she needed all the security blankets she could find.

Bolstered by the soothing sounds, she sat in front of her vanity and started to tackle making herself presentable. After doing her hair—a massive undertaking—she spent twenty minutes trying on every dress in her closet, with and without her grandmother's belt. In the end, she decided for basic black. Cool, sophisticated, slightly elegant.

After much internal debate, she ruled out the belt. For one, it just didn't do anything for the outfit. For another, she was a grown woman. She'd found her confidence now, hadn't she? And listening to the CD had calmed her nerve. Surely, she could go out for the evening without a security blanket.

She took another sip of wine. Instead of the belt, she'd rely on liquid courage.

At last dressed, she sat on her grandmother's pink chaise and focused again on her historical romance novel. Or at least the cover. She'd bought it for the story, but right now, she was more interested in the half-naked medieval lord on its front than the words that were on the pages.

Hale groaned as Tracy's fingers played across the cover of the book. She wasn't caressing him. Not really. But even so, he shivered from the thought of her fingers touching his flesh so intimately.

The look on her face was unmistakable. He'd seen it on dozens of women, all of whom had ended up in his bed.

Lust. Desire. *A sensual hunger.*

When he saw it, he wanted to leap for joy. Without question, Tracy wanted him, and the realization pleased him tremendously. Sure, the knowledge that she was attracted to him benefited his mission, but his joy stemmed from more than that. More than ego, too. Quite simply, he was attracted to the girl. He wanted her. And he'd hoped that she wanted him back.

To now know for certain that she did . . . Well, his body swelled with relief—and anticipation.

Then the truth bonked him on the head: she didn't actually want him. She wanted the sexy, buffed-up image he portrayed. And if her expression was any indication, this wasn't the first time she'd looked at his picture that way.

He remembered her reaction when they'd met on the set. Pleasure, surprise, and definite familiarity. And later, in the coffee shop, when she'd asked about his life as a cover model.

He'd been wrong when he'd told Elmer Tracy didn't know him. She *did*. And she'd had a crush on him just like so many of his fans did.

She desired him, and she had the belt.

Which meant he wasn't falling head over heels for a mortal after all. It was the belt that was making him feel this way!

Closing his eyes with relief, he leaned against the trunk of a majestic oak tree. *Thank Hera*. All that touchy-feely angst, all his raging emotions. They were an illusion, nothing more. Tracy wanted him—she'd wanted him since before he saw her. And it was because Tracy had Aphrodite's girdle that Hale wanted her right back.

The way she'd done to Leon, she'd put a spell on *him*, entrapped him in a web of ancient magic. Never in his whole life had he felt so relieved to be the victim of an enchantment. He wasn't actually *feeling* something for a mortal; he was simply under her control.

His mouth curled into a grin as he considered his predicament. A man under an enchantment couldn't be held responsible for his actions, could he? A man under an enchantment had guilt-free carte blanche to bend to the will

Join the Love Spell Romance Book Club
and **GET 2 FREE* BOOKS NOW–**
An $11.98 value!
Mail the Free* Book Certificate
Today!

Yes! I want to subscribe to the Love Spell Romance Book Club.

Please send me my **2 FREE* BOOKS**. I have enclosed $2.00 for shipping/handling. Every other month I'll receive the four newest Love Spell Romance selections to preview for 10 days. If I decide to keep them, I will pay the Special Members Only discounted price of just $4.49 each, a total of $17.96, plus $2.00 shipping/handling ($23.55 US in Canada). This is a **SAVINGS OF $6.00** off the bookstore price. There is no minimum number of books I must buy and I may cancel the program at any time. In any case, the **2 FREE* BOOKS** are mine to keep.

*In Canada, add $5.00 shipping and handling per order for the first shipment.For all future shipments to Canada, the cost of membership is $23.55 US, which includes shipping and handling. (All payments must be made in US dollars.)

NAME: _____

ADDRESS: _____

CITY: _____ **STATE:** _____

COUNTRY: _____ **ZIP:** _____

TELEPHONE: _____

E-MAIL: _____

SIGNATURE: _____

If under 18, Parent or Guardian must sign. Terms, prices, and conditions subject to change. Subscription subject to acceptance. Dorchester Publishing reserves the right to reject any order or cancel any subscription.

of the woman who'd cast the spell. In this case, he'd heard the woman in question say she wanted a fling. A wild, hot, steamy fling.

And that's exactly what Hale had planned. After all, his mission required a seduction, and Hale wasn't the type to turn his back on a mission. For the good of the cause, he was more than happy to make a few sacrifices.

No strings. No guilt. No funky, inexplicable emotions tugging at his gut.

Just him, Tracy, a very good time, and some feelings that—thankfully—would disappear the moment he completed his mission and got Aphrodite's girdle back.

Ding-ding-dong-dong! Dong-dong-ding-ding!

The annoying doorbell her grandmother had loved so much—an imitation of Big Ben—echoed through the house and Tracy sat bolt upright, guiltily throwing her paperback aside. Smoothing her skirt, she stood up, a little unstable after those two glasses of her favorite Chardonnay. Nibbling on her lower lip, she wondered how wrong it was to fantasize about one man while she waited to go out on a date with another.

Giving up on finding an answer, she rushed out of her room and down the stairs toward the entry hall. Mistress Bettina scampered out from the kitchen, her high-pitched bark echoing through the hall.

"Calm down, girl." Tracy bent down and grabbed her collar. The little dog quivered with excitement; she pretty much lived for the door chime. Considering that Tracy's first real date in months stood on the other side of that door, at the moment, Tracy knew exactly how Missy felt.

"Just a sec," she shouted, then checked her reflection in the antique mirror that hung near the door. Not bad, all things considered. Thanks to the wonders of modern cosmetics and that cooperative salesgirl—not to mention her own American Express card—Tracy had managed a few minor improvements. She'd spruced up her basically boring face. As for her hair, there wasn't much improvement in that department. Through liberal application of hairspray, she'd forced a few curls in her cursedly straight locks, but the odds of her new 'do surviving the night were slim.

Still, at the moment, she looked good. Not stunning. But good.

Hopefully, good was good enough.

Taking a deep breath, she pulled open the door, and there was Leon, his eyes warm and dreamy. "Hi." She swept her arm back, indicating the entrance hall. "Come on in."

Without saying a word, he followed her lead, stepping into the open doorway and then onto the marble flooring. He had the celebrity thing down pat: not a hair was out of place, not one single wrinkle marred his clothes.

Even though he looked good enough to eat, Tracy couldn't say she'd entirely enjoy the meal. Her fantasies about Hale had ruined her appetite. Hale might be less famous than Leon Palmer, but a thread of something purely and totally male added something to him that Leon just couldn't hope to attain. And right now, Tracy wanted a taste of it.

Leon cleared his throat. Tracy frowned, trying to get her thoughts under control. She was being silly, of course. She might imagine that Hale was standing right next to her, so close she could feel the heat from his body, but in reality, he was probably in some hotel, having drinks with a supermodel.

No, it was Leon—her date—who was standing in front of her looking like a dream. Leon, not Hale. No matter how many fantasies she might be having about that other, absent, man. Talk about your etiquette faux pas. Any minute now, Miss Manners, Emily Post, and Tracy's grandmother were going to yank Tracy's membership in the polite young ladies club.

With a frown, Tracy realized Leon still hadn't said anything. Looking up, she watched as the dreamy expression in his face faded, only to be replaced by something. What? Surprise? Revulsion?

She backed away, unsettled by the harshness in his face, and even more by the coldness in his eyes. The dreamy quality was gone, and he skimmed his gaze over her body. Hale had done the same thing, and the intense inspection had practically melted her on the spot. Under Leon's torturous examination, all she wanted was to cover herself and run from the room.

When their gazes met, she kept her eyes wide open, fighting back the burning onslaught of tears.

"I think there's been a mistake," he said. Once again, his gaze darted down, scoping her from neck to feet. "I can't go out with you tonight."

Apparently, she hadn't passed inspection. So much for a boost of belt-less confidence. "I see." Screw Miss Manners; Tracy didn't even try to fight back the note of fury that laced her voice. "Any particular reason why? My outfit not snazzy enough for you?"

She didn't know what she expected to see on his face—shock? an apology?—but whatever it was, she certainly didn't expect the befuddled expression that marred his usually perfect features.

"The outfit's . . . okay." He shrugged. "It's not your clothes. It's . . ." He stood up straighter, almost as if realizing he'd lost the upper hand and was fighting to get it back. "Look, Tracy. You're a nice girl, but there's nothing between us. Nothing at all. I'm not sure why I asked you out. Obviously I made a mistake. I'm sorry. I'll see you at work."

He turned to leave, then paused in the doorway and actually had the gall to turn back one last time to say. "And have a nice weekend."

Nice? *Nice?* He actually expected her to have a nice weekend after he'd snubbed her for the second time?

She sucked in a deep breath, readying herself to let loose and scream until Leon tumbled backward out the door and down the porch steps from the force of her fury, but someone else got there first. A deep, guttural growl came from behind her, then seemed to rush past in a gust of wind.

Tracy jumped back, at first scared and confused, then jubilant as Leon stumbled over his own feet, then crashed down the steps, facedown on the walk. A bubble of laughter rose in her chest, and she didn't even try to stifle it. It was mean, maybe—but at the moment, she didn't really care.

Leon pulled himself up, then turned around, and she saw the blood dripping from his nose. "You bitch!"

Her laughter stopped, replaced by anger. "Me? You're the one who begged for a second chance, and now you go and dump me. You're the one who tripped over your own feet. I've just been standing here."

"Something *tripped* me. Where's that damn mutt of yours?"

"Don't blame Missy for your clumsiness." Tracy glanced around, but she didn't see a sign of the fluffball. The dog must have scampered away after Tracy had opened the door.

"Well, something tripped me."

"You're a clutz, Leon. A clutz and a putz." With that, Tracy gave herself a couple of mental brownie points, stepped backward into her house, and slammed the door. *Jerk!*

Leaning back against the door, she wondered what the heck was going on. Leon had been so eager earlier, but now he was a cold fish. Just to be sure, she tilted her nose toward her armpit, but didn't smell anything offensive. Just soap, deodorant, and laundry detergent. She might not be beautiful, but her dress was flattering and she'd been reasonably happy with her appearance.

Leon doesn't know what he's missing, she thought. A tear trickled down her cheek, anyway, and she brushed it roughly away.

Okay, so Leon ran hot and cold. She didn't like it—heck, she didn't particularly like *him*—but she could deal with it. What was really odd was that something truly had seemed to trip him. She'd felt that rush of air, then seen him stumble over . . . well, nothing.

Was her house haunted? Was Grandma Tahlula hanging around protecting her? She shivered, not sure she liked the idea of sharing the house with a ghost. Not even a benevolent one.

A loud report echoed through the marble and oak foyer, and Tracy jumped, thinking the noise sounded like a . . . sneeze? She swiveled her head, searching for Missy—the poor dog might be catching cold—but she didn't see anything except Hale.

Hale?

She blinked, and when she looked again he was gone. *Okaaay.* She really needed to get her mind on something else. Clearly, she had Hale on the brain.

Shaking her head, she banished the foolishness. The house wasn't haunted, but it was drafty. She'd probably left a window open, and a cross-draft gust of wind had burst through the open door.

Sure. Right. That had to be it.

There were no ghosts, no guardian angel, in this house. And now no boyfriend. Just her and these drafty old rooms. She was all alone, and she might as well get used to it.

With that thought, Tracy slid down the wall until her butt hit the cold marble floor. Then she gave in to the flood of tears.

* * *

Claritin, Sudafed, *something*. He really needed to get his allergies under control. Only pure luck had saved him—that and the fact that Tracy was too upset by Leon to wonder about why she was seeing things.

At the moment, though, pharmaceuticals were the least of his worries. Tracy was miserable, and there wasn't anything he could do about it. Hale hated being powerless—*hated* it—and nothing in the world made him feel more useless than a crying woman. Especially when the woman in question was one he'd begun to care about. Even if the caring was an illusion, brought on by a magic belt.

Frustrated, he paced in front of Tracy, careful to tread softly so she wouldn't hear him. Already, he'd almost given himself away: first when he'd rushed Leon, and then again when he'd materialized from that monster sneeze. He'd managed to catch the sneeze and disappear before Tracy got too clean a look, but he hadn't experienced nearly as much restraint where Leon was concerned.

When he'd rushed the buffoon, he hadn't meant to yell, too, but somehow the sound had just burst forth. He'd had to swallow it, ending up gurgling more like a strangled ferret than a righteous defender of the downtrodden. He hadn't actually intended to bloody Leon's nose, either, but considering the way the little worm treated Tracy, it was the least he deserved.

No, Leon's injuries weren't his problem. He was much more concerned with making sure Tracy was all right. At the moment, he wasn't so sure.

She was still sitting on the cold floor of the foyer, her knees pulled up to her chest and her head bent over. He couldn't see her face, but he could tell from the way her shoulders were shaking that she was crying.

The need to put his arms around her and rock her nearly overwhelmed him, and he had to bite the inside of his cheek to stop himself. Instead of holding her, he sat on the tile next to her, hoping that somehow she'd feel he was there, even if she couldn't really know.

Maybe someday he could truly be there for her. Until then, this would have to do.

After a few more heaving sobs, Tracy lifted her head. Black mascara tracks snaked down from her red, puffy eyes. She sniffled, wiping her nose with the back of her hand as she pulled herself up to lean against the wall.

"Get a grip, Trace," she whispered.

He isn't worth it, Hale thought, wishing he could squeeze her hand.

"He's not worth it," she said to herself.

Hale smiled invisibly.

After a few minutes, Tracy pulled herself up and headed down the hall.

For the briefest of moments, Hale wanted to call it a night; but he couldn't leave Tracy alone to fend for herself. Allowing himself a single moment of hesitancy, he followed Tracy up the stairs into her bedroom.

First thing, Tracy headed for her bathroom and splashed cold water on her face. She looked as miserable as she felt, and she hated that even a man such as Leon would have that kind of power over her.

The cold water wasn't making any progress with her mascara-induced raccoon eyes, so she ended up breaking down and going for the full treatment, taking off her makeup with cold cream and a warm washcloth. Washing her face didn't seem natural unless she followed it up with brushing her teeth, and by the time she'd finished the whole bathroom routine, she was in her ratty old Disneyland T-shirt and ready for bed.

So what that it wasn't even nine o'clock? She'd had a crappy day and she deserved to lounge in bed with another glass of wine and a good book. With *Hale's* book, she thought, letting a tiny shiver of anticipation run up her spine.

Leon was real, but as Melissa had warned, he sure as hell didn't live up to his fantasy potential. So far, at least, Hale hadn't let her down. Maybe she only had fantasies, but right then, her fantasies were beating the heck out of reality.

With a deep sigh, she headed out of the bathroom and into her bedroom. She turned on the lamp, poured herself one last glass of wine, then clicked on her ocean CD. Grabbing the novel off the chaise lounge, she dove into bed and slid under the covers. She plumped a couple of pillows to put behind her, then settled back, ready to spend a few delicious hours lost in someone else's romance.

The story sucked her in, and after a few minutes, she was lost in the Middle Ages. No longer was she plain old Tracy. Instead, she was Ariana: the proud daughter of a besieged nobleman, forced to accept the help of her father's enemy.

Especially considering the image on the cover of the book, she had no trouble imagining Hale as the hero—arrogant, proud, protective. Fiercely loyal to the woman he loved.

Using her finger to mark her page, she closed the book and took a sip of wine as she examined the cover one more time. "Why couldn't you have asked me out instead of Leon?" she whispered.

Not that it would have mattered. She seemed to be cursed where men were concerned. If Hale had shown up at her door, tonight, Hale probably would have snubbed her.

She frowned, not liking that thought at all. Leon might recently have jumped up higher on her list, but it was Hale who had starred in her fantasies for a long time. And in those fantasies, he had always been the perfect gentleman. Well, maybe not entirely gentlemanly. She bit back a smile, remembering some particularly vivid fantasies.

Heck, already she was feeling hot and bothered—not to mention tipsy—and she hadn't done anything but lean back against her pillows and read a book with his picture on the cover. With a little moan, she closed her eyes and slid down into the bed. Hale's image floated above her, and she imagined his lips brushing against hers, his hands stroking her aroused flesh.

Suddenly too warm for comfort, Tracy pushed aside the bedcovers and ran her hands over her body. Her fingers dipped under the V-neck of her pajama top, and she caressed her own breasts. Closing her eyes, she imagined his fingers were tracing over her skin. Her nipples peaked, and she moaned with pleasure, feeling both naughty and a little bit drunk.

She wanted the real thing. Still, she could at least pretend this was the real thing. She could almost see Hale bending over her, his breath hot against her ear. His hands, hot and rough, caressed her body, skimming over the thin cotton of her shirt.

Shivering, she raised her hands above her head, her fingers gripping the polished wood of her headboard. Turning, she lost herself to the moment, her eyes drifting open dreamily.

Through a haze of passion, she saw him over her. She saw him right there in the mirror over her chest of drawers. He was still dressed in the sexy black T-shirt he'd been wearing earlier, but he'd lost the sportcoat. His strong arms were just as she'd imagined. Which made sense, of course; her imagination was running the show.

Even though she knew there was no way he could be in her room, the pragmatic part of her turned her gaze from the mirror to the bed. Nothing. She was all alone. It was just her, a romance novel, and one heck of a vivid fantasy.

Not too bad an ending for a perfectly awful evening, she thought. Then she turned her head back to the mirror, wanting to see again the fantasy she'd conjured.

She imagined his fingers touching her cheek, grazing over her skin, his face so close she could feel the heat of his breath against her neck. She watched, fascinated, as her imaginary lover traced the tips of his fingers up her leg, his touch softer than a whisper.

"Hale, oh, Hale."

The faintest of murmurs touched her ears, and she delighted in the completeness of her imagination. This man, this fantasy, was everything she'd imagined and more.

Smiling, she nestled down into her pillow and comforter. She wanted the real thing—now, more than ever. But all she had was a fantasy to make love to her. At least her fantasy complied.

Goose bumps tingled on her skin as he stroked and caressed her. A shiver wracked her body and she tensed, surprised at the force of her reaction. The dream Hale's onslaught didn't even slow. Instead, his lips brushed her cheek, then the hair at her temple, while his hand crept higher, seeking the dangerous, wonderful places beneath the hem of her short nightshirt.

Spellbound she pulled the thin cotton up, allowing him better access. Her own hands blazed a path up her leg, and she imagined that his fingers followed, her imagination doing such a fine job that she could actually feel the heat generated by his touch. Moaning, she writhed on the bed, the sheet twisting at her feet, as she lost herself to the fantasy. She trailed her fingertips up, playing with the soft skin of her stomach, then toying with the waistband of her panties.

Bless her parents for giving their daughter such a vivid imagination. Maybe Hale wasn't really here, but that didn't mean she couldn't feel him.

Oh, yeah, she felt him all over—stroking and caressing, making her hotter and hotter, but still not following her lead and exploring her most intimate places. No, his teasing touches were intimate, erotic, but he never touched her where she most wanted to be touched.

Considering he was a fantasy—*her* fantasy—she wondered about his hesitation. She arched her back, silently urging her fantasy lover on. Unsure of what she expected, she knew only that she wanted something. She wanted *more*, but she didn't know how to get it.

That, of course, was a lie. She knew how to get it, the real deal. But Hale wasn't there. Not really. And at the moment, she was just thankful that her imagination was so inventive and accommodating.

A wave of pleasure crashed over her and a moan ripped from her throat. She was thinking too much, too hard. She needed to just let go. To forget. To lose herself to everything but this exquisite pleasure.

Tomorrow, she'd concentrate on reality.

Tonight, she would just enjoy the fantasy.

Fire consumed Hale's entire body. Beneath him, Tracy Tannin was so hot, so ripe, and he longed to taste and explore her. His blood burned in his veins, seeking release, and he knew that she was just as close to the brink as he.

Just one quick thrust and he could satisfy them both. One thrust, followed by another, then another and another, until they lost themselves in a haze of lovemaking that wouldn't end until he'd taken her to the absolute highest peaks of pleasure.

A nice thought, except that she'd never know he was the one who'd sealed those peaks with her. Except . . . she'd called his name. He was in her fantasies, in her thoughts, and that knowledge thrilled him. He wanted this woman. And she wanted him. And being this close to her heightened that desire. He longed to sink inside her and give them both what they wanted.

Somehow, reason managed to soak into his brain through the cracks in his lust, and he remembered that he was invisible. It probably was not the coolest move to take Tracy all the way under the circumstances. She couldn't see him. Wouldn't know it was real. Would think he was only a figment of her imagin—

He caught his reflection in the mirror.

Hopping Hades! He hadn't even considered the possibility that she might see him in the mirror. How could he have been so careless? He *always* scoped out the possibility of mirrors!

Of course, there was a first time for everything, and he'd never made love to a woman while invisible before. Well, that wasn't exactly true. He'd never made love to a woman who didn't know he was there before. Otherwise, a touch of invisibility could add some definite sparks to an evening of sex.

But in this case, she didn't know he was there at all. What was he doing? What had he been thinking? This wasn't a seduction; it was an indulgence. His indulgence. He'd wanted to touch her—no, he'd *needed* to touch her. He'd needed to comfort her. Needed to show her how much a man could cherish her.

But now he needed to stop. Right now, she thought he was a fantasy. How long would it take for her to figure out the truth? Five minutes? Ten? With the next kiss?

But he was too far gone. He couldn't stop. He could only keep touching her, making love to her. Stifling a guttural moan, he slipped his fingers under the elastic waistband of her panties, then inched his fingers down as the skin on her lower belly tightened with anticipation. Just a little further and he'd—

No! It was a short burst of sanity, but he managed to latch on. He held tight, and only by calling on every ounce of strength in his body did he manage to wrest back some semblance of control.

Drawing in deep, quiet breaths, he tried to cool the fire in his veins. He shouldn't be doing this. Shouldn't be touching her, shouldn't be teasing her. Shouldn't be tasting her. In his head, he repeated the words over and over, hoping that with repetition would come reason.

Nope. Maybe he shouldn't, but, oh, how he wanted this.

"Hale," she whispered, her tongue darting out to moisten her lips.

His stomach knotted and his groin tightened. Damned if he wasn't lost. Knocked on his ass by one woman's feathery-soft whisper. Just looking at her had made him harder than he could ever remember being. Now, with her writhing slightly and making those little erotic noises . . .

His body stiffened and he stifled a groan. Suffice it to say, he was lost.

Maybe he shouldn't have touched her in the first place— no, no *maybe* about it—but he couldn't help himself. The sounds of the ocean had surrounded him, making him feel close to her even as the damn belt put a spell on him. He was powerless to resist. He ignored the voice that said he wouldn't have resisted even if he could.

Tracy's head was thrown back, her lips parted in passion. Hale propped himself up with his left hand, but the fingers of his right were still free to explore the soft skin at her waist.

Her hands stroked her belly, too, and he knew she believed his touch was merely a figment of her imagination. He leaned close, his lips brushing her hair as he breathed in her scent. She smelled fresh and feminine, and he closed his eyes, wanting to memorize the essence of her.

Something in himself reminded Hale that this wasn't real; he was responding to an enchantment, a spell. But Tracy wasn't wearing the belt right now; she was in a night-shirt. Another part of him shrieked.

There had to be some residual magic. Some remaining enchantment. There *had* to be. This was powerful magic after all. That's why he'd fallen for her. Even when she wasn't wearing the belt, the pull from the magic was so strong that he was completely and totally under her spell.

Yeah? Well, so what? If this was magic, he hoped she kept him bewitched for the rest of his life.

Bending over her, he stopped himself just before his lips brushed hers. He longed to explore her mouth, to taste and tempt and tease her . . . but no. He couldn't. He shouldn't.

Stiffening, he backed off just a hair, mourning every millimeter of distance he put between them. As much as she might want him—as much as he definitely wanted her—he couldn't do this. He was walking too fine a line between propriety and . . . something else. He wasn't sure what. All he knew was that if he made love to her without her knowing he was making love to her, he'd never be able to look her in the eye again.

And at the moment Hale wanted to look for a long, long time.

Knowing they'd both regret it, he slid off of her, the final touch of skin against skin coming near to driving him mad. Careful not to shake the mattress, he got off the bed, then stood in the middle of the room simply watching her.

A tiny moan escaped her, and she twisted in her guilt. Her hands stroked her body. Not slowly and languidly as before, but frantically, as if she were looking for something she'd lost. As if she were looking for him.

"I'm right here." The words he spoke without thought weren't even a whisper, but they seemed to calm her.

196

She turned her head, and their eyes met in the mirror. He fought the urge to run, to duck down. But she didn't believe he was real, and so he held fast, his gaze locked on hers.

"My Hale," she whispered. "What a nice fantasy you make."

His stomach tightened, and he clenched his fists against his immediate reaction to climb back into her bed. Soon, he'd give her what she really wanted—what they both wanted. And when he did that, they'd leave the lights on and he wouldn't turn invisible. That way he could see every luscious inch of her, and she'd be sure to see every inch of him.

Slowly, he moved away from her bed, watching as his reflection moved away from the mirror. He actually wanted a mortal. Actually *cared* about her—and not just in a platonic way. Thank Zeus this was only the result of an enchantment. An illusion. Nothing more.

No, there couldn't ever be anything real between them. But for the first time ever, he was content to share the fantasy.

Chapter Sixteen

With morning, came guilt. And Hale was suffering bucketsful. He'd slept the night on Tracy's couch. Well, *slept* was probably an overstatement; rather, he'd tossed and turned, thankful that Tracy hadn't awakened and decided to plop herself on the sofa for a little late-night television.

Of course, Missy had visited him, but he was able to explain to her—in simple doggie terms—why he was camped out in the living room. He wasn't sure the dog bought his story about keeping the place safe from the bad guys, but it didn't much matter. Missy certainly couldn't run to Tracy and tattle. Besides, the little beast seemed to like him, and she'd curled up at his feet, apparently undisturbed by the way he was tossing and turning.

Until last night, he'd assumed his lust for Tracy was simply a reaction to a pretty girl. At most, an annoying byproduct of whatever weird emotional malaise had gotten the better of him in California—in other words, temporary and controllable. But now . . .

Now he'd figured out about the belt; and that meant this might not be so controllable after all. In fact, Tracy was the one controlling him. Last night might have been heavenly while he was in the moment, but now that the haze of passion had lifted, Hale realized just how incredibly stupid he'd been.

Not only had his little invisible seduction been rude, it also could have landed him in one heck of a lot of trouble. Protectors were not allowed to go snooping around a mortal's house without prior authorization, and that was a minor offense compared to what he'd done! And the fact that he'd been suffering under the residue of the belt's magic was no excuse. Not that he'd necessarily call last night *suffering*. If Zephron found out—for that matter, if Tracy figured it out—well, he'd be on Probation so fast his head would spin.

And this wasn't just about him. There was the whole mission to consider. If he screwed this up, Hieronymous might get his hands on that belt. Then they'd all have worse things to worry about than seductions that didn't meet the Miss Manners seal of approval or the Mortal-Protector Treaty of 1970.

Never once had he put a mission in jeopardy, but he'd done it last night. And now that he was under Tracy's spell, the odds were good he'd do it again.

He didn't want to leave her—so help him, he was so far gone he wanted to stay near her no matter what the consequences—but under the circumstances, there was only one reasonable solution. He'd step back from the mission.

Zephron had wanted him to take the lead, but the Elder couldn't have known that Hale would be compromised by Aphrodite's spell. Which meant that Zoë should take over.

She could handle it; the odds were good, after all, that Tracy wasn't going to have the hots for Zoë.

Hale would do the right thing. Zoë would get the belt back, Hale could go back to sleeping with busty blond mortals while having absolutely no emotional connection with them whatsoever, and they'd all live happily ever after.

It was a perfect plan. All he needed was to enlist his sister's help. And so right before dawn, he headed for her house, then waited in the living room, determined to catch her the second she woke up.

The morning light hadn't quite made it through the curtains in the living room when Zoë padded in wearing an oversized T-shirt and white athletic socks. She yawned, headed for the kitchen, then yelped when Hale sat upright on the couch.

"Apollo's Apples!" She shot him an annoyed glare, and he stifled a laugh. "You scared me."

"I thought I trained you better than that." He'd come for her help, but that didn't mean he couldn't enjoy ribbing her. "What happened to always being prepared?"

"I never said I was a Boy Scout." She grinned. "Besides, I'm prepared. For the bad guys, I'm totally ready. For you . . ." She shrugged. "Maybe I just didn't want to strain myself."

He laughed, thoroughly enjoying the note of superiority lacing her voice. His little sister had come a long way. She was a skilled Protector, a married woman, and she played a mean game of Risk. Somewhere along the way, she'd become his friend even more than she'd ever been the little squirt he'd had to look after.

She squinted at him, concern etched on her face. "Are you okay?"

"I'm fine." He took a deep breath. This kind of thing wasn't easy for him. "I need some help."

A single eyebrow arched up, but she didn't make a smart-aleck comment. Instead, she just nodded. "Girl help? Or mission help?"

"Both."

"This calls for cocoa."

He raised an eyebrow. A year ago, her wacky super senses wouldn't have let her go near chocolate. "I'm impressed."

The corner of her mouth twitched. "Well, I'm still working on it. I'll make yours the normal way. Mine has more milk than chocolate." She tilted her head toward the kitchen. "Follow me."

Five minutes later, Hale was camped out at his sister's kitchen table, a steaming cup of hot chocolate in front of him, and a watered-down version of the same on the table for Zoë. She pulled out the chair opposite him, settled in, propped her elbows on the table, and looked Hale in the eye. "So give."

He glanced down the hall, not particularly wanting any other company while he was spilling his guts. "No one—"

"Taylor left about midnight. A stakeout on another case we're working. I don't expect him back until tonight. And Lane and I let Davy stay up late playing. They won't wake up for hours."

Hale nodded, but still didn't say anything. There just wasn't an easy way to phrase it.

"That was supposed to be your cue to talk," Zoë prompted.

"I'm working on it."

Her eyes got big. "That serious, huh?"

"I don't know." He leaned back in his chair, suddenly bone-tired. "I honestly don't know."

"Well, you said it involved the mission and a girl, right? So, that means the belt and Tracy."

"A brilliant conclusion. Marrying a private investigator did wonders for your powers of deduction," he gibed.

She made a face, but otherwise ignored his comment. "So . . . what? I know your problem can't be that you don't know how to initiate a seduction. You've never had female problems in your life."

Maybe not, but he was having problems now. "I haven't done the best job of getting close to her," he admitted. Actually, *getting close* hadn't been the problem at all. He'd gotten close, all right. So close he could still smell Tracy on his skin. *That* was the problem.

"Oh." She pursed her lips, considering. "Well, that's not good. You need to get close enough to persuade her to give up the belt. She focused on him, her teeth playing along her lower lip. What have you tried."

He shifted on the chair, not sure he wanted to discuss the details with his sister after all. Then again, confession was good for the soul—and it was either Zoë or Elmer. Between the two of them, he'd take Zoë any day. At worst, she'd become indignant on behalf of females everywhere. But then she'd get over it. Elmer would never let him live it down.

"Hale? What is it?" Her forehead creased, real concern reflecting in her eyes. "What did you do?"

"I started with your basic flirting," he said. Might as well start with the truth.

"Started with? Where'd it go from there?"

Right into her bedroom. But he didn't say that. He needed Zoë to understand how affected he was. How much the belt's spell had mesmerized him. If she didn't understand, she'd never agree to take over.

"The thing is, Zo, I need you on this mission. More than just as backup. I need you in there on the front line."

"Zephron said this was your baby." From the tone of her voice, he knew she wouldn't ignore Zephron's orders. Not without a damn good reason. Fortunately for Hale, he had a trump card. "Zephron didn't have all the facts."

"Uh-huh." She shot him a dubious look before taking a long sip of cocoa.

"Seriously. The girl has a crush on me."

At that, Zoë exploded into laughter, spewing cocoa on the table. "Oh, please!" She knelt on the chair, then sopped up the spilled liquid with her shirt. "That isn't exactly news. Half the female population has a crush on you. I even ran across a website devoted to you the other day. And I might be your sister, but I have to say you look pretty darn cute in a loincloth. Nice buns."

He groaned. He'd forgotten about that cover.

"I hardly think the fact that Tracy has a crush on you is a reason for you to abandon the mission." Zoë tilted her head as the corners of her mouth turned down in a scowl. "Though I will say that it's not like you to back out of a job for *any* reason. What's really going on?"

"Her crush *is* what's going on." Hale ran his hands through his hair, as frustrated by the truth as he was by the fact that he needed help. "She has a crush on me, and she has the belt. You do the math."

"Ohhhh." Zoë pressed two fingers over her lips. "So, since the belt makes anyone the wearer desires fall under her spell—"

"I'm a sitting duck," Hale finished.

"So, it's working? I mean, you like the girl? More than the usual"—she gesticulated—"lust?"

That was the understatement of the year. "She's amazing. There's something about her that makes me feel . . ." He shrugged. "I don't know. Wonderful, I guess. Which is terrible."

Zoë quirked a brow. "Wonderful is terrible?"

"Yes. And it's worse because even though I know it's an illusion, the little things make it seem real—her love of the ocean, her love of animals." He shrugged again. "The way she laughs at my stupid jokes. All these little things draw me to her. But even more, she's got this fire—this spark—but she doesn't even know it."

He frowned. "No, the belt makes me *think* she's special. It feels wonderful . . . and I hate it."

"Sounds perfect for the mission."

Hale got up to refill his hot chocolate and shot her an annoyed glance. "She's mortal—"

"You and your issues."

"Even if she weren't, this isn't real. It's a spell. I can't work a mission while I'm bewitched."

"Uh-huh." Zoë ran her fingers through her hair, standing the coppery strands on end.

"That's it? The entire scope of your sisterly advice is 'uh-huh'? Sisters are supposed to be interfering and opinionated. I'm in need of opinions here, Zo. I need a plan."

"I just don't see why you can't stay on the mission. I mean, it was your idea to romance the belt out from under her. And if you're enchanted . . ." She trailed off, grinning. "If you're enchanted, then you'll really enjoy it."

Taking a long swallow of cocoa, he counted to ten. So far, she really wasn't helping.

"Try and follow me, okay?" When she nodded, he continued. "If I didn't know I was under her spell, then maybe I could do that. But I do know, and it's driving me nuts."

"It's not like you're not used to dangerous missions."

"Dangerous, yes! But not this."

"Not what?"

He waved a hand. "Do you know what I did last night?" Too late, he realized he'd opened a door he wanted to remain shut.

Her eyes went wide. "Something totally off the charts if the tone of your voice is any indication."

"Yeah, well . . . you could say that."

"What?" She held her hands out, imploring. "I'm your sister. You have to tell me."

He paused. "You've heard of phone sex?"

"You called and talked dirty to her?"

He ignored that. "The point is that the participants can't see each other. Let's just say I took that to a whole 'nother level."

Remarkably, her eyes got even wider. "You didn't."

"I couldn't help myself. She's . . . amazing." He slammed his mug down on the table and stood up, totally frustrated with himself and the situation. "I told you I'm bewitched. I'm doing crazy things."

Zoë shook her head. "What's really driving you insane is feeling this way . . . and about a mortal." She leaned back in her chair, her grin totally self-satisfied. And she didn't look the least bit sorry for him. "I'm right, aren't I?"

"Yes!" The answer burst out of him. The whole thing frustrated him. That Tracy was mortal. That he desired her because of some ancient trinket. Hale wasn't one to buckle under to any sort of pressure. And now to have been bested by some fashion accessory . . . well, that really reeked. The only good thing was that at least it wasn't really *him* liking her. It was the belt. This was a curse. An enchantment. But it was better to be under a spell than to have fallen for a mortal.

Zoë laughed, the sound light and airy. "Oh, I wish Taylor were home to see this. And Daddy. You and a mortal. It's priceless!"

Hale scowled. Their father was hopelessly in love with Zoë's mom, Tessa. And that woman was as mortal as they came. "How much longer are you going to keep teasing me before you decide to help?"

She glanced at her unadorned wrist as if it had a watch. "Dunno. Maybe five or six more minutes."

He rubbed his temples, thinking that maybe it would have been a good idea to catch some sleep after all. A clear head was a requirement for tussling with Zoë. When he looked up, she was grinning.

"Would you stop it? This is serious. I'm in charge of this mission, and I've reached critical mass here."

With obvious effort, she managed to pull her features back into some semblance of control. "You're right. It is serious."

"Thank you. Finally."

"But it's not serious in the way you think it is." She paused, her lips pressed together.

Hale wasn't in the mood for guessing games. "What are you talking about?"

"You're not going to like it."

"I'm already under the spell of an ugly belt that's making me do irrational, stupid things. What could possibly be worse?"

He spoke lightly, but she didn't seem to notice the levity. She didn't even crack a smile. "I've been doing some research. You know, on the Net and with some books I got from the MLO. Fascinating stuff. Did you know that in the fifteenth century, the girdle—"

"Just spill it." *Enough, already.* "Whatever you're trying to say, just spit it out."

"Okay. But, remember—you asked me to." She took a deep breath, then looked him straight in the eye. "I gotta say, I'm getting a perverse sense of pleasure telling you this."

"Telling me *what?*"

"You're not under any spell, big brother."

"Of course I am," he said. Then he had the hideous feeling he knew what was coming. "I told you—"

"And I'm telling *you*. I've looked into this. No spell, Hale. Sorry."

He opened his mouth to argue some more, but couldn't quite form the words. He wanted to deny it, to yell that it wasn't true. But in fact, he'd been avoiding the truth. He'd been messing around with Tracy and she hadn't been wearing the belt. He'd known. He just hadn't wanted to admit it.

Now he had no choice.

"A mortal wearing the belt has no power over a Protector," Zoë explained. A devious grin touched her lips, and he knew she was enjoying this. "So, it looks like there's a mortal woman in your life, and you're fresh out of excuses."

Mordichai perched on the windowsill of Zoë's kitchen window, looking in while she and Hale had cocoa. So far, all he'd seen was Hale wandering around looking agitated and Zoë looking smug. Unfortunately, neither was talking loud enough for him to hear anything.

He considered pressing himself to the window, but at the moment he was a red-breasted sapsucker, and while he might have a nice set of tail feathers, his hearing wasn't as good as he might have hoped.

And if he tried to get closer, Zoë or Hale might notice him. A mortal would never be able to spot him, but his cousins certainly could. And anyone would think an eavesdropping bird pressed to the glass was odd.

Still, everything was okay. Just by being here, he'd learned what he needed to know. Hale was with Zoë and not with Tracy.

Now was his chance.

He thought about the slim brunette, wondering about the best way to get close to her. Yesterday when he'd perched on her trailer, the girl had been talking to that dust mop she called a dog. If she talked to one dog, why not another? Especially if the new dog was a stately, refined canine who whined and licked her face at all the appropriate intervals. Maybe a beagle. Or a Labrador.

No. His tail feathers twitched as he thought of the perfect dog: a collie. Mordichai was no Lassie, but he could do a damn fine impression.

His feathers ruffled as he considered his plan. First he'd be man's—or woman's—best friend. He'd learn what he could this morning. And then this evening he'd be the man of her dreams. A man who understood her needs and desires, almost as if she'd told him herself.

She'd forgotten to set her alarm, so Tracy didn't wake up until about noon. She hated getting such a late start, but the reason was worth it.

As she snuggled back in bed, she remembered just *how* worth it. Last night she'd had the most amazing fantasy of her life. Amazing, that is, until it had fizzled at the end, leaving her teetering on the brink and totally frustrated. For reasons she didn't quite grasp, the fantasy had lost a lot of its oomph.

Who would have thought that one's imagination could be just as fickle as some men?

Well, imagined or no, last night had whetted her appetite for the real thing. That was for sure.

Realization bopped her on the head and she sat bolt upright. *The real thing!* Hale was taking her out tonight. She needed clothes. Shoes. *Help*. She needed help. And she knew just the person to help her—Hale's sister, Zoë.

Her date with Leon had been a disaster, and she didn't intend to watch history repeat itself. Now, with a plan, she slipped out of bed and pulled on a pair of ratty sweats and a T-shirt. As she was heading out and downstairs to the kitchen, she caught a glimpse of herself in the mirror. She looked like a cross between a homeless person and a teenager in a grunge band.

She had no plans to bump into Hale, but you never know. And she certainly didn't want him to see her like this. First she headed into the bathroom and did the whole makeup-and-hair thing. Not that it made a huge improvement, but at least she wouldn't scare people in public. Then she headed to her closet with an eye to finding something casual yet fun and flirty. She began rummaging through her not-so-stellar collection of outfits. Boring. Boring. Dull. Boring. Needs ironing. A-ha!

A little red sundress she'd picked up from a studio resale shop. Someone had worn it on *The Young and the Restless*, and now it was Tracy's turn. Apropos, considering how restless she'd felt last night.

As soon as she'd slipped it over her head and zipped up the back, she remembered why she hadn't worn it before. The waistband was just a little too big. Well, darn. She was heading to her dresser to find a belt when she remembered her grandmother's, still hanging on the back of the chaise where she'd left it last night.

For a second, she just scowled at it, wondering. Maybe she should have worn it for her date with Leon. Maybe if she had, he wouldn't have been such a prick.

Or maybe he would still have been a prick, but she'd have had the confidence to respond coolly and reasonably, instead of bursting into tears in the foyer. She had no idea which was more likely, but she did know that the belt really did give her a shot of confidence, and she'd been sorely lacking in that last night.

So what if it was becoming a crutch? Some women wouldn't leave the house without mascara. From now on, she wouldn't leave without this belt.

Snapping it on, she assessed herself one last time in the mirror. Fortunately, the belt matched the dress perfectly, its gold color complementing nicely the little yellow flowers that dotted the red material.

She ran a brush through her hair—there wasn't much more she could do without a blowtorch and concrete—then headed to the kitchen to make coffee and a phone call. Hopefully, Zoë would be home and willing to help her.

She was in luck; Hale's sister answered on the first ring.

"What's up?" she asked, as soon as Tracy identified herself.

"I need your help," Tracy said. "Your brother's coming over tonight, and—"

"You haven't got a thing to wear," Zoë finished for her. Then she laughed.

"Exactly. And . . . well . . . you don't know this, but my guy IQ is in the bottom percentile. I'm hopeless."

"I doubt you're that bad."

"Trust me, I am," Tracy said. "So will you help me with the clothes? And anything else you can think of? I don't want to blow it with your brother like I did last night."

The girl on the other end of the line paused. "I'd love to help you, but I'm not exactly an expert. If you're bad, I'm . . . well, worse. But my friend Deena . . ." Zoë drifted off. "Yeah. Let me send my friends Deena and Lane to help you out."

"Are you sure?" Tracy wasn't completely certain she wanted to go shopping with perfect strangers.

"Oh, yeah. If anyone can pull together an outfit, Deena can."

"Well . . ."

"Trust me," Zoë said. "You couldn't find better help if you paid for it."

Tracy sucked in a breath. Why not. She didn't know Zoë well, but she trusted her. "Okay. If you say so. But do you think they'll want to help?"

Zoë laughed. "Honey, if the object is to dress you up so that my brother Hale is prostrate with lust, well, that's one project they would never want to miss out on."

Chapter Seventeen

Big trouble.

Huge. Massive. Overwhelming trouble.

Hale couldn't have been any worse off if he'd planned it.

And at the same time, he couldn't leave. Couldn't take his eyes off Tracy. So here he was—spending the afternoon stuck in the middle of the food court at the Century City Mall, of all places—watching the most adorable mortal in the world play with a stray collie. A mortal he had indescribable feelings for.

Zoë's pronouncement that the belt was ineffective on Protectors had only proven what he'd known—and been avoiding—deep down. He'd been hiding from the truth, but the simple fact was—these feelings he had for Tracy were, well, *real*. A shiver ran up his spine; he didn't like that conclusion at all. Rather than deal with the way he felt for the woman, he'd much rather resolve this mission and then head back to some beach where he could get his head on straight.

This situation was enough to give a guy the willies. And the really sad thing was, there wasn't a damn thing he could do about it.

As much as he'd wanted to be enchanted, the truth was, he'd never really felt like he was under a spell. Well, that wasn't entirely true. He *did* feel bewitched—but by the woman, not her fashion accessories.

Damn, he hated this feeling.

More than anything, he wanted to run far and fast, but he couldn't. This was his assignment, and he was stuck with it. Get the belt. Protect the girl. And if you happen to fall for her, well, too bad for you.

So here he was watching her wander through the outdoor mall, fighting the urge to go talk to her. He was here to protect her. That was all. Later, on their date, he'd work on seducing her—but only for the purpose of getting the belt.

He'd seduce her, yes. He'd seduce her because that was the quickest and easiest solution to this mission. And, frankly, he'd enjoy the process. But no matter how much he liked Tracy, he didn't intend to let himself get truly close. He'd keep some distance, in his head if not in his heart. He had to, for his own self-preservation.

In the end, he'd win this girl's affection. But he couldn't keep the prize. He couldn't, because Tracy Tannin was dangerous. He needed to keep that firmly in mind.

"He's just the cutest thing!" Stumbling under the weight of three shopping bags, Tracy knelt and petted the muzzle of the light brown collie with the green eyes that had been following her ever since they'd left the food court.

Beside her, Deena tapped her foot. "Come on, Trace. It's already five, and we still have miles to go before we sleep."

"But he's so adorable." With her eyes as wide as the collie's, she turned the dog's pointed face so that he was looking up at Deena. "Come on, Deena. Don't you want to be his friend?"

Deena's mouth twitched, and Tracy knew she was trying to keep a stern expression. She'd fail, of course. Tracy might have only met Deena a few hours ago, but she could already tell that the girl's carefree blond curls perfectly matched her attitude. Deena was as laid-back as they came. And Tracy had never once met a laid-back person who didn't fall under the spell of a homeless, adorable puppy dog with "take me home" eyes.

Giving in, Deena dropped to the ground, sitting cross-legged on the concrete and forcing the other shoppers to walk around them. The collie blinked, then put his furry little chin in her lap. When he whined, Deena's face softened and Tracy knew it was all over.

"He is pretty adorable, isn't he?" Deena asked.

As if he understood, the dog shuffled closer, practically demanding the blonde scratch his ears.

"I think he likes you," Tracy said.

"Hmmm."

Zoë's sister-in-law, Lane Kent, joined them, carrying three fruit smoothies from a stand in the food court. "Uh-oh. What did I miss?"

"Nothing," Tracy said. After her initial hesitation, she was thrilled that Zoë had sent these two to help her. Who better to get her ready for a date with Hale than women who knew him well? "Laddie here's just going to join us for the day."

"Laddie?" Lane and Deena asked in unison.

Tracy lifted a shoulder. "Well, it's a boy dog. So Lassie doesn't work. But he looks just like Lassie."

"Lassie *was* a boy. At least the dogs who played her were boys, I think."

Shooting Deena a stern glance, Lane put her hands on her hips. "Do you mind? I'd like to keep one or two of my childhood illusions alive."

"At any rate," Deena said, hoisting herself up off the ground, "don't you think we should find out who he belongs to? I mean, this is an odd place for a dog to be wandering around."

That was true enough. Century City Mall was a prestigious shopping area overflowing with wonderful stores—wonderful, that is, until the credit-card statement came in the mail. Plus, it had the added benefit of being an open-air mall. Instead of being enclosed in one giant building, all of the common areas and walkways were outside; but even though a dog could certainly wander around easier than he could in, say, the Beverly Center, loose dogs still weren't common. For one thing, the surrounding area wasn't particularly residential.

"I still think he's a stray," Tracy said. "He probably came at night to scope out the trash cans behind the restaurants, and he just hung around."

"But he's not mangy or anything," Lane said. She bent down and petted him, and Laddie preened. Then she urged him to lift one foot, and frowned when she saw the underside. "And the pads of his feet aren't too worn down. He must belong to somebody."

"Or maybe somebody abandoned him," Tracy proposed.

"Could be," Deena agreed. "Why don't we report him to security and leave your home phone and cell numbers, and then if anyone's looking for a lost dog, they can find him." She looked at her watch. "And I hope he's trained to wait outside stores, because we still have some serious shopping to do."

Every muscle in Tracy's body groaned in protest. "Rest. I need rest. Can't we at least sit and drink our smoothies?"

Deena checked her watch and tapped her foot. "We've barely even begun."

"Zoë should have warned you," Lane said, a note of apology in her voice. "Deena's a shopping pro."

"I could tell." So far, in a mini-whirlwind of activity, Deena had dragged Tracy in and out of Victoria's Secret and a half-dozen other shops. Now she was laden down with enough hose, lacy underwear, and exotic push-up bras to clothe an entire bordello. "Please," she begged. "Must . . . rest. Bones . . . weary."

Deena and Lane exchanged looks, then finally shrugged in agreement.

"Thank you," Tracy breathed. "You two are slave drivers." She grinned at them. "And I appreciate every minute of it. Left alone, I'm a shopping disaster." Standing back up, she urged Laddie toward one of the nearby tables. "Come on, boy."

She sank into a chair and gratefully took the Wild Strawberry smoothie Lane passed her.

"And you had Bouncing Banana," Lane said, passing a styrofoam cup to Deena. She took a sip of her own, then sat back in her chair with her eyes closed. "Mmmm. Heaven."

"What'd you get?" Tracy asked.

Lane opened her eyes long enough to wink. "Passion Fruit Playground." She shot Tracy a sly look. "Maybe I should have ordered it for you."

"Ha-ha." Tracy took a long slurp of her strawberry smoothie. "Just because I've got a little bit of a crush on the guy." Laddie whined and laid his head on her lap. She rubbed behind his ears. "Yeah, thanks boy. See? Laddie understands."

"Oh, I understand crushes," Deena said. "I had a monster crush on Hoop before he finally caved in and realized I existed on the planet. You just need to know what you're getting in for if you're falling for Hale."

Tracy cocked her head. "What do you mean?"

Lane and Deena exchanged glances. "Well, what is it you want in a guy?" the latter asked.

Tracy's mind drifted back to her fantasy the night before, and a tiny little smile touched her lips.

"*Other* than sex," Deena said.

"Is there anything other than sex?" Lane asked. "I don't remember."

"Fidelity." Deena said. "I trust Hoop completely. Well, everything but his taste in clothes."

"Humor." Tracy said, thinking about the tiger-poop incident. "A guy who can laugh with me and at himself."

"Okay, okay," Lane said. "Um . . . dependability. A guy who does what he says he's going to do."

"Not a bad list so far," Deena said. She looked at Tracy. "We're talking about *your* guy. Anything else?"

Tracy considered keeping her mouth shut. After all, she'd never really had a girl-to-girl talk with anyone other than Mel, and she hardly knew these women. But she liked them. And she trusted them. It might be a little premature to be planning a relationship right now, but that didn't mean she couldn't window-shop.

Taking the plunge, she said, "All I've ever really wanted is a guy who likes me for myself. A guy I can talk to. A guy I can wander around the house in front of wearing sweats and a T-shirt and still have him think I'm the hottest thing on the planet." She shrugged, feeling a little silly. "I know it's not particularly original, but it's what I want."

Laddie whined and nuzzled his head closer, as if in approval. Looking much less enthusiastic, Lane and Deena exchanged another of their mysterious glances.

"What?" Tracy asked. "What aren't you telling me?"

"It's just that . . ." Lane dwindled off, then took a deep breath and started again. "We're just a little concerned. Because even though Hale acts like he likes you—"

"He does?" Suddenly Tracy's day was looking up. She'd figured he liked her, but now she had confirmation from the trenches.

"With Hale you have to be careful," Deena said.

Tracy squinted, moving her gaze between the two of them. "What do you mean?"

Another glance, then Deena took a breath. "Hale's had his share of women."

"He's a cover model, after all," Lane said.

"And he's . . . well . . . a little conceited," Deena added, looking toward Lane for confirmation.

"Yeah, conceited. That's fair. And arrogant."

"And a know-it-all," Deena said.

"We love him," Lane said. "We really do. And once he's in your court, he's as loyal as they come."

"But getting to know him isn't easy," Deena warned. "Hale's a lot to put up with."

"Not that any of this matters to you, yet," Lane hastened to add. "It's just that you should probably know about his whole thing with women."

"He goes out with lots of them," Deena said again. "But that doesn't mean he's particularly crazy about mo—" She snapped her mouth shut, shooting a horrified look in Lane's direction.

"About what?" Tracy asked. Laddie's head popped up, his eyes wide and agitated.

"About . . . about . . . moving too fast," Lane said. She sat back in her seat, looking strangely pleased with herself. Deena exhaled, looking a bit less happy.

"Uh-huh." Not only was Tracy's head spinning from the weight of information they'd just piled on her, but she distinctly felt like she was missing out on something.

217

"Anyway," Deena said. "Don't move too fast with a guy like Hale. Watch your step, and watch your heart."

Tracy exhaled, finally understanding what they were worried about. "It's okay, you guys. I'm not interested in Hale like *that*. I told my best friend that very thing just a day or so ago. Last night solidified it. No more relationships. At least, not right now. I crash and burn."

Deena frowned, her forehead creasing above her Ray-Bans. "Then, what's going on with Hale? I thought you were all excited about this date."

"Oh, I am! But you're right. I already figured he's probably got women all over the country." She licked her lips. "The thing is, I've noticed him for years. On my books, I mean. And now I have the chance to . . . to . . ."

"To have a hot time with a romance cover model," Deena finished. "Well, hallelujah!" She tossed an amused look Lane's way. "She *wants* to be seduced. This is going to work out beautifully."

"What will?" Tracy asked, once again feeling like she'd missed part of the conversation.

Lane patted her hand. "You and Hale, of course. If that's all you want, you're going to get along great."

Deena stood up, apparently deciding the conversation was over. Tracy opened her mouth to ask about Hale, but the blonde cut her off. "Now we really ought to get you something to put on top of that underwear. And I'm thinking something other than that belt."

"I love this belt. It was my grandmother's"

"I have some of my grandmother's clothes," Deena said, "but that doesn't mean I wear them every day." She looked at Lane. "Besides, I don't think it's your style. Do you?"

Lane shook her head. "More *your* style, actually."

"You're right," Deena said. "It looks just like something I'd wear."

They were right. Even though Deena might have this shopping mall thing down pat, her own personal style seemed to lean toward more vintage selections.

"I don't suppose you'd be interested in selling it," Deena said.

Tracy shook her head and smiled. "Nope. Sentimental value." Considering that, and the fact that good things only seemed to happen to her when she was wearing it, she wasn't inclined to get rid of the belt any more than she wanted to put it back in a box. "Besides, I want to wear it. We'll just have to find clothes that go with it."

Lane and Deena exchanged a look, but didn't say anything.

With a sigh, Tracy scooted Laddie's head off her lap and retrieved her shopping bags. "Let's go find me the perfect wardrobe. My credit cards are just getting warmed up."

Invisible, and at the next table over, Hale watched the women. He was impressed that Deena had tried to snag the belt—even though, according to Zephron, her attempt probably wouldn't work. But even while he was pleased by the attempt, he was irritated by the conversation, and he drummed his fingers on the formica. Not that Lane or Deena had said anything inaccurate, but somehow, hearing the truth out loud annoyed him.

It *shouldn't* annoy him. He shouldn't care at all what Tracy thought of him, since he was planning to seduce the belt away and run. A drive-by seduction. Love 'em and leave 'em. Just like James Bond. Heck, just like himself.

It shouldn't bother him to hear aloud that he was simply going to be Tracy's Stud o' the Month.

Except it did. It bothered him a lot.

Damn.

Sitting down in the chair beside him, a haggard-looking attorney-type tried to convince his screaming child to eat a bite of hot dog.

"No, Daddy. It's yucky," the kid replied.

"Billy, what's Mommy going to think if you don't eat your dinner?"

"Icky." The kid banged his fist on the table. "Icky, icky, icky."

Hale half-watched the child while his thoughts drifted over what Tracy had said. She had specific parameters for what she wanted in a man. Serious parameters. He didn't fit her bill at all. The realization should have made him happy. If he wasn't Tracy's kind of guy, then there was no way they'd get involved—no matter what foolishness his emotions might be planning.

Yes, he should be happy. But he wasn't. He wasn't happy at all.

In fact, he was so busy being unhappy that he didn't notice the woman who walked up to join the attorney and his kid. She came near to sitting in his lap before he came to his senses and slid out of the chair, landing with a thud on the concrete.

"Did you hear that?" the woman asked, peering toward the noise, her face only inches from Hale's.

"I can't hear anything. I think Billy's ruptured my eardrums."

The woman laughed and sat upright again, then started talking babytalk to her child, who picked up his hot dog and took a bite.

Nice that their problems could be solved so easily. Hale didn't think his issues would be resolved nearly as neatly. He looked around, wondering where the trio of women had gone. He caught sight of them turning a corner at the end of the sidewalk, and he was on his feet and running after them in no time.

Deena was leading the way, of course, and Lane and Tracy were walking a few steps behind, chatting and laughing. The stray collie was sticking close to Tracy. Not that

Hale could blame it. Zeus knows, he certainly longed to be that close.

When they reached Ann Taylor, the group stopped and Hale sidled closer. He caught the tail end of their conversation—they were still talking about men—and regretted not having heard the rest of it. A few more pointers about what Tracy was looking for might not be a bad thing.

Not because he intended to change anything permanently, mind you. But if he was going to seduce the belt away from her, he needed ammo. That was all. He was just planning for his mission.

Mentally, he rolled his eyes at his own line of bull. Sure, he just wanted ammo. And Hieronymous was really just a misunderstood nice guy.

"So we'll hit Ann Taylor first," Deena was saying, "and then move on down the line until we find something perfect."

"Well, I like that," Tracy mentioned, pointing to a yellow dress in the window. Hale tried to picture her in it, and decided he wouldn't have any objection.

"Not bad," Deena said. "We'll add it to the pile. But we still need to find something with pizzazz. Something that will knock Hale's eyes out of their sockets." Lane and Tracy laughed, then all three went into the store, leaving the collie outside whining and Hale lusting. Tracy wearing something with pizzazz: That was something he definitely wanted to see.

He knew he shouldn't, but his feet itched to follow them into the store. Not that he'd sneak a peek into the dressing room—he didn't intend to go down that road again—but just to see Tracy when she stepped out to model the outfits. After all, it was his eye sockets that they were trying to torture. If he wanted a little advance warning, that was fair. Wasn't it?

Since he couldn't exactly pull the door open and walk in—folks tended to get a little nervous when non-automatic doors opened and shut by themselves—he headed in that direction, then leaned against the wall and waited for another customer to come by. To pass the time, he listened, trying to hear if the collie was saying anything interesting. Maybe he could find out if it was a stray, lost or abandoned. If it was desperate to get back to its owner, maybe Hale could save Tracy some heartache.

He cocked his head, listening, but didn't hear a thing. Odd. Most collies had a habit of talking to themselves; they were one of the more articulate breeds.

Not this collie. This dog was apparently the strong, silent type.

Perplexed, Hale moved closer. The dog was sitting right in front of the store, its rump planted on the concrete, as if Tracy were its master and always had been.

Talk about instant loyalty.

Then the dog yawned, its eyes closing and opening wide along with its mouth. Vivid green eyes. Eyes that seemed familiar. Eyes that he'd seen recently, at the coffee shop with Tracy.

Right then, Hale knew. Loyalty had nothing to do with it. This dog wasn't there to help Tracy. This dog was there for the belt.

That damn collie was his cousin, Mordichai, again.

The whole situation stank of Hieronymous. And Hale intended to get to the bottom of it.

Without materializing, he headed toward the dog. As he got closer, Mordi's little nose started twitching, and Hale knew he'd been found out.

The dog turned and gave a tiny little *arf*, easily translatable as, "What do you think you're doing, sneaking up on me like that?"

Hale snorted. "Me? Sneaking up on you?" he whispered. "What in Hades are *you* doing snooping around Tracy?"

Don't you mean snooping around the belt?

Hale stiffened, his fears confirmed—Mordi knew about the belt. He could best his cousin—easily—but he didn't relish the thought. Especially since he'd hoped that the guy had decided to straighten up and fly right. Instead, it looked like genetics had won out. Mordi was here doing his dad's dirty work.

"Go back and tell your dad I've got the belt under control. Hieronymous isn't getting his hands on it."

You really think that's who I'm here for? Dad? The plea in Mordi's voice was clear. *Why would I risk my own powers by stealing the belt for him? Risk my Probation? Risk my future? Cousin, I thought you knew me better.*

"For years I thought I knew you. Recently, I learned I didn't." And just because Mordi had a few tick marks on the "good" side of the scoreboard didn't mean Hale was suddenly going to start trusting him.

I thought we got past that little error in judgment on my part.

"Let's just say you're on probation in my mind, too."

Maybe I'm here to help.

"That's why you've been following Tracy? To help?" Hale echoed, wondering if it could be true. "How?"

We Probationers have a lot of hoops to jump through. Maybe I'm here to help you.

Hale wanted to hit Mordi with a few more questions. Like why Zephron would fail to mention that Mordi would be assisting the mission. A suspicious little fact, that. But right then, Tracy slipped out the door, completely laden with shopping bags, and started heading toward Mordi.

"Laddie!"

Mordi—good little shapeshifter that he was—squirmed all over and generally gave the impression of a mutt thrilled to death to see his master. *She just loves me, he barked.*

Hale rolled his eyes, though no one could see it. "You stick around," he hissed, his voice pitched only for a dog's ears. "This isn't over."

But this time, Mordi didn't answer. He just licked Tracy's face and gave a pleased look clearly suggesting that, no matter what Hale wanted, at this particular moment, Mordichai was the one getting up close and personal with Tracy.

Well, damn.

Chapter Eighteen

"Tracy!"

The voice came from behind her, and Tracy spun around from where she was cuddling Laddie to try and locate the source.

"Tracy! Over here!" *Leon*. Rushing right toward her?

The last person in the world she wanted to see after the utter humiliation of last night.

"What do you want?" She stood up, wiping her hands on her dress. Hopefully, he wanted to jump off a bridge into traffic. But she doubted it.

She glanced behind her, hoping Deena and Lane were there for moral support, but they were still inside the store, giving their own credit cards a major workout. Only Laddie was around. His eyes were wide and earnest.

"You look beautiful." Leon's puppy-dog expression matched Laddie's. Considering the hideous way he'd behaved at her house last night, she couldn't help but wonder if the guy was schizo. Then she wondered how much *The National Enquirer* would pay for an article about how America's latest heartthrob needed to be locked in a loony bin. Enough for her property taxes?

She imagined Leon in a straightjacket and a padded cell, and had to admit the thought was tempting. She'd never do it, of course, but she could cherish the image.

"Listen, Leon. I'm really not in the mood. I'm shopping with friends—"

"I'm a friend."

"The hell you are." It burst out of her on a spurt of anger. She considered taking it back, especially when she saw his puppy-dog eyes get all wounded, but the truth was the truth. "You've been a total jerk."

"I'm sorry," he said, real contrition in his voice. "It's just that, well, you make me nervous."

"I make *you* nervous?" The thought cheered her, and she wondered if she shouldn't give him another shot. *No.* Shaking her head, she reached for common sense and held on tight. "Forget it, Leon. You already fooled me twice. I'm not getting up to the plate to strike out. It's *not* going to happen."

Beside her, Laddie growled and bared his teeth, his eyes focusing on Leon's groin.

The blood drained from Leon's face, and he took a step backward.

She patted Laddie's head. "Good dog."

"Can't I even buy you a drink? A soda? A cookie?"

"No." She was rapidly moving from angered humiliation to simple anger. "I'd really appreciate it if you'd just leave."

"I can't. I—"

Something rushed by him then, and Tracy thought the something would rush by her, too, until she felt extra-large hands gripping her around the waist and pulling her to the ground. A burly man with flaming red hair, a pockmarked face, and serious bad breath was just inches away.

"Gimme purse," said a strangled, voice. It was somehow familiar. Like the guy who'd tried to mug her when she'd had the flat tire.

And what was even stranger was that he wasn't reaching for her purse at all. Again, he was fumbling at her waist. What was with these guys?

"Pervert!" Tracy screamed and kicked and clawed, but the guy was persistent. Not to mention heavy, and it was all she could do to struggle beneath him. "Get away from me!" she cried. Nothing. The guy didn't even budge. "Leon! Help!" She managed to turn her head, silently imploring the actor to be the hero he played on the television show.

But Leon didn't move. Just stood there with his eyes wide. Some hero. Had she really considered having a fling with this guy?

The redheaded cretin made another tug for her belt, managing to grab part of her dress. The muggers in the parking lot, they'd been reaching for her waist, too. She'd thought it was the tire iron they wanted, but . . .

He fumbled at the clasp of her belt. "Itsa not coming off. Take off. Give to me."

"Get off me!" Tracy yelled, in no mood to follow orders from a smelly mugger. She twisted out of his grasp, trying to pry his hands from the belt. No way was he getting her grandmother's belt. It simply was *not* going to happen.

Laddie, bless him, must have agreed, and he lunged at her assailant, sinking his teeth into the back of the man's thigh.

The mugger squealed and yanked once more at Tracy's waist. Miraculously, the belt stayed on tight, despite the fact that the clasp had never seemed too sturdy. Thank goodness.

And then the mugger got in her face, snarled, and ripped her purse off her arm. The move surprised Tracy, since up

Julie Kenner

until that point, he'd been totally uninterested in anything but the belt. Reacting immediately, she brought her knee up with every ounce of strength in her body, catching him right where it counts.

She bit back a satisfied, half-hysterical laugh, sure he'd grab his private parts, howl in pain, then keel over. But he didn't. For that matter, the guy hardly seemed fazed at all.

What the . . . ? She'd spent a hundred and fifty dollars and two weekends in a self-defense class for *that?* This guy was supposed to be out of commission. Instead, he was getting away.

And fast.

Already he'd managed to get off her and scurry a few yards away—her purse dangling from his arm—apparently totally unfazed by her oh-so-well-placed knee.

"No!" She was on her feet in an instant, running after him. Laddie was right beside her, yapping his head off.

The behemoth turned and snarled at her, and she knew—she just *knew*—she was going to have to let him get away. And there wasn't a darn thing she could do about it. But, right when she was sure all was lost, someone tall and dark streaked out of nowhere, knocking Super Creep to the ground. As the two went rolling end over end over, Laddie's yaps transformed into full-fledged barks and Tracy yelled encouragement to the stranger.

They flipped over, and she saw only the creep. Then she blinked, and . . . her dark-haired knight looked an awful lot like . . . Hale?

She peered closer, trying to get a good look without getting kicked by the flailing limbs. "Hale?"

The tussle stopped for just an instant, and their eyes met.

She swallowed, surprised by the force of her reaction. Once again, her hero had come to her rescue. And damned if she didn't like the feeling.

*   *   *

228

Bop! Ka-pow! Blam! Blooey!

Over and over Hale rolled with the mugger, his mind going a million miles a minute even as his fists were flying faster, each blow sinking into the Henchman's squishy flesh.

Damn Hieronymous. He'd sent a little Henchman invasion to Los Angeles, and apparently it was Hale's new job to stop them.

Fortunately, Henchmen might be known for being sneaky and slimy—under their human guise they looked a lot like walking squid—but good fighters, they weren't. Hale had little nervousness about besting the critter. The trick would be to overpower it without hinting to Tracy that he was any stronger or faster than your average guy.

Bop! Hale landed another wallop, the Henchman's nose squishing under the blow. *Blam!* He got it in the gut, his hand sinking where it had no business sinking.

A quick glance behind him confirmed that Tracy was watching the whole thing eagerly, gnawing on her lip as she jumped up and down, yelling encouragement to him.

Pow! Pop! A one-two punch, and the Henchman groaned. Hale assumed he'd hit him in some sensitive spot. Not that he could tell. The mugger might look human, but he felt like a glop of goo, and fighting goo wasn't easy. Even for a superhero.

The creature kicked and flailed, but Hale dodged his blows, and with Tracy cheering him on, he reached out and grabbed her purse, not sure why a Henchman would want it. Perhaps it was similar to spoils of war—if the beast couldn't take the belt to Hieronymous, he'd take the purse. The weird part was that Hale had no idea why the Henchman hadn't managed to get the belt off Tracy's waist. At the moment, though, he supposed it didn't matter. The belt was safe and Hale needed to recover Tracy's purse and snare the bad guy. Yet while he managed to close his fingers over the leather strap, the Henchman himself slipped from Hale's grip. In no time at all, the monster was gone, jiggling away down the stairs at the back of the mall.

Hale considered running after him, then decided it wasn't worth it. Instead, he'd corner Mordi and find out what exactly was going on. He glanced around for the dog, then sighed. Apparently, after sinking his teeth into the fight, Mordi had flown the coop, too.

Still, the fact that his cousin had helped Tracy at all gave Hale pause. Was Mordi really firmly entrenched in the Council now? Or was he still playing both sides of the fence?

He didn't have time to ponder the question, because Tracy launched herself at him and wrapped her arms around his neck. "You did it!" she yelled.

Considering the outcome hadn't ever really been up for debate, he felt a little hypocritical accepting her enthusiastic kisses. But not hypocritical enough to peel the girl off. If she wanted to thank him, who was he to say no? After all, Protectors protected. He'd just been doing his job.

All in all, it felt pretty nice.

Her arms were still around his neck when Tracy stopped dusting his cheek with kisses. Leaning back, she looked him in the eye, her expression almost horrified. "I'm so sorry." She let go, sliding off him and taking a step back. "I didn't mean—"

Before he had time to reconsider, he took her hand, pulling her close until her breasts were pressed against him. "Are you telling me I have to give those kisses back?"

He could feel her heart beating against his chest, its tempo increasing.

"No." A single, breathy word. "The kisses are yours to keep."

Deena stepped out from the storefront where she and Lane had just appeared. "Do you want to tell us what's going on?"

Hale shot them each a meaningful glance. "I'm going to take Tracy home. Whose car did you come in?"

"Tracy's," Lane said.

He turned to Tracy. "Give me your keys."

For a second, he thought she was going to protest, but then she dug into her purse and tossed him a key ring.

"Can you get into your house?"

Tracy nodded. "I have a spare."

"Here." He stepped closer to Lane. "Drive Deena home. Then head on back to my sister's. I'll give you the full scoop in the morning." When she nodded, he lowered his voice. "Tell Zoë what happened. Tell her the Henchmen aren't just in the Valley anymore."

As he expected, Lane's eyes went wide. She'd had her own little run-in with the Henchmen not too long ago, and Hale knew they didn't rank up there on her favorite persons list.

"So, are you two still going out tonight?" Deena asked. Leave it to her to cut to the chase.

He moved back to Tracy and curled an arm around her shoulder, drawing her close. "That depends on what she wants."

"I hope we are." Tracy tilted her head back, the beginnings of a smile on her lips. "I'm just shook up. I'm not hurt. I'd like to go out on the town."

Hale nodded, feeling foolishly proud of her. For a mortal, she was damn resilient.

"Well, you two have fun," Deena said. She turned to Lane. "Ready?"

While the girls backtracked to the entrance of the parking garage, Hale turned back to Tracy, then realized he had no idea what to say to her. Part of him wanted to lecture her on being safer—didn't she know she was a target for Hieronymous? But of course she didn't, and that was part of the point.

231

Another part of him wanted to pull her close and hold her tight.

And yet another part of him was wishing for an allergy attack so he could sneeze, disappear, and then run far and fast from this woman who was messing with his head.

Tracy solved the dilemma for him.

In one quick motion, she was on her toes, her arms around his neck. Then, before he even knew what to expect, she kissed him, her mouth firm against his.

He groaned, low in the back of his throat, as his arms tightened around her waist, pulling her closer. A soft, blissful sound escaped her, and Hale's body tensed simply from the knowledge that one simple kiss was affecting her as much as it was affecting him.

He didn't like this. He didn't need this. But, dammit, for just a few seconds he wanted the oblivion her lips promised. Wanted to not think about anything. Not that she was mortal. Not that he was supposed to be seducing her, as opposed to the other way around. Nothing.

For a few seconds of bliss, his world consisted only of her rose-petal-soft lips pressed against his mouth and the flowery scent of her shampoo.

And, for just an instant, Hale actually forgot that she was a mortal.

Chapter Nineteen

Tracy couldn't believe she'd been so bold. But, then again, she couldn't believe she'd been mugged right in the middle of Century City. The first mugging, in the Valley, she could almost understand. But here? They were walking distance of the Beverly Hills Police Department. And who got mugged in Beverly Hills?

Still, compared to throwing her arms around a man and kissing him, a mugging was practically a daily event in her life.

Part of her was mortified. The other part was proud of herself for taking the initiative. But it was the mortified part that won out; she pulled back. Now she stood in front of Hale, staring down at her new pedicure, certain her cheeks were on fire.

"Um . . ." She cleared her throat and tried again. "Anyway. Thanks. For fighting that guy and getting my purse back. That's twice now that you've saved me." Deciding her toenails had been inspected enough, she peeked up at him. "Guess you really are a superhero," she joked.

"Would I lie?" Somehow, he looked just as awkward as she felt.

"Right. Well." This time she checked out her manicure. It wasn't in nearly as good a shape, and she'd broken two nails wrestling with the mugger. "I guess we should get back to my house. You, uh, probably have stuff to do before you move in tonight."

He shrugged, then stepped closer. "Not really. Make me a better offer."

The old Tracy would have just blushed from her toes to the ends of her hair. The new, belt-toting Tracy had a slightly bolder streak, bless her devilish little heart. Sucking in a breathful of courage, she nodded. "Okay. I will. There's no point in shopping anymore, so why don't you take me out for an afternoon on the town."

"Why isn't there any point in shopping?"

"Because you're here, of course." She hoped her smile seemed inviting and flirtatious, but it probably just looked goofy.

"Come again?"

"I was shopping for tonight. Deena and Lane were my dating fashion consultants."

"Oh." And then, with more inflection. "Oh!" He reached out, a devious gleam in his eye. "Then let me see what you've got in there."

Almost too late, she realized he was reaching for her shopping bags. Filled with exotic, teeny-tiny underwear. In a rainbow of racy colors.

She jumped back, clutching the bag to her chest. "Oh, no. Really. It's boring. Just girl stuff."

She got a hint of a smile, just enough to display his dimple. "I'm a big fan of girl stuff." He took another step closer, and heat pooled in the backs of her knees. "And I'm planning to get to know all about *your* girl stuff soon. Very soon."

Oh, my. "Yes . . . well . . ." She was being positively foolish. After all, the man was playing with her. Wasn't this exactly the sort of flirty banter she'd been fantasizing about?

Of course it was. And instead of grabbing the bull by the horns—or the man by the whatever—she was acting like a dreamy-eyed schoolgirl. She should be acting like a sexually knowledgeable Hollywood starlet.

Well, no time like the present for a little improvisation. Taking a deep breath, Tracy summoned her courage, then slipped her bag behind her back and moved in closer.

His heat teased her and she almost lost her nerve, but then she tilted her head back and looked deep into his fathomless blue eyes. "You can look if you want. But it's just underwear. Pretty boring in a bag. Especially when, if you're a good boy, I'll show you the real thing."

"Oh, I think I can be a *very* good boy," he said. He leaned closer with what could only be described as hunger in his eyes.

If she'd expected him to be knocked silly by her boldness, she was sorely disappointed. Instead, the man looked positively intrigued, and Tracy had to wonder what fine mess she'd gotten herself into.

Still, she had to grin. She wanted him, no doubt about it, and he clearly wanted her, too. If she was lucky, her "fine mess" might prove very fine indeed.

"How much longer do you think we can keep this up?" she asked. "This back-and-forth, I mean. Sooner or later, one of us is going to run out of snappy comebacks."

"I can go all night," Hale said. He caught her in his smoldering gaze.

"Big talk from a big guy." Two points for her. That was definitely a Tahlula kind of thing to say. She was getting the hang of this.

"Sweetheart, I play to win."

"Oh, yeah?" She cocked her head. "But what about after you get the trophy? What happens then, champ?"

She'd expected a laugh, or at least a response, so she was surprised when there was nothing but silence.

"Hale?"

He waved her concern away.

She was confused. "I didn't mean to touch a nerve."

His forehead creased. "You didn't. Don't worry about it. I'm fine. Just distracted."

She wasn't sure she believed him, but he gave a quick flash of his cover-model smile before she could question him again. "Besides, what man wouldn't be distracted around a woman like you?"

"You'd be surprised."

"Considering you're the most distracting mo—" He coughed. "*Woman* I've run across in a long time, I probably *would* be surprised. Especially if you're saying that all men don't agree with my assessment."

"Let's just say your competition isn't exactly breaking down my door."

At least, not until recently. She let her mind drift back over the last few days. Leon—sort of. The coffee shop guy. Walter. That cop. Burke. Hale. Even that polished-looking fellow she'd met at the mall. Moopi or Mordi or something. Hale's cousin—the guy who made animal films. It was as if all the men on the planet had suddenly realized she existed.

"I find that hard to believe."

"Believe it."

She'd gone from being invisible to being so radioactive she practically glowed. If the scenario weren't so suspicious, it would be intriguing.

But right now, she wasn't in the mood to analyze. Instead, she was in the mood to enjoy. And absolutely nothing was going to stop her. Not nerves, not logic, not muggers. Not anything.

Looping her arm through her date's, Tracy aimed what she hoped was a saucy grin in his direction. "But none of that matters. Right now, I want to have a good time. And I want you to be the one I have it with."

Hale let her words float over him. Exactly the kind of words he'd spoken to so many females, so many times. He should be happy. Hell, he should be *ecstatic*.

So why in Hades did he feel about two inches tall?

Mentally, he shook his head, needing to get over it. Tracy had just said she wanted exactly what he wanted—and needed for his mission. No strings. No commitments. Just a wild time and enough warm, fuzzy moments to convince her to hand over the belt.

Life really couldn't be more perfect. Could it?

He headed through the central area of the mall, Tracy's arm still looped through his own. His assignment practically required him to have an affair with this woman, and that was what he was going to do. A dirty job, but somebody had to do it.

So what if he felt something for her beyond attraction. He knew better than to try and take it anywhere. Mortals and Protectors were like oil and water. Mortals left. They couldn't stand the heat, so they got the hell out of the kitchen.

Or the Protector ended up turning down the heat to a slow simmer for fear the mortal would somehow get burned. He thought of his father, Donis, now back with Tessa after twenty-five years. Donis hadn't been on active duty in almost a year. Instead, he was spending "*quality time*" with Tessa. Yeah, right. To Hale's ear, that sounded like a fancy way of saying he'd let himself be put out to pasture.

"Penny for your thoughts." Tracy's soft voice pulled him out of his reverie.

"Sorry. I was distracted."

"Earlier you said *I* was distracting you. Guess I'm not that unique after all."

At her fake pout, he laughed, amazed at how much he enjoyed hanging out with this woman. He stroked a finger up her bare arm, relishing the way she shivered under his touch. "Trust me, sweetheart. You're one hell of a distraction."

She gave him a long look. "Good. I want to be."

Hale pulled her close, then realized they'd stopped near a Brookstone, and the gadgets and gizmos in the window caught his attention. Tugging on her hand, he led her into the store.

"What are we doing?"

"Taking care of you," he said. And that's *all* he was doing. Just being a Protector. A little preventative medicine. At least, that's what he told himself as he searched for a repair kit to leave in Tracy's car. He found one easily enough, a little kit with jumper cables, some goo that filled up flat tires, a jack, and some other paraphernalia. He schlepped it all to the cash register as Tracy looked on, her eyes wide.

"For me?"

"It's either this or buy you a new car." He was tempted to do that, actually, but he doubted she'd accept.

"Oh." A frown creased her forehead, then cleared and she raised herself up on her tiptoes to plant a soft kiss on his cheek. "I think that's the sweetest thing anyone's ever done for me. Thank you."

His heart twisted, and he reminded himself that he was simply protecting her. That was all. His job. "You're welcome."

After he'd paid up, they wandered out of the store. He looked around, needing to shake this flood of emotions and get back on track with his seduction plan. "So, what do you want to do now?" he asked.

She looked amused. "You asked me out, remember? I'm looking to you to provide me with a whole evening's worth of entertainment."

"Well, yeah. But it's still early. What I have planned for tonight will blow your socks off." At the moment, he didn't have anything planned. "But I haven't had any time to come up with something equally fabulous for the afternoon."

She leaned closer, and his body tightened in response to her warmth. "No? Too bad. Guess you'll have to think fast."

"Okay. I've got it. The perfect afternoon's entertainment."

Tilting her head, she looked up at him, one eyebrow cocked. "You do think fast."

He nodded. "It's a little game I like to play called Guess What I'm Thinking."

The corner of her mouth twitched, and he considered leaning down to kiss it.

"What do I get if I guess right?" she asked.

"Anything you want, sweetheart. Anything at all."

"Really?" She looked up at him, one eyebrow cocked.

"Cross my heart."

"I think I like this game." She licked her lips. "*If* I win."

"Don't worry about that. If we decide to play, I think we can safely say the fix is in." In one quick motion, he slipped his arm around her waist and pulled her close.

She gasped, her look of pleased surprise giving him more satisfaction than anything in a long time. "Something I can help you with, mister?"

"Actually, there's something I can help *you* with."

"Oh?" Again, that sexy little twitch at the corner of her mouth. "And what exactly is that?"

"You've got this thing, right here." He traced the corner of her lip with the tip of his index finger, barely grazing her skin. A low moan settled in her throat, and he knew he'd touched a nerve. Not wanting to threaten the moment, he urged her closer, until their hips met and he had to fight the desire to grind against her and lose himself in passion.

"A thing?" she repeated, her voice breathy. With her tongue, she traced the edge of her mouth, until she caught the edge of his finger. "This thing?" she teased.

Almost as if to punish him, she turned her head, then drew his finger into her mouth. The combination of the sweet, wet warmth and the sucking sensation nearly did him in. His body hardened, this woman affecting him stronger and faster than any he'd touched. And he'd touched plenty.

He groaned, resisting the urge to rock against her. Hell, more than that, he was fighting the urge to pull her skirt up and sink himself into her. She might like it—from the way she acted, it was a good bet she'd be as enthusiastic as he was—but outside a mall on a Saturday afternoon was hardly the place for a close encounter. No matter how desperate he was, she deserved better.

Still, pressed together as they were, she undoubtedly knew the reaction she'd caused. And she didn't show the slightest signs of relenting.

Well, as they said, no good deed goes unpunished. And he intended to punish her in the most erotic of ways. Before she could protest, he withdrew his finger and leaned in close. He heard and felt her startled intake of breath as he pressed his lips to the corner of her mouth. "Right here," he murmured. "This little twitch. But I think I can take care of it for you."

"You can?" More breath than voice, her whisper tickled his ear. "How?"

"A unique new therapy. Surprise therapy." And with that, he pressed his mouth hard against hers, taking advantage of her surprise to dip his tongue inside and taste her sweetness. She responded greedily, her arms going automatically around his neck, her mouth opening further to allow him better access.

Rational thought abandoned him. Somewhere, in the thinking part of his mind, he knew he should be rejoicing. He'd set out to seduce this woman, and so far he was right on target. But he didn't care. Not about the mission. Not that she was mortal. Not about anything except losing himself to her.

Oh, yes. Belt or not, this woman had definitely bewitched him.

241

Chapter Twenty

"Mmmm." Even to her own ears, Tracy's low murmur seemed dreamy. She was far gone, and she knew it. "If this is the appetizer, I'm not sure I'll survive the main course."

He pulled back just slightly, but from the look in his eyes, she knew Hale didn't enjoy the increased distance between them any more than she did. "Maybe we should stop. I'd hate for you to fill up before we get to dessert."

"I guess that depends what's for dessert."

"Pure, hot decadence," he whispered, leaning in to kiss the side of her neck.

Closing her eyes, she tilted her head back, giving him better access. "Decadence, huh? You certainly know the way to a woman's heart."

"Sweetheart, that dish is my specialty."

"Yeah, that's pretty much what Deena and Lane said." She spoke the words with a chuckle in her voice, but he seemed to tense anyway, and she wondered if she'd struck a nerve. Presumably, he was afraid she wanted some sort of long-term commitment. An honest fear, she supposed, since that's what most women wanted.

But right now, she didn't. She was having too much fun exploring her growing newfound confidence. Plus, the thought of anything permanent with Hale . . . well, really. She was just flattered he wanted her for now. Even if she had fantasies of something longer-lasting, she knew it wouldn't really happen. Just because he did something nice for her by buying the car kit, didn't mean they were establishing any sort of relationship. He was just being kind. Considering she was just Tracy and he was *Hale*—the object of desire for women all over the world—forever was pretty much out of the question. Wasn't it?

"So, where are we going?"

He stroked her cheek. "I guess you'll just have to wait and see."

Amused, she said, "I can wait. I'm patient." Then, lifting herself on her tiptoes, she whispered in his ear, "How are we going to get there?"

"We're walking."

Walking? In Los Angeles? No one walked in Los Angeles. "We're not near anything. Where are we walking to?"

"The Century Plaza Hotel." He held out his arm for her. "I thought I'd buy you a drink."

Oh, that sounded good. "I can handle a drink."

"Can you handle a walk?"

"Sure."

The hotel was just up the road from the mall, across the street from the twin towers that had housed the pretend offices of Remington Steele years ago. Tracy supposed that if the neighborhood was good enough for Pierce Brosnan, it was good enough for her.

She and Hale strolled in comfortable silence until they hit Century Park East. Feeling devilish, she took his hand.

Not exactly a wanton action, but it made her feel bold and provocative nonetheless. When he squeezed her fingers, it made her feel light-headed.

As they approached the hotel, a doorman opened the ornate glass door, and they walked through into a lobby of tasteful opulence. "You have a room here? I'm impressed."

"Well, tonight I have a room here."

She cocked her head. "Tonight?"

"Tomorrow I'm in a house—*your* house. Remember?"

She laughed. "Right." Then she swallowed as the situation hit home. She was alone with Hale in a four-star hotel. The situation was the ultimate in decadence . . . and was delightful.

He nodded toward the lobby bar. "Why don't you grab us some seats while I check my messages."

She agreed, and quickly headed off in that direction.

Hale arrived at the table she'd procured at the same time the waitress returned. Champagne, please," he said. "Dom. Put it on my room tab."

Tracy started to argue—a bottle of Dom wasn't exactly cheap—but then she managed to keep her mouth shut. If this man wanted to buy her champagne, she was going to let him.

The small, round marble table provided almost no buffer between them, and when she scooted her chair closer, her breath caught as her knee bumped against his. Instinctively, she started to pull away, then felt his hand close over the thin cotton material of her sundress. For a fleeting moment, she wished she'd worn a miniskirt.

His fingers traced a circular pattern on her knee, and she lost herself to the sensation until somewhere in the back of her brain she realized he was talking.

Oh. Words. She squinted, trying to will her mind to listen. "—about being an animal trainer."

Work stuff. Small talk. That was good. She could talk about work on autopilot and still let part of her brain get lost in the wonder of his touch.

"I love it. I told you. I've always loved animals. And I've always loved Hollywood, too. My grandmother was an early film star—Tahlula Tannin." Hale nodded in recognition, and she continued. "Anyway, when my grandmother was older, she starred in a sitcom that had an animal cast. Mel worked for the company that did the training, and I hung out on the set."

"So that's how you met Mel?"

His fingers were still stroking, and it took her a second to realize it had been a question. "What? Oh! Yes, in a roundabout way. I went and worked for a vet for a while, then for another local company that trained animals. Last year, when Mel bought Paws In Production from her boss, she hired me. We'd been friends, but once we started working together, we became even closer."

Stroke, stroke. The man's touch was driving her crazy. She gnawed on her lower lip, fighting the urge to leap over the table and demand more.

"She sounds like a good friend."

"Oh, she is. Once my grandmother died, I pretty much just had Mel."

"You and your grandmother were close?" The stroking stopped, and Tracy mentally breathed a sigh of relief. She tried to get her thoughts to return to a state of semi-normalcy.

"Oh, yeah." She'd tried to describe her relationship with her grandmother before, but never managed to find words adequate. "She raised me, you know. She was Mom and Dad and best friend all rolled into one. She let me get away with murder in some ways even while keeping me on a strict leash in the important ones." She blinked back fresh tears. "Sorry. The whole thing makes me sentimental."

"Don't apologize for loving your family."

The smile she flashed him felt weak, but her whole heart was in it. "My grandmother was wonderful." Leaning sideways from the table, she pointed to her belt, wanting to explain her grandmother's odd gift to this man. "This was hers. I found it recently." She shrugged. "That's why I've been wearing it so much lately."

Instead of looking bored, Hale seemed genuinely interested. "It's beautiful. Antique?"

She nodded. "I should probably frame it. Maybe in a shadow box or something. I'm stupid to wear it; I couldn't bear to lose it. And I guess it must be worth something, since that guy you saved me from wanted it. Maybe it's real gold."

"Your grandmother willed it to you? Interesting legacy."

"Even more interesting since I just found it."

"What do you mean?"

"It was in a box in the attic. All the specific stuff mentioned in her will was inventoried by the lawyers. But this wasn't in the will. I mean, it was, since I inherited everything that didn't go to anyone else. But it wasn't a specific bequest." She frowned, remembering the engraving. "And there was a message, so she definitely meant for me to have it."

Hale's blue eyes were bright as he leaned closer. "A message?"

"Yeah. Like a riddle. Something like, Be careful what you wish for. And it was addressed to me." She shook her head, not intending to get lost in that quagmire again. "Not like my grandmother at all. She was very up-front. Riddles weren't exactly her thing."

"Interesting." He stroked her hand. "Why don't you let me borrow it for a few days? I know some people in the antique business. Maybe they can give you some information about it." He looked deep into her eyes. "And you know you can trust me. I'll take good care of it."

Tracy hesitated. She *was* curious about the belt. If Hale knew someone who could tell her its history, or even what it was worth, it might be a good idea to let him take it.

Her hand slipped to her waist, and her fingers closed over the clasp. But she couldn't bring herself to unfasten the thing.

Odd.

She tried once more. Again, she couldn't bring herself to do it.

"Sorry," she finally said, not quite sure why she was hesitating, but willing to trust her instincts. "I just can't bear to part with it. Its value to me is sentimental, you know." She grinned, feeling a little foolish. "That, and it seems to give me a jolt of confidence. Pop psychology, you know." She shrugged. "Anyway, it's nice of you, but no, thanks. I'd rather keep it close to me. I'd be devastated if it got lost."

He nodded, though he looked a little disappointed he couldn't help. "I understand."

"What I really want is to know the story behind her message, and I don't think you can help me there."

"Probably not," he admitted. "There must have been things about your grandmother's life you weren't aware of."

"I suppose." She munched on a pretzel as she considered the proposition. "When you get right down to it, I guess, everyone has secrets. Don't you think?"

"I know they do."

She leaned closer. "Yeah? Well, what are your secrets?"

"I already told you the biggest one." He grinned. "I'm a superhero."

A laugh escaped her. "Sorry. I forgot."

"Forgot?" His face morphed into an expression of mock-offense. Then he held up an arm and flexed his muscles. "How *could* you forget?"

"Hard to believe, I know."

They laughed together for a moment until his eyes turned serious again. "So, you lost your parents when you were young?"

She nodded. "I barely remember them."

"Me, too." One shoulder moved in a shrug. "My mom. My dad's still around." He took her hand. "It's not easy."

She blinked back a tear, surprising herself. "No, it's not." But she was glad he understood. Somehow it made her feel closer to him.

"It was just you and your grandmother for a while . . . then you and Mel?"

"Pretty much."

"No boyfriends to turn to?"

She met his eyes, but couldn't bear to hold the gaze and ended up looking down to where she was methodically shredding her cocktail napkin. "No. Nothing serious. Well, one. Walter. You know, from the coffee shop. But it didn't last."

"You dumped him."

"Hardly. He quite unceremoniously walked out on me."

"Really? I can't imagine that. But good riddance."

At that, she had to grin. "Yeah, well, even if you don't believe me, I've never exactly been a male-magnet."

"You don't need to be a magnet, Tracy. All you need to find is that one guy."

"Sometimes that's harder than it sounds."

The waitress arrived and poured them each a glass of champagne. Hale held his up in a toast, his eyes soft and warm. "To the successful conclusion of your search."

Although she managed to stay calm and sip her champagne after they clinked glasses, Tracy's mind was going a million miles an hour.

Did he mean good luck concluding her manhunt in the future? Or did he mean now? *Him.* Hale. That he was the conclusion of her search?

She didn't know, and she tried not to let her eager little brain latch onto the second possibility. She had such lousy luck with men. Always jumping to conclusions and getting hurt. First Walter. Then Leon. She stifled a shudder. She wasn't going to make the same mistake with Hale. This was a fling, and that's all it was.

And with a fling she was more than justified in making the first, bold move.

Leaning across the table, she took his free hand. "Thank you for the champagne. And for rescuing me. And for inviting me out tonight. It's been a truly adventurous day."

Above the table, he squeezed her hand. Below the table, his fingers urged the thin material of her dress up, leaving her knee and the top of her thigh exposed. She stifled a gasp as his fingers slipped down, softly grazing the sensitive spot beneath her knee.

"What if I told you the adventure wasn't quite over?" he asked, his voice low and inviting. "Would that be good? Or bad?"

She swallowed, her mouth suddenly dry. He hadn't said so in words, but she knew exactly what kind of adventures he was talking about. And at the moment, she couldn't think of one single thing she wanted more.

"It would be good," she whispered, willing her voice to work. "It would be very, very good."

Hale breathed a sigh of relief.

So far so good. The only question now was how did he parlay seduction into Tracy's agreement to give him the belt? So far, he'd just assumed that getting close to Tracy would be sufficient. Certainly he'd never had any trouble in the past getting what he wanted from women he seduced. Yet, somehow, this was different. Tracy Tannin had a core that he liked, even respected. And that was something new.

249

He still wanted to sleep with her, sure. He wanted that desperately. But the mission wasn't a factor at all. There was a desire he felt, born of more than sexual attraction or devotion to duty. And that realization left him reeling.

On top of that little problem, he also felt a twinge of guilt. The belt meant the world to Tracy, and his job was to take it away. Essentially, to hurt her. His mission called for it, and so he had to do it. But that didn't mean he had to like it.

And there was still work to do. He'd thought they'd made some sort of connection. The way she looked at him, the kiss at the mall—all those things had suggested to him that there was something between them. A bond, as Zephron would call it. But when he'd asked for the belt, she'd turned him down flat. She'd *almost* given it to him—he'd seen the decision in her eyes—but then she'd said no. Which meant he hadn't yet done what he needed to do. He still had to get closer. Which meant it was time to ramp up his seduction efforts.

Tracy took another sip of champagne and leaned closer to him, almost conspiratorially. "So, what kind of adventure? Are you going to take me on some sort of superhero journey?"

"The thought had occurred to me." But, no. He didn't want to perform for Tracy, like he had for other women; didn't want to do tricks. He just wanted her. Her skin against his. Her lips touching his. Their bodies, mingling until he wasn't sure where he ended and she began.

Standing up, he took her hand. He needed to get her in private. And soon. "Come on."

Her eyes widened, but she followed him outside to the valet stand. "Where are we going?" she asked.

"Someplace I think you'll like." He gave the bellman his valet ticket, then ushered Tracy into his Ferrari as soon as it pulled up into the circular drive.

Fortunately, he'd kept his room at the Malibu hotel. Since he hadn't known how long the mission would last— and he *was* still in California—it had seemed silly to cancel it. And though he was now staying at the ritzier and more conveniently located Century Park East hotel, he'd harbored hopes of finishing his mission and returning to enjoy a vacation there.

His Ferrari zipped through traffic and took the curves to Malibu like a dream. Through the entire drive, Tracy just sat there, a grin on her face, as she tried to guess their destination.

"The ocean!" she said as they came over a curve, the deep blue waters of the Pacific coming into view. From the look on her face, he knew he'd made the right decision. "You brought me to the ocean!"

"You said you liked it."

"And you remembered." She reached over, resting her hand on his as he worked the gear shift. "Thank you."

A knot rose in his throat and he told himself that he was doing this for the mission, not for her. But somehow, he didn't quite believe it. Something was building in him—a desire, a happiness, something he couldn't explain.

He pulled up in front of the Malibu hotel and turned the car over to the valet, then led her through the lobby and into the elevator. He hit the button to make the doors close, then he pulled her into his arms.

"Dammit, Tracy. You're driving me crazy." It was a desire he'd never felt so strongly. He wasn't sure what reaction he'd been expecting, but the sound of her delighted laughter wasn't it.

"Really?" she asked.

He couldn't manage a response. Especially when she stepped up next to him, so close she could tell for herself just how crazy she was making him. Her hand slipped down between their bodies, stroking him until Hale thought he'd have to strangle any person who dared join them on the elevator.

"Well, well," she said. "Maybe you are a little crazy."

"I'll show you crazy." In one bold movement, he pressed her back against the paneled wall. She moaned, low in her throat. He moved closer, longing to feel her skin against his. He closed his mouth over hers, the sweetness making him dizzy. "Tracy." He whispered her name, rejoicing when she snuggled closer. The elevator door dinged and opened again.

"What floor are you on?"

His mind went blank. He'd forgotten to hit that button.

Laughing, she pushed him away with the palm of her hands. "We need to get you some oxygen so you can think better."

Normal thought returned as their distance increased. "Fifteen," he said. Then more firmly, "Yeah. Room fifteen-ten."

"So press the button, mister."

He did, stretching his arm around her to reach the control panel. But instead of standing back upright again, he shifted closer and, with the tip of his finger, slipped her hair behind her ear. "Maybe I should just hit the stop button."

"Why?" Her question came out on a single breath, tickling the skin on his neck.

"Elevators can be so very erotic, don't you think?"

Her back was against the paneling, her head tilted up. "I . . . I guess I never thought about it."

Her lips, soft and perfect, were only inches from his, and Hale bent over, wanting to taste perfection.

"Well, you don't need to think," he murmured. "Just let me show you."

Her lips parted in sweet compliance with his silent demand. The palm of his hand caught her waist, pulling her close. Though he was several inches taller, they fit together perfectly.

She squirmed against him, the physical manifestation of her need delighting him, and he cupped her rear, reveling in her excitement even as he silently cursed the fact that they were fully dressed and in a public place.

"Yes," she whispered, her eyes closed.

"Yes, what?"

"Very erotic." She opened her eyes, passion burning in her green irises. "But please, can't we get to your room now?"

He seconded that desire and, fortunately for both of them, the elevator slid to a stop; the doors opened to reveal an empty hallway. Good, since considering how intertwined their bodies were, they'd be giving quite a show to any innocent bystanders.

They stumbled out, and it was all he could do to keep his fingers off the buttons of her sundress.

"Where?" Tracy gasped. The word was more demand than question.

Her eyes met his, and they both started laughing.

"We're pathetic," Tracy said after she caught her breath. "It's like we're in high school or something. Just two completely horny little kids."

"I'd say that about sums it up." Except it was so much more than just lust—at least on Hale's part. He wanted to cherish this woman by making love to her. Oh, he wanted to satisfy himself in the process—that was a given—but when the night was over, he wanted Tracy to realize just how special she was.

"You'd think we could make it to the door before attacking each other," she was saying. There was laughter behind her words, but also a trace of nervousness. Suddenly, he understood. She *did* feel like a girl on a first date. Awkward and unsure. Afraid the guy didn't really like her.

Well, that was one misconception Hale intended to dispense with. And pronto. As they reached his door, he fished in the back pocket of his jeans for his card key. The light came on red. He tried again. Still red.

"Let me try." Her luck wasn't any better.

"Here," he said, taking the card. "Third time's a charm." Only it wasn't. The light was still red. Just as red as his passion for Tracy, and if he didn't get inside that hotel room, they'd both end up arrested for public indecency.

Time for some serious action.

"Should we go back and tell the front desk?" Tracy asked.

"Let me try one more time." Telekinetic skills were standard for Protectors, but manipulating objects he couldn't see was difficult. His only chance was that he'd done this sort of thing before. Slipping the card back in the slot, he let his mind picture the locking mechanism on the inside of the door. With intense concentration, he twisted it, hoping Tracy had no clue as to what he was doing.

"It's still red," she said. "Oh! Wait. It just turned green."

He'd done it. And he pushed the door open before the lock had a chance to fall back into place. "We're in."

Barely had she entered the room when he caught her around the waist, pulling her close as the door shut behind them.

"All alone in your room." Her tone was innocent, but she snuggled closer as she spoke, her hips writhing against his in a motion that was anything but demure. "What have you got in store for me now?"

"I guess you'll just have to wait and see," he said. "But I can promise that you'll enjoy it."

Chapter Twenty-one

Enjoy it? That was the understatement of the year. The mere feel of his body against hers practically sent her into erotic convulsions. Enjoy it? Oh, yeah. She'd definitely enjoy this.

His lips grazed her neck, and Tracy moaned, wanting to concentrate on the feeling, to absorb every little touch and shiver so that she could later recall every moment. But it was impossible; they were moving too fast, were acting too wild, and all she could do was lose herself to the sensation.

"Oh, Hale." She barely recognized the dreamy voice that escaped her lips.

With a gentle hand, he steered her to the French doors on the far side of the room. Opening them, he led her onto the balcony, and she breathed in the fresh sea breeze. The late afternoon sun reflected off the blue water, the foam from the waves dancing in the sun's golden rays. From the fifteenth floor, she had an amazing view, and to her, the ocean seemed to stretch on forever.

Hale couldn't have brought her anyplace more special even if he'd had years to plan.

He'd done this for her, and the realization warmed her. A man who could make her laugh, could fix her car, and could manage the most romantic afternoon imaginable—who would have thought she'd ever be on a date with such a guy? She didn't know what would happen tomorrow, but right now, she intended to enjoy the moment.

His arms closed around her waist, and she leaned back against him.

"Tell me what you want," he whispered.

That was easy. "You. I want you. Please."

"Say pretty please."

Even though her eyes were closed, she could hear the grin in his voice.

"Pretty please." Her voice sounded hoarse. It didn't matter, though. The words worked just as fast as *abracadabra* worked to pull a rabbit out of a hat.

She gasped as he pressed her up against the rail, his lips ravaging hers, and his hands slipped up under her dress. She had no idea how he'd managed to get her skirt up, but he had, and now his fingers danced along the elastic of her panties.

"You're sure?"

"Mmm-hmm." She couldn't manage real words, so she hoped he understood her little groan. He had to, because surely she would die if he did anything as foolish as stop now.

One quick twist of the material, and her panties were history. She wished she'd changed into some of the decadent, lacy pieces still in her shopping bag, but the simple fact was, it didn't matter. Hale certainly didn't care.

For a moment, darkness fell over her, and then she realized he was pulling the dress over her head even as he urged her back from the rail and out of view of the bathers below. The cool air tickled her skin, and she boldly pulled him closer, wanting his warmth, his heat.

Only one foot was on the floor, the other was wrapped around the back of his legs, and she held on tight, wishing they could be closer, one person. She wanted to know him, to know everything about him, but she didn't know how to tell him. And so she simply moaned, hoping he understood.

Bless him, he seemed to understand perfectly. His hands grazed her bare arm, slipping her bra strap down until he'd loosened the cups and revealed the slopes of her breasts. She'd always thought of them as too small, but Hale simply gazed down, then into her eyes.

"Beautiful," he murmured. Dipping down to taste and tease her with his tongue, he laved the swell of her breast.

She tried not to tremble under the intensity of his touch, and only when the bra fell away did she realize that his hands had slipped to her back and unfastened the clasp. She was naked, pressed against the door frame by a fully clothed man at least twice her size. But she didn't feel overwhelmed or embarrassed. Instead, she felt beautiful. Beautiful and special and a dozen other emotions she'd never experienced before.

"Please," she whispered.

"Please what?" His voice teased her ear, sending shivers racing down her spine. "Tell me what you want."

"You. Everything. You."

Her head tilted back as he covered her neck with kisses, his tongue dipping lower and lower in its sensuous assault. And when she was certain that every bone in her body had melted, he picked her up and carried her to the bed, placing her gently in the middle.

"No fair. I'm naked and you're not."

"Not for long," he promised.

She watched, mesmerized, as he peeled off his shirt, then kicked off his shoes. He stripped off his jeans next, revealing rock-hard thighs and evidence of his arousal that was just as solid. When his underwear dropped to the floor, she gasped. She wanted this, true, but somehow knowing he wanted it too—seeing just how much he desired her—made everything more real. More special.

She held out her arms, and before she could even blink, he was there, his burning skin pressed against hers.

"Touch me," he said, guiding her hands to his velvety smooth maleness. She did, reveling in the response of it too her touch, and in the soft noises from the back of his throat.

With Hale, she felt more cherished than she'd ever felt, yet at the same time she felt bolder, in control. Empowered. It was wholly a new experience. She longed for it to last forever.

Wow. They hadn't even reached the main course, and already she was hoping for seconds.

With a low growl, he flipped them both over so that she was straddling him, the sensitive insides of her thighs pressed against his tight, firm waist. His hands were all over her. Stroking, teasing. She arched back as his fingers caressed her breasts, her own hand stroking his taut thigh.

The passion on his face was raw, and a swell of foolish pride rose inside her knowing that she was the cause of such deep emotion. Bending over, she kissed him, bold and possessive, her tongue seeking entrance to his mouth. She wanted to know everything, to explore everything with him, and the sounds he made told her that he'd take her wherever she wanted to go.

"Now," he whispered, the one simple word arousing her even more.

He didn't give her time to respond, just grasped her hips and lifted. She arched back, then cried out as he brought her down, maneuvering his hips up to impale her on him. They moved together, lost in a delicious haze of passion, their bodies slick with sweat despite the coolness of the room.

A frenzy of primitive urges welled inside Tracy, and she pressed against him, seeking a satisfaction that she knew only Hale could bring. She focused on the sensations ripping through her, wishing she could capture the moment as he drew her nearer and nearer to some exquisite pinnacle.

Mentally, she reached out, her mind seeking release as much as her body, and when her climax finally came, its force seemed enough to tear her from his arms. She held on tight, not wanting to ever let go, as waves of pleasure crested over her.

When she could breathe normally again, she curled up next to him, her fingers drawing patterns on his chest as her eyes drifted shut under the lure of sleep.

And as he stroked her back, whispering her name, Tracy knew she'd found her own little slice of heaven.

Tracy snuggled closer in her sleep, and without thinking, Hale tightened his arm around her shoulder, content to just lie there and look at her. They hadn't made it out of the hotel last night, had made love throughout the night, yet he wasn't sated, and it was everything he could do not to wake Tracy up and take her once again. He wanted to lose himself in her over and over, again and ag—

Then he remembered. Protection. They hadn't used any protection. He *never* did that—forgot. Ever. The fear of having a child—worse, of having a half-mortal child—had always kept him vigilant. Hale simply didn't lose himself in the heat of the moment. Not like that. Not like he had with Tracy.

He ran his hands through his hair. Hera help him, with Tracy, he'd completely let go. He made a strangled noise in the back of his throat. He'd lost himself in her. He'd never lost himself to a woman before, but he'd gone over the edge with this one. Willingly. Boldly. Over and over again.

Maybe it was lust. Maybe it was chemistry. Maybe it was those damn pesky pheromones doing their little thing. He didn't know and, frankly, he didn't care. No matter what the cause, the bottom line was the same. The woman had gotten under his skin. He was going to be thinking about her day and night. Wondering what she was thinking. Focusing on her instead of his duty.

It wasn't a situation Hale wanted to be in. It wasn't a situation he could *let* himself be in.

He needed to extricate himself. Needed some distance.

Needed to let her know in no uncertain terms that what they had going here was just sex.

No matter how much he might be craving more.

On the other hand, no matter how much he wanted to untangle himself, he did have to admit his seduction scheme had worked. They'd connected—and he couldn't just walk away. That would jeopardize the mission! Which left him in a bit of a quandary: What in Hades was he going to do now?

For a few more minutes, he let himself enjoy watching her. Her hair fanned across the pillow, framing her face as she drifted in the peace of sleep. A smile touched her lips, and he wondered if she was dreaming of him.

No. No sentiment. Just practicality and the mission. His training. His job. His life as a Protector.

Bracing himself, he woke her up.

Her sleepy smile almost dissolved the steel of his conviction, and he fought the temptation to make love with her again. But he needed some distance if he was going to figure out this mess, and he held fast. "Want some breakfast?"

"No breakfast in bed?" she asked, rolling closer and sliding her hand onto his thigh.

His body tightened in response, and he had to force himself to move away. "The brunch in the café's supposed to be great."

Her brow furrowed, a little v appearing above her nose as she pulled her hand back. She must have recognized the change in him, yet she didn't argue, just nodded and slipped out of bed to throw on the sundress she'd left hanging over the armchair. "Then let's go have breakfast." And that was that. She didn't try to persuade him to remain in bed, to . . .

He reminded himself that this was for the best. Hadn't she told Mel just a few short days ago that all she wanted was a fling?

She had. And that's all Hale had wanted, too. He hadn't wanted the kind of relationship where you wake up in the morning craving the other person, where food becomes secondary. Where *everything* becomes secondary.

But now . . . Now, what he wanted didn't jibe with what he *wanted*. He wanted a fling. Down and dirty sex. A few nights of doing the wild thing with a woman who made him feel like he'd never felt before.

Unfortunately, at the same time, he wanted Tracy. All of her. Forever. And it wasn't something he wanted to want.

She slipped on her shoes then turned to him, her face tight and her eyes confused and sad. The look almost killed him. "I'm ready," she said.

He nodded, fighting the urge to cross the room and pull her into his arms. "Let's go."

They headed down, and when they reached the lobby, her face lit up. She grabbed his arm. "Can you wait here for one second?" she asked, then headed across the room where she embraced a tall, blond man with an aristocratic nose wearing perfectly ironed slacks. Hale hated him on the spot.

The man returned Tracy's smile, his pleasure at seeing her coming through loud and clear, even from across the lobby where Hale was seething.

Their laughter drifted toward him, and Hale seethed some more.

They were flirting. Flirting! The knowledge ate into his stomach like acid, and he cringed, put-off by how much it hurt to see Tracy flirting with another man. She'd said she only wanted a fling, and now he had proof positive that she meant it. Why else would she flirt with another man in front of him?

Well, wonderful. That's what he wanted, too. Hell, that's what he'd intended to remind her. He should be grateful. There was just sex between them. Nothing more. Any bond that was between them was physical—*sexual*. Not emotional. That's what they both wanted. Right? *Right*.

His jaw tightened as he focused on his mission. He'd parlay their intense sexual connection into persuasion, just like he'd been planning. No problem. The mission was perfectly on track. And that, of course, was good.

Even so, he fought a scowl as she headed back his way. What in Hades was wrong with him?

"That was Troy," she said, although he was barely listening. "His grandfather and my grandmother used to star in movies together. I thought he'd moved to London. What a great surprise seeing him again."

"Hmmm." Hale was in no mood to talk about other men, and he kept quiet as he led her into the restaurant.

Some other cover models Hale recognized from shoots were at a corner booth, nibbling on dry toast and sipping Evian. There was probably a shoot going on somewhere around here. Automatically, he held up one hand and gave them a quick wave and a winning smile. A wiry redhead who'd appeared recently on the cover of *Cosmopolitan* winked at him, then stood up to come over.

Hale fought a cringe. He'd reacted out of instinct, waving to the girls, but now he felt a twinge of guilt at showing any sort of interest in other women with Tracy by his side. He quashed the feeling immediately. Tracy didn't care. Why should she? She'd just made it perfectly clear that this was just a fling, so the fact that there might be other women he knew or wanted should mean absolutely nothing to her. They were both free as birds. Just two consenting adults having a good time.

Too bad he could only see having this kind of good time with Tracy. But that was something he intended to get over, and get over quick.

So, it was a good thing that she'd flirted with Troy and he'd waved to the models. He wanted to make it absolutely clear to all concerned—including himself—that he and Tracy weren't an item. They'd spent a fabulous, mind-numbing night together, forged a physical bond like he'd never experienced. But that was it. That was all. Just sex. Done. End of story. And when they got back to the room, they'd have a few repeat performances. Tighten the seduction up a bit. And then he'd ask her for the belt. Voila! Mission accomplished.

The model—Amber or something like that—sashayed over. "Hale, darling." She leaned in, presenting him with an air kiss to each cheek. "Kiss, kiss." He took her hand, determined to be just as free and easy as he'd been for the last thirty-some-odd years of his life. She aimed an invitation in the form of a smile his way, then turned to Tracy and squeezed into the booth next to him, her hip brushing up against his. "Who's your little friend?" she asked.

"Tracy trains the animals on a sitcom I'm doing some work on," he said. Not entirely true, but it was easier than explaining Elmer.

Amber perked up, probably smelling a back door into an acting career. Tracy didn't look nearly as pleased. In fact, she'd gone from looking irritated to downright pissed.

"I just love working with animals," Amber said, turning her full attention Tracy's way.

"Lucky for you," Tracy said, shooting Hale a scathing glare. "I'm sure a lot of the men you work with qualify."

"Oh," Amber said, apparently not hearing the sarcasm. "I suppose a few of them are, but—"

"If you'll excuse me." Before Hale could catch her, Tracy was up and walking toward the restaurant exit.

"Tracy!" he called. But he forced himself to stay put.

She turned back. "Don't get up." Her tight smile lacked any of the warmth of last night. "I'll see you later." Her eyes met those of the model next to him. "I'm just popping back up to *our* room to get something I forgot."

"Men are pigs," Mel said, her voice echoing over the phone line. "That's all there is to it."

Utterly miserable, Tracy nodded. With one hand, she pressed her cell phone against her ear as she crouched in the handicapped stall in the hotel lobby bathroom. "You got that right." She pulled off about five yards of toilet paper and wiped her eyes, then blew her nose.

"Aw, honey. You did say you only wanted a fling."

Tracy sniffled. "But I never told *him* that. And who cares what I said, anyway? Did I sign some pact in blood? Aren't I allowed to change my mind?"

A pause, then. "*Did* you change your mind?"

"No. Yes. I don't know." And she didn't. Being with Hale made her feel lighter—happier—than she'd felt in a long, long time. With him, she didn't feel alone anymore. She tried to explain to Mel, but wasn't sure that the words were working. "At first, I really thought I just wanted a wild night. But little by little . . ." She trailed off with a sigh. "Mel, he brought me to the ocean. I thought . . . I hoped . . ."

"Sounds like you've really fallen for the guy."

Tracy released a groan saturated with misery. "Yeah." She paused. "Or maybe I've just fallen for the fact that he seems to like me. It's not like I've had a long and storied love life." She sighed. "Until recently. The thing is, lately there seem to be a lot of men interested. But as soon as I show any interest in return, these guys start blowing hot and cold. First Leon, now Hale." She cringed, hating the thought that one was anything like the other. But the facts were the facts.

"And he's moving in," she added. "I can't believe I agreed to let him move in. How am I supposed to live under the same roof with him?"

"Well, like you said, it's a big house. You'll probably never even run into each other."

Tracy rolled her eyes. "You're not helping."

"Sorry. Maybe it's not as bad as you think. Maybe he was just being polite. You said he knew that model, right?"

She shrugged, then realized Mel couldn't see her. "Maybe. But, no. You weren't there. I slept with the guy. I'm now qualified to tell who he's flirting with." She pressed her head against the cool metal of the stall. "Oh, Mel. You're right. I've fallen for this guy, even if he is a jerk. What am I going to do?"

"I don't know, kid. I really don't know."

Resigned, Tracy clicked off, then hung out in the stall a little longer. It was a bit weird, sure, but it was the one place she knew she wouldn't run into Hale.

She should head back up to his room and leave him a note, but at the moment, all she really wanted was to go home. She had her purse, so it wasn't like there was anything keeping her here. With that thought, she slipped out of the bathroom, hugged the wall until she got to the main entrance, stepped out into the light, and then headed for the taxi stand.

Five minutes later, she was still waiting for a taxi.

"Sorry, miss," the bellman said. "One should be along shortly."

"You need a ride?"

Twisting around, she looked up to face Hale's cousin. The guy who'd said he was producing the film that needed an animal trainer. He was standing next to her, smiling.

"Oh. Hi. Um . . ." For the life of her, she couldn't remember his name.

"Mordi." He held out a hand. "I'm happy to give you a ride."

His hand closed around hers, warm and strong, but all she could think about was comparing it to Hale's. Tears welled in her eyes and she blinked them back.

"Tracy?" He frowned. "Are you okay?"

Sniffing and blinking, she nodded. "Sorry. It's been a long night, and an even longer morning." She conjured a smile from somewhere. "Yes. Thank you. I'd love a ride."

Finally, a break! Mordi practically leapt for joy as the valet pulled up with his Porsche. He opened the door for Tracy and she slid in, still looking miserable. And damned if he didn't feel sorry for her.

Shaking his head, he walked around to the driver's side, tipped the valet, then headed out. He needed to take advantage of this moment. Clearly she'd had some sort of tiff with Hale—and, when you thought about it, what reasonable-minded woman wouldn't? The guy was way too full of himself where the ladies were concerned.

Mordi grinned. This was his opportunity. His break. This was his moment to prove himself once and for all.

Determined, he shifted gears and headed for the freeway, trying to drive casually. No sense alerting the girl that anything was up.

After a few seconds of silence, he turned to her. "So where are we going?"

"My house, please."

He nodded. Time to start his Oprah-esque routine. Get to know the girl. Get into her heart. Get the belt. Trying out his most charming smile, he turned and closed his hand over hers. "You just relax and enjoy the ride."

Dammit! Hale stormed through his hotel room, searching for Tracy—to no avail. He'd rushed up here to find his hotel card key still didn't work, and she wasn't waiting for him. She'd lied. She'd said she was coming up to the room, but she'd lied.

And now she was somewhere in Los Angeles, completely unprotected.

All because he'd acted like an ass. She'd seen an old friend, and he'd lost touch with reality. She hadn't been flirting; he'd just let his emotions overcome his common sense. He'd been a jerk and, worse, he'd hurt Tracy.

For the first time in his career, he'd screwed up a mission, and damned if he didn't now what to do now. He needed to find Tracy and the belt. He needed to make sure she was safe. To make sure Uncle H and his band of creepy Henchmen didn't get to her. Hell, he needed to hold her in his arms.

Dammit, dammit, dammit!

He was still pacing and cursing when his cell phone rang, the tone announcing that the call was coming in over the Council network.

"Yes?"

"It's Zoë. Where are you?"

"At a hotel."

"Is Tracy with you?"

"She skipped out." He closed his eyes, silently hoping she was simply walking off steam.

Zoë sucked in a loud breath.

"What is it, Zo?"

"Get over here now. I'm at Tracy's house with Lane."

She hung up before he could question her, but from the tone in her voice, he knew better than to argue. Fearing something had happened to Tracy, he started for the door. He was just about to pull it shut behind him when he noticed it—*the belt*. Draped over the armchair in the corner, just where she'd left it last night.

If he took it, would he be risking his powers? He wasn't stealing it, but he was taking it without Tracy's knowledge. Did that count?

At the moment, he wished Aphrodite had written a rule manual. He really didn't have a grasp of this damn thing's tricks. Of course, if Tracy was just in the gift shop, it was a moot point. She would ask for it back. But if she'd had a run-in with a bad guy of the Hieronymous sort . . .

Hale needed to know what was going on before he could make a reasonable decision.

Rushing to the elevator, he was down to the lobby in no time. Of course, just being there didn't exactly do him any good, and he swiveled around, trying to decide where to start his quest.

He settled on the front desk, but no one there remembered seeing Tracy. After trying the restaurant, the bar, and the gift shop, he finally popped his head into the ladies' room. That little endeavor earned him a couple of nasty looks, but no Tracy.

It wasn't until he stepped outside and talked to the bellman that he finally cut a break.

"Cute little thing in a red sundress?" said the lanky grayhaired hotel employee, who was probably pushing sixty. He leaned against the bell stand. "Yes, sir. I remember her coming in with you, and I remember her leaving with that other gentleman." He leaned closer, as if about to engage in some secret divulgence. Either that or he was angling for a tip. "Not a bad-looking guy, but I gotta say, I don't know what she saw in him compared to you." He puffed up his chest. "Now, if she'd left you for me . . ."

Hale handed him a five. "So what did this Lothario look like?"

"Tall. Dark. Held himself sorta regal-like. Had a real polished way of talking." He shrugged. "She seemed to know him, but I wouldn't worry yet, Romeo. Maybe they're just old friends."

"Trust me," Hale said, his stomach churning. "It's time to worry."

Mordi! The name echoed through Hale's mind as he raced back up to his room, bursting through the door at a speed he usually saved for cross-country travel.

Still no Tracy.

But the belt still hung over the armrest of the chair.

He crossed to it, trying to act casual, but feeling a little nervous about approaching the thing when it wasn't around Tracy's waist. As soon as he got close enough, he grazed his fingers over it in the lightest of movements. No lightning bolts, no nothing.

Hmmm. He didn't know the rules, but he had to assume that taking the belt to return it to Tracy wouldn't be a violation.

Besides, as things stood, he didn't have much choice. Mordi had Tracy. Mordi was Hieronymous's son. The next step in the equation was pretty obvious. Once Mordi realized Tracy didn't have the belt with her, he'd come traipsing back here—whether he was working for his father or not.

Which meant Hale could either wait to confront his cousin. Or he could take the belt, keep it away from Mordi and Uncle H, and return it to Tracy just as soon as he got her back.

Because he *did* intend to get her back.

Of course, waiting wasn't really an option. Mordi was no fool. If he'd lured Tracy into his car, then he'd been to the hotel last night. He likely surmised what had happened. And he knew Hale well enough to know Hale wouldn't just sit by and let his uncle abuse a girl he'd been with. He sighed, thinking of the way he'd acted earlier. No, he wouldn't let Hieronymous hurt Tracy—no matter how he himself had hurt her this morning.

Mordi was probably taking Tracy to Uncle H right now. And worse, any minute he'd demand that Hale deliver the belt in trade.

Hale had no intention of delivering anything to Mordi, but Mordi didn't need to know that. And if having the belt gave him that extra insurance in getting Tracy back, then so be it.

His fingers brushed the cool metal, and Hale stifled a cringe. He wasn't stealing this. He was simply taking it into protective custody to return to Tracy as soon as he found her. That's all. Nothing nefarious.

He considered saying the explanation out loud—just to make sure its enchantment was on the same page that he was—but time was wasting. Taking the belt this way was a risk, true. But it was a small one. And for Tracy it was a risk he was willing to take.

Before he could change his mind, he closed his hand around the belt, said a silent apology to Aphrodite, grabbed it up, and waited. Nothing. No lightning bolts. No deep voices from Mount Olympus. No dizzy feelings as he transformed from superhero to mortal.

Well, that was good.

Now for a quick test. He glanced around the room, looking for something to levitate, and finally decided on the pillows on the bed. In his mind, he tested their weight, then

applied the slightest of pressure. Up they sprang. His telekinetic skills were working A-OK.

Another quick test, and he confirmed that his power of
invisibility was working fine, too.

Presumably speed, strength, agility, and all the rest were
functioning as well. Which only left his ability to understand animals. Considering he'd gone and abandoned Elmer for over a day, and the ruckus that would cause, he
almost wished that power *would* disappear—at least temporarily. The ferret was really rather peevish when he felt
abandoned.

But that was something he could worry about later. Right
now, he needed to find out what trouble was brewing at
Tracy's house, and he needed to get there fast. His Ferrari
was fast, but his propulsion cloak was better. Turning invisible, he whipped the cloak around his shoulders and
took off from the balcony.

As the superhero flies, it wasn't very far to Tracy's house.
In under five minutes he'd managed a perfect landing in
her front yard. Not bothering to take off the cloak as he
materialized, he raced to the front door and burst
through—not sure what he was expecting, but hoping it
wasn't the worst. He became visible.

Except for Davy tormenting Elmer with plastic cars on
the entrance hall floor, no one was around to greet him.
Well, damn.

*It's about time you got here! Do you know how long I've
been playing with this kid?* Elmer shrieked. *And playing
trucks? Don't you think I'm a little old for this?*

Hale ignored the ferret. "Zoë? Lane?" His voice echoed
through the silent house. "Where are they?" he asked Elmer
after a second.

*Waiting for you, and leaving poor old Elmer to watch the
kid.*

Despite his fear that something terrible had happened, Hale still had to smile at the thought of the ferret as a reluctant babysitter.

"Unca Hale." Davy toddled over, his arms out to be picked up. Automatically, Hale hoisted the kid, then pushed him back to get a good look at his freshly washed little face.

"Where's your mommy, big guy?"

"Kitcha." One chubby arm pointed to the right, and Hale headed in that direction. Elmer skittered behind them.

Deep in conversation, Zoë and Lane didn't even notice when he walked in.

"It could just be a coincidence," Lane was saying.

"Could be. But I doubt it." Zoë ran her hands through her hair. "I want to know where she is. And whether or not the belt's with her."

"It's not."

At Hale's pronouncement, both women turned to him. Immediately, Lane jumped to her feet and took Davy away.

He nodded, then said, "I've got it."

Zoë blinked. "You've got the belt? How? She gave it to you? Then we're done. It's all ov—"

"No. I *took* it."

All the color drained from Zoë's face. "You what? Are you crazy? You'll be—"

"I'm fine. I didn't *steal* it. I just took it. She left it in my room, and I saw it when you called. I grabbed it." He looked his sister in the eye. "Now tell me what's going on."

His sister and Lane exchanged glances, then Zoë met his eyes. "I think you should follow me."

Chapter Twenty-two

"It's all like this," Zoë said, watching Hale's face as he took in the disaster area that made up Tracy's bedroom. It looked like a gang of marauders had whipped through. Clothes everywhere. Furniture slashed. Glass shattered. "Her room and the attic. All the other rooms."

"The whole house," Lane agreed. "We just got the entrance and the kitchen put back together. And Taylor and Hoop are cleaning the attic with Deena."

Hale looked at both of them in turn, and Zoë noticed the way the color faded from his face as he held on tight to the doorjamb. "When?"

"This morning," Lane said. "We came by to see how Tracy's date with you had gone. The door was open and . . ." She ended with a shrug.

"Hieronymous," Hale said, and he met Zoë's eyes. "Uncle H sent someone to ransack the house."

Zoë nodded. "At least Tracy was with you." She paused. "Uh, until you lost her."

Hale dropped onto the bed and started rubbing his temples.

"You wanna tell me what happened?"

Hale looked decidedly uncomfortable, and Zoë had the feeling that this wasn't about the mission at all. That look was about Tracy and Hale—and a brand new bunch of feelings her brother just didn't want to think about.

She turned to Lane. "Maybe you and Davy should see if the guys need any help."

Lane nodded and took her child away.

As soon as she'd left the room, Hale's eyes met Zoë's. "She left me. She ended up with *him*—Mordi. We need to find her before she agrees to give him the belt."

"But you already have the belt."

Hale nodded. "But she didn't *give* it to me. It's still Tracy's, and she can agree to hand it over to anyone."

Zoe propped a hand on her hip, feeling mildly peeved. "That's it? That's your worry? That Mordi will sweet talk the belt away?"

"Yes, exactly. What else would it be?"

She sighed. "You might fool Lane, big brother. But not me. Since when have you ever been worried about Mordi? About anyone, for that matter. This is more than just the job. Tell me what's really going on inside your head."

On the bed beside Hale, Elmer started chattering, and even though Zoë couldn't understand a word, she knew the tone of a lecture when she heard one.

"Zo." Through the harsh tone of his voice, Hale's concern was coming through loud and clear. "Can't we do this later? We need to find her."

"Zephron's already on it. He's tracking her by satellite. I contacted him right after we talked on the phone." She aimed a gentle look in his direction. "You know there's nothing more we can do."

"We can scour this town. Fly over it. You can look through every roof. I can peer in every window. Hell, Zoë, we can go door to door."

Zoë was amazed by her brother's vehemence. "If she's with Mordi, she could be in Venezuela by now."

He blinked. "Venezuela?"

"Wherever." She waved her hand, frustrated. "The point is, they could be anywhere."

"We can't just sit here not knowing." Hale's voice was frantic.

"Apollo's Apples, Hale. Just tell me." Their eyes met and locked. "Tell me, or I'll tell you."

"What? What will you tell me?"

"That you're in love with her, of course."

Her words started a whole new round of chattering from Elmer, but the only reaction she got from Hale was more rubbing of his temples. Damn her brother. She'd never met anyone more stubborn.

"You might as well admit it. It's as obvious as . . . well . . . as the mess in this room."

But her stubborn, stupid brother didn't admit it. Instead he just looked her in the eye, managing to look sad and annoyed at the same time.

"Mighty Zeus! You're so stubborn. You've got this whole we're-superior-to-mortals thing going too far. Taylor's right. I swear, you might as well join Hieronymous. That's pretty much his party line."

Anger flashed in Hale's eyes, but still he said nothing.

"Well, say something already," she demanded.

At first he didn't say anything, then he looked away. When he glanced back again, the intensity in his eyes made her gasp.

"Why do you think Taylor's not going to leave you?"

Not at all the question she expected, Zoë sank down onto Tracy's now-unstuffed chaise lounge. "I just *know*," she said at last.

"Are you absolutely sure?"

Zoë frowned, trying to read her brother. His whole life he'd made a point of telling her that mortal-Protector relationships didn't work. Mortals leave, he'd say. And why bother with them, anyway, since Protectors were so much better. Sex with them was fine, but a relationship with a mortal was slumming.

She'd always assumed his short-lived flings with mortal women had been the product of his overdeveloped sense of superiority. But now she wondered. Did he dump women before women dumped him? Was his lifestyle a way of staying in control? Of not making the mistake their father made and falling for a mortal woman who'd left at the first sign of any weirdness? Considering their lifestyles, weirdness was certainly a daily occurrence.

"Zoë? I'm right, aren't I? You don't know that Taylor's not leaving. He might leave tomorrow."

She shook her head. "But he won't. I know it in my heart."

"And you think that's enough?"

She looked him in the eye. "Yeah, Hale. I do. You have to have faith in something. Isn't that what love's all about?"

Hale ran his fingers though his hair. "I don't know, Zo. I just don't know." He looked like he wanted to have faith, Zeus help her, he really did. But Zoë knew that a leap like this . . . Leaping off a building was one thing for Hale. Taking a leap that put his heart—and his ego—at risk . . . Well, that was something entirely different.

Zoë met her brother's gaze again, but at last his shoulders slumped. "Oh, Zoë. I can't."

She felt a hitch in her throat. "You're missing out on a lot."

"Maybe. Or maybe I'm just smarter."

The corner of Zoë's mouth turned up at the return of her brother's old bravado. "I have faith in you, though." In one quick step, she was at his side, her lips on his cheek in a soft kiss. "You'll do the right thing."

She stepped back, her heart dancing and full of mischief. "It's about time you grew up, big brother."

Mordi maneuvered his convertible down the Pacific Coast Highway, still unable to believe his luck. The one thing he'd needed more than anything—time alone with Tracy— had just been dumped in his lap. Or, more specifically, the front seat of his Porsche.

Twisting around, he glanced at her. The wind had whipped her long, fine hair into a frenzy, and she had one hand over her head as she tried to hold it in place. With her sunglasses on, he couldn't see her eyes, but from the slump of her shoulders, he knew she wasn't having the best of times.

Considering she'd entered the hotel last night with Hale and left this morning alone, the reason for her bad mood seemed obvious: his cousin and his oh-so-delicate way with women.

Mordi remembered well enough what Tracy had said in the food court. She wanted a man who loved her for herself, no matter who she was. Not exactly an on-point description of Hale. Not by a long shot. He was a one-night kind of guy. Perfect for such a mission as wresting away a belt like Aphrodite's girdle through kisses and complements, but awful for a long-term commitment.

Thinking of the belt, Mordi glanced at the girl's waist, then frowned. Nothing. No belt. Not even the slightest hint of gold. He sighed. Wasn't that just his luck? His first chance to try to sweet-talk the belt away from this girl, and she didn't even have it! Which raised an interesting question:

Had she left it somewhere? Or had Hale succeeded already?

"Thanks for driving me," she said. She turned in her seat and flashed him a genuine, albeit watery, smile. "Sorry I'm such poor company."

"Not at all." Reaching over, he patted her hand, trying to muster a supportive expression. All the magazines said women wanted a man they could talk to. And Tracy had said it, too. Well, by Zeus, he was going to be that man. "Do you want to talk about it?"

There. That sounded very Alan Alda. If he was lucky, by the end of the drive she'd have warmed up to him and spilled her heart. He'd convince her Hale wasn't the man for her, and then ask her out on a date. By tomorrow night, he'd manage to get the belt from her, and Mordi would be the hero du jour.

Her shoulders rose and fell in a dejected little shrug. "There's not a lot to say. I just spent the night with a guy, and I thought it went great—until this morning, when I realized that my idea of great and his idea of great didn't mesh."

"I'm sorry." He frowned, trying to figure out what might have happened. If Hale was trying to get the belt, surely he wouldn't have snubbed the girl. Then again, Mordi had seen the way Hale treated mortals. But the way Hale had been looking at this girl when Mordi had been spying . . .

"I probably shouldn't even be talking to you about it," she said. "You're Zoë's cousin, right?"

He tried out his most debonair smile. "Something wrong with that? You don't like my genes?"

She laughed, and he was glad to put her at ease. "No. I mean, yes." She gave herself a little shake. "I mean, there's nothing wrong with your heritage. It's just that if you're Zoë's cousin, then you're Hale's cousin, too."

"And he's the guy you're talking about?" Mordi made himself look surprised. "Well, that's your problem."

Turning in her seat, she looked at him over the rim of her sunglasses. "You think he's wrong for me?"

Mordi wondered how much hesitation would produce the proper effect. "Not at all." He paused. Two seconds. Three seconds. That seemed about right. "Except . . ."

"What?"

"Nothing."

She sat up straighter. "No. It's okay. Please tell me." She frowned. "Heck, I may have already heard it."

"You mean from Deena and Lane at the mall." He spoke the words without thinking. Immediately, she turned to him, her eyes wide.

"How on earth did you know about that?"

"Excellent question." He scrambled for something reasonable. Hidden cameras? ESP? Certainly he couldn't say he'd been her newfound friend Laddie. "I know Lane," he finally answered. "She and I go way back." Considering their last encounter, when Mordi had been trying to steal her necklace, he doubted Lane would claim him as a friend. But "way back" was more or less accurate. And it would make sense that Zoë's cousin would know Zoë's sister-in-law.

"Oh." Tracy didn't look convinced, but neither did she push the point. "Well, then you know what she thinks about Hale. Is it true?"

He frowned. The girl had jumped straight to the heart of the matter. Which could only mean one thing. She had it bad for his cousin.

Yet as much as Mordi wanted to malign Hale and get in good with Tracy, he couldn't quite bring himself to do it. Frowning, he tapped a finger on the steering wheel. His father wouldn't hesitate. Hieronymous would take this opportunity and run with it.

But if there was one long, hard, painful lesson that Mordi was learning, it was that he simply didn't take after the man. He'd spent his whole life trying, but he'd never quite made it. And when push came to shove, all this annoying *niceness* came out.

Hale might be a womanizer, but unless Mordi had been seeing things, his cousin had been smitten with this mortal. Did he really want to ruin that? Or try to ruin it?

"I guess it's true," she said, clearly taking his silence as concession. "He's a player. A shallow, cold-hearted player."

Mordi made a decision. "Yes and no. The man's got a roving eye, I'll give you that. But unless I'm imagining things, his gaze stopped roving when he met you."

A surprised smile danced on her mouth before fading. "You're just saying that to be nice. How could you possibly know?"

That was a very good question. He'd been disguised in the coffee shop, and he'd been a dog at the mall. When was he supposed to have witnessed this great love affair in bloom?

"Actually, Hale told me." It was an out-and-out lie, but he couldn't think of anything better.

"Really?" Tracy's delight spread across her face, and he decided on the spot that he didn't regret his falsehood.

"Cross my heart."

"So, why did he act like such a jerk this morning?"

"Because my cousin's an idiot." There. *That* wasn't a lie. And it should make up for some of the doozies he'd been telling.

Instead of answering, Tracy just cocked her head. "A little harsh, don't you think?"

"Not at all. The man's nuts about you, and look at how he behaves."

"Yes, but—"

"And you're crazy about him."

She opened her mouth, then shut it again. "That obvious, huh?"

"Pretty apparent."

She scowled.

"Don't fight it. Just go with it." He stifled a cringe. That really *did* sound like Oprah. Who knew method acting would come so easily to him? Scary!

"But Hale was such a jerk."

"Yeah, but you know *why* he was."

"I do?"

"Of course you do. Don't all women?" So far so good. But what was he doing, sabotaging his own plan to salvage his cousin's love life?

She licked her lips, one hand clutching the door handle as Mordi took a curve at sixty miles an hour. "Fear of commitment, you mean? That's what all the women's magazines are always blaming."

Mordi had no personal knowledge—he'd never fallen under the spell of any woman, Protector or mortal—but it sounded good. "Exactly."

"So what should I do?"

"Just be patient."

"Patient?" she repeated, her eyes wide. "Don't do anything? Not exactly the proactive type, are you?"

Actually, he wasn't. But he was becoming more so. And any day now he was going to proactive himself right out of the whole situation with his father. "Just trust me," he said. "You need to be patient, and you need to tell him how you feel. And you need to be willing to fight for it." He paused. "Remember the first bit. With Hale, you'll need all the patience you can get."

She turned in her seat, twisting around to face him, her expression soft. For a moment, she didn't say anything. Then she glanced down at her clasped hands. "Thank you."

Mordi nodded and focused on the road. He might have done his good deed for the year, but he'd also counseled his way out of any chance of getting a date with Tracy. Clearly, his seduction skills needed work. Although his matchmaking skills seemed to be functioning at full capacity. Not exactly the types of job skills that were going to make Dad proud.

Well, maybe he'd still wind up with the belt. Or maybe he wouldn't. Right now, though, he wasn't going to do anything more than deliver Tracy Tannin back to her house—and to Hale.

His fingers tightened around the steering wheel. Damn, he hated being such a softie.

Doing nothing felt worse than doing something stupid, and as Hale paced around the entrance hall of Tracy's house, he knew that any minute now he was going to go do something stupid. He couldn't wait any longer. He couldn't. He knew Mordi had Tracy. He knew Mordi was Hieronymous's flunkie. Ergo, Hieronymous had Tracy. Which meant that Hale ought to just fly to Manhattan, bust into Uncle H's high-tech haven, and rescue her.

"Give it up, man. There's no way to rescue someone when you don't know where they are." Taylor's words filtered through the red-hot haze of his thoughts.

Slowly, Hale turned to face his brother-in-law. "Is it that obvious what I want to do? Or have you been talking with your wife?"

"A little of both."

Since the entrance hall was the only room near the front of the house that had been cleaned, Hale had carried a sofa in and the girls had covered it with a sheet to hide the rips in the upholstery. Aphrodite's girdle was draped over the back of the sofa—Hale didn't want it out of his sight—

and it glittered and gleamed in the afternoon light streaming in through the window.

Hoop had already made himself at home on the couch, and now Taylor dropped down onto it, managing to wake Elmer, who shot him a dirty look, turned three times, and settled back in. Hale ignored all three of them and kept on pacing.

"Besides," Taylor added. "It's obvious you're hot for this girl. Of course you're nervous—"

"I'm not hot for her."

"Bull—" Behind them, Hoop coughed into his palm— an age-old trick—but his sentiments were clear enough.

Oh yeah, Hale, Elmer chittered. *You're hot for Tracy. It's pretty funny, actually. The supercool superhero bowled over by a twenty-something chick who talks with the animals.* He managed a little ferret snicker. *It's perfect.*

Taylor aimed his thumb in Elmer's direction. "What's with the rat?"

Humans. Harrumph.

"The usual. Ignore him."

"So," Hoop said congenially. "If you were hot for this girl, what would you do?"

Hale ran his fingers through his hair, still not quite believing he could be even half seriously thinking about this. Or admitting his feelings to these clowns. But he was. "What would *you* do?"

"Me?" Hoop made a face. "Hell, I don't know. I'm not the poor slob to be asking. I'm no superhero, and I've never been desperate for a woman in my life. Deena pursued me; I just finally gave in."

Taylor and Hale exchanged a glance. Anyone with eyes could see that Hoop was crazy about his girl.

"Uh-huh," Taylor said.

Hoop just shrugged, grinned, and settled a pillow more firmly behind his neck. At the moment, Hale envied him.

He was one man who knew exactly what he wanted—his business and his girl. And they were both safe.

Hale wasn't even ready to admit he wanted Tracy. At least, not out loud. Not long-term. But he did want her safe.

"The first thing you should do," Taylor said, "is admit you love this girl. Zoë'll hound you until you admit it."

"It's not my sister I'm worried about." Hale said, trying to shift the conversation away from his feelings and back to reality. "It's Tracy. Where she is and who she's with." He leaned over and started rummaging through his Council pack.

What are you doing? Elmer asked.

"Getting my Propulsion Cloak." He looked at the ferret, Taylor, and Hoop in turn. "I'm going to New York."

In an instant, Hoop was off the couch and on his feet. "Don't do it, buddy. Zoë's got Zephron and the MLO satellite on this thing. Do you really think any of us would be so calm if we thought there was anything we could be doing?"

"Hoop's right," Taylor added. "They've got Hieronymous's place staked out, and they're using every spy satellite in the atmosphere to try and find your gal. There's nothing you can do. They'll let you know when there is."

"Except if I fly to New York, I'd feel like I'm actually doing something." Hale slammed his fist against the wall, accidentally punching a hole in the Sheetrock.

"Good thing this place already needs some repairs," Hoop said in a deadpan.

"Sorry," Hale said, to no one in particular.

"You destroying the place?" Zoë, Deena, and Lane traipsed in, all three of them covered in dust and a fine layer of sweat. "Lot of thanks that is for us putting your girlfriend's place back together."

Hale scowled at his sister.

"Henchmen," Zoë said, her voice derisive. "They'll destroy anything, even when it's not necessary. At least they only locked Tracy's dog in the closet." Hale noticed that Mistress Betina had scampered in, looking distrustful.

"This wasn't Mordi?" Taylor asked.

"No. For one, he was probably watching Tracy all night. For another, I may have a bad thing to say about Mordi every once in a while, but he's not this stupid—and he doesn't *stink*."

Hale sniffed the air, noticing as he did so that Taylor, Hoop, Deena, and Lane were all doing it, too. "Stink?"

"Trust me," Zoë said, tapping her super-sensitive nose. "There were Henchmen in this house." Her nose wrinkled. "It positively reeks in here."

Hale resumed his pacing—at least he was *moving*—before finally stopping in front of the door. Henchmen. More of them. Destroying Tracy's house. Tracy with Mordi. "Forget it. I've had enough. I'm going to find her."

"Hale . . ." Lane stepped up and closed her hand over his.

"No, I'm going." He couldn't stand the sympathy in her eyes. He had to do something. If Tracy wasn't with Hieronymous, Hale could be back in L.A. within the hour. But sitting around here, waiting for other Protectors to find Tracy . . . He couldn't do it anymore.

"You may not have to," Zoë cried. She'd rushed to the window, and they all turned to look at her. She spun back, her face triumphant, but a little confused. "She's here."

His sister's words cut straight to Hale's heart. "*Here*?"

"Yup. Coming up the drive now."

Hale peered out the window and, sure enough, he saw a Porsche cruising up toward the house. "And Tracy's in there?"

"With Mordi," she agreed. "Yup."

Bless his sister and her eyesight.

And damn Mordi for taking Tracy in the first place.

He went to the door, his hand poised over the doorknob as he waited for just the right moment.

Footsteps.

Closer, then closer.

When he could tell they were right outside the door, he yanked it open, ignoring Tracy's startled expression as he launched himself at Mordichai. He crashed into his cousin and over and over they rolled, until Mordi finally managed to slip out of Hale's grasp and back away. Mordi gasped as he tried to catch his breath.

"What in Hades are you doing?" Mordi yelled, standing up to brush the leaves and twigs from his linen suit.

"What am *I* doing?" Hale spat. "What are you doing with Tracy?"

"Bringing her back to you. What does it look like I'm doing?"

It was a perfectly reasonable response, but Hale wasn't having any of it. His fist was still itching to make contact with Mordi's face, and he lunged forward, intent on that goal.

"Hale, no! Mordi was just driving me home!"

Too late, Tracy's words penetrated his mind. Two other things stopped him from rushing Mordi, though—Zoë's grasp on the back of his jeans, and the fireball Mordi conjured in self-defense.

"Hale!" Tracy's scream broke though the maelstrom in his head, not to mention the flame that engulfed him. Thankfully, Mordi'd had the presence of mind to make it a warning. The flame had been illusory: hot, but harmless.

"I'm okay," he grunted, not thinking. "It's not real fire."

The second the words were out of his mouth, he twisted around, turning to look into Tracy's eyes. They were confused. And no wonder; conjured illusory fireballs weren't exactly normal occurrences in the mortal world. And certainly not in Beverly Hills.

Tracy's hands went to her hips, and one eyebrow raised. "Okay," she finally said. "I give up. What in the name of Heaven is going on?"

Chapter Twenty-three

"Something really weird," Tracy continued, glaring at the seven people, one ferret, and a dog camped out in her entrance hall, "is going on. And I want to know what."

"Sweetheart," Hale said. "Nothing's going on. I think you should just—"

"Don't you sweetheart me!" She turned to face him head on, digging deep for the courage she'd never found with Walter. But Hale meant something to her, and if she had any shot at all in repairing this relationship, she couldn't be a doormat. "Right now, what you think doesn't matter. You gave up that right when you turned cold on me this morning, then sealed your fate when you exchanged kissy-faces with Miss Supermodel."

Zoë aimed a raised eyebrow in her brother's direction. Hale just shrugged and, Tracy was happy to see, looked utterly miserable.

288

She took a deep breath, pleased with herself for sounding calm, and tried not to look around for support. "Now, I want to know what's going on. What's *really* going on."

Zoë and Hale looked at each other, while Deena and another man Tracy presumed to be the blonde's guy, Hoop, did the same. Lane stared at Davy, sleeping in her arms, and Mordi glared at Hale's ferret. Missy just snored on the floor.

"Somebody?" She tapped her foot on the marble flooring. "Hale?"

He didn't quite meet her eyes. "There's nothing going on, sweetheart."

Elmer perked up, chattering away from his perch on the armrest.

"Will you knock it off?" Hale said, turning to the ferret.

"Nothing, huh?" She glanced from him to Elmer.

Hale shrugged, but glared at the ferret.

"You're all in my house, know each other, someone tried to mug me"—she held up two fingers—"twice. And men have started paying attention to me." She pointed at Hale. "And you talk to ferrets. And this one," she added turning to glare at Mordi, "throws fire. Fire! So *what* is going on? Are you all circus performers?"

Again, Zoë and Hale just shrugged. The rest of the crowd remained stone-faced.

"Fine. Don't tell me. I'll guess." It wasn't so difficult to figure out, she supposed. Weird stuff had started happening to her since she'd found her grandmother's belt. She aimed a glance at each of her guests in turn. "This has something to do with Tahlula's belt, doesn't it?"

She had no idea how it possibly could, but that seemed the only reasonable explanation. No. Strike that. There was no *reasonable* explanation. But the belt had to be the link between all this weirdness. Either that, or she was losing it.

289

"How on earth could your a belt have anything to do with men paying attention to you?" Lane asked.

"Or you getting mugged, for that matter," Deena added. "I mean, it's a truly funky-looking belt. You think muggers would want it?"

"Both times they grabbed for it." Tracy responded. "Not my purse. Not me. My waist. For the belt. Somebody wants this thing, and I think I know why."

Neither Hale nor Zoë looked at each other, and Tracy knew she had to be on the right track. She started pacing the room, feeling a bit like Perry Mason at the end of a case. "So, will one of you tell me, or do I have to guess?"

"I vote for guessing," Hale said.

"Me, too," Zoë added, holding hands with a man Tracy presumed was her husband, Taylor.

"Works for me," Deena's man added.

Taylor and Lane both nodded. Mordi just rolled his eyes, crossed his arms over his chest, and sank further into the sofa cushions. Davy twisted in his mother's arms. Elmer rolled over, and Missy didn't wake up.

Tracy closed her eyes and counted to ten. "Fine. I'll guess." All she knew about the belt was that it boosted her confidence, it had a mysterious message from her grandmother . . . and about the time her grandmother had started wearing the belt in publicity photos her popularity had increased exponentially.

Her train of thought was interrupted when she saw the belt in question draped over the sofa. She should have been surprised to see it there—she'd forgotten she'd left it in the hotel room, she'd been so mad—but she wasn't.

Ignoring the seven alert pairs of eyes that followed her as she moved around the room, Tracy headed for the sofa, then twisted the belt between her fingers. She'd thought her confidence when she wore the thing had been a placebo effect. The belt was a crutch that pushed her into her own little confidence zone. That's why everybody she ran into seemed to stumble all over themselves to make her happy.

But that was some pretty darned potent self-confidence she'd had. So potent that now she had to wonder if there wasn't more to it.

Like maybe magic?

Mentally, she rolled her eyes. She felt silly for thinking it, and even sillier saying it out loud, but she really didn't have any other explanation. "Magic," she explained, trying to keep her voice firm and confident, even though she knew these people would brush off her silly comment. After all, a belt couldn't be magic. Could it?

The reactions from her guests weren't exactly as she'd expected. Well, except for Missy and Davy, who slept through the entire thing. Everyone else acted agitated. Elmer ran up the back of the sofa to perch above Hale. Taylor closed his hand over Zoë's, while she and Hale shared another one of their surreptitious glances. Deena grabbed Hoop's knee, Lane let her head flop back against the sofa, and Mordi massaged the bridge of his nose.

"No way," Tracy said. These people were acting like she'd just got it *right*. But she couldn't be right.

Could she?

"Tell her," Zoë said.

"Zo . . ." Hale didn't look too keen about the "tell her" plan.

"Zoë's right," Taylor said. "At this point, you might as well tell her everything."

"Everything?" Tracy asked. She frowned. "Do I need to sit down?"

Lane nodded. "I would if I were you."

"For crying out loud, Hale," Deena yelped. "Do you think you could be a little less abrupt?"

"What?" Tracy squinted at Deena, trying to figure out what she was talking about. Then it occurred to her to turn and follow the line of the blond woman's sight.

Oh, my. All of a sudden her knees went weak. So it was probably fortunate that a chair was floating through the air, making its way toward her. The second it settled behind her, she collapsed onto it, the sound of Missy's frantic barking ringing in her ears.

"Magic," she whispered. "I was right."

"Telekinesis, actually," Hale said. "You know, the ability to move stuff with your mind. Or with my mind, actually." He flashed her that cocky grin she so adored. "You can do a lot of things, but I'm pretty sure you can't do that."

"Yeah," she said, gripping the bottom of her chair so she didn't topple over. "I'm pretty sure, too."

"Don't worry," Taylor said. "You'll get used to it after a while."

"Used to what? And what does this have to do with my belt?"

"Your belt's an artifact," Hale said. He got up and moved to stand behind her. "And there's some rather bad guys who want to get a hold of it." He squeezed her shoulders. "And you."

"And that's why you jumped Mordi?" she asked, turning to squint at Hale's cousin. "Because you think he's one of the bad guys?" He'd been nice to her. But then so had they all. And they were all evidently in this together. Whatever *this* was.

She tilted her head back, staring at Hale's face while she waited for his answer, but he wasn't looking at her. Instead, he was looking at Mordi, the crease in his forehead suggesting he was thinking very hard.

"The jury's still out on that," Hale said at last.

"Hmmm." Tracy wasn't so sure. In her mind, anyone who could and would provide astute advice about her love life was firmly entrenched on the good side. But that wasn't a topic she intended to raise. Not now, anyway.

She turned back to Hale. "So what kind of artifact?"

"Extremely old," he answered. "Thousands of years. And it's been lost. Somehow your grandmother got a hold of it."

"Okaaaay." It wasn't really, but she was willing to go with the flow for now. "And what do *you* have to do with the thing? Are you part of some magical, mystical police unit that retrieves artifacts?" She tilted her head back again to await his response.

Another one of those looks passed between Hale and Zoë.

"Um, guys?" Tracy lifted her hand, waving a bit to get their attention. "I was kidding."

"Maybe you were and maybe you weren't," Deena said.

"You might as well start at the beginning," Zoë said to her brother. "It'll make more sense that way."

Hale gave Tracy's shoulders one last squeeze, then moved in front of her. His touch left an echo on her skin, and she longed to reach up and stroke that part of her shoulder he'd touched, but she managed to stifle the urge. Now wasn't the time for lust. She wasn't entirely sure what it was the time for, but lust was clearly out.

He stood in front of her. Tall, proud. And his face was deadly serious. Whatever the truth was, she was about to hear it.

"I'm a Protector. I guess you'd call me a superhero."

"Oh, come on, guys. You said you were going to tell me the truth." They were going to drag this on all night.

"He's serious, Tracy," Lane said. She nodded toward the chair. "Remember?"

The chair had floated through the air, but one floating chair did not a superhero make.

"Tracy," Hale said. "I'm serious." He looked her deep in the eyes. And then he was gone. *Poof.* Just like that.

Jumping up out of her chair, she gaped, then just stood there shaking her head, feeling a bit like Dorothy in *The Wizard of Oz*—complaining about the way people came and went so quickly.

Pop! He was back. Standing right in front of her, as solid as a rock.

"I really am a superhero." He grinned. "I've been telling you that for days."

"You have," she admitted. And, suddenly, as weird as it seemed, it all fit.

She sank back into her chair. Figures. If she'd thought he was inaccessible as a cover model, now his no-chance-in-hell-of-a-long-term-commitment factor had just increased exponentially. The man was a superhero. A living, breathing superhero. Way, way, way out of her league.

No wonder he'd decided he didn't want her.

Except Mordi seemed to think he did. She licked her lips, a glimmer of hope shining in her mind. She'd seen real desire in his eyes—at least last night. So, maybe there was some hope. Even if it was foolish, couldn't she at least cling to that?

She tilted her head and met his eyes. "A superhero, huh? So are you all superheroes? Have I wandered into the middle of a *Superfriends* cartoon?"

"Not exactly," Hale said. Then he fell silent.

"So how does this superhero thing work? You have powers?"

Hale nodded.

Tracy turned to Lane. "How about you? What powers do you have?"

Lane just shrugged. "Don't look at me. The only power I have is the ability to entertain a five-year-old while cooking spaghetti. It's not much, but occasionally it's useful."

"It's just Zoë and Hale," Hoop said, a grin dancing on his lips. "They're the only superfreaks we got." He started humming the old '80s tune.

Zoë rolled her eyes. "Thanks a lot."

"Uh, hello?" Mordi leaned forward on the couch to glare at Hoop. "What am I? Invisible?"

"No," Hoop said. "That's Hale."

"I take it you're a superhero, too," Tracy asked, turning to Mordi.

"If they are, I am."

Tracy turned to Zoë. "So, if Hale can turn invisible and Mordi can do stuff with fire, what can you do?"

Zoë shrugged. "Not much."

"Yeah, right," Deena said. "Keep an eye on her. If she takes off those glasses, she could tell you what color underwear you're wearing."

"Yes," Zoë said, her voice exasperated. "But I *wouldn't*."

"Yeah, but that's not the point," Deena countered. "She asked what you could do, and you can—"

"I've got it." Tracy held up a hand, then stood up herself, pacing as she tried to harness her new nervous energy. "Wow."

She was still trying to process the information. Frankly, she thought she was doing a darn good job, considering that before this, the last really amazing thing that had been dumped in her lap was Walter walking away four years ago. "I guess you really were telling me the truth."

Hale lifted a shoulder. "Technically. But I didn't want you to know. I thought I could complete my mission without you finding out."

"Your mission. Tell me about that."

"Protect you. Recover the belt."

"A little more detail would be nice. Like, who are you protecting me from, and why do you need to recover a belt my grandmother's had since she was young?"

"I told you. It's an artifact."

Mordi snorted.

"I think your cousin believes there's more," Tracy said.

"It's an artifact that his father wants to get his hands on," Hale added, scowling at Mordi. His cousin just shrugged and flicked a piece of lint off his tailored slacks.

"And you were protecting me because..." Tracy prompted.

"Because my father tends to get what he wants," Mordi put in. "That's just the kind of guy he is."

"I take it he's not one of the good guys?"

"Hieronymous definitely ranks among the bad guys," Hale agreed.

Mordi crossed his arms over his chest and scowled.

"Okay. So you came here to protect me so this Hero-mynus guy—"

"Hieronymous."

"Whatever. So he won't get my grandmother's belt."

"Right."

"Well, why does he want it in the first place? Deena's right. It's not exactly fashionable, and if it's magic, it doesn't seem to be too powerful. I mean, my life's been a bit odd since I found it, but most of that can probably be attributed to all you guys following me around. Well, mostly."

They all exchanged glances, and Tracy sighed. "Enough with the secret looks, okay? Just tell me." She held up a hand. "No, let me guess. It makes the wearer irresistible."

Hale frowned. "Pretty close. Are you familiar at all with mythology?"

Tracy's head was spinning already, but she decided to ignore it. "Some. Why?"

"How about Aphrodite?"

"Sure. Goddess of love. Something about being naked in a giant seashell."

"Well, I'm not sure about the seashell," Hale said, "but she was Zoë's and my great-great-great-and-then-some grandmother."

"Oh." Tracy blinked. "Well, sure she was. I mean, why be superheroes if you can be gods and goddesses."

"Oh," Deena piped in. "That was just their cover story."

Tracy had no idea how to respond to *that*. "Cover story?"

"Yeah. See, those old Greeks weren't really gods and goddesses, they were just this other . . . well . . . race, I guess. And since they could talk to animals—"

Tracy turned to Hale, who nodded.

"—and turn into animals, and see through things, and all sorts of other stuff, we humans all just take them for gods and goddesses." Deena turned to Zoë. "Right?"

"Pretty much."

"The point," Hale said, "is that Aphrodite had a belt. Mythology calls it Aphrodite's girdle, and it's real."

"This belt." Tracy held it up. "So, what's it do?" She faced each of them in turn.

Finally, Mordi spoke. "Like you said. It makes the wearer irresistible to whomever he or she desires. And it makes it so that she gets whatever she wants."

"Oh." Well, that certainly explained a lot. No wonder lamebrain Leon and all those others had been so friendly. "But why would this evil Herobidons guy want it? Is his love life in shambles?"

"On a Protector, it's different," Mordi said.

"It's not a question of who the wearer desires," Hale added. "It's everyone. Everyone—Protectors, mortals, *everyone*—would bend to his will."

"Oh." That sounded pretty bad.

"He wants to take over the world," Deena said. She shot an enigmatic look Mordi's direction. "Zoë had a little tassle with him last year. Not a nice guy. Delusions of grandeur. A real nutcase."

Tracy was confused. "But if y'all are these super dudes, why hasn't he popped in and just taken it? I mean, I appreciate the protection and all, but surely he could have managed to get the belt from me by now."

"He can't steal it," Mordi explained. "The Protector who steals it, loses his powers." He shrugged. "And he can't kill you."

Tracy's knees went weak. That particular possibility hadn't occurred to her. "Uh, why not?"

"If you die wearing the belt, its characteristics die with you. It becomes nothing more than a piece of old junk."

"But those muggers . . ."

"Trying to get it from you," Hale said. "Hieronymous can't steal it, but he can receive stolen property from those minions without losing his powers." He shrugged. "Or, you can give it to someone. But except for those options, there's not a lot Hieronymous can do."

"Oh." She was beginning to feel like her vocabulary had shrunk to that one word. And then, in a flash of inspiration, it all made sense. Turning to Hale, she gnawed on her lower lip, sure she'd realized the truth, though not really wanting to face it. "That's why you're here. Not just to protect me, but to try and get the belt from me. That's why you kept asking about it." Her eyes scanned the room. "And the rest of you, too."

Hale's eyes closed, and when he opened them again, she knew she was right. "Yes. I'm sorry, Tracy. It's my job. I came here hoping to convince you to give me the belt. It needs to be turned over to the Council where it can be safe. Protected from Hieronymous. Not a danger to anybody—least of all you."

His words sunk in as she realized one more horrific implication. She'd been wearing the belt all this time. When he'd helped her with those first muggers. And she'd been wearing it again at the mall. But she hadn't been wearing it this morning; and it was this morning that Hale had turned cold and distant.

With her hand over her mouth, she stifled the urge to be sick. Instead, she took a deep breath. After all, she had to know. "So that's what it was, then." She gestured between the two of them. "You. Me. It was all the belt. Nothing real." She blinked back tears as a cold darkness settled over her. "Nothing real at all." Taking a deep breath, she met his eyes. "I'm right, aren't I? You don't really feel anything for me. It's just the belt. I wanted you, and so you wanted me." She felt so silly, so humiliated.

He didn't say anything, and she saw the way his fingers dug into the armrest of the sofa.

"Hale, please. I need to know the truth."

After an eternity of minutes, he nodded. "I'm sorry, Tracy. I do like you. But anything more than that . . . Well, the belt's magic is pretty damn potent."

Chapter Twenty-four

Hale felt about two inches tall. And not just because Zoë and Lane were shooting him the evil eye. Heck, even Mordi was looking at him like he was a lunatic.

Zoë opened her mouth. "Hale—"

He held up a hand, cutting her off before she could say anything else. "She deserves the truth, Zoë." Tracy did deserve the truth, but that didn't mean he could face it. To save himself, he had to tell her a lie.

His sister took a deep breath, and for a minute, Hale was sure she was going to tell Tracy the truth. But then Zoë pressed her lips tight together, her eyes cold and angry.

Hale quashed another wave of guilt. He'd done what he needed to do. What else could he say? That the belt didn't affect Protectors and that, yes, he was truly infatuated with her?

Why in Hades would he put his heart on the line like that for something that wouldn't—that *couldn't*—last. He

300

and Tracy came from two different worlds. And it was a fact of life that only a rare few mortals could handle the stress that came with being with a Protector. Maybe Tracy was one of the few. Hale didn't know. But it wasn't a risk he intended to take.

Besides, he didn't want to be tied down to anyone, right? Why would he get himself in a position where he would be expected to have a real relationship? He was young. He was good-looking. And he could have his pick of women.

A little voice in the back of his mind pointed out that he'd already picked Tracy, but he shouted the voice into submission.

All in all, a little white lie was best. For him, and for Tracy.

None of which changed the fact that he felt like an absolute heel.

I can't believe you're just going to—

He turned to glare at Elmer, and the little guy clamped his jaw tight. He'd already lectured himself; he didn't need a ferret doing it for him.

When he looked back to Tracy, her lips were tight and colorless. She blinked, her eyes bright with unshed tears, and he fought the urge to take her into his arms and tell her the truth. To recant.

No. He'd done the right thing—was doing the right thing—for himself, and for Tracy. He needed to believe that, needed to hold onto it tight.

"Well," she finally said. "Thank you for telling me."

"Tracy—"

"Don't worry about it." She smiled at him, the smile of a stranger. "It all makes perfect sense." She wiped her palms on her skirt and stood up, then started pacing. "So what now? Elmer's still in the show, right? So I'll be seeing you next week."

"And I'm still moving in," he said.

301

She looked at him as if he had two heads. "Excuse me? I don't think so."

"I'm afraid so." No way was he leaving her on her own. "Unless you want to give me the belt right now, I'm sticking around to protect you. And yes, he's still in the show, which means we need to work on training Elmer."

At his name, Elmer's head popped up. *If you even think about taking me off that show . . . This is my big break, after all!*

"You son of a—" She slammed her palms against the back of her chair. "You dump all this on me, tell me you don't even care for me, then say you're still moving in? I don't think so."

"Maybe we should go work on cleaning the rest of the house," Zoë said. At Tracy's look of surprise she added, "Oh. I guess now would be a good time to tell you that Hieronymous sent some guys to trash this place. But don't worry. We're almost done putting it all back." While Tracy blinked, Zoë stood up, and the whole gang followed, each of them—especially Mordi—looking relieved to escape. Everyone except for Elmer and Missy, who remained put on the sofa and the floor, respectively.

Hale caught the dog's eye, but she just bared her teeth, then turned her big, brown eyes to Tracy. He sighed. So much for any friendship between them.

Now that he was alone with Tracy, it was everything he could do not to go to her, not to put his arms around her and tell her how sorry he was. He hated to see anyone hurting—hated it—and yet he'd just hurt Tracy more than that creep Leon ever had.

"I'm staying, Tracy," he said. "Whether you believe it or not, I do care about you. Just not . . . that way. But I'm not going to let anything happen to you." He looked her in the eye. "Unless, of course, you give me the belt. Then Hieronymous will stop bothering you and I can go."

"You're just like Leon, you know that?" she spat.

Hale cringed, but he didn't argue. At the moment, he felt about as low as that little worm. "If you want me gone, Trace, just give me the belt," he repeated.

"No."

"Then, I'm staying."

"No, you're not. It's my house."

"How are you going to stop me? The police?" He turned invisible, and she gasped. "They'll never find me."

She opened her mouth, but didn't say anything. Instead, a single tear rolled down her cheek.

"Give me the belt and you'll never see me again." He had to force the words out halfheartedly.

A single tear trickled down her cheek. "No. You want to stay? Stay. There's not a damn thing I can do about it. But this is a big house, and I expect you to keep out of my way. But I'm hanging onto the belt. I already told you it means a lot to me. Besides, my whole life I've wanted to be noticed. Now, suddenly I've got television stars and cover models and coffee-shop guys drooling all over me."

"It's dangerous," Hale confided. "Hieronymous will keep sending his minions."

"They can't kill me. You said so yourself."

"They can come pretty damn close."

She licked her lips, and he could tell she was digging in for a fight. "Right now, I'm really not interested in them. Or you, for that matter." She stood up straighter, as if she was gathering courage. "I had a great time with you last night, even if it all was an illusion."

Her tears were falling in earnest now, and he balled his fist against the urge to comfort her. He had to be strong, for them both.

"Maybe that's all I'll ever have," she continued. "An illusion. But if that's the case, then I intend to go out with a bang." She lifted her chin, looking him straight in the eye. "I'm keeping the belt, Hale. And I'm going to use it, too."

"Superheroes?" Mel sat on Tracy's now-repaired bed, her fingers lost in Missy's fur.

"Technically, they're called Protectors. But it seems to be the same difference."

"And the belt is magic."

"Looks that way."

"No wonder your grandmother was so popular."

"I know." Tracy closed her eyes and leaned back against the chaise lounge. She'd covered it with a quilt, but even so, the loose springs poked at her through the ripped material. "She cheated. I can't believe my grandmother actually cheated." She wiped away a single tear. "I always thought her fans loved her for *her*. It never even occurred to me it was all a lie."

"But it wasn't a lie," Mel said, leaning forward. "She quit wearing the belt, right?"

Tracy shrugged. "That's what Hale said."

"And there's no pictures of her wearing it except early on."

"So?"

"So, she really *was* loved. Maybe she just needed something to boost her confidence at the beginning." Her friend smiled at her. "Maybe that's all you needed, too."

"Yeah, well, *my* confidence hasn't been boosted. Quite the opposite, actually." Her chin started to quiver, and she bit down on her lower lip. Tears threatened again. Damn herself for caring so much about what Hale thought!

"You're making a mistake," Mel said.

"About what? About Hale? I don't think so."

"Yes, about Hale. And about not giving the belt back. Haven't you even paid any attention to that inscription your grandmother wrote?"

She'd paid attention, all right. She'd wished for Hale, and look where it had gotten her. "I'm tired of being invisible, Mel. I'm tired of it. And Grandma left me the belt for a reason." She held her head up, reassuring herself as much as Mel. "She left it to me, and I'm going to use it."

Mel just shook her head.

"What?"

"You're in love with the guy. Such a short amount of time, and you're really in love with the guy."

"Hale? Don't be silly," Tracy snapped.

"Lie to him all you want," Mel said, "but don't lie to me. I know the symptoms. And the wound goes too deep to have been inflicted by some guy you just care for a little." She pulled her legs up, sitting cross-legged on the bed. "Yup. You're in love with him."

Tracy opened her mouth to argue, but the words didn't come. How could she argue with the truth? "I really thought he liked me, Mel. And I liked him. And I was so very, very wrong."

"Bullshit."

Tracy wiped away an escaped tear. "Excuse me?"

"You heard me. I said bullshit. Hale *does* like you. Heck, he *loves* you. Belt or no belt, that guy cares about you."

"No. I mean, he told me. Everything was the belt. He likes me, sure, but—"

"Bullsh—"

Tracy held up her hand. "I got the point."

"All I'm saying is that you weren't wearing the belt that first day you told me about with him. Remember? He jump-started your car. He was flirting with you then, you said."

True. But that didn't mean anything. "The guy flirts with women. That's what he does." She remembered the *kiss-kiss* with the model from the hotel. "Believe me. I've seen him in his true form."

305

Mel just sat back and pulled Missy up into her lap. "Mark my words," she said. "He really likes you. I don't know why he won't admit it, but it's true. And if you try hard enough, I think you can get him to admit it out loud."

Tracy wished Mel were right, but knew she wasn't. It didn't matter, though. Hale might not really like her—heck, *no* guy might really like her—but she intended to have what she'd set out for at the beginning of this whole stupid adventure. She was going to charm the socks off as many men as she could. Have flings with whomever she wanted.

If she couldn't have reality, she'd take fantasy. After all, fantasies were the only things that had gotten her through the last twenty-seven years.

Hale hovered around Tracy all day on Monday at the set. Part of her was delighted he was there, but a bigger part of her knew it was only because she was wearing the belt.

He'd said she had power over any man she desired, and she'd tried—oh, how she'd tried—to not want him anymore. But it just wasn't possible. By mid-afternoon, it was beginning to drive her crazy.

"You don't need to be here, you know." She glanced at the ferret perched on his shoulder. "We're not even close to shooting Elmer's scenes."

"Protection, remember?" He glanced pointedly at her waist, then let his gaze trail slowly back up until their eyes met. His were smoldering. She hoped hers were cold and distant, but she had a feeling she wasn't that lucky.

"I'm fine here. It's a closed set. Now, please, go home."

"Not gonna happen. Besides, I need to let Elmer get used to the lights." A devious grin touched his lips. "I'm not just here for you, Tracy. This is about work, too."

"Fine. Whatever." She scowled, determined to get some mileage out of the belt whether he was there or not. "Just don't cramp my style."

She spun away, wishing her hair were thicker and bouncier. What she'd *wanted* to do was flip it over her shoulder in a carefree gesture as she turned back to the craft-services table. What she'd ended up doing was giving herself a crick in her neck. Her hair, of course, just hung there limply.

"Your neck okay?" Gary, the assistant director, moved closer.

"Yeah. I'm fine. Thanks. Just a little crick." She cocked her head, considering. Gary was awfully cute, but Tracy had always assumed he was gay. Now, she wondered if maybe she'd been wrong. Or, maybe, with the belt it didn't matter.

Testing her theory, she inched closer to Gary. Out of the corner of her eye, she saw Hale scowl and cross his arms over his chest. Well, too bad for him. He wanted to hang around? She didn't intend to change her plans just because he was stubborn.

Moving closer, she aimed a smile at Gary. "Actually, it is a little sore. I don't suppose you could . . ." She trailed off, hoping the man got the message.

He did. His face lit up, and suddenly, his hand was on her neck, massaging the sore spot. The massage felt absolutely delicious. Nothing else felt right at all.

"Um, Trace. I've been meaning to ask you. Have you got a date yet to the company picnic?"

Every year, this production company held a picnic at Griffith Park. Through brute force of will, Tracy managed to not look at Hale. "Actually, Gary, I don't."

"Really?" The inflection in his voice skyrocketed, as if she'd just said she truly believed the world was flat. "Well, then, would you care to go with me?"

"Sur—"

"No." Hale stepped forward and slipped his arm around her waist. "Sorry, Gary. She's going with me."

"No, I'm not." She turned back to Gary. "I'm not going with him."

"Yes, you are. And Gary was just leaving. Weren't you, Gary?" Hale pulled himself up to his full six-plus feet. His broad shoulders loomed over the assistant director's five-foot-eight, thin frame. All in all, Gary didn't stand a chance.

"Um, yeah," Gary said, already taking a step backward.

A moment later, as Gary hightailed it out of there, Tracy whipped around to face Hale, her face burning with anger. "What the hell do you think you're doing?"

"My job."

"Your job?" She put her hands on her hips and waited for an explanation.

"Yes. My job. Protecting you."

"From Gary. From sweet Gary who wouldn't hurt a fly."

Hale just shrugged. "I call 'em as I see 'em."

"Uh-huh. Let's set up some rules, okay, Superstud? Rule number one. You can protect me from muggers and evil superheroes. Fine. I've got no problem with that. But don't protect me from dates. That's not your job."

"He didn't really want to go out with you."

"Yeah?" She cocked her head. "How do you know?"

His hand slipped around her waist, and she fought a shiver. She backed away, needing to break contact.

"The belt, Tracy. Remember? He asked you out because of the belt."

Even though he was right—hell, she'd orchestrated it—a fresh wave of anger and hurt washed over her. "And that's all it'll ever be, won't it? Because why should anyone notice me otherwise? That's what you're saying, isn't it?"

He flinched, as if she'd slapped him, but didn't say anything.

"Well? Isn't it? I mean, *you* certainly wouldn't have fallen for me if I hadn't put you under some spell." Tears were rolling down her cheeks, but she didn't bother to wipe them away. "That's all I'm ever going to have, Hale. So, dammit, leave me alone and let me have it."

"Tracy . . ." He reached out to her, his voice soft and warm, and she had to fight the urge to run into his arms and bury her face against his chest. But he didn't really care. Not really. Everything was an illusion, him most of all.

"Ms. Tannin." It was a new voice. She wiped her eyes and turned around in time to see Burke heading toward her. "There you are, Tracy."

"Hi, Burke. Are you ready for the horses?"

"No, no. Not for a few more hours." He draped his arm around her shoulder and pulled her aside. "I wanted to talk about your career."

She frowned. "My career?"

"I've been watching you and, frankly, I think you're the backbone behind Paws In Production."

"Well, no . . ." She scowled. "It's Mel's company. She runs everything."

"Ridiculous. You're perfectly capable. And I want you on my team. Permanently."

The man was talking nonsense. "I'm not sure I'm following."

"This production company does plenty of work with animals. There's absolutely no sense in engaging the services of an outside trainer for every show. What I propose is that you give Mel your resignation, and come work for me."

"But, but . . ." This was a nightmare. Just the other day, she'd wished for him to like her work, sure. But not at Mel's expense. "But the animals are all Mel's."

Sadly, that was the best argument she could come up with on the spur of the moment.

"We'll buy more. You'll have a budget. Quite a hefty one, too."

"But Mel's worked so hard for you."

"*You've* worked hard for me." He patted her on the arm. "Just think about it, okay?"

He left before she could argue anymore. She turned back to face Hale, sure she looked as baffled as she felt. "What the heck is going on?" she asked.

"He loves you. Why wouldn't he? You're wearing the belt."

"Yes, but it's supposed to be about me. It's not supposed to hurt my friends."

He didn't look particularly sympathetic. "You know what they say . . ." He trailed off, not finishing the sentence.

He didn't need to. She knew what he was thinking. She'd been thinking it herself. Her grandmother's words, coming back to haunt her. *Be careful what you wish for.* She sighed. Wasn't that the truth? Right then, all she really wanted was Hale—and look at all the trouble *that* wish had caused her.

Would you leave? You're making the girl nervous.

"I'm not going anywhere," Hale said.

Tracy peered at Elmer. "What's he saying?"

"He wants me to leave." Shooting had ended for the day, and they were in Mrs. Dolittle's living room. Tracy was working with Elmer to teach him all the various commands he'd need to know for his Hollywood debut.

"That makes two of us."

He frowned, hating the way he cringed inside upon hearing that she didn't want him there. Not that she should want him around after the way he'd behaved.

He shrugged. "I'm staying."

She matched his shrug. "Suit yourself." She turned to Elmer, flashing the little guy the very smile Hale had hoped she'd turn on him. "Okay, Elmer, it's really easy. I tap my fingers like this"—she tapped two fingers on the tabletop—"and you climb up Leon's sleeve."

She tapped, and Elmer climbed up Hale, who was standing in for the obroxions actor.

When he reached Hale's shoulder, Tracy applauded, smiling. "I've got to say, it's going to be a pleasure watching Elmer scale Leon. He doesn't like ferrets."

"Speaking of Leon," Hale said. "I haven't seen him around you."

Tracy blushed. "Yes, well. I'm pretty much over him."

"Good."

She didn't answer, but her cheeks flushed. She nodded toward Elmer, clearly trying to steer the conversation away from who she liked and who she didn't. "Working with Elmer is going to make me look like the world's best trainer."

"One of the benefits of working with Protector-bred animals."

Protector-bred? Excuse me? I don't think all of the animals affiliated with the Council would do nearly as good a job, thank you very much!

"Now what's he saying?"

"He's saying it's not his relationship with us Protectors, but his innate acting skills."

She laughed, apparently forgetting that she was mad at him, then turned to scratch Elmer under the chin. "In this case, I think he's absolutely right."

Elmer sighed, his face reflecting pure ferret heaven. *I love this woman. You should marry this woman.*

"*Now* what's he saying?"

"That your scratching is perfect," Hale lied.

"Well, good." After a few more scratches, Elmer climbed down.

What now, sugar?

"He's ready for the next trick, I guess?"

Hale nodded, and they started the routine all over again. Tracy showed Elmer each of the calls and signals she used

311

to get the other animals to behave in a certain way.

"Stupid ferret tricks," Hale said, after a few minutes, delighted when she laughed at his lame joke. Elmer looked miffed.

"Pretty much." She shot Hale a genuine smile. "I think he's ready. So long as you're there, he should do just fine. If he has any questions, you can translate. We'll just have to make sure it's not obvious."

Knowing he was taking a risk, he took her hand. "Sweetheart, I plan on being there the whole time."

Instead of pulling away, she met his eyes, and he saw longing burning there. Along with a hurt that he knew he'd caused.

"Right there to protect me."

When he nodded, she pulled her hand away. It slipped away from his like silk across his skin.

"That's what I figured," she said.

After a second, she stood up, then planted a little kiss on Elmer's furry forehead. "I'm heading back to the trailer. Good night Elmer." A hesitant smile touched her lips as she nodded in his direction. "Night, Hale."

And then she was gone, leaving Hale alone on the set with Elmer.

You're blowing it big-time, buddy.

Hale ignored the ferret. His head knew exactly what he was doing. It was his heart that kept trying to make him mess up. And Hale knew better than to trust his heart.

Chapter Twenty-five

Hale tossed and turned in bed and finally gave up. He needed to walk, needed to do something to get her out of his system.

Cracking his door, he peered out into the hall. No one. Not that he was expecting anyone; Tracy was probably sleeping like a baby. After all, he was the one feeling guilty.

He was just heading toward the stairs when he heard her, moving through the hall below him. Instantly he dematerialized.

What he should do was go back into his room, shut the door, and leave her alone. Following her while he was invisible was rude and inconsiderate. Not as rude as what he'd done the *last* time he'd turned invisible around her—thank Heavens she hadn't figured *that* out—but still definitely not high on the politeness scale.

Unfortunately, what was right was warring with what he wanted. Oh, at the moment how he wanted Tracy! Barring

313

the real thing, however, he'd settle for another look at her. Besides, he was already drowning in guilt. A tiny bit more wouldn't make a difference.

Knowing it wasn't the best justification, but lacking anything better, he headed toward the stairs, ready to follow wherever Tracy might lead.

The intense quiet of the house had been grating on Tracy's nerves, keeping her from sleep. She wished for the sound of a television, a washing machine, a marching band. Anything to keep her from her thoughts.

As it was, she'd tossed and turned for hours thinking about Hale sleeping so close under the same roof.

How could *he* sleep?

She stifled a snort. That was easy. He could sleep because he didn't care. She was the one who cared and, apparently, caring translated into insomnia. Figuring she had only three options—lie in bed and fantasize about Hale, get up and drive to the ocean, or get up and eat—she'd finally pulled herself up off the bed and padded down the stairs to the kitchen. At three o'clock in the morning, a drive to the ocean would be foolhardy—no matter how much she craved the soothing sound of the surf and the delicious feel of the waves breaking across her toes. Since the beach was out of the question, she settled on the next best thing: milk, cookies, and the warm familiarity of the kitchen.

More than anything, she didn't want to be alone in bed with her fantasies of Hale. Just thinking about him conjured his scent, and she breathed deep, unsure if she was imagining him, or if in only a few short hours his musky cologne had already permeated her halls. She hoped for the latter. There was something comforting about sensing he was there with each breath she took. Even if Hale wasn't permanent, she wanted his memory to be.

A renegade tear trailed down her cheek, and she wiped it away.

Mel had said he loved her, but how could that be true? He'd made it clear his attention was just because of the belt. *The belt.* It wasn't her. And how could she argue with her past failures?

In her mind, she went over all the times she'd been wearing the belt. When they'd gone out for coffee. When . . .

She frowned. When they'd made love, she hadn't been wearing the belt. She'd taken it off and draped it over the chair. That first time, too. Mel was right. He *had* been flirting. And that was before she'd even pulled it out of her grandmother's box again and decided to wear it.

And taking her to the ocean and buying her the car kit— those weren't lust things. Or even something he'd had to do to keep her safe. No; he'd been sweet. Caring. Even romantic.

Frowning, she moved to the stove, trying to get her mind around what common sense was telling her. As she walked, something brushed against her cheek. She whipped around. Nothing. She shivered, not feeling alone at all, but also not feeling scared.

Just the opposite, actually. In fact, she felt cherished. How?

"Hale?" She peered around the kitchen, looking for some sign that he was there, invisible, and watching her. Nothing. No sounds of breathing. No ghostly glimmers. No telltale reflections in the teakettle. Nothing.

Suddenly, she remembered that night in her room. She'd seen him in the mirror, and she'd assumed he was a fantasy. But no dream lover had ever been that sweet, that perfect.

No, he'd wanted her even then, and he'd been overwhelmed enough to come to her and play the role she'd already had going in her head.

The logical part of her brain told her she should be furious. He'd been spying, and he'd taken advantage. But the rest of her—the part that loved him incontestably and was hopeful he loved her—only felt flattered. He'd made her feel special without her even knowing he was there. How many people would do that? And obviously he couldn't have found his own release. It had all been about her.

Unfortunately, he didn't seem to be here now, and no amount of hoping and wishing would make him appear. Which made sense, really. After all, it was three in the morning. He was surely sound asleep in his room. She was the neurotic nutcase who couldn't sleep.

No, Hale wasn't in the room, but that didn't mean that he wasn't here with her. She'd awakened for a reason. Her subconscious had a message for her, and it was time she listened to what it was saying. Heck, to what Mel had been saying. *Hale did love her.* She just had to believe it.

She let the thought in, and all of a sudden she was sure of it. Just like she knew her own name. Just like she knew that she loved him. Truly. Perfectly. Magically. She knew it simply from the way he looked at her, the way he touched her. No enchantment could do that. Especially when, if what he told her about the belt was true, a good chunk of the time he hadn't even been enchanted around her.

No, the belt wasn't anything except an excuse.

Which raised an interesting question. Why had he lied to her?

Because you're you, and Hale's Hale. He probably just couldn't see himself with her. Heck, he was probably astounded with himself for falling for a girl like her. And he'd latched onto the belt as the easiest escape route.

Which meant that even though he wanted her, he didn't *want* her.

Well, wasn't that the story of her life?

Losing her appetite, Tracy turned off the fire under her kettle and headed back to bed. Even a man who loved her didn't want her. What kind of odds did that leave for her love life once Hale was out of it?

And for that matter, did she really care? She wanted Hale, no one else. That's when she decided she didn't intend to give up without a fight.

She didn't have a plan, but as she slipped back into her room and crawled back under her covers, she came up with the next best thing: Zoë. In the morning, she'd talk to Zoë. If anyone knew how to get Hale to open up, surely his sister would.

As Tracy drifted off to sleep, she opened her eyes just long enough to gaze into her mirror. There, on the chaise lounge, she imagined that she saw Hale watching her. Protecting her. She didn't know if it was a dream or reality, but at the moment, either was enough.

A smile touched her lips and she snuggled deeper into her pillow, sure that he really did love her. She just had to teach him to act like it.

"You have failed me yet again." Hieronymous paced in front of his windows, gazing down at the pathetic mortals wandering back and forth on the street below.

"Yes, Sir. I'm sorry, Sir."

Hieronymous whipped around, not liking the hint of uppity-ness in his son's voice. "Do you think this is funny? How often do you think an opportunity like this comes along? That belt would provide me with a chance—a real chance—to gather my minions and overthrow the Council."

"I know that, sir." The color had drained from Mordichai's face. Good. His son should be nervous. "I am sorry."

Striding toward Mordi, Hieronymous tested a smile. "Sorry isn't sufficient, son." He wanted to strangle the boy, but he didn't. He needed Mordi. If not for this mission, then in the future. Mordi was in with the Council, and that made him a valuable asset. "I need to know that you are still with me." He pressed his hand against his son's shoulder. "That we're still a team."

"Or course, Sir."

Mordi didn't meet his eyes, and so Hieronymous slipped a finger under the boy's chin and tipped his head up.

"What's that? I don't think I quite heard you."

This time, Mordi met his gaze head-on, his green eyes blazing. "I said, of course I'm still with you, Sir. You're my father. Where else would I be?"

"Where else indeed?" With the answer he wanted in hand, Hieronymous backed off, his silk cloak fluttering behind him. "I'm glad to hear that, *son*. I was rather concerned when my sources informed me that you had the woman in your grips . . . and yet I don't have the belt in my hand."

"She didn't have the belt with her. I didn't have any way of finding out where it was. I made an attempt, but circumstances—"

"I am not interested in circumstances. I am interested in results." He drummed his fingers on his desk, the steady rhythm calming his nerves.

"Yes, Sir."

"I hope I am making myself clear."

"Of course, Sir."

"Good. Then we're agreed. You will return to Los Angeles. You will get the girl. She will be wearing the belt. You will bring the girl to the new location where Clyde and I will meet you to persuade the girl to relinquish it." He looked Mordichai in the eye, hoping for some sign of the strength he knew must flow in the boy's blood. Seeing an inkling of backbone, he nodded, pleased.

"You will do this," he said, turning back to the window and the parasitic mortals scurrying below, "or the next talk we have will not be nearly this pleasant."

"He's been out there all morning." Tracy stood at the kitchen window, nodding toward the far side of the yard. Fortunately, she had enough property that no one could see in from the street, because what they would see would surely send the tabloid photographers running.

"He's actually doing yard work?" Zoë asked.

"And at the speed of light. He's already completely re-landscaped the west side of the house—and I'm talking replanting trees and laying down granite pathways—and now he's starting over here."

Lane peered toward the window. "What exactly is he doing?"

"I'm not sure," Tracy said. "I think he's installing a koi pond. At any rate, it's pretty amazing."

"Not as amazing as you think," Zoë said, a smile touching her lips.

They headed back to the kitchen table. "What do you mean?"

Zoë shook her head. "Just that he cares about you. And that this is his warped but sincere way of showing it."

Tracy nodded. *Now or never.* "Actually, that's kind of why I asked you to come over this morning."

"I was wondering. Aren't you supposed to be at work?"

"No scenes with the animals today, so it's a freebie." She nodded toward Elmer, who was sacked out in the candy dish on the kitchen table. "I'm supposed to be rehearsing him. Instead, I'm still angsting about your brother."

"He has that effect on people."

"Should I leave?" Lane asked.

Tracy shook her head. The more people who could give her insight into Hale's psyche, the better.

Speaking of people, the doorbell rang, then they heard the door open. Tracy aimed a shrug in Zoë and Lane's direction. "The more the merrier, right?"

"Hey, girl? You in here?"

"In the kitchen, Mel."

About two seconds later, Tracy's boss appeared, hauling Penelope in an animal kennel with one hand, a box of donuts tucked under her other arm. "I have a meeting with some Disney folks this afternoon and Chris called in sick. I can't leave the expectant mom all alone."

Tracy nodded at her one empty chair. "No problem. Do you have time to hang out? We're dishing about my love life."

Mel sat down, plunking Penelope's kennel on the floor next to her. Elmer immediately perked up, his little nose twitching. After a second, he crawled to the edge of the table, peered over, and then hopped down onto the kennel. In a few seconds, the two ferrets were chattering away.

"Great. Hale's ferret's got a better handle on his personal life than I do."

"Hon," Mel said. "Everyone has a better handle on their personal life than you."

Tracy scowled at her, but didn't argue. "Okay," she agreed deciding to just take the plunge. "Here's the thing." She took a deep breath. "I've decided Hale really loves me."

"I told you," Mel said.

"Yeah, well, maybe the belt's affecting him a little bit, but it can't be affecting him as much as he thinks, because there've been at least two occasions where I wasn't wearing it that . . ." She pressed her lips together. "I was thinking about it last night. Unless there's some leftover enchantment—"

"There's not," Zoë interrupted.

Tracy blinked at her. "What?"

"There's no leftover enchantment. There's not even any enchantment in the first place."

"But . . . ? Of course there is. Henchmen, remember? Magic belt. Aphrodite. That's why you guys are here."

Zoë and Lane exchanged glances, then Lane nodded.

"Worn by a mortal, the belt has no power over a Protector," Zoë said.

"Oh." The words sunk in. "Oh!" But if the belt didn't affect Hale, then . . . She scowled. "Does Hale know that?"

Zoë nodded. "He knows."

"And he told me he was enchanted anyway. I knew it. He loves me and just won't admit it. Why?"

Lane spoke up. "The thing is, Hale's got mortal issues."

Zoë nodded. "He does. It's true."

"He's a hotshot Protector, so he thinks he's better than we are. Once he makes friends with you, he's fabulous. But getting there." Her eyes widened. "Jeez. It's torture."

"Is that it?" Tracy asked. "He's got a superiority complex?"

"Not exactly," Zoë answered. She turned to Lane. "There's a little of that, I'm sure, but mostly I think it's a defense mechanism." She shrugged. "We don't talk about it a whole lot, but if I had to play Dr. Freud, I'd say he's afraid you're going to leave. He's afraid to get close. He's latched onto this belt thing and he's using it as a crutch."

"He thinks *I'm* going to leave?" Tracy couldn't believe it. "What? He thinks I'm going to do better than a superhero? A gorgeous cover model? A man who makes me laugh and makes me feel safe?" She shook her head. "After years of being with someone like Walter who couldn't keep his eyes in their sockets, suddenly, I'm the one branded with being a quitter?"

"Ironic, huh?" Mel said. "Your biggest neurosis, and the guy you fall for is suffering the same thing."

Tracy tilted her head back. "More than ironic. It's pathetic." She sat up straighter. "No. I wouldn't go anywhere. But why on earth wouldn't Hale? I mean, look at him." She pressed her lips together, the familiar insecurity weighing down on her once again. "Seriously, even if I was to get him to admit he loves me, what's to say he's going to stay? And why would he stay with me?"

Zoë reached over and took her hand. "Because that's what people in love do." Her lip curved up in a gentle smile. "I seem to be having this conversation a lot lately, but sometimes you just have to put your faith in the other person."

"I want to. I really do. But he's been blowing hot and cold. Like Walter. Like Leon."

"Do you really think Hale's like either of them?" Mel asked.

She sighed. "He hasn't acted much better than them . . . But, no. I'm just scared." She looked at each of the women in turn. "If I do confront him, and he does love me, but he doesn't stay . . ." She shrugged, not knowing what else to say.

"At least you'll have tried," Lane said. "You'll have put your heart on the line. You'll have taken a chance."

"When you get right down to it, what more can any of us do?" Zoë asked.

Tracy nodded, trying to absorb it all. She did want him. Oh, how she wanted him. But she didn't want to be hurt. Not again.

Taking a deep breath, she turned to Zoë. "So, why does he think I'll leave?"

"It has to do with my mother." Zoë explained how her mother, Tessa, walked away when she was pregnant. She'd walked the day she found out about Zoë and Hale's father's superpowers.

"And they're not the only mortal-Protector couple with troubles," Zoë continued. "It's hard. I think all the troubles are in relief for Hale because he'd just lost his mom, and he was kind of pinning his hopes on mine when she left." She shrugged. "Anyway, who can ever really tell what's in a guy's head? The point is, he's crazy about you. And you two should be together."

"So what should I do? Confront him?"

Elmer started squeaking, and Mel picked him up, stroking his furry little head.

"Too bad we can't understand him," Zoë said. "He probably knows my brother better than anyone."

Elmer made some more frantic gestures, then started nudging Mel's waist. She shrugged. "Not getting it."

"I am," Tracy said. She leaned over to grab Elmer, then plopped him onto the table. "He's saying I should wear the belt."

The ferret started scurrying around in circles. Not exactly enthusiastic agreement, but close.

"No," Zoë realized. "Not the belt. *A* belt. A duplicate."

Tracy frowned. "A duplicate? How? Why?"

Zoë ignored her. "That's perfect," she agreed, as Elmer bounced up and down. "And I know just where to find one." She stood up, pulling out her cell phone. "I just have to make one quick call."

Chapter Twenty-six

The sun was beginning to set as Hale finished laying the stones around the koi pond. He'd been unable to find the kind of marble he wanted, so he'd flown over to Texas earlier in the day and brought back some granite.

All in all, he was pleased with the way the yard was shaping up. He hoped Tracy was, too. After all, it was the least he could do for her.

Not that he was doing it just for her. Spending twelve hours landscaping her entire yard had been therapeutic for him, as well. Even on no sleep, he'd needed to get out and work with his hands.

Last night, it had taken a supreme act of will to simply sit on her chaise lounge and watch her sleep. He'd longed to curl up next to her. Longed to tell her he'd lied, and that he was sorry.

And that he loved her.

But those weren't words he intended to say. He knew what was best for him. He'd always known. And he also knew to trust his instincts.

It was just hell that, for the first time in his life, his finely honed instincts seemed to be torturing instead of protecting him.

With a sigh, he hauled the last of the tools back inside the gardener's shed. Though the yard had lights, he couldn't stay out here forever. Zoë had come to be with Tracy during the day, but it would still be Hale's job to watch over her at night. No matter how torturous that might be.

Shutting the door behind him, he turned back around, ready to head down the newly laid flagstone path toward the house.

"Hiya, stranger."

Tracy stood in front of him.

"Hey," he said. She didn't look angry. In fact, she looked happy to see him, and the realization pleased him more than he'd anticipated. He waved his hand at the yard. "What do you think?"

She moved closer to him. "I think you've done an amazing job." Her hand reached out, stroking his bare chest. "I'd have to say you're the best landscaper I've ever had."

His pulse beat in his throat. This wasn't what he'd been expecting. She'd been angry—no, *furious*—about his "confession." He'd hurt her. And for a day she'd been avoiding him. So why the sudden seductress routine?

"I want you," she said. She skimmed her hand down her simple sundress, stopping at her waist. The gold of Aphrodite's belt sparkled in the light of the rising moon. "And if this is what I have to do to have you, then so be it."

He swallowed. "Tracy."

325

She pressed a finger over his lips. "Don't argue. There's no point, remember? I'm wearing the belt, so I get what I desire. *Who* I desire. And that's you, Hale."

"It's not real." His voice choked on the lie.

"I don't care. I want you." She slipped tight against him, and automatically he closed his arms around her. "And right now, I'm in a position to get what I want."

He was strong. Zeus knew he was one of the strongest Protectors on the Council, but he was powerless to resist this woman. She'd trapped him in his own lie, and worse, Hera help him, he didn't want to become untangled. This might be the last time he touched her, held her. And he wanted it. Wanted it so bad he could almost feel the desire burning in his veins.

Stumbling backward, he led her to the garden shed, yanking open the door and leading her into the darkened room. The back section held camping equipment, and an old cot was stored there, probably for the estate's former gardener. In no time, Hale had thrown a sleeping bag over the dusty cot; then he grabbed Tracy by the shoulders and threw her down, too.

"You're sure?" he growled. "This is a dangerous game you're playing."

Her eyes were wide, innocent. But more than that, excited. "Quit stalling. I told you what I want. You." In a bold move, she pulled her skirt up, revealing first an enticing bit of thigh, and then an even more enticing view. She'd neglected to wear panties.

Sweet Hera, the woman had set out to drive him insane.

But who was he to argue with one who so clearly had a plan? His jeans seemed to fall away and in an instant, certainly before she could change her mind, he embraced her, already painfully hard and in no mood to wait even a second longer.

"Do you want me?" she whispered, her voice teasing.

He rubbed against her, drawing supreme satisfaction from the way she drew in a breath and arched back, her eyes closed and her pulse throbbing in her neck.

"What do you think?"

"Then what are you waiting for?"

Hale doubted he could have held out any longer anyway, but with her sensuous demand ringing in his ears, he was lost. In one quick thrust, he entered her, losing himself in her hot, wet depths and giving them both what they longed for.

As he took her, she screamed out his name. Not sweet and gentle, their coupling was hot and wild and indescribably satisfying. Her skin burned beneath his, her legs wound around his waist. She cried out, urging him on, throbbing around him as she found her own climax. And when he was spent, when he finally collapsed against her, she pressed gentle kisses against his forehead.

"Tracy," he murmured. "Oh, Tracy." He leaned up, propping himself on his elbow. "Why?"

"Because you love me." Her skin was still flushed—she was the color of a woman who'd been taken to heights of passion and back again—but her face reflected no hesitation. Her words were just a simple statement of fact.

Hale swallowed, unable to face the truth, and certainly unwilling to reveal it.

"We've already been over this. It's the belt." His hands skimmed over her waist, still clothed and bound with the golden accessory.

"It's not the belt, Hale."

"Of course it is."

She sat up, leaning against the bed frame. Her skin glowed pink from lovemaking. "No. I'm saying *this* isn't the belt." She unclasped it and handed it to him. "It's a duplicate."

Standing up, he took it with some trepidation, his hands closing around the gold mesh. Upon inspection, he knew she was right. The back held no inscription from her grandmother.

"What? Why?"

"Don't you think I should be the one asking you that question?" she asked. "Protectors aren't affected by a mortal wearing the belt. I know. I talked with Zoë."

Hale cringed, irritated with his sister, but not surprised. After all, no one else could have gotten Tracy the duplicate so quickly.

"Why did you lie?"

He had no choice but to tell her the truth. With a sigh, he sat back down on the bed. "It seemed easier."

"Easier than what? Than loving me?"

Hera help him, yes. He nodded.

"But you do love me. And I love you." She blinked, releasing a single tear to trail down her check.

"It's not enough, Tracy." He took her hand, hating that he was hurting her, the woman who'd become his friend and lover. "I wish it was."

"Why not?" Her voice was calm, but even so he could hear the underlying anger and frustration. "Because I might leave? I won't." She reached out to grasp his hand, her fingers closing around his, warm and reassuring. "I'm not going anywhere. Not even when you're a pain in the rear like this. I'm staying right here."

"You can't know that. No one can." Though it killed him to do it, he stood up, ripping his fingers free. "I'm sorry, Tracy. I love you. Hera help me, I do. But I can't . . ." He shook his head, turning away, unable to face her. "Zoë was wrong to have told you. It would have been better if you'd never known."

"Better? Or easier for you?" The cot creaked, and he knew she was standing up. "I never thought it was possible."

"What?"

"A cowardly superhero." The door opened, and he fought the urge to turn and look at her. "But that's what you are, Hale. You're a coward."

And with that truth still echoing in the shed she slammed the door. The noise masked the sound of Hale's fist pounding against the wall as he tried to beat the frustration out of his system.

Her tears flowed in earnest now, and Tracy wiped them away with the back of her hand. She'd been so sure her plan would work. She'd thought he would realize she knew his secret, admit he loved her, and then they'd live happily ever after.

So much for fairy tales.

In the real world, apparently, love was just a four-letter word.

She should have known. For her at least, true love had never been an option. She'd foolishly thought that everything had changed with Hale. But now she knew how stupid she was.

Well, that's what she got for falling for a superhero with issues.

Still sniffling, she threaded her way down the darkened path. The bushes and shrubs of Tara Too, beautifully landscaped now, and which had seemed friendly when she'd approached Hale, now seemed ominous and menacing. Shivering despite the warm summer breeze, she rubbed her hands over her bare arms and tried to tell herself she was being silly. A woman scorned, suddenly her whole world turned to black? Shouldn't she be stronger?

Maybe so, but she didn't know how, and at the moment, she wasn't inclined to learn. She wanted Hale, and that's all she wanted. Wanted his love. But it wasn't something she was ever going to get.

At least he'd given her a couple of nice memories.

She ran her hands over the tops of the birds-of-paradise, the sturdy flowers tickling her palms as she tried to decide if she wanted to go back into the house. Mel was long gone. Lane and Zoë, who stayed to give support and protect her, and find out how the plan went, were watching television. Davy was surely asleep. She could join them, of course, but she really wanted to just be alone.

Instead of turning left at the fork in the path, she turned right, following the path that would lead her to the swimming pool. Hale had done himself proud there, too. The once-murky water now glistened in the moonlight, and the algae that had covered the cement sides had been stripped clean.

The whole estate had been transformed into a magical fantasyland. Too bad her one true wish would not come true.

She knew Hale had followed her, to protect her, but that he wouldn't let her know that. She sighed, wishing she could take comfort in his presence, but the hurt was still too fresh.

Taking off her shoes, she dangled her feet in the pool's cool water, wishing it could ease the passion burning in her. Unrequited passion, apparently. A flurry of ripples spread out from where she'd broken the surface and, for some stupid, silly reason, that reminded her of Hale. What he'd done was touch her, and he'd sent ripples shooting through her life. He might leave, but she'd never be the same again.

Something tickled her face, and she reached up to brush whatever it was away, only then realizing she was crying again. No big surprise. For the last couple of days, crying seemed to be her natural state of existence. Heck, she'd probably lost five pounds in water weight alone.

Sniffling, she tried to pull herself together. Sitting in the dark moping couldn't be healthy. She'd tried to win Hale. She'd failed. Now she should go inside, be with her friends, and regroup. Besides, being alone with Hale, knowing he was watching her, only made her sad.

She headed back to the house, determined to pull herself out of her funk. But when she got inside, she couldn't bring herself to join Lane and Zoë. They were watching *The Way We Were,* and somehow, that just didn't fit her mood.

Instead, she called out to let them know she was back, then headed for her bedroom and parked herself in front of the full-length mirror. Her tousled hair and swollen lips didn't exactly make a fashion statement, but she did look like a woman who'd just been made love to.

Sadly, it was probably for the last time.

Behind her, Aphrodite's real belt gleamed from its perch on the chaise lounge, taunting her. Her grandmother's warning had been prescient, and now she picked up the belt and ran her finger over the carefully inscribed words.

"What you wish for," Tracy whispered. All she wished for was for someone to love her. No, not someone. Hale.

But wishes didn't always come true.

Feeling a little silly, she exchanged belts, securing the clasp tight around her waist. She did a little pirouette in front of the mirror.

"Too bad you don't affect Protectors," she said. Considering she'd hit rock bottom, at the moment, she'd be more than willing to use the powers of the belt to make herself irresistible. Cheating, maybe. But she didn't really care. She wanted him, and she'd run out of ideas. The ball had been hit firmly into his court, and he'd refused to return it.

There were times when life truly, truly sucked.

She was just about to succumb to another whopper of a crying jag when there was a tap at the window. She peered at it, but no one was there.

Hale!

Immediately, she raced over and threw up the sash, and was rewarded by a movement in the air—someone climbing in the window.

Missy suddenly appeared around her ankles, a low growl in her throat.

"Hush, little girl," Tracy told the dog. "It's Hale."

"Sorry, it's not." Mordi materialized in front of her. "Prototype invisibility and propulsion cloak. Pretty nifty, huh?"

"Oh." She had no idea what he wanted, but the fact that he'd come in through a window made her more than a little hesitant, and she took a step backward. "Hale's not here, and Zoë's downstairs."

"Actually," Mordi said, "I came to see you."

"I'm not the best company right right now . . ." She trailed off, hoping he'd get the hint and leave.

"Not having the best of days?"

"That's the understatement of the year."

"Hale?"

"How'd you guess?"

"I'm sorry to hear that. I truly hoped the two of you would get this worked out.

But as I said, my cousin can be an idiot about a lot of things."

She nodded. "Unfortunately, he can."

A moment of silence, and then; "I'm sorry, Tracy."

With a little shrug, she tried out a smile. Maybe he really had come to check on her. "It's not your fault."

"No, I'm afraid it is."

Squinting, she looked him in the eyes, then backed further away when she saw something unexpected there. "Mordi? What are you doing?"

"I'm truly, truly sorry. I have to do this. Hera help me, I have to."

The next thing she knew, his hand was over her mouth and his cloak was wrapped around her shoulder. He sprang forward, and—with Missy's frantic barks echoing beneath them—they were off the ground and zooming above Los Angeles.

Tracy never even had time to scream.

Nothing looked wrong, but even so, ice-cold dread settled in Hale's stomach as he walked up the front path to the house. He stepped cautiously over the threshold, only to be met by Missy's excited yapping. The dog raced down the stairs to greet him. He tuned her out, more interested in determining where Tracy was.

He'd followed her through the grounds, watching until she'd entered the house. Once she was safe inside, he'd gone back to work finishing her yard. Had she sneaked out without him or Zoë noticing?

"Tracy?" No answer. He tried again, louder. "Tracy!"

"What's going on?" Zoë's head appeared around the corner from the living room.

"Is Tracy with you?"

"She's in her bedroom." His sister pressed her lips together, looking concerned. "What happened?"

"She found me. And we fought. And now I can't find her."

"Oh, Hale. You need to—"

He held up a hand. Now wasn't the time for lectures. "I don't need to do anything but find her."

"Right. Sorry."

Missy's continued barking broke their silence.

"What's she saying?" Zoë asked.

"I don't know. I wasn't listen—" He closed his eyes, realizing he might have just wasted valuable time, and knelt in front of the fluffball. "Hey, girl. Sorry. What's that you're trying to tell me?"

She yipped and yapped and he struggled to understand her primitive speech, made even more inarticulate by the fact that the dog was more than a little pissed off at being ignored.

Considering the information she had, she had a right to be pissed. "Mordichai," he repeated. He closed his eyes, his heart twisting from a raw fear that pulsed in his veins. "Mordichai took her."

Standing up, he met Zoë's eyes, knowing only one thing for certain. He loved Tracy. With all his heart and soul, he loved her. And he was going to get her back.

Chapter Twenty-seven

"She's a lovely little thing, don't you think?" Hieronymous stroked Tracy's cheek, and the girl flinched, turning her face as if she wanted nothing more than to melt into the damp stone walls to which she was bound.

Mordi grunted in agreement, wishing he could crawl under one of the stones in the floor.

The prison room in this faux castle was simple. A single window high above the Pacific. Four walls, each lined with permanently affixed manacles. One door, laden with heavy, unpickable locks. One chair, upholstered in red velvet, for Hieronymous. And one ratty mattress stretched out on the floor for those instances when Hieronymous's softer side was touched and his prisoner was allowed a bit of shut-eye.

The castle was definitely not *Metropolitan Home* but it was surprisingly functional for having been built as a movie set. Apparently, the movie mogul who'd built the place years ago had a passion for swashbuckler movies. He'd built the thing, filmed a few movies, then converted it to his house and the backlot to his own private playground after his company had gone belly-up.

Hieronymous—or one of his companies, rather—had picked the place up for a song.

Despite having been built by an eccentric millionaire with a love of castles, there were still modern touches. The cameras, for example, that hung in every corner of the room. Eventually, the technophilic Hieronymous intended to wire the entire castle. Right now, only this chamber had been rigged. The alcove beyond the door and the rest of the castle were still technologically challenged.

Mordi fought the urge to unbind Tracy and to rush her out past his father. But that wouldn't help her or him. He had a role, he'd chosen his path, and now he needed to play his part.

"We're so pleased to have you as our first guest," Hieronymous said. He turned to Mordi. "Aren't we, son?"

"Thrilled."

"First guest?" Tracy snapped. "You might want to consider better accommodations before throwing any house parties. And if I were you, I'd seriously consider hiring a decorator."

Hieronymous scowled and took a step back.

Mordi faked a yawn, using his hand to hide his grin. Thank Hera, Tracy's spunk hadn't left her. She'd need it for dealing with his father. And with Clyde.

"Comments like that aren't good for your health." Speak of the devil. Daddy Dearest's number-one minion, Clyde the Creep, stepped into the chamber. "I looked for years to find just the perfect place."

"If you're into creepy-crawlies. Sure. It's perfect."

Clyde took a menacing step toward her, but Hieronymous held up a hand, stopping him. "Clyde, please. There's no need to intimidate our guest." He tilted his head, clearly inspecting her from toes to hair. "For that matter, you must be uncomfortable."

He spoke as if she were simply sitting on an extremely hard chair, rather than being stretched so tight that she balanced on her tiptoes with her wrists far above her head.

"Mordi, there's no reason for Tracy to be bound. She's our guest after all. Let her down."

Mordichai nodded, then slipped the key from his pocket. He moved slowly, as if he wasn't in any hurry to help her out, then started to fumble with the lock at her wrist. "Just stay calm," he whispered, hoping his father couldn't hear him. "Stay calm and it will all be over soon."

If he'd hoped for some sense of connection between them, he was sorely disappointed. The look she aimed at him was scathing, and full of hurt, and once again Mordi cursed the birthright that had led him to this situation.

As soon as she was released, Tracy sank to the floor, then crawled to the mattress and started massaging her wrists. "What do you want with me?" She aimed the question directly at Hieronymous, and Mordi was impressed that she looked him in the eye.

"What do I want? Well, my dear, I think it's obvious. I want the belt."

"I—"

"Come, come. Hale and Zoë have been putting nasty thoughts into your head. There's a bit of a family feud, I'll admit, but I'm really not such a bad guy." He turned to Clyde. "The tray, please."

Clyde passed a silver tray, covered with a silver dome lid. Hieronymous pulled the lid off, revealing a sumptuous turkey dinner, complete with gravy, dressing, and cranberry sauce.

Tracy's eyebrows went up, but she didn't say anything.

He put the tray in her hands. "It's Thanksgiving, my dear. Do what I ask, and you won't believe the blessings that will be heaped upon you."

"In other words, give you the belt, and I'll be treated differently than all the other mortals you're planning to enslave."

"But of course. Concessions can always be made."

She licked her lips, her eyes darting down to the food. "I see. And you want . . ."

"Simply the belt, of course. Such a small thing, really."

"Right." She licked her lips, then nodded at the food. "May I?"

"Certainly, my dear. I didn't bring it in just to torture you."

There wasn't a fork or a knife on the tray, but Tracy didn't hesitate. She reached for the stuffing, got a few fingersful, then lifted it to her mouth. Mordi held his breath, wondering if she was truly going to accept food from his father.

He should have known better, of course. Tracy apparently had the backbone he'd lacked his entire life. In one quick movement, she flipped her hand around, flinging the stuffing onto Hieronymous's face.

"Oops," she said. "Looks like it got away from me."

Mordi's father leapt to his feet, his cloak swirling about him. "That was a stupid thing to do." His words were measured, harsh, and Mordi cringed. He knew that tone.

Tracy managed to hold her own. "What was stupid was kidnapping me. Hale will save me, you know."

"Will he? He'll have to find you first, and don't think that will be an easy chore."

"It doesn't matter. You're not getting the belt."

"We'll see about that." He turned to Clyde. "Confine her again."

Tracy struggled, but in the end, she was no match for Clyde. In no time, he had her pinned to the wall.

338

Hieronymous turned to Mordi. "Open the trapdoor and let Harry in."

Mordi nodded, not wanting to, but helpless to resist his father's command. Bending over, he tugged at the thick metal ring on the floor until the heavy wooden door opened and Harry—Hieronymous's favorite Henchman—popped into the room.

"The belt," Hieronymous said, pointing to Tracy. "Separate the young lady from the belt."

Harry slithered over, his slimy body leaving a wet imprint on the floor. When he reached Tracy, he grasped her around the waist, his tentacles fondling the belt as Tracy struggled uselessly against her bonds. Tears streamed down her face, and Mordi had to force himself to stay put, to not lunge forward and grab the belt the second it fell from Tracy's waist.

Except it wasn't falling. It wasn't budging at all.

"Get . . . the . . . belt." Tight fury laced Hieronymous's voice.

"Can't get. Itsa not coming."

"Fool!" Mordi's father's arm shot out, striking Harry's head with a resounding *squish* and propelling the Henchman out the window. Silence. Then *ker-plop* as his doughy, squid-like body hit the ocean below. Mordi had no idea why Harry hadn't been able to take the belt, but at the moment, it didn't matter. All that mattered was that the belt was still tight around Tracy's waist . . . and Hieronymous was pissed.

Tracy cringed, her eyes darting between Clyde and Hieronymous as she gnawed on her lower lip.

Hieronymous just stood there, staring at Tracy, his face expressionless. Then he smiled, and Mordi went cold. "Apparently I won't be acquiring the belt through one of my Henchmen. Too bad, too. It would have been so much more pleasant for you."

Tracy liked her lips. "What do you mean?"

"It looks like I have only one choice," he said, picking the tray up from the floor. Hieronymous leaned closer, his nose almost touching Tracy's. She managed to hold his gaze, but her deathly pale skin revealed just how scared she was.

"What?" Her question, barely voiced, drifted to Mordi.

"I should think it's obvious. Clearly, I'm going to have to persuade you to give it to me." The leader of the Outcasts's smile turned ice cold, and Mordi shuddered. "I wonder if three or four days without food won't make you more cognizant of the joys of sharing."

Mordi shuddered.

"A castle? South of Santa Monica?" Hale stared at the computer screen, unable to believe what he was seeing. "What in the name of Hades is Clyde doing with a castle?"

They were sitting in Tracy's kitchen working from Hale's laptop, and now Zoë slid her chair over to look around his shoulder and read the e-mail from Zephron aloud. "Council intelligence has determined that Clyde, a known Hieronymous associate and Outcast, recently inspected for the purpose of purchasing an abandoned movie set, including functional castle. Intended use is as yet undetermined." She turned to face Hale. "What intelligence? Who's this from?"

"Does it matter? It's the best lead we have." He stood up, pulling his Council pack off the table. They'd been trying to find Tracy all night, had called Zephron, and this was the first break they'd gotten.

"I'm going with you," Zoë said.

"No. It might be a trap. I want you to wait here. Call Zephron. Let him know I may need backup. And if I don't report back in an hour, you know the drill." He kissed his sister's cheek, then caught her eye. "If something happens to me, you may have to rescue her on your own." He couldn't even bring himself to voice the possibility that something might happen to Tracy.

Zoë put her hand on his arm. "She'll be all right."

"What if she's not? I never even told her I love her." He shook his head. "Well, I did. And then I told her it didn't matter. That it wasn't enough." Closing his eyes, he drew in a strangled breath. "Not enough? Hell, it's everything."

"Don't tell me. Tell her."

"That's my plan."

Within seconds, he'd put on his cloak and was racing down the Pacific Coast Highway. On any normal day, it would be a pleasant flight. Invigorating, even. But today—this morning—all he could think about was Tracy. He'd been a fool. And now his foolishness was coming back to haunt him in the most horrible of ways.

He'd been afraid to care, afraid she'd leave. But deep in his heart, he now believed she wouldn't. And he had for some time, even though he hadn't let himself believe it. She loved him as much as he loved her. He wouldn't go anywhere, so why assume she would?

Because he'd been looking for an excuse, that's why. Any excuse to insulate himself from the very terror he was feeling right now—that the mortal he loved might be taken or harmed or used as bait. But he'd been stupid. Short-sighted. He'd turned Tracy away, and still she wasn't safe. She could never be perfectly safe. Because as long as he loved her, she'd always be vulnerable. And so would his heart.

Together, they could lean on each other.

He wanted many, many years of leaning.

He could only hope that, after being kidnapped by Hi-eronymous and held prisoner in a castle, she wouldn't want to wash her hands of him altogether. After all, she might blame him, blame him for this terrible world he'd brought into her life. Somehow, though, deep in his heart, he knew she wouldn't. No matter what she went through, she loved him. And she'd stay with him, forever. She'd been trying to explain that to him.

He had no idea who the Council's spy on Hieronymous's turf was, but he said a silent thank-you. Without him, Hale might have found Tracy too late.

Of course he hadn't found her yet, but something told him he was on the right track. Especially when the castle came into view. Elegant but dilapidated, it seemed perfectly suited to his uncle Hieronymous.

This *had* to be it. Tracy was in there somewhere. He didn't know where to look, but he'd find her. Considering how many times he'd dressed up as the castle laird for a romance novel, it seemed somehow appropriate that this should be the site of his rescue of Tracy. For, even if he had to comb every square inch from the dungeon to the tower, Hale intended to find her.

The sun was high in the sky, but Tracy couldn't control her shivering. Hunger, terror, and exhaustion were all taking their toll, and she wanted nothing more than to lie down and sleep. But sleep was an impossibility and lying down was even less feasible. She was pinioned upright to a cold, stone wall.

Even now, she couldn't believe she was trapped in some European castle, but that sure seemed to be the situation. Mordi had blindfolded her for the journey, and she could no longer see out the window, so she didn't know where exactly she was, but she'd bet Scotland. Not that it mattered. Wherever she was, she was in trouble.

She'd read more than her share of romance novels set in Scottish castles. Surely one had a scene where the heroine broke free of manacles. But darned if she could think of one.

Not that she'd had any opportunity to try to escape. She'd been kept under constant surveillance by Hieronymous and his minions since she got here.

She still couldn't believe she'd misjudged Mordi. He'd seemed to sincerely want to help her and Hale. Finding out that he was nothing more than a Hieronymous flunkie had certainly been a major letdown.

"Master. Our little problem has arrived."

Little problem? That had to be Hale. Tracy tried hard to keep the smile from her face.

"Don't count your chickens yet, my dear," Hieronymous snapped. "I assure you Clyde is more than capable of ridding the castle of my silly nephew."

Apparently, she hadn't managed to keep that smile under wraps after all.

"I, however, must be running along." Hieronymous reached out and took her hand, then raised it to his lips and kissed the tips of her fingers. Tracy bit back a wave of revulsion as he leaned close and whispered, "You see, I must maintain no connection to this place. If anyone asks, I will simply have been in my Manhattan hideaway, unaware of what my son and Clyde were doing to you poor, defenseless little mortal."

"I'll be more than happy to clue them in."

He laughed, then patted her cheek. "You do that, my dear. And while they might believe you, they won't be able to raise a hand against me. You see, even though your beloved Hale's Council seems to have such love of you mortals, you can't testify against a Protector. Not even against an Outcast. I'm afraid, my dear, that their laws protect me. I'll be back once this situation is . . . handled." He smiled then, and, ridiculously, *Mack the Knife* started running through her head: *And he keeps them, pearly white*.

Dear Lord, she must be hysterical.

She tried to think of something else to say, something to stop him, to keep him there until Hale found her. But there were no words, and soon he disappeared, flying out the window, his cloak flapping behind him until he was little more than a pinpoint in the sky.

Clyde glowered at her from the corner, and Tracy shivered again. She turned to Mordi, who was closer.

"Why did your father say that Hale was no match for Clyde?"

"Every Protector has powers. Clyde has all the innate Protector skills—speed, strength, agility—but they're enhanced."

"Oh."

Mordi looked unhappy. "In other words, Clyde could probably cream us all."

"Oh," she repeated. She glanced at Clyde and smiled weakly. He didn't smile back. "Great."

"Tracy!" someone called.

Hale! His voice far away, but clearly in the castle.

"I'm up here," she shouted. "Somewhere in the tower. But be careful."

"Is Mordi with you?"

"Yes," she yelled back, glaring at Mordi. He didn't try to stop her. "And someone named Clyde." She glanced over. The Outcast appeared amused by Hale's plan of attack.

"Are you okay?" His voice was getting closer.

"I'm fine. For now. Please. Be careful." She'd never chewed on her fingernails, but at the moment, she wished she could rip a hand free from the manacles and have a nibble.

Hurried footsteps. Closer, then closer still.

"Did they get the belt?"

"No. They tried using a Henchman. It won't come off. I might as well be wearing ruby slippers." She laughed. Not that anything was funny, but considering she'd been yanked from her house, flown to Scotland, and tortured by a demented ex-superhero, a few hysterics were probably in order. "It's still firmly around my waist."

"I'll have you and your waist out of here in no time." His voice was just beyond the threshold.

Clyde moved toward the door.

"No," Mordi said. He turned to look up, facing the cameras in the corners. "Hale and I have a history. I get the first shot at him."

A thin grin spread across Clyde's face. "You think that you—a mere halfling—can best Hale?"

"I think I can, yes."

"As you wish." Disdain dripped from his voice, and Tracy made a mental note to ask Hale what was going on between those two. Assuming he got her out of here, of course.

The door burst open. Tracy held her breath, expecting Hale to burst through, too. Instead . . . nothing.

She frowned.

Then Mordi keeled over, clutching his stomach in pain.

"Hale!" She wanted to clap, but her manacled hands prevented it. Instead, she wriggled with pleasure. Hale would get her out of here. He'd save her. She had no doubt at all.

His disembodied voice drifted toward her. "Hey, sweetheart. How are you doing?"

Mordi tried to straighten up, then collapsed as something knocked out his knees from behind. Clyde watched, amused, from the side.

"A lot better now that you're here," she answered.

"When this is over, we need to talk."

"Yeah?" She liked the sound of that.

"Yeah."

"About what?"

Mordi was standing back up again, and once more, down he went.

Tracy stifled a giggle, suddenly in a remarkably chipper mood.

"About the fact that I love you." Hale's words zinged straight to her heart. "And I've been an idiot."

"Yes, you have," Mordi said. This time when he stood up, he focused on Hale's voice. "You haven't been playing fair," he said, launching himself at the other Protector.

"Hale!" Tracy cried.

"I'm okay, babe. Mordi and I have been down this road before. I always win."

"Not this time," Mordi grunted.

Tracy struggled, a little whine growing in her throat, but her manacles held fast. She wasn't going anywhere. Damn.

Clyde had kicked back in the chair and seemed to be enjoying the show. All he seemed to need was a bucket of popcorn.

Somehow, Mordi managed to get Hale around the . . . neck? He tumbled to the ground, holding on, and over and over he rolled until he actually reached the threshold and tumbled out of the room. Tracy could hear him and Hale struggling, but, try as she might, she couldn't see a thing. Which meant that she could only hold her breath and hope that the man who eventually came back into the room was the one she loved. Hale. She looked over at Clyde. It looked like he was thinking the same thing.

"You conniving little twit," Hale yelled, slamming his fist again into Mordi's gut. They'd grown up together, and Hale was certain of winning. Beating Mordi on the field of battle wasn't any trick at all.

Clyde, though . . . Clyde was a completely different story.

Mordi rolled, trying to avoid Hale's kicks and punches while he held on. His efforts rolled them into the far corners of the hallway outside Tracy's cell.

"I had no choice," Mordi gasped out.

Hale broke free and turned visible. "Sweet Hera, you're a cool liar. I was actually beginning to believe you'd changed. I even thought you liked Tracy."

"I *do*," Mordi hissed. "Will you listen to me?"

Hale wasn't having any of it. Once again, he threw himself forward. The two Protectors both struck the wall, the force of their impact knocking several stones loose.

"Dammit, Hale, I need to tell you something." Hale ignored his cousin, gripping Mordi by his neck until the little viper's next words were little more than a squeak. "Why do you think I got us out here?"

"You've put me and the woman I love in danger. Why in Hades should I let you say anything?"

"Because there aren't any cameras out here in the alcove," Mordi gasped, his voice little more than a whisper. "My father can't see a thing."

It wasn't at all the response Hale was expecting. "What the hell are you talking about?"

Mordi opened his mouth, but nothing came out except a wheeze.

Hale pinned him down, using both arms to press Mordi's shoulders to the wall, and his knee to keep firm pressure on his gut. "Talk."

"Keep your voice down," Mordi said, "I don't know how sensitive the mikes are in Tracy's room."

"If you don't start talking now, you're never going to know anything about anything," Hale said, increasing the pressure with his knee. But even so, he spoke in a whisper. This might be a trap, but the crafty little bastard had caught his attention.

"Who the hell do you think sent Zephron the location of this castle? Who do you think is spying on Hieronymous from the inside?"

"You?" Hale shook his head. "I'm not buying it, Mordi. I know what you've done, remember? I watched you help

347

your father try to take over the world and battle Zoë. You stole Tracy. I think I know you well enough to know what to believe."

"I had hoped that you did." This time, Mordi sounded cool and collected, and for an instant, Hale's resolve cracked. "Throw us against the next wall," he said.

"What?"

"Clyde. We need to sound like we're fighting. Throw us against the next wall."

Hale shrugged, then, keeping a grip on Mordi, lunged across the room. It sent a few more rocks clattering to the floor as Mordi's back impacted on the stone.

"You could be a little more gentle," Mordi hissed.

"You're on Probation," Hale said, reminding himself why he couldn't trust his cousin. "There's a reason for that. You have a little difficulty distinguishing the good guys from the bad guys."

"I *am* one of the good guys. I was going to recover the belt for the Council. *Me.* For once in my life I was going to manage to do something the great Hale couldn't do. And do it by using my father."

Hale swallowed. *This* was starting to sound more like the cousin he knew. "Why the hell should I believe you?"

Mordi tilted his head up, and Hale saw the intensity reflected in those vivid green eyes. "Do you think I like being on Probation? Being tested over and over again like my loyalty is in question?"

"Your loyalty *is* in question." Hale kicked a few rocks down the stairs. On the off chance Mordi was telling the truth, he didn't want Clyde's suspicions raised. Not that Clyde was the brightest bulb, but still.

"I also considered keeping it for myself," Mordi admitted, not meeting Hale's eyes.

"The belt?"

348

A single nod. "My father thought I was getting it for him. Zephron thought I was simply a mole in my father's organization." A smile touched his lips. "At first I merely wanted to show you up. Me. Mordichai. Hieronymous's son. I wanted to be the one to return the belt to the Council. But then—"

"You thought you'd just keep it and have a run at world domination yourself."

"Why not? It's better than being on Probation the rest of my life."

"That's exactly why you are on Probation."

Mordi sighed. "Don't I know it." Another intense gaze. "But I didn't try to keep it. I sent that message."

"You also kidnapped Tracy."

"I had to. If I hadn't, I would have lost my usefulness as a mole. If there's one thing my father is not, it's stupid." He took a deep breath. "I'm the one who got you here. So you could save Tracy *and* the belt. I don't have a chance in Hades against Clyde." He shrugged. "Hell, maybe neither do you, for that matter."

"Okay. Help me. If you're really on my side, help me defeat Clyde."

"No can do, cousin."

Hale felt annoyed. "Why am I not surprised?"

"Think, Hale. If I fight Clyde, my cover's blown. I can't. I'm sorry, but I can't."

"Convenient," Hale said. He just couldn't bring himself to trust his cousin.

"Dammit, Hale. What do I have to do to convince you?"

"I don't think there's *anything* you can do. You've cried wolf just a little too often."

Mordi closed his eyes. "Then so be it." Twisting violently to the right, he managed to free himself from Hale's grip.

Hale cursed. He'd let his hold go slack as he listened to Mordi's absurd story. Even more absurdly, he'd actually been wanting to believe his cousin. Now, Mordi was showing his true colors.

Mordi bounded back, on guard just at the edge of the stairs.

"I don't want to fight you, Cousin," Hale said. "Just leave. Leave, and we'll deal with this another day."

"No," Mordi said.

"Then you've made your decision." Hale moved forward, but as he did, a ball of fire bloomed in Mordi's hand. Real fire, not the fake kind his cousin often summoned. Hale hesitated. He could defeat Mordi—even with fire—but that made it more difficult. And he still had Clyde to confront. The Outcast was in the cell with Tracy.

Thinking of Tracy, Hale realized he needed to just go for it. He rushed forward, planning to fall into a roll as soon as Mordi pitched the fireball. Mordi tossed. Hale crouched, rolling on the floor, but as he did he realized that the fireball had been thrown clear. It burst into a flurry of sparks on the far side of the room.

Mordi hadn't even aimed at him. . . .

Had he been telling the truth after all? There wasn't time to think about it now. And he could never be completely certain.

"I'm sorry," Hale said, pulling his fist back. With all of his strength, he let fly. Mordi didn't even raise a hand in defense. Only when his cousin fell to the ground unconscious did Hale decide that maybe Mordi had been telling the truth after all.

That creep Clyde looked all too comfortable in that upholstered red chair. Especially since Tracy was so decidedly uncomfortable in her current position. She strained sideways, trying to see something—anything—through the doorway.

Nothing.

And then she saw a burst of flame as a fireball exploded.

She held her breath. Mordi conjured fire. Did that mean he'd hit Hale? Closing her eyes, she said a silent prayer. Please, no. She'd just gotten him again. She couldn't lose him. Not now. Not ever.

The silence in the castle was deafening. There was nothing in the room except the scrape of her manacles against the wall and the sound of Clyde's breathing. Nothing in the alcove—just a terrifying silence that sank in her stomach like a rock.

The sound of her breathing grated against her ears, and now her heartbeat seemed to echo through the room. Where was he? Her skin felt cold and clammy, and she wondered if she was in shock.

"It sounds like your little hero isn't so much of a hero after all," Clyde sneered, drumming his fingers on his chair's wooden armrest.

She writhed against her manacles, wishing more than anything she could get her fingers around his neck. "He'll win."

"The silence would suggest otherwise. I admit I'm surprised. I certainly didn't think Mordichai could defeat an accomplished Protector like your Hale. But it sounds like he did just that." An awful, wide sneer crossed the thug's face. "Of course, it doesn't sound like he made it, either." Clyde shrugged. "Pity."

"Hale is fine. You'll see. He'll wipe that sneer off your face."

"You have quite a mouth, young lady." Clyde looked at his watch. "We'll see how enthusiastic you are after a few more days with no food or water."

Tracy swallowed. Already her mouth was parched. In a few days without water, she'd likely be unconscious. Or dead.

351

Suddenly, his chair lifted into the air, and the look of confused surprise on Clyde's face almost made this whole terrible encounter worthwhile. Almost.

The chair hung there for a moment, then whizzed across the room, landing with a crash on the opposite wall. It shattered, and Clyde tumbled to the ground in a flurry of black cape and leather shoes. When he looked up, an expression of astounded horror lined his face.

"Ha!" Tracy yelled. "I told you."

Clyde climbed to his knees. "Where are you, you invisible coward?"

No answer.

Tracy scanned the room, looking for some inkling of Hale's whereabouts. Nothing.

Clyde twirled around, his cape fluttering, as he tried to find Hale, too. From the frustrated look on his face, Tracy assumed he wasn't having any better luck.

A stone on the floor rose and flew straight at Clyde. The Outcast jumped sideways, but not fast enough, and it struck the side of his body.

He spun around. "Show yourself, you miserable coward!"

"I'm right here, Clydie-boy."

Hale, Tracy thought. His voice was so close to her. And then not just his voice, but the man himself. He materialized, leaning against the wall right next to her.

Tracy stifled a laugh. Like Clyde, she'd assumed he'd been invisible while lifting the chair and tossing the rock. He'd been invisible, all right. But he hadn't lifted anything. He'd levitated the things while standing right next to her.

As Clyde scowled, Hale tilted his head back and looked at her. "Guess it's time for me to do my job and rescue the fair princess from the tower."

"Guess so." Even under the circumstances, Tracy couldn't keep the delighted smile off her lips.

"I love you," he said.

Her smile grew even broader. "I know." She nodded toward Clyde. "Now go beat the crap out of the bad guy."

Damned inconvenient he had to fight Clyde. All Hale wanted to do was gather Tracy in his arms and make love to her.

It was even more inconvenient since the odds were definitely in Clyde's favor. On pure strength alone, he was no match for the brute. Already he was exhausted from the trip here and the battle with Mordi. But his one advantage was his ability to turn invisible, and Hale intended to use it.

Clyde rushed forward. Hale dematerialized, but the other man still knocked him to the ground. Over and over they rolled, Clyde grappling with a foe he couldn't see, but still managing to keep Hale's legs pinned down.

Finally, Hale managed to get a single strike in—at Clyde's nose. As the Outcast recoiled, Hale hopped to his feet. His enemy followed suit, half-crouching as he slowly turned, ready to defend himself wherever the attack might appear.

Seizing the advantage, Hale rushed Clyde when his back was turned. He threw the Outcast to the ground and got a lock around his neck. The brute gasped and wheezed as he stood, thrashing about with every ounce of his inordinate strength, but Hale hung on.

Clyde threw himself backward against the wall. Since Hale was clinging to his back, that meant Hale was squashed. He kicked, pressing his heel into Clyde's groin until the creep gasped and lurched forward, releasing Hale from his trapped state.

Hale slid off, rolling sideways as silently as possible. Clyde again circled, once more trying to find him.

Julie Kenner

"I know you're here, little man." A singsong voice. "Come out and play." A pause. "Or are you afraid the big, bad Outcast will beat you to a pulp?"

Hale kept his mouth shut, not intending to let Clyde bait him into revealing his whereabouts.

Another turn of the circle, then another. Finally, when Clyde's rear end was right there, Hale shot his leg out, catching the burly Outcast at the base of the spine. The blow sent him tumbling.

Hale had expected Clyde would immediately hop back to his feet, but the other man surprised him, lying unmoving on the floor. Hale crept forward, peering down, trying to decide if the brute was playing dead.

No signs of life.

Silently, he leaned forward. Nothing. No movement. No breathing. Nothing. He kicked him. No movement.

That was easy! The big dumb Outcast would never stand for such treatment if he were awake.

Turning visible, he went to Tracy. "I can't tell if he's dead or just knocked out, but right now, I don't care." He took a step toward her. "Let's get out of here and get that belt to the Council before he wakes up."

She nodded, but the look of relief on her face faded as she went pale. She screamed, her body jerking futilely as she tried to point.

He whipped around. Visible, he was one heck of a big target. *Ka-choing!* Clyde sprang forward, his fist catching Hale in the throat.

Choking, Hale stumbled backward, the force of the blow knocking him partially through the stone outer wall of the castle. He pulled out, throwing himself at Clyde so that the two went tumbling, landing in a heap on the mattress under the window.

"You can't win," Clyde sneered. "You know I'm stronger. Compared to me, you're practically a mortal."

354

"And what the hell's wrong with that?" Hale asked, his body energized by the fury that burned in his blood.

Clyde sneered. "Why, my boy, I thought if anyone knew, you did."

Automatically, Hale's eyes darted to Tracy. Tight and thin, her colorless lips revealed her worry. But her eyes met his, and in them he saw trust bloom.

"Sorry, Clyde. I can't think of a thing." In one swift motion, he raised his legs and pushed, catching his foe at the hips and off-balancing him. The Outcast stumbled backward, toward Tracy, and Hale silently willed her to understand.

Bless her heart, she did. As Clyde approached, she grabbed onto the chains above her hands, lifted her legs, and kicked for all she was worth.

Like a puck on an air-hockey table, Clyde was thrown back toward Hale. In a flash, Hale grabbed him by the shoulders, flipped him over, and sent him crashing through the too-small window.

Bits of rock and mortar went flying and, after a few seconds, a resounding splash echoed up from the ocean below.

Hale turned to Tracy. "That's only temporary. He'll be back soon." He grinned, then held up Clyde's propulsion cloak, which he'd held onto. "Of course, he won't be back *too* soon."

"What about Mordi?"

"He's fine. Passed out, but fine. But he's going to have a hell of a headache—and a heck of a lot of explaining to the Council and his father." He kissed Tracy's nose. "Not our problem. We need to go."

"I'm all for getting the hell out of Dodge. I mean, I've always wanted to see Scotland, but this isn't really what I had in mind."

355

He headed toward her, ready to rip her free from the chains, when he realized what she'd said. "Scotland?"

"Well, yeah. I just assumed. Is this Ireland or England?"

He laughed. "Try Los Angeles, sweetheart. Clyde's taking a swim in the cold waters of the Pacific."

Her shoulders sagged and she looked somewhat disappointed. "No way. And here I thought I'd finally had the chance to be the heroine in one of your romance novels."

Stifling a grin, he kissed the tip of her nose. "You are, Tracy. With the belt, without the belt, you're the only woman for me. The only heroine for me. And I love you."

The corner of her mouth twitched. "The only one?"

Hale shrugged, embarrassed at how stupid he'd acted before. "Well, from here on out anyway. I can't change the past, but I promise I won't ever repeat it."

A single tear trickled down Tracy's cheek. "I love you," she whispered.

"I know." He ripped the manacles open, freeing one of her wrists and then the other. "Time to fly back?"

She looked dazed. "Where?"

He kissed her on the nose, wanting to kiss her everywhere. But there was plenty of time for that later. "Our home. I just moved in, remember? You're not getting rid of me this easily. In fact, I think I might be there to stay."

"Yeah?"

He nodded. "Yeah. If you'll have me."

She beamed. "Let's get home. The sooner the better."

Hale hopped up to the window, then held out an arm for her, not feeling completely whole until he'd lifted her up and wrapped her in his embrace. "I hope you don't mind flying economy," he said.

"I think I can handle it." She kissed his cheek. "Just one thing, though." Reaching down she unhooked the belt, then pressed the cool metal into his hand. "We need to deliver this to your Council on the way." Her smile went straight to his heart. "I don't need it anymore."

Tracy held on tight to Hale's hand as they delivered Aphrodite's girdle to Zephron. Any tighter, actually, and Hale would have wondered if she'd somehow absorbed a portion of his super strength. She might have spent her youth around celebrities, but apparently that didn't mean Tracy was comfortable with superhero leaders—no matter how grandfatherly they might look.

"Thank you, Miss Tannin," Zephron said with a smile. "I assure you, the Council will keep your grandmother's belt safe."

She exhaled, and Hale silently thanked Zephron for putting her at ease. "I know you will," she said. "I'm just happy it's away from the bad guys." She frowned. "Speaking of . . ."

Zephron nodded. "Yes. Clyde and Mordichai."

"What's going to happen to them?" Tracy asked.

"Clyde has disappeared. We will find him, of course. The moment he uses his powers, we will be able to hone in on him." Zephron shrugged. "And until then . . . well, he'll have a chance to see how mortals live."

"What about Mordi?" Hale asked.

"Your cousin. That is trickier. Despite what he told you in the castle, we still do not know his true intentions. Did he intend to acquire the belt to return it to us? Was he truly working for his father? Or did our young Mordichai plan to use the belt for his own purposes?" The Elder shook his head. "We don't know. But the Council is investigating."

"He was kind to me," Tracy put in. "He could have tried to drive a wedge between me and Hale, but instead he told me Hale cared about me." That was news to Hale, and he silently thanked his cousin. "If he needs a character witness," Tracy continued, "you can call me."

Zephron smiled at her. "You are a special woman, Tracy Tannin. I hope you realize that."

Tracy didn't answer, but when Hale squeezed her hand, she squeezed back. Zephron was right, of course, and Hale intended to remind her how special she was every day for the rest of their lives.

The Elder turned to him. "And you, Hale. You are due to be congratulated for your successful mission." A small smile twitched on his lips, and Hale had the impression that Zephron was holding something back. He'd thought that once before—the day the Elder had assigned him this mission. He hadn't asked then, but now he needed to know. "What? Am I missing something?"

Zephron fingered the belt. "Let's just say that I was certain you were the appropriate Protector to give this task."

At that, Hale had to laugh. "I was the most *in*appropriate Protector. Heck, we're lucky Hieronymous didn't prevail. You sent me—a guy who had some pretty hefty mortal issues—on a mission to befriend a mortal."

"Ah," the old man said. "It's even worse than that. I sent you to fall in love with a mortal."

Hale blinked. He certainly hadn't been expecting Zephron to say that. "Excuse me?"

Zephron looked at Tracy. "Do you understand?"

To Hale's surprise, she nodded. "I think so. I figured it out in the castle."

Hale gaped as he waited for her to continue.

"Not anyone could persuade me to give up the belt. Even torturing me wouldn't do it, although I guess Hieronymous didn't know that." She licked her lips. "Aphrodite was the goddess of love. I was only going to give the belt up to someone I loved."

Hale frowned, then looked to Zephron for confirmation. The Elder nodded.

"It all makes sense," Tracy continued. "Although I didn't realize it until that Henchman couldn't get it off me but I could take it off to give to you. I'd wanted to give it to you earlier, in the hotel bar. Something held me back. I wasn't in love with you yet." She smiled. "I was close. But I wasn't there yet."

Hale looked at Zephron, his eyes wide. "Then, you knew I'd fall in love with Tracy? Or that she'd fall in love with me?"

The Elder shook his head. "No. I did not even know if that was how the belt truly worked. I told you, we did not have the full information. But I suspected. It was a risk, of course, sending you. Your 'issues' as you call them made you a questionable choice. But at the same time, I believed that you were ready to overcome them. You just needed the right woman. And I believed Ms. Tannin here not only had the belt, but was that woman." He caught Hale's eyes. "So I assigned you. And I hoped."

"Hoped?" Tracy echoed.

"Yes, I admit to taking a risk." He smiled at her, his eyes warm and caring. "Considering the outcome, it is a risk I'm glad I took." His eyes moved between Hale and Tracy. "I wish you many happy years. Perhaps there will be a new halfling on the horizon soon. . . ."

Children? Hale swallowed and tugged at his collar, the idea more appealing than he would have thought. And also more terrifying.

Tracy laughed and squeezed his hand. "Don't worry. I'll let you get used to the idea of being in love with a mortal before we start planning kids."

"Sweetheart, I didn't fall in love with a mortal. I fell in love with Tracy Tannin." He stroked her cheek, imagining himself holding her child . . . *their* child. He had to admit he liked the image.

Her smile zinged straight to his heart as she said: "And I didn't fall in love with a superhero or a cover model. I fell in love with you." Then she asked with a soft laugh, "So, do you think Elmer's ready to be an uncle?"

Hale chuckled, hugging her close. "So long as he gets his vacation and occasional infusions of HBO, I think he'll do just fine."

Epilogue

Tracy laughed as Hale tugged at the bowtie around his neck. It was the first time she'd seen him in a tux, and when he'd walked into Tara-too's private screening room, her first reaction was to melt at his feet. Her second was to rip it off him, forget the party, and stay in bed all night.

"Don't laugh," he growled. "I saw you yanking at your pantyhose earlier."

"I hate the damn things. They must have been invented by men." She aimed a pretend scowl his way. "Remind me again why we're doing this?"

He moved closer, sweeping her into an embrace. "It's Elmer's big night. His acting debut. And you had the bright idea of throwing a party to celebrate his episode of *Mrs. Dolittle*."

"I know that," she said. "But why am I wearing panty-hose?"

Hale laughed. "The ferret has attitude. Since he's wearing a tux, he insisted we dress up too." He pulled back, his eyes roaming over her body. "I plan to thank him for it. You look stunning."

"Yeah?"

"Yeah." He bent her over his arm, planting a long, slow kiss on her lips.

"Without the belt, I'm just another girl." Even in her awkward position, she managed a shrug. "And not even an average girl. Just plain old Tracy. Heck, Leon hasn't even given me a second look." Not that she wanted Leon's eyes on her, but she had to admit that the belt had been nice for her ego.

"Believe me, sweetheart, there's nothing plain about you. You're beautiful—inside and out. I knew it from the first moment I saw you. Even though I fought like hell." He kissed the tip of her nose. "Besides, you don't need any other men looking at you. Your fiancé's the jealous type. And a jealous superhero can be a dangerous thing."

That's one of the things she loved about Hale: he always knew the right thing to say. And he made her believe she was beautiful. "Have I told you today how much I love you?" she asked.

"Even if you did," he said, "it bears repeating."

"Break it up, you two." Mel's voice filtered into the room, followed by the click of her heels as she hurried in, a ferret on each shoulder. "The show starts in fifteen minutes."

Elmer—decked out in his own little tux and tiny sunglasses—started chittering as Hale pulled Tracy back to a standing position.

"What's he saying?" she asked.

"That if we forget to tape the show, he's going to disown both of us."

Penelope chimed in.

"The same?"

"She just doesn't want us to miss the beginning. This is Elmer's big night, after all."

Tracy looked at her watch. "We've still got a few minutes. Where's Zoë and everyone?"

"The kitchen." Mel glanced around the room at the catered buffet Tracy had ordered that afternoon. "All this, and Hoop wanted popcorn."

Elmer jumped down to one of the seats and started tapping his paw. Penelope hopped down as well and snuggled up close. The show had taped two weeks before, and even in that short time, her delicate condition had become more apparent. Elmer, who'd developed some surprisingly gentlemanly qualities, scooted over to give her more room on the seat.

"Hey, hey. Let's get this show on the road." Hoop stormed in with Deena on his heels. Taylor and Zoë followed, with Lane and Davy bringing up the rear. Hoop aimed a smile toward Tracy and Hale. "Great party, you two. And Hale, congrats on your miraculous recovery."

Tracy chuckled as Hale scowled, clearly clueless.

"Recovery?"

"Your acute mortal-itis," Taylor explained. "Looks like you're cured."

At that, Hale laughed, then pulled Tracy closer. "With *this* mortal, maybe. The rest of you losers I only put up with because my sister makes me."

Zoë laughed. "I take the Fifth."

"And we don't believe you," Lane added. "You've blown it now, Hale. We know the truth."

Deena winked. "But don't worry. Your secret's safe with us."

Hale aimed a mock-stern glance toward them all, even as Elmer started hopping up and down, chittering away.

"What now?" Tracy asked.

363

"He says to shut up. We may have kept the world safe from Hieronymous, but he's guest-starred in a television show." Hale grinned. "Can't argue with that." A frown creased his forehead. "Of course, now he's begging Marty to line him up a job in commercials. What do you think? Could Elmer endorse a line of clothing?"

Tracy tugged at his hand, ignoring the neurotic ferret. "Come here, mister." She led him out of the room and into the hallway. "We still have five minutes before showtime, and there's something I want to do."

"I'm not sure we can do that in five minutes."

She tried to ignore him, but couldn't help the smile that touched her lips. "Not that. This." She hit 'play' on the jambox she'd left by the door, and the low strains of Frank Sinatra singing "It Had To Be You" echoed through the hall.

"Dance with me."

Caressing her cheek, he smiled. "Anything for you, sweetheart. Anything at all."

He swept her into his arms and they twirled on the floor in time with the music. Just the two of them, alone with the magic.

With a sigh, she rested her head against his shoulder. She'd finally made it. This was the dance she'd always fantasized about. With the man she'd fantasized about.

Only this time, it was a fantasy come true.

Aphrodite's Kiss
Julie Kenner

Crazy as it sounds, on her twenty-fifth birthday Zoe has the chance to become a superhero. But x-ray vision and the ability to fly are only two things to consider. There is also her newfound heightened sensitivity. If she can hardly eat a chocolate bar without convulsing in ecstasy, how is she to give herself the birthday gift she's really set her heart on— George Taylor? The handsome P.I.'s dark exterior hides a truly sweet center, and Zoe feels certain that his mere touch will send her spiraling into oblivion. But the man is looking for an average Jane no matter what he claims. He can never love a superhero-to-be—can he? Zoe has to know. With her super powers, she can only see through his clothing; to strip bare the workings of his heart, she'll have to rely on something a little more potent.

___52438-4 $5.99 US/$6.99 CAN

The Cat's Fancy
Julie Kenner

Straight-laced Nicholas Goodman's life is going just fine. A hotshot attorney in a huge law firm, Nick has money, success, and a girlfriend whose father just happens to be his biggest client. All the aspects of his life are tucked neatly into nice little corners, just the way Nick likes it. Until he opens his door and finds a completely naked, slightly befuddled green-eyed beauty on his doorstep.

Maggie has found the man of her dreams—Nick Goodman. He is smart and sexy, and she knows he loves her. Maggie's only problem is . . . well, she isn't entirely human. But Maggie is determined, and through the power of love she is given a chance—and a lithe woman's body. She has one week to convince Nicholas to admit that he loves her. One week to prove that a guy like Nick can fall for "a girl like Maggie." One week to prove that a cat's fancy can be the love of a lifetime.

___52397-3 $5.99 US/$6.99 CAN

Dorchester Publishing Co., Inc.
P.O. Box 6640
Wayne, PA 19087-8640

Please add $1.75 for shipping and handling for the first book and $.50 for each book thereafter. NY, NYC, and PA residents, please add appropriate sales tax. No cash, stamps, or C.O.D.s. All orders shipped within 6 weeks via postal service book rate. Canadian orders require $2.00 extra postage and must be paid in U.S. dollars through a U.S. banking facility.

Name_____
Address_____
City_____State_____Zip_____
I have enclosed $_____ in payment for the checked book(s).
Payment <u>must</u> accompany all orders. ❑ Please send a free catalog.
CHECK OUT OUR WEBSITE! www.dorchesterpub.com

Everyone loves a little meddling *help* from Mom...

A Mother's ~~Day~~ *Way*
Romance Anthology

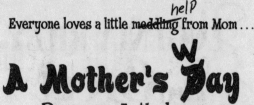

♥

Lisa Cach, Susan Grant,
Julie Kenner, Lynsay Sands

Is it the king who commands Lord Jonathon to wed, or is it the dia-bolical scheme of his marriage-minded mama? After escaping her restrictive schooling, Miss Evelina Johnson wants to sow her wild oats. Mrs. Johnson plants different ideas. Andie never expects the man of her dreams to fall from the sky—but when he does, her mother will make sure the earth moves! Jennifer Martin has always wanted to marry the man she loves, but her mom knows the only ones worth having are superheroes. Whether you're a medieval lord or a marketing liaison, whether you're from Bath or Betelgeuse, it never hurts to have some help with your love life. Come see why a little meddling can be a wonderful thing—and why every day should be Mother's way.

___52471-6 $5.99 US/$7.99 CAN

EUGENIA RILEY
The Great Baby Caper

Courtney Kelly knows her boss is crazy. But never does she dream that the dotty chairman will send her on a wacky scavenger hunt and expect her to marry Mark Billingham, or lose her coveted promotion. But one night of reckless passion in Mark's arms leaves Courtney with the daunting discovery that the real prize will be delivered in about nine months!

A charming and sexy British entrepreneur, Mark is determined to convince his independent-minded new wife that he didn't marry her just to placate his outrageous grandfather. Amid the chaos of clashing careers and pending parenthood, Mark and Courtney will have to conduct their courtship after the fact and hunt down the most elusive quarry of all—love.

TRISH JENSEN

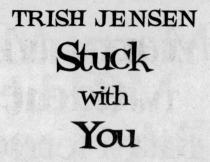

Stuck
with
You

Paige Hart and Ross Bennett can't stand each other. There has been nothing but bad blood between these two lawyers . . . until a courthouse bombing throws them together. Exposed to the same rare and little-understood Tibetan Concupiscence Virus, the two archenemies are quarantined for seven days in one hospital room. As if that isn't bad enough, the virus's main side effect is to wreak havoc on human hormones. Paige and Ross find themselves irresistibly drawn to one another. Succumbing to their wildest desires, they swear it must be a temporary and bug-induced attraction, but even after they part ways, they can't seem to forget each other. Which begs the question: Did the lustful litigators contract the disease after all? Or have they been acting under the influence of another fever altogether—the love bug?

___52442-8 $5.99 US/$6.99 CAN

Marry Me, Maddie
Rita Herron

Maddie Summers is tired of waiting. To force her fiancé into making a decision, she takes him on a talk show and gives him a choice: Marry me, or move on. The line he gives makes her realize it is time to star in her own life. But stealing the show will require a script change worthy of a Tony. Her supporting cast is composed of two loving but overprotective brothers, her blue-blood ex-boyfriend, and her brothers' best friend: sexy bad-boy Chase Holloway—the only one who seems to recognize that a certain knock-kneed kid sister has grown up to be a knockout lady. And Chase doesn't seem to know how to bow out, even when the competition for her hand heats up. Instead, he promises to perform a song and dance, even ad-lib if necessary to demonstrate he is her true leading man.

___52433-3 $5.50 US/$6.50 CAN

Baby, Oh Baby!

ROBIN WELLS

The hunk who appears on Annie's doorstep is a looker. The tall attorney's aura is clouded, and she can see that he's been suffering for some time. But all that is going to change, because a new—no, two new people are going to come into his life.

Jake Chastaine knows how things are supposed to be, and that doesn't include fertility clinic mixups or having fathered a child with a woman he'd never met. And looking at the vivid redhead who's the mother, Jake realizes he's missed out on something spectacular. Everyone knows how things are supposed to be—first comes love, then comes marriage, then the baby in the baby carriage. Maybe this time, things are going to happen a little differently.

KATHLEEN NANCE
THE WARRIOR

Callie Gabriel, a fiercely independent vegetarian chef, manages her own restaurant and stars in a cooking show with a devoted following. Though she knows men only lead to heartache, she can't help wanting to break through Armond Marceux's veneer of casual elegance to the primal desires that lurk beneath.

Armond returns from an undercover FBI assignment a broken man, his memories stolen by the criminal he sought to bring in. His mind can't remember Callie or their night of wild lovemaking, but his body can never forget the feel of her curves against him. And even though Callie insists she doesn't need him, Armond needs her—for she is the key to stirring not only his memories, but also his passions.

___52417-1 $5.99 US/$6.99 CAN

THE TRICKSTER
KATHLEEN NANCE

Long after she's given up on his return, Matthew Mark Hennessy strolls back into Joy Taylor's life, bolder than Hermes when he stole Apollo's cattle. But Joy is no longer the girl who had so easily trusted him with her heart. An aspiring chef, she has no intention of being distracted by the fireworks the magician sparks in her. But with a kiss silkier than her custard cream, he melts away her defenses. And she knows the master showman has performed the greatest trick of all: setting her heart afire.

Mark has traveled to Louisiana to uncover the truth, not to rekindle an old passion. But Joy sets him sizzling. It is not her cooking that has him salivating, but the sway of her hips. And though magicians never divulge their secrets, Joy tempts him to confide his innermost desires. In a flash Mark realizes their passion is no illusion, but the magic of true love.